Sarah Rosenbaum's
Dachau Redemption

Sarah Rosenbaum's
Dachau Redemption

Gerry Feld

All Cover designs and art work created by FrinaArt
Editing and Proof reading by Lori Hawkins
Interior design and typesetting by Roseanna M. White

Published by Ingram/Spark Content Group
Global Head Quarters in La Vergne, Tn. U.S.A.

Printed in the U.S.A.

ISBN Soft cover: 978-0-578-76423-8
ISBN e-book: 978-0-578-76424-

Preface

The Holocaust was the single worst man-made tragedy in the history of mankind. It boggles the mind that any one nation on this earth, could have developed such a diabolical scheme to destroy innocent human beings in such a gruesome and systematic manner. What is more unbelievable, is that the monsters that created the plan found enough people willing to carry out the horrendous operation that led to the slaughter of over six million souls.

The more I considered writing this story, the more I wondered how to bring it to life, while keeping in mind that a sense of dignity must be maintained for those who suffered through it.

I had not yet written very much when I came across the cover design for the book created by FrinaArt. The graphics from the cover told my entire story. I was mesmerized by the eyes of that young woman, and instantly realized they were the eyes of Sarah Rosenbaum, the main character of my story who you are about to meet.

Although the camps still exist as a testament to the evil that permeated every aspect of Hitler's Third Reich, the voices of the survivors are fading as the survivors pass away. Luckily, we have thousands of written and recorded testimonies that we can and must rely on as evidence to the greatest tragedy of mankind.

Even now there are revisionists at work, attempting to rewrite history by stating that the Holocaust never occurred. We must never forget the reality of this tragedy. It is our duty to teach younger generations the facts of the Holocaust, including what brought it about, enlightening each generation to ensure that such a thing could never happen again.

Dedication

This story is dedicated to all the souls that perished at the hands of the dreaded German S.S. during World War Two. Some died in shooting pits, some died in mobile gas chambers, and some died in cramped ghettos, but the largest number died in extermination camps. No one will ever fully realize the terror, horror and humiliation these innocent people were forced to endure.

I also wish to dedicate this story to the late Lee T. Johnson, who was a very good friend of mine, a scholar of all things World War Two, and author of the World War Two book, "Wood-McLennan U.S.O." He never tired of listening to my plans or ideas for my story, and he always gave me valuable feedback. His opinions, insight and knowledge of the war were remarkable. Regrettably, Lee passed away in August of 2020 before I was finished with the book.

As with all of my writing, I need to thank my wife JoAnn, for her patience and understanding during the many hours I sat at my computer writing or researching. She is always a great sounding board when I am stuck and not sure where to turn. During the many down times when I had lost my way, it was her support and ideas that helped me find the path once again.

First they came for the communists, and I did not speak out—Because I was not a communist.

Then they came for the socialists, and I did not speak out—Because I was not a socialist.

Then they came for the trade unionists, and I did not speak out—Because I was not a trade unionist.

Then they came for the Jews, and I did not speak out—Because I was not a Jew.

Then they came for me—and there was no one left to speak for me.

MARTIN NIEMOLLER,
German Protestant Pastor,
1892 – 1984

TABLE OF CONTENTS

Chapter One
An Empty Slate

Where does the tormented soul go when it no longer finds peace on earth? Where does the pain go when all life ceases to exist? Where does man find solace from the evil he has created?

Today, the large brick ovens in the crematorium of Building X at Dachau sit silent and empty. There is no complete record of the number of bodies that were consumed in the unquenchable flames that roared day and night. Nor is there a trace of the thick putrid black smoke that poured endlessly from the tall brick chimneys. There is not even a sign of the German soldiers or Jewish kapos that operated the hungry ovens day in and day out. It was as if death had taken a holiday.

However, it was not as if there were no bodies waiting to be cremated. You see the death rate in the camp had well out paced the ability of the ovens to keep up. Now that the storage building next door was full of victims, it became necessary to stack the dead in piles about five feet high near the crematorium. The Germans had hoped they would be able to dispose of all the bodies before the camp was overrun by the allies, but that simply was not going to be the case.

But today, all work in this factory of death had come to a stop. The only living soul around this monument of horrors, was a young woman named Sarah Rosenbaum. She sat, oblivious to the horrors and stench that surrounded her, as she woke up leaning against the front wall of Building X. She had quietly spent the night there, refusing to let go of the hand of Galenka Goldman, a woman who had passed away the day before, and now belonged to the nearly endless stack of lifeless corpses waiting for the all-consuming flames. Unlike most of the women in the barracks Sarah was assigned to, Galenka had treated her with compassion, as she understood the hate and bitterness raging in the young girl's soul. In the end, Sarah returned the favor a hundred times over, not only for Galenka, but for many other women, now long gone and forgotten, after waiting their turn to be disposed of in this wasteland of death.

As Sarah rubbed her eyes, her mind could not grasp what was happening. Sometime during the night as she slept, the crematorium had been turned off, and the kapos and guards had left. But for where?

Scanning the camp carefully this morning, Sarah felt an eerie silence of the type that almost made one's skin crawl. Where were the snarling dogs? Where were the angry guards with rifles and riot batons, that beat the prisoners every day as they fought over the scraps of food tossed to them like swine on a farm? In a state of fear and uncertainty, Sarah looked up toward a nearby guard tower, where the ever-alert soldiers waited to fire a burst from their machine guns at anyone foolish enough to dare approach the fence or the front gate, but even the tower was empty. Only the deadly machine gun menaced her soul, with its barrel still pointed down at her.

The only thing present in the camp this odd morning was silence, a strange and bitter silence that didn't even allow the wind to whistle through the dreaded electrified fence. The only thing that existed was the all-consuming odor of death and decay that lingered like an evil cloud over this man-made hell.

After kissing Galenka's cold and withered hand one last time, Sarah stood up. She walked toward the tall fence surrounding the camp. It was an ugly fence, of taut electrified barbed wire. A fence of death that had killed many prisoners who threw themselves against it, choosing to end their lives rather than continue the horrific suffering.

Closing her eyes and holding her breath, Sarah placed her hand on the wire, but it was cold to the touch. It no longer snapped and hummed, no longer electrified, it no longer chose to kill. Stumbling backward in fear away from the fence, Sarah fell to her knees, her legs no longer willing to hold her upright. Struggling with every ounce of energy she could muster, Sarah grabbed onto a fence post, using it to pull herself back up. Slowly, she raised her head and gazed into the brilliant blue sky, where the sun appeared to be spinning in circles. Realizing her tortured and abused body had given all it could, Sarah fell to the ground, her desire to live all but gone. Now she just waited for death to overtake her. It would be a sweet death, a death that would forever end the agony she had suffered for so long, a death that would free her from her captives, a death that would finally reunite her with her family, and today, that was all that mattered.

As the early morning fog began to burn off, it appeared that only the stacks of rotting corpses lining the way to the now quiet crematorium, were all that was left of an ancient culture that was chosen to be separated from all humanity, erased forever. They no longer cried out in pain, they no longer fought for a scrap of bread, they no longer felt the brutality of the guards. Their empty wide eyes would stare for eternity, their gaping mouths unceasingly questioned why; were now a silent testimony to what had become of a tortured people.

But then a door opened, allowing a single skeleton-like individual to stumble from the darkness of a shabby barracks into the daylight. It peered from left to right, unsure of what to make of the silence. It stood still as if planted in place.

Slowly more walking skeletons began to appear in the gathering sunlight, shading their eyes with skin covered sticks, once the useful arms used to create and hold their children. They looked toward the office of the commandant, where decisions on who lived and died each day were made, but it too was quiet. They looked up toward the now empty guard towers, but could not bring themselves to understand why they would be empty. Surely the hate-filled soldiers would not just walk away, leaving this witness to the world what the men of the Third Reich were capable of.

A single man standing silently in the middle of this abyss of insanity pointed a bony hand toward the main gate. Then another pointed, and another, and soon, a few brave, lice-covered, filthy skeletons dressed in rags with oozing sores and gaping eyes, slid their bruised and battered feet across the ground to investigate who these people were, standing in horror outside the gate.

It was obvious that no one inside this camp of horrors had any idea it was April 29, 1945, the day of their liberation. To them it was just going to be another day of torment, suffering and starvation as they waited for death to make them just another statistic of Dachau.

Those who were too scared, too weak, or no longer cared, huddled on the ground as they clutched one another outside their barracks. Those on death's doorstep no longer had the strength or desire to rise up from their filthy, lice infested bunks to see what was happening. They all simply waited to see what new kind of horror was going to be heaped upon them by these strange men that just stood there and stared.

Captain Edgar Woolridge, a member of the forty-fifth division of the United States 7th Army, stood motionless as he looked into the depths of depravity.

"What the hell, Lieutenant? What have we stumbled across?" He asked the question of Lt. Clark Edwards who stood beside him, shaking his head in total disbelief as he made the sign of the cross.

The lieutenant frozen in place could not respond, as one of the wretched figures now stood in front of him, just inside the wire. The figure poked his shrunken hand through the fence, attempting to touch the Lieutenant's arm as he mumbled something incoherent.

"That's Yiddish sir. All the Jews in my neighborhood back in Brooklyn spoke the same language. Give me a second, I'll get Sgt. Mendelson up here, he should be able to translate for us since he's Jewish," Lt. Edwards responded, as he quickly turned and ran off in search of his sergeant.

Several minutes later, Mendelson arrived at the main gate, looking totally terrified. After gathering his thoughts, he asked the man who he was and where he came from.

As the ghostly figure began to slowly respond, a group of ten more starved men, covered with oozing bloody sores, arrived at the gate, all attempting to tell their stories at the same time. Mendelson was overwhelmed at what was happening, as more and more of these deplorable looking people made their way forward.

Sergeant Mendelson turned toward Capt. Woolridge. "Sir, we have stumbled upon a concentration camp. Most of these people are

Jews, one of them claims to be a French soldier. They say there are Jews here from all over Europe, and some political prisoners. They want to know if the Germans are coming back and what we are going to do with them."

As the sergeant finished speaking, Lt. Alvin Chambers, the battalion surgeon, walked up to the gate and stood beside Capt. Woolridge.

"Sir, these people are in an extremely dangerous condition. If we give them too much food, they will die. Their bodies simply no longer have the ability to digest large amounts of food. We will have to start them slow, but their medical conditions are so horrible, they still may not survive. But water is essential, we must give them water as soon as we can if we are going to save any of them.

Still in shock, Capt. Woolridge had his communications center notify division and seventh Army headquarters as to what they had found, and requested every available doctor and medic, along with hospital tents, medications, and all additional medical equipment that could be spared.

After a water tanker was brought forward to the gate, Dr. Chambers and his staff began helping soldiers dispense the precious liquid to everyone in the camp. Regrettably, even the cool clean water was enough to kill some of the survivors if they drank too much or too fast.

At the same time, soldiers from Headquarters Company began breaking open the horrific smelling rail cars that sat on the siding outside the camp. They were horrified to find the fifty cars stuffed with the corpses of men, women and children, that had perished while waiting to be unloaded inside the camp. There was no way of knowing how long the cars had been sitting on the siding. The stench was so incredible that many of the tough combat veterans either vomited or passed out. The doors were quickly slammed shut until the decision could be made as to what to do with them.

While speaking with some of the survivors, American interrogators soon came to understand the duties of the kapos inside the camp. They were Jews or political prisoners that had agreed to do all the dirty work the Germans did not want to do. For doing these jobs, they were rewarded with more food, cleaner barracks and other privileges. They were easily identified by the different uniforms and caps they always wore. Most of them that had been set free by the Germans when they left, and had already been rounded up wandering the countryside around the camp. Captain Woolridge ordered they be brought back into the camp to help clean up the mess.

As three soldiers marched the first five kapos back into the camp, they were stunned as the weak, sick survivors found the sheer strength to descend upon them with a vengeance. The soldiers were overwhelmed, unable to control the ghastly mob that grew quickly, displaying an anger that intensified by the second. More soldiers ran to the brawl, attempting to pull the kapos free, but it was too late for three of them. Once the last two injured kapos were pulled back out of the camp, the soldiers stood in silence and shock, as they watched more survivors arrive to kick at the bodies of the dead men. It was eerie to watch these weak starving people create a rotating procession around the bodies and kick or yell at the corpses as they passed by. The soldiers made no attempt to stop the procession or remove the disfigured bodies until the survivors had returned to their barracks. Captain Woolridge wrote an immediate order that the kapos would be escorted in and out daily by armed guards, while the survivors were confined to their barracks.

Although every survivor in the camp had reason to hate these people, the captain would not allow any more killings if he could help it. He knew well enough that the day would come when the kapos would all be hunted down and killed. There would be no place on earth where they would ever be safe.

Soldiers from Alpha Company started the painstaking process of walking through the camp checking all the bodies on the ground to see if any of them were still alive. When they found one, they would call out for a stretcher team to take the person to the medical teams. At the rear of the camp near the fence, a young sergeant walked up to a body he was positive had to be dead. Placing his hand on the throat of the girl, he was surprised to find she was alive, and yelled out, "I got a live one here, she has a pulse."

As the stretcher team attempted to pick up Sarah, she screamed as loud as she could, while trying to fight off the soldiers with what little energy remained in her sick weary body. She clawed and scratched as she yelled, "No, don't take me to the box! Please don't do it, please no, I'll behave!"

She quit resisting when she looked up to see the kind face of a young American soldier. He brushed her hair with the back of his hand as he said, "Shhhh, shhhh my child, everything will be alright, everything will be alright." Although, he was speaking to her in a language she did not understand, she trusted his warm smile and kind attempts to calm her soul. After the soldiers placed her on the stretcher, Sarah reached out her hand to grab hold of the soldier that had spoken to her. Looking up at him she simply said, "Danke," before passing out.

Opening her eyes nearly two days later, she looked curiously at the IV bottle hanging above her, attached to a plastic hose that ran to a needle in her arm. Sarah then observed an older man, maybe fifty, wearing a long white coat. It was a very clean coat, drawing her attention because she hadn't seen anything that brilliantly white and clean in years. Smiling, the man walked over and felt her pulse.

In very good Hebrew, he stated, "I am Doctor Acker from America, I was born and raised in a strict Jewish family. How are you feeling? How old are you? What is your name?"

Sarah's mind spun as she realized she was being asked questions about things no one had cared about for a very long time. Did they even matter now, why did he want to know?

"I must think now, how old am I? How old was I when the Germans came to take my family away." Those things, once so important to a child, had somehow become vague at best, lost in a world she wanted only to forget.

After a moment of thought, she attempted to put the words together to respond to the kind, smiling man. Forcing the best frail smile possible she replied in Hebrew. "I am Sarah Rosenbaum, I am thirteen years old. I have not eaten in so long, I do not remember last time I had bread. Please give me something to eat, even just a crust of bread, please!"

Sarah hated coming to the point where she had to beg simply for a crust of bread, but now her overwhelming desire for food was all that mattered.

Doctor Acker looked at her and shook his head as he replied. "We need you to drink water right now and a little food tomorrow. Too much food will harm you, it is best we wait."

Angrily, Sarah pushed him to the side and pulled the needle from her arm. She jumped up from the blanket she was laying on, gathered every ounce of strength possible in her condition, and stumbled out the door of the tent. After walking about fifteen feet, Sarah stopped and looked around. She was surprised to find herself right back where she was when all of this began.

She stood there motionless, as she watched armed American soldiers keeping an eye on captured German soldiers, kapos, and civilians from the local towns, that were loading some of the eight thousand corpses that were stacked in the camp onto trucks to be buried. Somewhere in that mass of tangled corpses was Galenka. Terrified she would never see her friend again, Sarah once again stumbled forward screaming, "Galenka, Galenka, I'm sorry!"

One of the American soldiers grabbed her, trying to keep her from running into the area they were attempting to clean up.

Sarah cried as she beat her small withered hands into the soldier's chest. "Galenka, Galenka, where are you?"

With all her energy spent, once more Sarah dropped to the ground, exhausted as she wept.

Several hours later she once again awoke under the same tent, on the same blanket she had run from earlier. Kneeling beside her once again was Dr. Acker. Shaking his head, he spoke gently.

"You have amazing strength for the shape you are in. Your will to live is stronger than you can imagine right now. Stay here and work with us, and we will get you back on your feet once more." After a moment of silence he continued. "Who is Galenka? Is she family, a friend?"

Sarah rolled her head to the right so she would not have to face the doctor. "She is no one you will understand or ever know."

Nodding his head, Dr. Acker was not ready to give up. "Sarah, you are the youngest person we have found in this camp. Where did you come from? Do you have any family still alive that you know of?"

Sarah laid still, refusing to answer as memories of her family rambled through her mind in a jumbled order. It felt like an eternity since she had crawled under that box car and ran. She wished her brother Jonathon would have gone with her, but he may not have survived anyway, so what was the use of wishing.

Doctor Acker thought for a moment before asking another

question. He was hoping to find the right thread that would unravel her story. "Sarah, where was your home town?"

Looking up at Dr. Acker, Sarah replied, "Straubing, I came from Straubing. Hitler did not come for us as quickly as he did in other parts of Germany. We thought maybe he would let us be, but that was not to happen. I escaped on my birthday when I was just seven. You can never understand what it's like to be hunted like a wild animal, to eat roots from plants in the forest, or to watch people you love get slaughtered just because we were Jews. But I will survive, I must. I want to punish those that did this, even though Galenka taught me to forgive. She loved unconditionally, she never hated the German soldiers for what they did to us, she prayed for them, she prayed God would forgive them, and she asked me to pray with her. I did, because she asked me to, but the suffering was too much at the time. I still did not understand Galenka. I think now I am starting to see that my Galenka was right all along. If we could survive and pray to our God of Abraham we would be rescued and set free. Someday, I may fully understand, and once again find peace in my heart, as Galenka pleaded with me to do. She tried hard to help me find my God, our God of Israel, and trust in him instead of hate him. I promised poor Galenka over and over I would do that if I survived, and live as she asked me to do. I have a scrap of her clothing and a lock of her hair by my bunk. I will take her memory home as she asked and bury it in Israel someday. This I must do to be whole again."

After a moment of silence, Sarah slowly sat up on the cot and looked intently at Dr. Acker. "I was not the youngest child in the camp. There were other little children in the camp a while back, eight of them were in our barracks, I helped look after them. They were just innocent little children, they were no threat to anyone, and they all went up in the smoke.

Calling over an investigator, Dr. Acker pulled his stool closer to Sarah. "Tell me, what happened to the other children. Take your time."

"One day, I was playing games outside of the barracks with the children like I always did when we were allowed out. Sergeant Wilhelm, a hateful man walked over near us. I called the children together because I feared what he might do to them. One little girl named Rena ran up to him and called him big Papa. That outraged him like I had never seen before. He pulled his black jack from his belt and struck her on the top of the head, killing her instantly.

The next day a new doctor that had arrived in the camp came by to look over the children. I knew he had killed other children in the camp by doing experiments on them. I was not about to allow him to touch my children, so I pushed him. When he came toward me, I pushed him backwards again. Before I realized what was going on, Sgt. Wilhelm's men knocked me down and dragged me to the punishment box. After I was locked in the box, the doctor ordered the guards to take the children to the hospital. One of the women, Levana, protested and fought back desperately. She was beaten by the guards, and when she could protest no more, one of the soldiers struck her on the side of the head with his rifle butt. She was taken to the crematorium to be burned."

The investigator looked down at Sarah. "There is no gas chamber here, how did they die?"

Sarah closed her eyes as she shook her head. "The doctor did all kinds of experiments on them like the others. Most died right away, those that hung on were taken behind Building X where they were shot. Pop, pop, pop, one gun shot after another until they were all dead. Then, like everyone else they were burned by the kapos."

The investigator shook his head. "Other than Sgt. Wilhelm, do you know the names of any other soldiers that helped in this matter?"

"Yes, I am sorry to say that Cpl. Barnard who had treated me kindly at times was with them. The rest I did not know."

The following day a medic handed Sarah a small piece of dark bread along with a cup of tepid water. "Eat slowly, Sarah. If your body can handle this, I will get you more in a while."

Even though her instinct was to shove the entire piece in her mouth all at once, she nibbled on it as the medic had requested, knowing there was more to come, and that now she would not have to fight for it like a dog.

By the time darkness began to settle over the camp, Sarah had eaten two small pieces of bread. However, still in survival mode, she had hidden the third piece under her pillow in case they chose not to feed her again. By the fifth day Sarah was doing much better, although her body still reacted negatively to the food if she ate too much too fast, as was the problem with all the survivors.

Ten days after being rescued, Sarah went for a walk with one of the medics. She was surprised to see that the stacks of corpses had been completely removed. The barracks had all been deloused and cleaned, and fresh mats had been passed out to the people that were still forced to stay in the camp for now. Returning to the hospital tent, a woman dressed in very nice clothing approached Sarah. Taking hold of Sarah's hand, the woman began to cry.

"I am so sorry for what happened here, I am so sorry we did nothing to help you. We—"

Sarah pulled her hand back from the German woman as she glared at her in anger. "You could not smell what was happening here? You could not see the smoke? I am sorry, but I do not believe you cared then, and I do not believe you care now. You are trying to mend your own soul to make you feel good about yourself. But this place is full of souls that will never find peace that you could have saved. Your words mean nothing, they are empty and without meaning. Go, go to your home and live with your pain, your pain means nothing to me."

As tears rolled down the woman's face, she looked intently at Sarah. "I have lost a husband and a son to this war. Believe me when—"

"I will never believe you or feel sorry for your loss. I am thirteen and have lost everybody that meant anything to me. You seek forgiveness here from us? As I said, go to your home and live with your pain, because your pain and loss is not ours!"

Backing away, the woman turned and walked back out the main gate. After watching the woman leave, Sarah returned to her cot. She was angry with the woman for trying to seek peace in her soul at the expense of all those that had died here, and she was angry at all the Germans, her country-folk that lived near by. She knew some of them had worked in the camp, so everyone knew exactly what was going on inside those walls.

As night settled over Dachau, Sarah was awakened by cries coming from the camp. Slowly, she stood up and walked out of the tent. As she strolled toward the barracks, she realized the sounds were not coming from the run-down structures. Instead, it came from the ground, the sky, and the stars; it circled around her like a whirl wind. Thousands of faces of the dead, crying out for food, crying out for their families rolled unceasingly across the heavens. Placing her hands over her ears she yelled, "Make it stop, make it stop!"

Then there was silence, dead silence, and the stars had been covered by a layer of clouds that blocked out the light. In the darkness she felt fear, in the darkness she saw the faces of the S.S. guards laughing at her, pointing at her, calling her a Jew bitch. Turning back toward the tent she saw Galenka, standing erect and dressed in a white garment. Holding out her arms she smiled. "Peace my child, pray as I have taught you. Find peace in your soul."

Before Sarah could respond she was gone. Standing near the entrance to the tent, she looked back toward the camp. All the faces were gone now and the wind she experienced was still. All that remained was the stench that had permeated every structure and the very ground she stood on. Here the wind was not your friend, here the wind was a constant reminder of hatred, bigotry, and brutality that would forever haunt this camp. Here the wind was not filled with fresh air, here it was filled with a disgusting odor that sucked the life out of your soul. The wind neither cooled or warmed you in Dachau, instead it always carried the unearthly moans of the thousands that perished here. This was a land where the living would forever be guests of the dead, and the wind would always sing its mournful song.

Chapter Two
Straubing Germany

It would be hard to find a more wonderful place to grow up than in the area around Straubing, Germany in the 1930's. It was a peaceful town with a southern Bavarian charm that captivated everyone that visited the area. The city was nestled along the beautiful Danube River, with the dark enchanting Bohemian Forest just a short distance to the east.

Paul and Margot Rosenbaum were delighted to settle in the growing community where there were good schools, ample room to raise a family, and a small but thriving Jewish community where they could practice their faith. Working as an accountant for the city of Straubing, Paul earned a good salary, allowing Margot to stay home to raise their three children Rose, Jonathon and Sarah, while tending to their large vegetable garden.

Being of devout Jewish ancestry, Paul and Margot demanded their children attended Sabbath services regularly, study the Talmud and read from the Torah daily.

However, at age six, Sarah began to protest when it was time to attend Temple services or read the daily lessons her mother prepared for her. Like most children in the area, Sarah would rather be off hiking along the river and singing songs with her friends, than studying her ancient religion.

Although stories regarding raids on Jewish communities were told at the synagogue, no one ever felt threatened in Straubing. From time to time convoys of German war equipment would pass by their community, but no one became alarmed. After all, Germany had used large parts of the forest for their war games over the years, dating back to World War One. No matter what was going on, the soldiers always appeared to be very kind, handing out candy to the children that waved and yelled at them as they traveled along the road.

The soldiers always enjoyed watching Jonathon and other boys from the community marching along the road in good step, carrying tree branches over their shoulders for rifles. Even though Margot was not happy with Jonathon's plans, she knew full well he wanted to join the army as soon as he was old enough. He loved being part of the Hitler Youth where they could camp in the forest, cook their meals over an open fire, sing songs, and perform tough physical exercises that challenged their minds and young bodies. Little did Margot know, but Jewish boys all over Germany were now exempt from membership in the Hitler Youth. In Straubing, their banker Herr Brown was in charge of the local Youth Organization. He liked Jonathon and the other two Jewish boys that were members of the group, so he quietly defied the orders from Berlin, allowing the boys to remain members. Figuring no one would ever check his records, the religion listed for each boy was Methodist.

No one appeared to be at all concerned when the German Army took over an old construction yard south of Straubing on April first. They told city officials it would be easier on them if they could store some of their equipment in the yard, instead of towing it back and forth each time they were going to train. Since the yard was surrounded by a large growth of fir trees, no one could see that the primary tenants at the facility were Waffen S.S. soldiers. Each night, some of the soldiers would come to Straubing to have drinks in the bars, or eat at one of the small cafes. All the while they were gathering information on the residents of the city, identifying the people of wealth and influence.

At City Hall, the Commandant of the camp began spending large amounts of time looking over the platting of the city to see who owned which properties. He explained it away, saying that the Government might be interested in building a larger base or maybe even an airfield nearby. Paul always complied with the requests for documents, but their presence and their secretive conversations always made him nervous and uncomfortable. Several times they spoke with him regarding subversives that were known to be hiding in the forest, but each time he told the officers he knew nothing about any such people.

On May 10, 1939, Sarah hurried home from school, excited about celebrating her seventh birthday. Rushing into the house, the aroma of a freshly baked cake made her smile.

"Can I see it? Can I see the cake, Mother?" Sarah squealed with delight.

Her mother smiled as she finished washing the large mixing bowl, "Cake? What are you talking about? Why would we be eating cake on a Tuesday night? Where would we get the ingredients? Times are not good my little one."

Sarah smiled as she tugged on her mother's apron, "Please Mama, let me have a quick look."

Her mother did not answer, and the smile on her face had completely disappeared as she watched two black Mercedes sedans pull up in front of their home. Everyone in Germany knew that the only people that drove such vehicles were high ranking S.S. officers or the Gestapo, the dreaded state police.

Placing her hand on her daughter's shoulder, Margot said, "Sweetheart, go change your clothes. Go do it now and do not argue."

Before another word could be said, there was a hard knock at the front door.

Sarah swiveled in the direction of the living room yelling, "I'll get it, Mama."

"No Sarah! Go to your room as I said, go now!" Her mother demanded with a stern look on her face as she pointed toward the staircase.

Once again there was a hard knock on the front door as a man's voice called out. "Open at once or we will come in!"

Margot walked briskly to the front door, not wanting to irritate the Gestapo agents any more than they already were.

Opening the door, she half bowed as she said, "Excuse me, Herr Captain, I was dealing with an unruly child. Please, forgive me."

Sharply, Captain Muellor raised his right arm as he boldly stated, "Heil Hitler."

Nodding her head, Margot replied, "Yes, would you care to come in and have a seat. I can brew you some coffee if you would care to have some."

Glaring at Mrs. Rosenbaum, he yelled, "Do you not pay homage to our Fuhrer, our sacred leader?"

Nervously shaking, Margot raised her right arm as she replied, "Yes, Heil Hitler. I'm sorry Herr Captain, it will not happen again, I promise."

Pushing past her, Captain Muellor walked into the comfortable home along with his aid, Lt. Beckman. "Mrs. Rosenbaum, we are here to inform you that your husband has been arrested and is on his way to Dachau reeducation camp. He has been speaking out against the Third Reich and our glorious Fuhrer while attending secret meetings with people that are hiding out in the forest. So, now we must clean out this rat nest of traitors here in the Fatherland."

Lieutenant Beckman handed Margot an order written on official Nazi stationary, signed by Heinrich Himmler. "You will be deported from the Fatherland tomorrow morning at the prescribed time. You will be sent to a new farming area in Austria where you will till the land and grow farm produce for the Army. Each family member can carry one bag of clothing, the rest of your belongings will be shipped to you with in the month. Anyone on this list not complying with this order, or anyone on the list attempting to leave Straubing will be shot on sight. Do I make myself clear, Mrs. Rosenbaum?"

Margot's hands shook as she read the order. "Yes, it is clear Herr Lieutenant. We will not give you any trouble."

"Good. That is good, Mrs. Rosenbaum. The more you comply, the quicker you will be with your husband. I do not understand why you Jews think you can do as you wish and subvert the natural laws of our Fuhrer. Good day," Major Muellor replied as he walked back out of the house.

Sitting down on the sofa, Margot began to cry. She knew nothing about these secret meetings Paul was alleged to have been attending, or any anti-Nazi organizations living in the forest. Paul had made it quite clear on many occasions, that if all the Jews in the community kept quiet and minded their own business, Hitler would have no reason to mess with them. Now, something had gone drastically wrong.

At first, Margot decided to put the kids in their car and drive them to her folk's place near Augsburg, however S.S. Units from the construction yard had now been deployed, blocking all the roads leading out of Straubing.

Returning to their home, Sarah looked at her family. "We are all packed and ready to go. Tonight, let's cross the river and make our way to the forest. No one will see us go. We can hide there until we can get to Grandma and Grandpa's place. No one will miss us and we will be safe."

Margot looked at her daughter while shaking her head. "If we do that, we will never see your father again, they will kill him for sure. They have promised we will meet up with him when we get to Austria. Besides, there are only about a hundred Jews here. They will miss us right away, and start a search. It will not go well for the rest of our friends or us, when they chase us down."

Jonathon, the oldest child agreed with their mother. "Sarah, you need to understand that our God will be looking out for us, he will never let anything bad happen to his chosen people. He has shown us his mercy how many times throughout our history. He will keep us in his embrace."

Smiling, Margot placed her arm around her son. "You have learned well. Yes, we need to keep faith in our God of Israel that he will protect us. With him at our side, we have nothing to fear."

Sarah listened to everything that was said, but felt in her heart that the God of Abraham, Isaac and Jacob she had read so much about was already abandoning them. Why should they need to be resettled far away? What had they done wrong? Why were heavily armed men being sent to take them? Why would the roads be blocked, preventing their escape? Nothing looked right to her.

Looking over at Rose who had said nothing, Sarah questioned her. "Rose, don't you think going to the woods would be a good idea? We would be safer there."

Margot stood motionless, waiting for her eldest daughter to respond.

Standing up, Rose walked over to her younger sister. "I think you feel this would be a great adventure for all of us. But it would be hard and we would need to find food and dry places to sleep and much more. It would not be the adventure you think it would be. I think Mother and Jonathon are right. We must do as we are told for our own good."

As prescribed in the letter, all of the 102 Jewish people living in or near by Straubing assembled in the town square around 10:00am the following morning. Each person was carrying some type of traveling bag containing clothing, food and sacred family heirlooms.

A few minutes later a convoy of trucks arrived in the square. Soldiers dropped the tailgates and began to yell for the assembled crowd to load up. When one of the soldiers hit a crying child, Rabbi Kaplan stepped forward.

"That is not called for. We have assembled as we were ordered. I have assured Captain Muellor that everyone is accounted for. You need not strike the children!"

Without saying a word, the soldier leveled his Mauser at the Rabbi and shot him right between the eyes. Everyone began to scream, as those in trucks began to climb back down, and others standing nearby attempted to run away. A few stronger young men tackled several soldiers, attempting to take away their weapons. In seconds, shots rang out in every direction as bodies fell to the street.

Captain Muellor stepped up onto a concrete bench by the fountain, firing several shots from his pistol into the air. When everyone stopped, he called out.

"Listen to me! There will be no more resisting. Get on the trucks as you were told. I assure you it is in your best interest to comply."

Margot held onto Sarah and Rose as she looked at the angry soldiers standing nearby. Looking at Jonathon, she pleaded, "Please get on the truck, we will see your father in a few days, and then we will be whole again."

With the trucks loaded, the convoy left Straubing, driving west to the major train yard at Munich. Leaning against her mother, Sarah knew she would always remember her seventh birthday, if she lived long enough. For now, her beautifully frosted cake was still in the upper cabinet where her mother had placed it to keep prying fingers from getting at it. The sausages they were going to have for supper were still in the ice box and would probably waste away there, and the odds of sleeping in her own comfortable bed again appeared to be stacked against her.

Sarah first looked up at her mother who was attempting to console Rose and Jonathon as she recited passages from the Torah. Then looking around the truck she saw neighbors and friends crying as they recited scripture or read from prayer books. What difference did all these prayers make right now, as no one was listening on the other end. She felt a sense of doom lingering over the small convoy of trucks as they bounced along the road, guarded by armed military vehicles.

Sarah made up her mind that if the chance came to escape, she would take it, even if it meant leaving the rest of her family behind. They all believed they would see their father in Austria, but Sarah felt an uneasiness about the German promise. She would run, she would live, she would be strong. She would not be cowed into believing what the Germans were offering. If it were true, why were Rabbi Kaplan and the others shot dead so quickly. No, this was bad, and it was going to get worse before this day was over. She knew in her heart their only chance to survive was to run, but Mother, Rose and Jonathon would never take that risk. But the will to survive was strong in Sarah's heart, and no matter what it required, she was going to escape the evil Nazi soldiers and their snarling dogs. However long it took.

Chapter Three
Escape

Arriving at Munich, the rail yard was in total turmoil as the S.S. soldiers struggled with all the newly arriving captives. Hundreds of Jews from all over Germany were being pushed into cattle cars, as soldiers shot anyone attempting to run or refusing to cooperate. Dogs barked and bit old men and women as they hobbled forward to the train cars. Soldiers carrying truncheons and heavy batons, swung their tools of death at anyone they felt was slowing down the process. They broke bones and crushed skulls, leaving shattered bodies all around the loading platform. Those that were still alive and couldn't get up were shot.

Margot tightly grabbed hold of her girls, while keeping Jonathon in front of her, not wanting them to get lost in this desperate, tragic sea of humanity. She followed directions, nodding her head and not saying a word that might anger the soldiers who were just waiting for their chance to attack the helpless throng.

Arriving at rail car number 23, a soldier pushed Margot toward the car as he yelled, "Move, move, we don't have all day! The sooner you get on the cars, the sooner you get to the resettlement camp."

By now, Margot was all too sure they were not headed toward the land of milk and honey the Germans had been promising. Was it possible that little Sarah's misgivings had been accurate all along?

It began to appear that the rumors Rabbi Kaplan attempted to dispel in the Synagogue last week regarding the execution of all Jews in Germany may have been accurate. No one, especially Margot and Paul had wanted to believe those horrid rumors, but still, they persisted week after week. When Jonathon suggested they drive down to Chaument in France to stay with their father's sister and family on the large farm, Paul had refused to leave the home they had built. Now Paul was among the many Jews that were missing, and she and her children were about to be loaded on a filthy rail car to be deported.

Getting a spot along the back wall of the rail car turned out to be a blessing, as the small window slot above them would offer fresh air once the door was sealed. Women and kids screamed as the soldiers kept pushing more and more people onto the already overloaded car.

"Mommy, I'm being squished, I can't breathe down here!" Sarah called out above the many voices that protested in unison, as the massive steel door was rolled shut, blocking out all daylight, except what could enter through the small barbed wire covered window slots.

"I know, honey, I know. Please be patient, Sarah. Once we get moving it will be better," Margot promised, although at this point, she was certain that nothing would be getting better.

Margot was absolutely right, and everything went from bad to worse in short order. As the hot relenting sun beat down on the steel car, the temperature inside rose to unbearable heights. Some people fainted and had to be held up by family members, while others became sick and began to vomit on the floor or on people around them. Before long the stench of human excrement added to the odor of vomit fouling the air inside the car so badly, it was nearly impossible to breathe at all, causing even more people to get sick or faint.

Nearly an hour after loading into car 23, the train began to slowly move forward to its designated terminal. The screams of the desperate people had slowly died away, to be replaced with sobbing, moaning of the sick, and the sound of people reciting scripture out loud. Parents attempted to reassure their children, while old people clutched each other knowing they were going to die together before this day was over.

To help keep Sarah under control, from time to time Jonathon would raise her up toward the window slot, allowing her to inhale fresher air and see the countryside as it passed by. That worked for about the first two hours before she started to protest. "Mother, I need to go pee. I want to go to the bathroom, I really need to go bad."

Margot shook her head as she placed her hand on her daughter's head. "Honey, there is no bathroom, you will have to pee where you are standing, I'm so sorry."

Sarah looked up at her mother, "No. I will not do that. I am a big girl, and big girls don't pee on themselves!"

An older woman standing next to Sarah called out, "None of us are happy being here in this car. Just do as your mother says and quit whining. You should be saving your breath to pray for God to reach out and save us, as you have been taught in the temple. Now, be still!"

Before Margot could respond, Sarah yelled back at the woman, "God is not on this train, he is nowhere around here. He has walked off and left us, you'll see, he will not save any of us!"

Immediately, Rose gave her little sister a quick slap on the face. "The God of Israel is not dead. It angers me when you say that. He is testing us to see if we are worthy of his love. You are wrong, you will see, God will pull us from this torture and raise us up above the ones who hate us, you must believe, Sarah."

Sarah was about to reply to her sister, when she realized smoke was beginning to fill the car, as a horrible high-pitched squeal came from the right front corner of the box. The sound of running footsteps could be heard on the roof as German soldiers ran back and forth.

With a thunderous boom, and a massive jerk forcing everyone toward the front of the car, the train began to slow. Now the smoke billowed into the car through the floor boards and window slot at a rapid rate. Everyone coughed and wheezed as the smoke became thicker, darkening the light that had come in through the window slots.

Outside the voices of excited German soldiers alerted everyone inside that something bad had taken place. Moments later, the latch that held the massive steel door in place swung to the side, as anxious soldiers began rolling the door open.

"Get out, get out!" An angry sergeant yelled as he pulled people off the car, dropping them to the ground. Margot grabbed Sarah by the hair, stopping her from rushing forward as she screamed and stomped her feet.

When they finally were able to get to the edge of the car, several younger men helped Margot and the girls down, as Jonathon jumped clear. Looking under the car, Jonathon was able to see that the wheel bearing must have frozen, creating enough heat to burn off the wheel journal, causing the assembly to collapse.

Sarah's quick eyes scanned the area from side to side, attempting to figure out what the German soldiers were going to do. She had made up her mind, she was not getting back onto any other car, no matter what her mother said.

After several minutes, the burly sergeant walked over to the people who were quietly seated in the ditch.

"We are just a mile from Weissenburg where we can get you onto another train. You will need to walk until we get there. Anyone who attempts to escape will be shot, no questions asked. Now stand up and start walking."

The people had walked about three car lengths, when several men threw themselves under the parked rail cars attempting to roll across the tracks to freedom. Shots quickly rang out as guards on the far side of the train cut them down before they could get very far.

Margot was stunned as the man walking next to her yelled out. "Now is the time, run my people, save yourselves!"

Instantly, a bullet shattered the back of his head after an angry soldier fired point blank from just a few feet behind him. Margot, now covered in blood, dropped to the ground, pulling Rose and Sarah with her. Jonathon attempted to cover his mother with his body, as several more soldiers came running forward, attempting to control the terrified people now scattering in every direction. Bullets whizzed through the air, hitting target after target, littering the ground with the people of Straubing that Margot knew so well. Dogs chased people, grabbing on to legs or arms, dragging them to the ground so soldiers could easily run up to the victims and shoot them in the head.

As Margot momentarily released Sarah's hand, a tiny voice inside her head spoke up.

Run, run for your life and don't look back.

Instantly, Sarah rolled under the nearest box car and over the tracks. Jonathon yelled at her to come back, as Margot screamed in terror at her youngest child. Coming out on the far side of the car, it was clear to see there were not enough German guards to handle all the people that were attempting to escape. Looking over at her family Sarah yelled, "Come on, follow me! We can make it, come on, hurry, we must go!"

Margot shook her head, yelling, "Baby, they will kill us all, please come back to me!"

Looking over at Jonathon, Margot yelled, "No, don't follow her, Jonathon. I need you, please stay with us, don't go!"

Jonathon's heart was beating out of control as he watched his little sister roll down into the tall grass on the far side of the train. What chance would a seven-year-old girl hope to have on her own? She should have someone to watch out for her, and he knew he was the one that should be there to keep her safe. As he began to crawl under the car, Margot and Rose grabbed his ankles.

"They will kill the both of you if you go. Stay here, Jonathon." Margot screamed passionately as she clung desperately to her son's ankle. Losing her youngest daughter was painful enough, but she was not going to lose her son, too, in what she considered an ill-fated attempt to escape the angry German soldiers.

With Rose having a death grip on Jonathon's right leg, she cried and screamed for him not to go. After several moments he crawled back out from under the car and into the waiting arms of his heartsick, desperate mother.

Sarah poked her head up from the tall grass in the ditch. Two German soldiers were chasing down a man to her left, as another soldier was forcing people back under the car to her right. Just as she was about to stand up, someone grabbed her arm.

"Not now, roll down the hill some more, get close to those little trees. Then take my hand and we will run like the wind."

Sarah looked over to see a boy just a little older than Jonathon laying right behind her. Nodding her head, she began rolling through the tall grass as he did the same. When they reached the small trees, he took hold of her hand while whispering, "Now, we go now!"

As Jonathon laid his head on his mother's shoulder, he stared intently across the tracks, hoping to see one more sign of his little sister. A second later he saw the little body of his sister disappearing into the woods, holding on to the hand of a young boy. He smiled as tears ran down his cheeks. Softly, he said, "Run Sarah, run. Don't look back, just live, Sarah."

Sarah gathered in deep breaths of air as she rapidly placed one foot in front of the other, running faster than she had ever run before. A shot rang out, striking a tree just to her left, as she continued stretching out her little legs as far as they would go, in order to keep up the rapid pace being set by the boy. Low hanging branches from fir trees struck her in the face, but she made no attempt to slow down or whine about it. All around her, bullets whizzed over her head, striking trees or other escapees taking the same route. Although her ears were ringing and her little heart was pounding, she continued gulping in tremendous amounts of air as she forced her legs forward. All around her she could still hear yells of people being killed, as pursuing soldiers continually fired. The farther they ran, the darker the forest became, until it appeared as if it were early evening.

Without warning, the boy pushed her into a hole in the ground that was created when a tree had been blown over by the wind. Grabbing Sarah by the waist, the boy shoved her into a hollow spot in between the thick branches. Putting his index finger up to his lips, he shook his head and said, "Shhh, be very quiet."

Nodding her head, Sarah closed her eyes, as her racing pulse made it feel like her neck was going to explode. The boy burrowed a bit deeper into the thick branches and remaining completely still, watched the forest behind them.

Several minutes later he slid back out to Sarah. "I think they turned back, I don't see anyone, although I'm sure they are out there somewhere."

With a smile on an otherwise sad face, the boy looked at Sarah. "My name is Isaac Levin, I came from Penzberg. My mother, father and brother were also in that car. They shot my father right after we jumped off, because he pushed a guard that tossed my mother to the ground. I ran as fast as I could toward the rear of the train and dove under a car as the German's shot two men behind me. I rolled into the tall grass and waited for the right time to run, as you did. I keep thinking I should have stayed with Peter and my mother, but I knew we would all die."

"How old are you?" Sarah inquired, as she looked into the boys brown eyes."

"Twelve, but please don't be scared of me, I will not hurt you," Isaac responded with a kind smile as he placed his hand on Sarah's shoulder. "I don't know where we are going, but we will get there together. How old are you?"

Sarah explained her age and story to Isaac, as tears rolled down her cheeks. She longed to be held by her mother and to be with Rose and Jonathon, although somehow she felt they were in a far worse place.

After taking another good look around the area, Isaac stood up. "We should be on our way, more Germans may come looking for us. Let's just keep heading east. I know the Bohemian Forest is by the Czechoslovakian border. Father always told me we had crazy relatives living there. Maybe we can find them and have a good place to stay. What do you think of that idea, Sarah?"

Sarah stared straight ahead for a moment before answering. "My grandparents live near Augsburg, we could go there. They will take good care of us.

Isaac shook his head. "Sarah, if they are clearing out Jews from small towns like Penzberg, surely they will do the same to Augsburg if they have not already done so. The chances of escaping the grip of the Nazis a second time will be much harder, if not impossible. We must go to the forest."

Sarah longed to see her grandparents and it made her sad to think of them being loaded on rail cars and hauled away never to be seen again. Standing up she nodded her head. "Alright Isaac, we shall head to the forest. Maybe there are other Jews who have taken up refuge there also."

Carefully, Isaac and Sarah left the hole and began walking east. About an hour later they could hear the sound of trucks driving on a road that cut the forest off from a large cornfield. Isaac knelt down, quickly pulling Sarah to the ground behind a large tree.

"Stay here and do not stand up. Let me crawl forward to see what's going on. I will be back for you as soon as I know what's happening." Isaac explained giving Sarah his best reassuring smile.

Crawling the last fifty yards to the road, Isaac took cover behind a tree stump. He observed several German troop trucks and scout cars driving slowly along a dirt road. Just to the south of them, a large group of soldiers climbed down from a truck and began making their way into the forest. Quickly, Isaac crawled back to Sarah. "Germans are beginning to search the forest all along the road. We cannot stay here, we must get across the road and into the corn field, then run as fast as we can."

"Won't they be searching the corn field, too? We might get caught right away," Sarah replied, as her little body shook with fear.

"It's our only chance. If we stay here or go back the way we came, they will find us for sure. We need to get across that road, that is our only chance," Isaac replied, as he understood the possibility for capture was increasing by the minute.

Reluctantly, Sarah agreed, understanding that Isaac was doing his best to keep them free and alive, while being terribly scared himself.

Arriving back by the tree stump, Isaac could see the truck that had dropped off the soldiers had driven away to the north. But there was still the patrolling scout car to deal with, along with the soldier standing behind the large machine gun mounted in the back of the vehicle.

Isaac and Sarah were frozen in place as the scout car idled by their position less than ten yards away. The driver pulled to the side of the road, as two soldiers came walking out of the forest dragging a man behind them. Isaac recognized him as a bank clerk from Penzberg, who had been in the car with them. After securing his hands and feet, they threw him into the back of the scout car near the gunner's feet. Turning around, the driver headed north at a good rate of speed. After watching the two soldiers disappear back into the forest, Isaac took Sarah by the hand. "Now Sarah, now!"

As quick as lightening, the two children bolted across the dirt road diving in to the tall grass at the edge of the field. Isaac looked north as Sarah looked south to where the soldiers had been. Seeing nothing, they jumped up and ran through the large field until they came to a farm yard.

Everything was eerily quiet. There were no dogs barking, no chickens clucking, and no cows in the small corral by the barn. Isaac sat down beside Sarah. "We need a place to spend the night, plus those billowing storm clouds are going to dump a lot of rain on us in the next hour or so. We either need to see if the house is occupied, or we can hide out in the barn. What do you think?"

"I like the idea of the barn. It will give us a better chance to escape if we need to run." Sarah responded, although she would have much preferred the house.

Nodding his head, Isaac took Sarah by the arm, leading her back into the corn field for cover until they were directly behind the barn. After scanning the area, Isaac and Sarah dashed into the rear door of the barn. There were no animals, but there was plenty of straw and horse blankets they could use to make a comfortable, warm bed for the night.

Sarah walked around the barn checking out everything, and looking for things they might be able to use when they left. Coming to a window looking out over the yard behind the house she called out, "Isaac, you better come over here."

Isaac walked over to the window and gasped. Hanging from a tree behind the house, were the bodies of two older people. It was evident they had been there for some time.

Turning away, Isaac took a deep breath. "Come on, let's go check out the house, it will be warmer than the barn tonight, and maybe we'll find some food in the kitchen."

Sarah nodded. "What should we do about them, they scare me."

Isaac half smiled. "They are dead, Sarah. They cannot hurt you, and besides, they most likely were Jews that would have gladly helped us if they had been alive. It is best that we leave them as they are. The Germans can see them from the east as they approach the house. If the bodies are moved, they will know someone is here. Come, let's run to the house."

They were only in the house about five minutes when the heavens opened up, dropping copious amounts of rain on the parched field crops behind the farm house. It was apparent that people had gone through the house after the couple had been murdered. Most everything that was useful had been removed and the cupboards and pantry were nearly empty. However, they had found enough canned fruits and vegetables, along with a small stick of dried sausage, to fill their empty stomachs.

When they had eaten their fill, they strolled around the house trying to decide where they would spend the night. In an upstairs bedroom they found several quilts and blankets that were stacked on the floor, and never taken. Isaac pulled them into a closet and began arranging them.

Around three in the morning, Sarah suddenly sat up, poking Isaac, "There's someone in the house," she whispered. "I heard voices downstairs."

Isaac listened for a moment before looking over at Sarah. "I think we should stick together in case we need to run. Stay behind me and do as I tell you, and remember the cornfield will be our best route of escape. If we get separated, run there as fast as you can and I will find you."

Picking up a large French knife he had found in the kitchen, Isaac led Sarah quietly down the stairs. Arriving at the bottom, he listened intently. It was clear that one of the people was a woman that was attempting to console a child. Feeling confident there was no immediate risk, Isaac pushed open the heavy wooden door and entered the large kitchen.

The woman shrieked and backed up against the wall as she pulled a small girl into her arms. "Please, we mean you no harm, we just needed to get out of the rain. I was afraid my daughter would get sick if we did not find shelter and your door was open." The woman pleaded as she shook in fear.

Isaac placed the knife on a broken chair that was sitting nearby. Holding up his hands, he replied, "And we mean you no harm, either. Are you a Jew?"

The woman's eyes were filled with terror when she heard the question. She gazed at the two scared and dirty children for a moment before responding. "Yes, Isabelle is all I have left. My husband and son were killed by the Nazis. Please don't hurt us."

Sarah stepped forward as she gazed upon the terrified woman. "We are Jews, too. We escaped when the train broke down earlier today. We do not know where they were taking us, but said we would be happy there. But I never believed them."

The woman let out a sigh of relief as she let go of her daughter. "So, you do not live here and are all alone?"

Isaac nodded his head. "The owners are hanging from a tree out back. We came here like you to escape the storm. We are headed for the Bohemian Forest where there are people that can help us. Do you need something to eat, there are still some canned vegetables in the pantry. You can help yourself, but don't start a fire or light a candle."

Sarah dashed up the stairs to get some dry blankets for the woman and her child while they ate from one of the remaining jars. Returning, Sarah helped Isabelle get out of her wet clothing. "Where are you headed? You can go with us if you want."

Isaac was angry with Sarah's invitation. "Sarah, it will be easier for two children to sneak around the countryside. Having an adult and another child will endanger us all and make us easier to identify. They will have to find their own way, that's the way it has to be."

The woman nodded her head. "He is right, child. We can make our own way, we got this far over the last few days. We will figure it out and find the right direction."

Isaac looked perplexed at the woman. "The last few days? Were you not on the train that broke down yesterday?"

Shaking her head, she looked intently at Sarah and Isaac. "I have seen hell, and that is where you were headed. You do not want to see what I have seen happening to our people, you do not! I will make the soldiers kill us before they take us back there. You should be afraid, very afraid."

Isaac stepped close to the woman. "Where have you been and what did you see?"

The woman looked at Sarah, "Maybe she should not hear. My daughter has not spoken since we escaped from the camp, she saw far too much."

Sarah stepped forward, "I can handle whatever you say. I know God has abandoned the Jews like he did before we were taken to Egypt as slaves. We are a worthless forsaken people."

The woman was stunned by Sarah's response, but honestly could fully understand why she felt that way.

"My name is Anna Benowitz, my family came from Tilburg, Holland. My husband was a diamond cutter for a large jewelry company. When the German's came, we were rounded up and placed in makeshift camps at first. Then we were loaded on trains and taken to a camp called Buchenwald, which is most likely where you were headed. They put us in horrible barracks that were infested with rats and lice. People died from starvation, overwork and brutality. They had ovens where they cremated bodies by the hundreds every day.

We were spared because of my husband's expertise with diamonds and other expensive stones. Then one day we were put back on a train bound for Dachau where the Germans had compiled large amounts of expensive jewelry from Jews and other prisoners. After a month they wanted to take my husband to a special work site in Berlin, but the camp commander did not want me and my daughter to go, as he did not want us talking about what we had seen. But the men from Berlin won out. They put us in a truck along with several other gemologists and countless bags of jewelry to be sorted and graded.

We were near Neumarkt when the front tire on the truck blew, causing us to slide in the ditch and roll over. When the roof on the truck broke free, my husband grabbed Thomas as I grabbed Isabelle, and we began to run as did the other men. But all too soon the bullets started flying. I saw my husband and son go down, so I held Isabelle tight and ran all the faster until the shooting stopped. We have been wandering and hiding since then, not sure which direction to go." Anna took Isabelle into her arms and hugged her as she cried. "We will be alright, we have survived thus far."

Sarah looked angrily at Isaac. "No, they will go with us, we cannot abandon them!"

Shaking his head, Isaac replied. "Fine, we will go together in the morning then. Come upstairs, we have more blankets where you can get warm and sleep for a while. Picking up the French knife, Isaac led them to the second-floor closet.

The morning dawned dark and windy but the rain had finally stopped. After finishing the canned vegetables, Sarah led everyone out to the barn and into the corn field where Isaac took the lead.

The first day went rather well as they were able to stay hidden in fields and wooded areas, with no signs of soldiers or military patrols. Anna was aware of what roots or bulbs were edible in the forest, so she pointed them out as they went along. Sarah was not very happy with the choice of food, as she dreamed of her birthday cake up in the cupboard that she would never touch. They prepared to sleep in an empty cow barn that evening, far from any house or prying eyes.

As Anna laid down on a large horse blanket next to Isabelle, she gestured for Sarah to lay down beside her. Although it was not her mother, having an adult woman to sleep with gave Sarah a sense of peace, something she would need to hold on to for a long time.

Chapter Four
Fear and Safety

Arriving at the bank of the Naab River, Sarah felt like she was going home. Her family had made several trips to Regensburg over the last couple of years to enjoy swimming in the river, while visiting many of the historical sites such as the Thurn und Taxis Palace. It was a very Christian community with few Jews, if any, so everyone in the area was suspect.

As the current of the river was slow this time of year, it was easy to wade through the knee-deep water. Arriving on the east side of the river, Anna asked if they could stop for a few minutes to rest, as Isabelle was tired. They had barely sat down when a man with a shotgun and a stern looking woman happened upon them. The woman stared at them for a moment before looking at her husband.

"Jews, all of them. I can smell them from here. We must notify the Gestapo that we have captured some runaways. They will appreciate our help and pay us a handsome bonus."

The man mumbled something to his wife that was incoherent to Isaac, as the man's teeth were clamped tightly on a large pipe that hung from his little round mouth.

"Get up!" The woman ordered as her husband kept the double-barreled shot gun trained on their four captives. "Walk back along the river and do not try to run, my husband will gut you like the pathetic animals you are."

They had walked about a hundred yards when Isaac could see a small cottage built back from the river a short way. Back behind the cottage was a small storage shed with a heavy wooden door. The woman removed the wooden shim that held a strong beam in place over the door. Isaac allowed Anna and the girls to enter first as he kept his eye on the angry looking man.

"Get in or die!" The man yelled as he glared angrily, but Isaac did not move. As the woman leaned forward to push Isaac into the shed, the man lowered the barrel of his gun. Like a tightly wound spring, Isaac pulled the French knife from under his jacket, spun around, planting it straight into the man's throat. The shot gun fell to the ground as the man placed both hands over his throat, attempting to control the gushing blood. The woman screamed in horror and reached for her husband as he began to fall backwards.

Anna rushed forward from the shed, striking the woman across the back of the head with an ax handle she picked up in the shed. Angered and fearful, she struck the woman over and over until finally she fell to her knees gasping for air, as she looked at the motionless woman.

As Isaac picked up the shotgun, Anna looked at him. "Is she dead."

Isaac looked down at the woman's shattered skull and replied. "Yes, I must say she is gone."

Quickly, Isaac removed the balance of the ammunition from the man's vest, as Anna readied the girls to go. Afraid for their safety, they ran east into the small woods behind the cottage, not stopping until they reached a north-south macadam covered road that was very busy with military traffic.

Isaac led them back into the woods a short distance where they found a safe spot behind a fallen tree.

"What do we do now, Isaac? There are soldiers everywhere. We're not safe here. I think we should find another way," Sarah stated, as she watched another truck rumble past.

Isaac shook his head. "One way or the other we have to cross this road if we are going to get into the deep forest, there is no other choice." For the first time since meeting Anna and Isabelle, Isaac was regretting his decision to bring them along. It would definitely be easier for two children to escape across this road than four people, one of them being an adult. But he clearly understood they could no longer abandon them.

As the sun began to set, traffic on the road began to die down, but it was still too dangerous to cross. Isaac hoped once darkness covered the area, they would be able to make a mad dash for the safety of the forest.

About an hour later, Isaac and Sarah cautiously moved closer to the road, so they could watch headlights and figure out when it was safest to run. Around ten o'clock there was not a headlight to be seen. Turning back toward the fallen tree, he called out, "Now, we need to go now, run!"

Anna quickly pulled her sleepy daughter up from the ground and charged around the stump as fast as she could run. Isaac grabbed Sarah's hand as they dashed across the road, running straight into the dark forbidding forest.

Once they were out of sight from the road, Isaac stopped everyone. "We need to camp here for the night. We cannot see where we are going or what might be out there that we need to avoid. I know this is not the best, but it will have to do."

As dawn broke in the east, Isaac was awakened by the sound of heavy tanks rumbling down the road. He awakened Sarah and Anna and prepared them to continue on, although they were all very hungry and cold.

Holding the shotgun at the ready, Isaac slowly began walking deeper into the forest, with Sarah right beside him. About an hour later, a voice called out in Yiddish, "tell them to stop." Isaac peered around the dark forest, but could see no signs of life.

Anna stepped forward, responding in Yiddish, "We mean you no harm, we are Jews like you. We need help, I have three children with me."

Slowly, three men wearing worn old clothing appeared out of the shadows holding German military weapons. "Where have you come from?" A man with a long beard inquired.

Isaac gave a quick explanation, hoping it would put the men at ease and get them to lower their weapons, but they continued standing like statues, not moving a muscle. So, Isaac lowered the shotgun, placing it on the ground in front of him.

The man with the long beard came forward, picking up the weapon. Looking it over he smiled, "It's a nice piece, this cost someone a lot of money, I take it this was not yours. Where did you get it?"

The man who owned it had no need of it where he went, so I took it," Isaac responded nervously, not sure what was going to happen next.

Laughing, the bearded man asked, "Did you send the owner to hell?"

Without changing his facial expression, Isaac pulled the French knife from his jacket, gripping it firmly. "Yes, it was his life or ours. I chose to live."

Handing the shotgun back to Isaac the bearded man half smiled. "You are one of us. Come, we can use a man like you."

Trying not to act scared, Isaac followed the bearded man and his compatriots deeper into the forest until they came to a fast running stream where an encampment of small huts and tents had been set up. The bearded man had Anna, Sarah and Isabelle stay with three women as he took Isaac across the stream to several more tents.

A tall man with a shaved head walked forward. "I am Ishmael, leader of our group. Who might you be, young man."

"I am Isaac Levin, from Penzberg. I hear I have family in this forest, and I would like to find them." Isaac declared more boldly than he thought he was capable of doing.

Ishmael nodded as he rubbed his chin. "First thing to remember, young Isaac, is that no one here has a last name. That will get you in trouble. Use only your first name, you will be Isaac from Penzburg, and only use your town when searching for someone. Now, I do know two people in other groups with that last name. But we try not to cross into other territories too often for a visit. It's safer for all if no one knows who is here, and how many of us there are. However, tomorrow if you want, I will see if we can find them. Otherwise, we will accept the four of you into our band. You are welcome to stay."

Isaac smiled as he shook hands with Ishmael. "I accept your offer. We will join your band. It is not necessary to find my relatives.

The ones you spoke of may not even be related. Best not to take additional risks."

Ishmael looked at the bearded man, "Yosef, let them use the army tent we captured. It will go to good use for the four of them."

The women in the camp were very generous, giving some of the little they had to make the tent as comfortable as possible. As nightfall claimed the forest, Sarah was happy to have some type of enclosure around them, to keep them dry from the morning dew and chilly wind. Settling in next to Anna, she wondered what had happened to her own mother, but now she feared the worst.

Throughout the fall into winter, Sarah and Anna worked with the women to wash clothing and cook meals from whatever the men could bring in from the forest.

Isaac took his turn walking patrols, hunting and standing guard in the tall trees. He never questioned an order, but neither did he fully trust some of the men in the band. He feared they were breaching the security of the forest to steal things from the military and private citizens who lived nearby. That kind of behavior was sure to bring retribution at some point in time.

Near the end of January of 1940, just as winter was at its harshest, two men from the band attempted to sneak into a barn and kill some chickens, or grab a small goat. However, the farmer and his son happened to be near, and chased them back into the forest. They returned to camp without letting anyone know what had happened.

Just after dawn the following day, a large convoy of trucks stopped on the road that Isaac, Sarah and Anna had crossed several months ago. A large contingency of troops and dogs exited the trucks as black uniformed S.S. soldiers and officers began yelling out orders.

Back at the encampment, men who were high in the trees sounded the alarm as they began to withdraw. Everyone knew within a short time their huts and tents would be piles of ash and most of their cooking equipment would be smashed.

Anna took Isabelle by the arm, crossed the stream and began running east with most of the women. Sarah ran up to Isaac where he was stationed to cover the west side of the encampment.

"Come Isaac, we must go, we will be captured or killed if we stay here. We must go, there is nothing and no one left to protect," Sarah pleaded, as she listened to the barking dogs coming closer and closer.

Isaac nodded his head. "In a moment, I must help our people escape."

Just as he finished speaking, an S.S. soldier guiding two snarling dogs came into view about ten yards in front of them. Isaac took in a deep breath and waited a second more before firing the first barrel. The soldier crumbled to the ground as the lead dog let out a yelp. Quickly refocusing his attention on the second dog, he pulled the trigger. The animal instantly dropped to the ground as the buck shot ripped into its side.

Grabbing Sarah by the arm he yelled, "Run!"

They ran at full speed past the burning tents and huts that Yosef's men had set on fire. The billowing smoke added perfect cover for the remaining camp inhabitants to flee as the soldiers began firing their automatic weapons.

After crossing the stream, Isaac pulled Sarah up behind a large tree where he reloaded his weapon. After looking back to see where the soldiers were, he once again took Sarah by the arm and ran for their lives.

By nightfall they had joined up with Josef and several of his men, and a few women. Sarah slept with the women as Isaac took turns watching the forest for danger, and it was not far away.

Throughout the night, more trucks filled with soldiers had arrived. They had spread out over a large section of the forest, hunting down Jews from some of the other camps. Several planes flew overhead, firing machine guns any time pilots saw movement out in front of the troops.

About mid-afternoon Sarah was exhausted, cold, and weak from hunger. As they stopped to take a break, she laid down on the ground looking up at Isaac. "I am too weak and tired, you must go on without me. Save yourself, Isaac."

Angrily, Isaac pulled Sarah to her feet. "Dying is giving Hitler what he wants. We must live to tell our story, to start a new life, to raise new families. Sarah, our faith tells us what we must do."

Sarah shook her head. "Don't tell me you really still believe all of what we were taught in the Temple. Where is God now? Where is the promised land? We are just bait for the army rifles and their camps. We will all die and no one will care. Go on alone, I choose to stay here and die, no more running, or pretending we can survive."

Isaac was stunned when Sarah laid back down and told him to leave, because he could hear the crash of the soldiers breaking through the underbrush as they neared their position. His head pounded knowing his shotgun was no match for the modern firepower the soldiers carried. Now it was run, or stay here and die with Sarah, and he had come too far to quit. Turning east, he began running as fast as he could go, as bullets snapped close by. He wanted desperately to look back and see what had happened to Sarah, but he knew slowing down would mean instant death.

Coming to a small ravine, Isaac dropped down behind several large boulders and stared back to the west, looking for any Germans that might have been on his scent. Although he saw nobody, he knew full well that German soldiers were still on the prowl, as he could hear occasional gunshots and screams echoing throughout the dark forest. But most of all he wondered about Sarah. He had promised he would look out for her when she left her family, and now he had abandoned her when there was no one left to save her. Tears rolled down his face as the pain in his heart overwhelmed him.

Chapter Five
Buchenwald

Margot, Rose and Jonathon huddled together in the ditch beside the train, with several more women and children and a few older people. All the while soldiers shot anyone from the train that even appeared to be making an attempt to run. When the firing stopped, a group of sixty-five more survivors were marched back to the ditch, where angry soldiers stood guard pointing their rifles at them.

"How many do you have?" An officer called out as he walked up to one of the soldiers.

"There are eighty-two total, Herr Captain. What do you want me to do with them?" the soldier inquired as he pointed his machine gun at the last survivors and smiled.

The officer was quiet for a moment as he looked at the bodies covering the ground. "We have a large mess to clean up here already. Find room in the cars toward the front of the train to stuff them into. Pull off some dead if that helps to make room. Do not shoot anymore unless we have no choice."

It didn't take long for the soldiers to find room in other cars for the survivors. Luckily, Margot and the children were able to stay together, when the soldiers found a car with six dead people near the door. As soon as all the doors were properly sealed, the train once more began moving north, pulling just the front half of the train.

Standing by the door now, Margot and the children found themselves in total darkness as they listened to the moans and cries of the people stuffed tightly in the foul-smelling cattle car. However now Margot was short one daughter, her youngest, barely seven and ill-equipped to survive alone under such brutal conditions. She prayed desperately for God to watch out for her Sarah, while hoping she would find her way to freedom.

The final leg of the trip to Buchenwald took about four hours. The engine hissed and belched thick black smoke as it rolled up to the unloading platforms inside the walls of the camp. Fear filled the cars as soldiers screamed, dogs barked, and occasional gun shots were followed by the wailing of terrified Jews as they were pushed and prodded forward on the platform.

Then it was Margot's turn to exit the car. As soon as the door was pushed open, she grabbed Rose and Jonathon by the hand, pulling them down to the platform with a thud. Two dogs snarled and charged toward Jonathon, when he lost his footing falling forward. Rose grabbed him by the arm, yelling,

"Get up, Jonathon, get up. Those dogs will rip you to pieces!"

Jonathon's ankle was swollen and hurt badly after twisting it when he landed on the platform. However, he stood up quickly, and attempted to walk forward, just as one of the dogs tore into his left leg. He let out a tremendous scream as blood gushed from the torn piece of flesh that hung from the back of his leg. Margot grabbed her son, holding him up as she sneered at the soldier with the dog who stood several feet away laughing.

"Leave me mother, I can't walk on that leg. You and Rose go on before the soldiers do something worse to you. I will find you later, I'll be alright."

"No. We shall stay together, Jonathon, we are a family, where one goes, we all go. We must be strong so we can see your father again. He must be here in this wretched place," Margot screamed above all the commotion on the platform.

Arriving at a station where an officer was directing the people, Margot attempted to follow the line to her right before a soldier stopped her. The officer on the podium glared at her before looking down at Jonathon's injured leg.

"Stupid Jew, there is no way he can work like that, he will need medical attention. He goes to the right, the rest of you to the left."

Margot reached out for the officer's arm, pleading to allow her and Rose to walk with Jonathon to the aid station, but the angry officer refused.

"You will go where we tell you to go. You will not argue and you will learn to cooperate while you are here. Now move!"

Rose screamed, "Jonathon, Jonathon come back!" as she watched her brother being pushed away with a large group of mostly older people that obviously would not be able to do any kind of strenuous work. In a moment he was out of sight, disappearing into an ever-increasing number of people being directed into the right-hand line.

Jonathon stumbled along on his sprained ankle as blood continued running down the back of his leg. Soldiers along the walkway used the butts of their rifles to push the slower people forward as they yelled insults. Just a short distance in front of him, a young mother attempted to console her baby that was crying out with hunger pains. Lord only knows how long the poor child had gone since the last time it was fed. An S.S. Soldier ripped the baby from its mother's arms and threw it on the ground, before smashing its skull with his hob nailed boot. With an evil look on his face, he pushed the woman forward while yelling,

"We won't be bringing any more Jewish filth into the world in this place. Now you will need to pay the price for illegally breeding like a dog."

Jonathon shuddered, what was wrong with these people? They were Germans just like the woman and her child. How could a German be so barbaric to another fellow German? How could you destroy a child with the heel of your boot and feel nothing? No matter how hard he tried, Jonathon could not understand what was happening in his beautiful country.

Approaching a large building, two soldiers separated the men from the women forcing them into designated rooms. Once inside, a soldier climbed up on a platform. Looking over the men he called out. "You will need to undress and place your clothing on the benches.

We will then cut your hair so you can be disinfected of lice and other vermin in the showers. Now strip!"

After removing his clothing Jonathon stepped in line to have his hair cut. But it was easy to see they were not getting just haircuts, everyone young and old was getting their heads completely shaved, along with the long beards many Jewish men wore.

At the front of the line, Jonathon observed two S.S. men standing by a huge steel door. They appeared to be laughing as they kept a keen eye on the growing line of men, watching for anyone that might be getting out of control.

After a bell rang, the heavy doors were pulled open by the soldiers as they yelled, "Get in the showers, move, hurry up, you will get soap and a towel when you get inside. Keep going, we do not have all day to shower you."

As Jonathon stepped into the room, he and many other men instantly knew something was not right. Although the floor was wet, none of the shower heads were dripping water, no one was passing out soap and the room smelled of human excrement. Not sure what to do, Jonathon spun around, attempting to push his way back through the surging terrified men. He had almost made it back toward the door when he was hit from behind by the butt of a rifle.

"Where are you going, Jew? If you can't follow orders, I'll just shoot you right now. Is that what you want?"

Staring back up at the soldier, Jonathon nodded his head. "Yes, shoot me, it is finished one way or the other. Let us finish it here."

After the soldier struck Jonathon in the stomach with his rifle, a second soldier came along pulling Jonathon from the cold concrete floor. "Get moving Jew, we've saved room for you."

Once the soldier had pushed Jonathon farther into the room, the large steel door was closed. Every one stood nervously waiting for the water to begin pouring from the shower heads, as heavy boots could be heard walking on the roof above. Moments later the cover from the main vent above was pulled off. A man wearing a mask began pouring pellets down onto a wire mesh screen where they began to disintegrate into a cloud of smoke with a hellish smell. Men reached up toward the mesh, as if attempting to grab the pellets, other men climbed up over their backs attempting to do the same thing. Yells and screams filled the room as one after another, bodies fell to the floor convulsing violently. Jonathon reached for his throat as his airway began to constrict. Backing into a corner near the big door he slid down the wall gasping for air. Closing his eyes, he could see Sarah running into the woods with the boy.

"Be free, Sarah, run free, run free," Jonathon whispered as his head dropped forward.

Moments later the room was quiet. Nothing moved as the Zyklon-B Gas had once again performed its diabolical work. Minutes later, huge blowers started to suck the dangerous gas out of the building so workers could remove the bodies. When the blowers quit, the doors on the far side of the gas chamber were opened. Jewish men called kapos, who were employed on camp work details, entered the room wearing makeshift covers over their faces to protect them from any residual gas that might be lingering. They began by picking up the bodies around the perimeter of the room. Once all the easily accessible bodies were removed, the men would literally have to rip apart the bodies that were intertwined in the center of the room. It was ghastly work, but it offered life over death to the men chosen for the jobs.

Jonathon's body was picked up by a kapo and placed on a steel cart along with three others. Another kapo dropped an empty cart for the workers, as he pulled the loaded one to the crematorium.

Since the train Jonathon arrived on was late, there were not a large amount of bodies waiting to be cremated from earlier gassings. So, Jonathon's body was immediately placed on a steel stretcher along with the body of the baby that the guard had killed earlier, and shoved into the blast furnace. Once the door was closed, the fire roared to life, consuming everything but bits of bone and teeth, that would be ground up later by kapos. As the raging fire consumed their mortal bodies, thick black smoke and ash rose from the massive chimneys, drifting their spirits off in whichever direction the wind was blowing that day.

As Buchenwald did not keep women at that time, Margot and Rose were taken to what was called a transitional barracks for the night. They were given a meal of soup that was mostly water with a few pieces of vegetable floating in it, and a very hard, dried up piece of bread. In the morning they were placed on a small train that took all the women to one of many satellite camps nearby to work. The camp Margot and Rose were taken to was near Wiemar.

Thankfully, the conditions at the work camp were slightly better than Buchenwald. Margot was assigned to work in a factory that produced parts for undercarriages of German fighter aircraft and dive bombers. It was strenuous work for women, but Margot became determined to do whatever it took to survive.

Rose was assigned a job in the kitchen, making meals for the workers. Although it meant death if she were caught, Rose would shove an extra crust of bread in her mouth whenever she felt it was safe. That way she would eat only part of her daily ration, giving the rest to her mother to keep her strong.

Most of the women in the camp had the same mind set as Margot. Doing their jobs properly and without creating problems meant life, at least for the time being. But there were always women that either refused to cooperate, or would attempt to sabotage the German war effort, and that created problems for everyone.

Late one day after Margot had been working in the plant for several months, an inspector found several hydraulic cylinders missing an important bushing that could cause all the fluid to leak out upon landing. After checking all the crates ready for shipment, they found ten more defective units. The superintendent of the plant immediately notified the S.S. officer in charge of the camp workers. He watched the assembly line from an overhead cat walk for over an hour, before observing two women on Margot's line failing to install the bushing.

Calling over three guards, the women on the line were removed from their jobs and marched out of the plant to an area by the loading docks. Margot and several other women protested, saying they had no idea the bushing was missing, and they had no way of knowing by the time the cylinders came to them for installation. The S.S. lieutenant listened intently to their explanations as the plant manager pleaded with the angry officer to spare the women that were doing the job properly, as replacing all of them would set back production, and that was not acceptable in Berlin.

After pacing back and forth for several moments the lieutenant looked at his sergeant. "And how do you feel about all of this?"

The sergeant clicked his heels together as he replied. "Sir, my brother is a pilot in the Luftwaffe. I would not want him landing with these landing gears. It could kill him. What is the life of a Jewess over the life of a patriotic Luftwaffe pilot?"

After nodding his head, the lieutenant looked at the plant manager. "Surely my sergeant's question weighs more heavily on my decision than your concerns to keep up production.

Turning to his sergeant, the officer nodded his head. "Do it!"

Seconds later, all three S.S. guards opened fire on the ten women. Margot dropped to the ground gasping for breath as tears filled her eyes. She knew from the beginning it would possibly come to something like this, but had prayed fervently to survive. As a shadow came across her face she looked up. One of the soldiers was standing over her with a pistol in his hand. Closing her eyes, she began to pray as a single gunshot echoed off the walls of the factory.

When the work detail arrived back from the factory, they explained to Rose what had happened to her mother. That evening Rose joined the women from the barracks on the floor, reciting the prayers of Kaddish for their friends who had been executed.

A kindly woman named Mary took Rose under her protection, giving her some sense of peace now that she was alone. Rose knew all too well that her mother had now joined Jonathon's ashes in the sky above the camp and her soul had been set free. Although Sarah's escape had angered her at the time, she was happy now that she had taken the chance. Tonight, Rose laid on her filthy mat, wondering where her little sister was. Had she been able to survive against the pursuing soldiers? Had she found people to take care of her? Was she free and safe? All those things went through her mind though she understood the odds were against a little girl of just seven. In her mind she saw Sarah dancing near a stream with flowers in her hair, enjoying other children she had met, somewhere far away from Germany and the hatred that had filled so many people. However, her heart told her that was nothing more than a dream, as everything was against her silly, persistent little sister. But no matter what her heart tried to tell her, the thought of Sarah dancing by that stream gave Rose the comfort she needed to fall asleep tonight.

Although Mary and several other women in the camp watched over Rose, she missed her mother very much, and from time to time contemplated suicide. Her plan would be quick and painless. All she had to do was walk up to a guard and spit on him, and she would be shot in the head instantly.

However, an inner voice kept crying out to her, "Survive, you must survive!"

Although working in the kitchen was a safer and cleaner job than most positions, the S.S. corporal in charge of the kitchen had become ruthless. She had the soldiers search each worker several times a day, looking for the least scrap of bread they may be concealing for someone else. If a worker dropped anything on the floor, their ration was cut for the day. One of the oldest guards named Helga, hated the young Jewish girls with a passion. She had no problem striking them while she laughed, or beating her target of the day unmercifully with the baton she carried just for fun. If she broke bones, she simply called for soldiers to take the girl away, as she could no longer work. Rose had been struck by the brutal woman on several occasions, though never seriously injured, but she realized her day was coming.

That afternoon when she made her way back to the barracks, the lieutenant in charge of the work details was walking through the yard. Walking up to the young officer, Rose bowed down to him while saying, "Heil Hitler Herr Lieutenant! May I speak with you."

The officer looked Rose over before he backed away a few feet. "What do you need, do you not know your place in this camp yet? Do you need to be taught a lesson?"

Rose was now wishing she would have just avoided the idea of asking for a new job. As she trembled, the officer yelled at her again.

"Girl, what do you want? Don't just stand there and act like a fool!"

"Herr Lieutenant, I have been working in the kitchen since I arrived. I was wondering if I could get a job in the plane factory? I am still strong, I can work hard." Rose blurted out, waiting for the soldier standing beside the officer to strike her.

Laughing, the lieutenant slapped her across the face with his leather riding gloves. "A Jewess asking for a favor? Asking me of all people for a favor. Who do you think you are? You are nothing but a tramp and a whore, now go to your barracks before I have you shot!"

Rose quickly turned and ran as fast as she could for her barracks, expecting to have a bullet hit her in the back before she could get in the door. Shaking and nearly out of control, she sat down on her filthy mat and cried. She knew she had just placed a target on her back, and that Helga would know all about it when she arrived for work the next day. Totally scared, Rose slept less than she did most nights, sure this would be her last night on earth.

When the guards arrived in the morning to assemble the work details, the sergeant pulled her away from the kitchen crew and pushed her to the ground. When he was finished with the morning count he turned to Rose. "You are going to the sorting building from now on, you will learn to speak only when spoken to. Follow me."

Rose had heard of the sorting room and wanted no part of it. Every piece of personal property brought by the Jews passed through this building, along with hair that needed sorting by color, teeth that needed to have gold extracted, and ears still containing piercings that required removal. Like the teeth, much of the clothing was blood soaked and had to be cleaned. Countless fingers and toes were found in the buckets of rings that needed sorting and sizing. She now wished she had kept her mouth shut.

The most degrading part of this job was the cavity search each worker had to go through at the end of each day. The searches were conducted by female S.S. soldiers that were just as brutal and demeaning as their male counterparts. Of course, if a worker was caught attempting to smuggle anything out of the building, it was instant death.

Rose longed to be back in the kitchen, where she was able to grab small pieces of bread or rutabagas that were used in the watery soup. It was never much, but just enough to keep her hunger somewhat under control. All she had now was the meager rations every other prisoner in the camp was fed, and she began to feel her strength starting to slip away.

As winter invaded Buchenwald, everything went from bad to worse. The guards handed out small lumps of coal for heating each of the barracks. The women attempted to add small pieces of wood they could break loose from the bunks or floor boards to lengthen the time they had a little heat. But most often the fire was gone in less than an hour.

Everyone was sick with colds and flu, but there was no medical treatment available. At night the women huddled together on their mats for warmth, covering themselves with the few thin motheaten blankets they were given. Each morning when they were awakened by the guards, they would drag the bodies of women that had not survived the night to the yard. This time of year, not a night passed that someone in the barracks did not die, and most often there was more than one.

Now Rose liked going to her job a little more than normal. The guards in the sorting building did not like being cold, so they stoked the little stove quite often, allowing the building to remain somewhat comfortable.

By the end of December Rose had become quite sick, and was not able to go to work. She laid on her mat getting weaker every day, despite some of the women giving her a part of their rations. There was no doubt in her mind that the end was near. With everyone gone to work, Rose laid silently on her mat, listening to the raging wind that drove an ample amount of snow around the windows into the barracks. The more she listened, the more she was sure she could hear her mother whispering on the wind, asking her to come home. No longer did she hear that little voice inside calling out for her to survive, that voice had disappeared months ago, and Rose no longer saw any reason to hold on.

About midday, Rose struggled to force herself up off her mat. Painfully, she walked through the barracks toward the door. As the snow swirled around the yard like dancing demons, Rose walked along the side of the barracks toward the large wooden bench she had sat upon so often. After pushing the snow aside with her withered hand, she sat down.

As the women returned from work that afternoon, Mary looked strangely toward the bench, unable to make out what was there. Walking over with several guards, they found Rose's frozen body leaning up against the building covered with snow. Mary knelt down beside the girl she loved so much, and picking up her hand, she wept. Within minutes, several kapos arrived to take Rose to the crematorium.

Chapter Six
Constant Fear

Sarah opened her eyes as the sounds of heavy footsteps and the snarling of dogs became closer by the second. It was too late to stand up and run, and Isaac was long gone. She was totally alone for the first time since running from the train, and there was nothing she could do to change it now.

Fear filled her body as a soldier stood above her looking down at her with contempt in his soul. "Sergeant, I found us a little Jew girl over here. She appears to be all alone."

The sergeant walked over toward the soldier asking. "What is your name, child?"

Sarah refused to answer as the sergeant scared her more than any other soldier she had ever seen. He had the look in his eye of someone who loved to see people suffer at his hands.

Stepping up to Sarah, the sergeant ran his hands through her snarled hair. "You could be very cute if you had a bath and your hair was brushed out nicely. Maybe I could take care of those things for you. What do you say about that?"

Angered by his sergeant's advances, the soldier rebuked his leader. "She's just a child, can't be more than six or seven. Leave her alone, let's turn her in to the lieutenant!"

The sergeant laughed as he ran his hand over the side of Sarah's face. "Corporal, you do not often get the chance to have such a lovely child all to yourself, without someone getting in your way. I think I have scored a real prize and you will not tell the lieutenant or anyone else. Do I make myself clear, corporal?"

Shaking his head, the corporal and the soldier with him slowly made their way forward, leaving Sarah alone with their depraved leader. Sitting down on a tree stump the sergeant began unbuttoning Sarah's shirt as he said, "I think we should see what the merchandise looks—"

He never finished his sentence as an arrow pierced his chest, sending him tumbling backwards. Sarah stood spellbound for a moment before a heavy hand came down on her shoulder. Looking up she saw the face of Yosef smiling at her.

"Come quickly child!" he whispered, as he took her small hand.

Moving rapidly through the forest, two more men carrying rifles joined Yosef as they headed due south. Sarah's lungs were burning and her legs were getting tired, but she knew better than to complain. She knew these men had placed their lives on the line to save her from a fate worse than death, and she appreciated it.

Arriving at a small clearing, Sarah saw a large group of people assembled eating a small meal. Some were from the camp she had been in, but now there were many Jews from other camps that had been overrun by the soldiers. Ishmael was sitting on a tree stump making more arrows as he hummed a song Sarah slightly remembered from going to the synagogue.

Looking up at Yosef, Ishmael smiled. "Tell us what you have seen, my friend."

Shaking his head, Yosef replied. "There are hundreds of them, we killed two with arrows. This is a good plan you came up with, Ishmael. They do not make a sound to give away your location."

Ishmael smiled as he stood up. "Continue, please."

"Other than Sarah, I don't think they found anyone else. They were pretty disgusted with trekking through the cold forest, though I can't say that they will be leaving soon."

Nodding his head, Ishmael walked over to Sarah. "And Isaac, did the soldiers get him?"

"No, I laid down and told Isaac I couldn't go on any longer, and that I would just wait to die. He argued with me, but I refused to get back up. He ran to the east and I have not seen him since. I was wrong, I should have gone with him," Sarah explained, as a tear rolled down her cheek.

Ishmael smiled as he knelt down to give Sarah a hug. "You are safe now, child. God sent Yosef to find you and here you are. I'm sure Isaac will regret leaving you."

Sarah shook her head. "I don't believe in this God who is to be our king. Look where we are, look how we live, even Isaac abandoned me. No, there can be no one looking out for us anymore."

Ishmael placed his strong hands on her little shoulders. "Someday Sarah, you will understand and you will know our God again. Have faith my child."

Just as Ishmael finished speaking, a band of men came from the east. The man who appeared to be the leader walked up to Ishmael. "We have walked to the border of Slovakia. We have seen no signs of soldiers. But there are guards that drive a very rutted road along the border. They don't appear to have any regular schedule. But I'm afraid mines could have been planted on both sides of the border after the Germans invaded, but none of us can be certain. Another Jew we ran into who came from the south, told us the road to Domazlice is guarded by German S.S. troops at the border crossing."

Ishmael nodded his head. "That is a lot of information, my brother. Rest now and eat, we will talk later about what we should do."

After a nervous night, Sarah was invited to join some of the other children in a small breakfast. She watched with anticipation as Ishmael sent a group of men back toward the Czechoslovakian border with knives and sharp sticks. By evening they returned, carrying a bag containing German antipersonnel mines they had dug up along the border.

Ishmael called the congregation together for a meeting. Climbing onto a tree stump, he explained. "Our brothers have cleaned a clear path across the border into the Slovakian forest. They have marked the path so we can cross safely. Anyone who wishes to remain here can do so, and we will wish you all the best. All those who wish to cross with me into Slovakia, please assemble to my left. We will move as soon as it grows dark. I am told by a good source that we can find some safety around the town of Strakonice."

Sarah was scared without Isaac, but felt like Josef and his wife were good people to cling to for the time being. So, she joined them as they assembled with the group that decided to follow Ishmael.

After much discussion, just twenty-five people decided to cross over into Czechoslovakia that night. Josef and his brother Ari, escorted two people at a time to the safe crossing point where Ishmael and two other men awaited. Although no border guards appeared to be on duty, Ishmael felt something was terribly wrong. Josef begged him to get the people across as quickly as possible, but once again Ishmael was reluctant. He realized the heavy fog could not only cover their movements, it could also cover the presence of soldiers patrolling the border trail.

A man named Izak approached Ishmael. "Everyone wants to go, my brother, they are getting restless. We must do something soon, or they will scatter back into the forest and get captured or step on mines. You must make a decision."

Ishmael shook his head, "What you cannot see can hurt you. I do not wish to have the blood of these people on my hands when it is not necessary, Izak. We shall wait until we know it is safe."

Angrily, Izak walked back into the forest, feeling Ishmael was being overly cautious. After speaking with the people, Izak brought them all up to the crossing point. "We have spoken and all agree, we are going to cross over now."

Turning to Josef, Izak nodded his head, "Then take the first four with you if that is their wish. I will send the rest in small groups until we are all across. It is the only way."

Josef smiled as he motioned for the first four people to follow him across the border. They had barely walked about twenty yards when voices called out from the fog, "Halt, stay where you are!"

"Run, run!" Josef called out, as two heavy machine guns began spraying bullets around the crossing. One man jumped off the trail stepping on a land mine, killing himself and seriously wounding his wife. The other couple stood frozen in place, watching in horror as Josef continued calling for them to run toward him. A second later, machine gun fire tore into them as well.

An armored car appeared out of the mist with its gunner also spraying the woods with his deadly weapon. Screams filed the night as bullets tore into flesh, and soldiers with bayonets charged into the woods, stabbing the wounded and firing at anything that moved.

Sarah dove behind a tree as she watched several people around her getting hit by rifle fire. This was no time to play dead, as she could see the soldiers stabbing anyone that was on the ground. With every ounce of energy in her body, she stood up and ran quickly toward the south, weaving back and forth around trees, trying to avoid the bullets whizzing all around her. As if in a daze, her feet began to stumble and lose contact with the ground, and she felt herself spinning out of control, until she slammed in to the hard ground with a solid thud. All the sounds of screams and gunfire were suddenly intertwined with a loud roar that filled her head, making it feel as if it were going to explode.

Two days later Sarah awoke in a warm bed with a large bandage covering most of her head. Without being able to focus her vision, Sarah panicked as she attempted to sit up.

"No, no, you must lay still. You are not well enough to sit up yet." A woman's soft voice said calmly in German.

After Sarah laid back down, the woman asked, "What is your name, child? Where were you going last night? Where are your parents?"

Although her head was pounding beyond anything she had ever experienced before, she realized anything she said now could mean instant death at the hands of the S.S. soldiers. "I cannot see. Who are you and where am I? I don't remember anything."

After a moment of silence, the woman responded. "Your vision should come back over the next few days, A bullet grazed the side of your head. My name is Gretchen, my husband is Stefan. We found you crawling near the edge of the forest two days ago. Were you with the Jews that were shot in the forest?"

Gretchen's question scared Sarah to the core. "What people are you talking about, I was hiking with my family, I don't remember anything else."

"After changing the compress on Sarah's forehead, Gretchen leaned close to Sarah's ear. "Try and sleep now, child. You have nothing to fear from us, nothing will happen to you."

Once more, Sarah went in and out of consciousness for the next three days as Gretchen and her husband looked after her. When she finally regained full consciousness early the following morning, her sight was back to normal. Looking around the small bedroom, she was happy to see a window on the south wall she could easily crawl out off.

However, before Sarah could begin to get out of bed, the door opened. An attractive woman in her forties with long dark hair walked up to her. "Do you remember me? My name is Gretchen."

Sarah nodded her head, "Yes, I remember your voice. You have been kind to me, but I must go. I must find my parents and a safe place, I will only get you in trouble if I stay here."

Gretchen smiled as she looked down at Sarah. "Child, you are safe here. We know you are a Jew, and we don't care. We do not believe in Herr Hitler's idea of racial cleansing. Whatever we can do for you we will do. The soldiers have not been around our small farm in a long time. They all knew we had a daughter about your age, but she died during the winter from a virus. So, if they should come, they will think you are her. Her name was Helga, and we will call you that, so you get used to it."

Sarah exhaled a sigh of relief. Feeling guilty, Sarah looked at Gretchen. "I lied to you, I have no parents or family, they are all dead now. But what I need is to get to Vichy France. I have heard they are not rounding up Jews in areas controlled by the Free French and I want to go there."

"We knew you were alone, and we were sure your family was gone. But you must get better first, as you are in no condition to travel right now. Then we can see what can be done about getting you to Vichy," Gretchen replied with a smile that helped calm many of Sarah's deepest fears.

When Sarah was able to get out of bed, she found that her right leg was not working as it should be. Over the next few months, she worked on running and climbing the ladder in the barn up to the hay loft. Little by little the leg responded until it was nearly back to normal, although she now had a slight limp. Only once during that time did any soldiers visit the farm. When they checked over the family paper work, they were totally satisfied that Sarah was indeed the daughter, Helga.

As Christmas of 1940 approached, Sarah enjoyed helping Gretchen decorate the house and place a small fir tree Stefan had cut down in their family room. She didn't let the fact that she was Jewish interfere with the couples Christmas traditions, in fact, it gave her a feeling of belonging she had missed since losing her own family. As New Year's Eve began slipping away into the new year, Gretchen and Sarah went for a walk through the newly fallen snow. As they strolled into the barn to check on the animals, Gretchen turned toward Sarah.

"What is your wish for the new year, Sarah?"

Sarah stood quiet for a moment as she contemplated the question. "I have come to love you and Stefan very much. You have been very good to me, like my own family. I know I would not have survived without your help, and I am very grateful. I almost hate to say this, but I would still like to go to Vichy France, where my people are still free. I feel it in my bones, I must go there."

Gretchen smiled kindly toward Sarah. "Stefan and I both understand why you would still like to go there, although we would like you to stay with us forever. We have come to love you also, and no one will ever know who you really are as long as you stay here. We can discuss it more once spring arrives and travelling is easier."

By June, Sarah's leg was fully back to normal. She was becoming more restless, and decided she was going to southern France one way or the other. After a long talk with Gretchen and Stefan the decision was made to allow Sarah to make the trip.

Stephan went out to the barn and dug up a metal container he had buried under a straw pile. The box was filled with gold and silver coins that were worth countless thousands of Reich's Marks. Looking up at Sarah, Stephan explained.

"There was a man that came here months before we found you. He accused us of helping Jews escape into Czechoslovakia, and he was right. He wanted us to bring some Jews here so he could turn them over to the Gestapo and make big money. When we told him no, he said he was going to turn us in and make better money. A scuffle began, and I killed him. We buried him in the forest, hid his box, and stopped helping any more Jews, we were scared. So now we can use some of that money to get you forged documents. We want to help you get what you want, although we will miss you very much."

Over the next month Stefan filled out countless forms supplied by the German Government, that would allow his daughter to travel by herself to attend school in Paris. Meanwhile, an expert forger that lived deep in the forest, began creating all the documents Sarah would require, using the name of Helga.

The forger was happy to do the work for just one of the gold coins. It was more than he had made in over a year, but it was difficult work. He had to make a rail pass from Aigen, Germany to Munich, with a transfer pass for the train from Munich to Freiburg near the French border. He then had to create a permit to cross into German held France, and a rail ticket that would take her to Paris. Those documents were the toughest as they changed on a regular basis. He could not create a document for her to travel from Paris to Vichy France. That she would have to get permission to do from the local S.S. office or a corrupt French official, and there were many of them in Paris. But at least she would have gold coins to help grease some palms along the way.

On September 10th, Sarah climbed onto the train at Aigen. She called out for all the German officials to hear. "Bye Mom and Dad. I'll send you a letter when I get to Aunt Clara's place in Paris. I can't wait to start school. Thank you for all your help."

It wasn't hard for Gretchen to act like a grieving mother, since she had come to love Sarah very much. As tears rolled down her cheeks, she called out, "Be safe, Helga, you know we love you."

Before she could settle back in her seat, a female S.S. officer walked up to her. "Young lady, my name is Lieutenant Kimmler, you should have checked with me before taking your seat. I am responsible for all unattended children riding this train as it says on your ticket."

Sarah felt a twinge of fear as she looked at the back of her ticket. "I am sorry Lieutenant. I have never traveled before, and I never read the back of the ticket. My parents want me to go to school in Paris, but I did not want to leave them. I am honestly scared."

The lieutenant laughed a little as she looked at Sarah. "Yes, being just nine years old, you are actually very young to be traveling by yourself. Your father told me they did not have enough money for one of them to ride with you, so that is why they made these plans. No worries, Helga, everything will be just fine. Walk with me when we get to Munich, and I will get your transfer made."

As the officer walked away, Sarah crashed back into her seat and closed her eyes. It was as if everything they had worked on for so long was over before the train left the station.

Although the trip to Munich went well, Sarah could not get past her fear as several S.S. officers and the always questioning Gestapo agents sat across from her.

Arriving in Munich, Sarah found Lt. Kimmler and seven other children standing on the platform waiting for her. After collecting all their tickets, the lieutenant walked them over to a Gestapo desk where final verification of tickets was taking place.

The captain examined each ticket very carefully before handing them back to the lieutenant. After looking at Sarah's ticket, the officer smiled. "My daughter is in Paris, she is going to the same school you will be going to. You will enjoy it very much."

Sarah smiled. "Thank you, Captain. I hope to meet your daughter, it would be nice to have a friend."

The captain was just about to say something when the conductor called out for everyone to board the train. He just smiled at Sarah and patted her on the head as she walked off with the rest of the children. She felt like she was going to vomit, but was able to control herself as she climbed into the coach.

Sarah breathed a sigh of relief when she sat down, knowing a good part of the trip to Freiburg would be over night, and no one would bother a sleeping child. Although the train made several stops to take on water and pick up passengers, Sarah slept most of the time. When she did not sleep, she wondered what had happened to Isaac, Anna and Ishmael. She was sure Josef had been killed that night at the border crossing. She felt bad for Mazal and wondered what she would do without her husband.

Arriving at Freiburg, Lt. Kimmler handed Sarah and the other children over to a sergeant in the Wehrmacht, who drove them the last few miles to the French border. The security at the border was tight, as the S.S. and Gestapo agents were always on the lookout for army deserters, spies, or Jews masquerading as normal German or French civilians. She arrived just in time to see several Gestapo officers pushing three people they had arrested into the back of a truck and driving away. She fully understood that no one would ever hear from those poor people ever again.

After having her ticket analyzed several times, Sarah and the other children climbed aboard a French passenger car for the trip to Paris. She was not sure who was going to pick her up at the train station, so she had to be ready to play the game properly so as not to draw unwanted attention. Sarah was sure it was going to be someone from the Jewish underground that still operated in France, although their numbers were dwindling as the Gestapo continued searching for them.

The atmosphere inside the cars was much more relaxed than in the German cars. People laughed freely and paid little attention to the Gestapo and S.S. Officers, at times being almost totally disrespectful. Sarah found it amusing that these normally tough and belligerent men now felt intimidated by the people they had conquered. It made Sarah happy, as it was clear the French were conquered, but definitely not out of the fight by any means, and the German soldiers understood it clearly.

As the train began to slow just outside Paris, a tall bearded man wearing a shabby suit came walking down the aisle toward Sarah. When he was just one seat away, he dropped his glasses. As he reached over to pick them up, he whispered, "Get off the car as soon as you can, there will be a woman holding a small sign saying Chartres. Get away from the other children and go to her quickly. Say nothing, just follow her where she leads you."

Before Sarah could say a word, the man stood up with his glasses and said, "I am sorry to disturb you, Mademoiselle, I should just keep them on my face all the time."

Nodding her head politely, she said nothing and turned back toward the window. She wondered who the man was, and more importantly how did he know who she was? For the first time since leaving Aigen, a terrific sense of fear had overcome her. She felt the cold eyes of Lt. Kimmler burning a hole into the back of her head, and she fully realized the Lieutenant was S.S. clear through.

As the train came to a halt, Lt. Kimmler stood up, "Children, the Paris Station is always busy. Stay together right behind me and we will get to the bus just fine."

Sarah stood up and smiled at the German officer as if trying to convince her she was not going to be a problem. She quickly began rummaging around in her back pack as if looking for something, allowing the rest of the children to exit the car in front of her. As Sarah came down the steps to the platform, she was taken back as a large contingency of S.S. soldiers and Gestapo men were searching back packs, brief cases, and any packages the passengers were carrying. As she handed her back pack to a Gestapo agent he called out,

"Child, what is your name and who do you belong to? I do not have time for games, who are your parents?"

Before Sarah could respond, Lt. Kimmler stepped up to the angry man. "She is with me, Herr Captain. Her parents sent her to Paris to attend school with the rest of my charges. She is not who you are looking for."

"And how do you know who we are looking for? We already have one in custody," he responded as he pointed to the man with the beard that had warned her on the train.

Looking nervous, Lt. Kimmler nodded her head in understanding as she cleared her throat. "Herr Captain, I can assure you this child is of Aryan blood, she is not a Jew. I met her parents and they are proud German citizens, just looking to give their daughter a good education."

Raising his voice, the Captain stared at Lt. Kimmler. "You can assure me of nothing, Lieutenant. I decide who is a threat to our Fuhrer's dream for the Third Reich, and I think she is involved with the old man." Turning to a soldier behind him he yelled, "Detain her, take her out to the car. Do it now!"

Before Sarah could think of what to say, she was being dragged through the train station right past a nervous elderly woman holding up a sign that read, Chartres.

After a short wait, a female Gestapo agent slid into the car behind the steering wheel and drove off without saying a word. Although the car was passing many of the historical sites of Paris, Sarah never noticed a single one of them. Her total attention was focused on the angry Gestapo agent driving the car, and what her fate might be before this night was over.

About a half hour later the agent drove the car into the center of Paris. She turned into an alley behind a large building and stopped. Two S.S. soldiers opened the rear door of the car, ordering Sarah out. They took her to an office on the second floor of the building where they pushed her into a chair.

One soldier stood next to her while the other soldier picked up a phone and made a call. About ten minutes later a major wearing a Wehrmacht uniform stepped into the room. "Bring her into my office."

The S.S. soldier grabbed Sarah by the arm, leading her into a very ornate office with a large painting of Adolph Hitler hanging on the wall behind the desk. The major looked over Sarah's paperwork quickly before looking up.

"You see your Fuhrer on the wall and you say nothing?"

Shaking like a leaf, Sarah thrust her right hand into the air while calling out "Heil Hitler, Herr Major! I apologize, I'm scared, I do not know what is going on."

The major stared at Sarah for several minutes. "Or maybe your parents did not impress upon you what the proper greeting is for a loyal German?"

Sarah nearly snapped to attention. "No Major, they are good loyal Germans. That is why they wanted to give me the best education possible, so I can grow up and work for the Fatherland and my Fuhrer, to make our country greater."

The Major shrugged his shoulders as he grumbled something Sarah could not understand. He walked over to the window and looked down on the street below. "What do you think of Paris, Helga?"

"I do not think anything, Herr Major. I have been too scared to look around," Sarah replied, telling the honest truth.

Laughing, the turned to face her. "Ya, I guess I can understand that for a child your age. So, tell me, who was going to meet you at the train station?"

Frowning, Sarah looked questioningly at the major. "No one, Herr Major. I was with Lieutenant Kimmler. She was taking us to the school, I was the last one getting off the train. We were assigned to her since we were all too young to travel by ourselves. My parents did not have enough money to pay for train fare to come with me. It was hard enough for them to scratch up the money to pay for my schooling. They are simple farmers, Herr Major."

Pointing at the soldier he called out, "Let her sit, you can go."

After the soldier left, the major began looking over Sarah's traveling documents again. "What did it cost your parents to get you all the way to Paris and enroll you in school, Helga?"

Sarah attempted to look very sad. "When my grandmother died last year, she left money for my parents to make improvements on the farm. Instead, they spent just about all of it to get me in the school. What little they had left, they used to buy a new plow horse because one of ours was stolen and then killed."

After placing Sarah's documents on the desk, he looked at her intensely. "Who took your horse and why was it killed."

"One night, some filthy Jews took our horse as they tried to escape into Czechoslovakia. There were soldiers chasing them. Just before they crossed the border the soldiers opened fire. That is when our horse was killed," Sarah replied.

The major shook his head. "Ya, things like that happen way too often, but the day will come when the Jews will no longer be a problem here in Europe. Our Fuhrer is seeing to that."

Sarah smiled. "We will all live better then, Herr Major. My father and mother have said Germany will be a richer country once those people are gone."

Smiling, the major continued. "So, Helga, what am I to do with you now? I see no reason to hold you, and I see no connection between you and the man we captured on your train. I suppose we can get a hold of Lt. Kimmler and have her come here to pick you up. Would you like that, Helga?"

Nodding her head Sarah replied. "Yes, Herr Major. I am tired and hungry and in need of a hot bath. I still feel scared after all of this today."

Before the major could respond, there was a knock at the door.

"Enter!" The major called out as he stood up.

An S.S. soldier walked in. "Herr Major, we have a Doctor Stanman here from the New German Grammar school, wondering what is going on with a Helga Buchner. What do I tell him?"

"Good, good, send him right in," the major replied with a broad smile on his face. "See Helga, everything is falling into place for you. No more reason to be scared."

Sarah nearly fell out of the chair when she realized the man that was coming to pick her up was Ishmael, now sporting a full head of hair and a neatly shaved beard. Snapping to attention and raising his right arm smartly, Ishmael called out, "Good afternoon Herr Major, Heil Hitler."

Saluting back, the major replied, Heil Hitler Herr Doctor. As you can see, Helga is just fine. There was a minor problem on the train with some Jewish people. As you can understand we needed to figure out who was who."

Ishmael nodded his head. "We do many background checks, Herr Major, to make sure only Aryan children get into our schools. Helga has passed all those checks in good order. Plus, she is a gifted child that will make a great student for us."

The major walked around the desk and shook hands with Ishmael. "I am glad you arrived, otherwise I would have to arrange transport for Helga and it is a busy day for us." After handing Sarah's paper work to Ishmael. he looked down at her. "Go now, and make your parents proud."

Sarah jumped up from the chair and gave the major a big hug. "Thank you for being so nice to me. In a way you remind me of my grandfather."

The major patted Sarah on the back of her head. "He is a lucky man to be a grandfather to someone as sweet as you. Go now Helga. Heil Hitler."

Both Sarah and Ishmael saluted while calling out, "Heil Hitler, Herr Major."

Arriving back into the alley, Ishmael led Sarah to an older French Citroen and opened the door. Before Sarah climbed into the car, she leaned against the brick wall and vomited while crying.

Chapter Seven
Paris

Neither Sarah or Ishmael said a word to one another until they were several miles from the Security office. Finally, Sarah looked over at Ishmael. "I figured you, Anna and Josef were all dead. How did you escape? How did you get here to Paris? How did you know I was on the train? How did you know where to find me?"

Smiling, Ishmael responded. "Ah yes, that is our Sarah. Always filled with so many questions that need to be answered. But I have not yet heard a thank you for getting you out of the hands of the Germans. Are you not thankful?"

Sarah looked down for a moment. "Forgive me, I was wrong for not thanking you, I have been so scared today. I thought I would be killed for sure. Thank you, Ishmael"

Just as Ishmael turned into an empty factory near the edge of Paris, he began. "Anna is dead. She and Isabelle were executed in the forest. Josef was also killed, though I am not sure what happened to his wife. But I have heard that Isaac is still alive and somewhere here in France."

After driving into an underground garage, Ishmael sat back in his seat. "I knew it was not safe in the forest that day. When the shooting began, I tried to grab you, but you pulled away and I lost sight of you in the fog. I ran back into the forest and hid for several days by myself, as the Germans killed and killed and killed. There are many Jews lying dead in that forest. I wandered south and was able to sneak across the Austrian border to the town of Neufelden. I stole clothing I found hanging on wash lines in several neighborhoods at night. I found a part time job working for an old Austrian that did not ask too many questions. I helped load and unload barges on the Danube. After a month I found out there was a Jewish underground network close by. I found them and joined, becoming their eyes and ears in the city. One day, I accompanied a load to Linz, and that was my lucky break. I climbed onto a freight train that was parked in a yard near the Danube. I hid in a car filled with lumber that was going to Salzburg. In Salzburg I killed a German captain and took his uniform, money and military papers assigning him to a headquarters company in Paris. Once I was on the train, no one bothered to check my papers—all the way to France."

As Ishmael and Sarah walked from the car to a small room one level below the main floor, he continued. "At the border there were many checks looking for soldiers who were missing, and Jews that were trying to escape toward southern France. During the night I crossed the border near Selestat, France, then climbed aboard a passenger train just as it began departing the yard. I jumped from the train before it arrived in Paris and changed back into the clothes I had stolen. It took me several weeks, but I finally found this underground operation and joined it. Sarah, you may not like this, but after the Germans came for my family I became a con man and a thief, and I was good at it. I did many bad things to both Jews and Germans alike, as I tried to stay alive and free. Now that I have seen what the Germans are doing to our people, I have a need to repent, so I help our people whenever I can. I'd never physically hurt anyone before the war started, but now I will kill a Nazi if push comes to shove, that's just the way it has to be. Luckily for me, those skills I learned years ago pay big dividends today. Now you know my story."

"I do not know everything," Sarah exclaimed, as she took Ishmael by the arm. "How did you know I was on the train?"

"We have spies on that train from the border to Paris every day. We know who is on it, and what their jobs are. I was on the train with you as a Wehrmacht soldier returning from leave back home. I saw you before you climbed aboard. And Lt. Kimmler is no more, by the way, there was nothing I could do. She will no longer be a problem for us."

Sarah was stunned by Ishmael's story, but believed every word he had told her. She knew from the moment she met him that he was a man of many abilities that both should and should not be trusted. But now she felt safe around him once more.

In the deepest basement of the old factory, lived a group of thirty men and woman, along with five children. They were well armed and answered to a man they called Baruch.

Later that evening, Sarah found Ishmael smoking his cherished pipe as he kept guard on one of the entrances. Sarah sat down beside him and was quiet for a short time. Finally, she looked up and questioned him. "You have killed a lot of Germans now, does it give you satisfaction? I want to kill them because of what they did to my family and our people. I would like to get even with them."

"Yes child, it does give me satisfaction, but it also takes something from my soul, and I do not know if God will allow me to ever get it back," Ishmael responded, before pulling in more smoke from his pipe. Exhaling, he continued. "Life is not what it once was. I never thought I would kill even one man, but now I have killed way too many. Their blood is on my hands, as the blood of the Jewish people is on theirs. I know there will be more killing. But I want to live, I want all these people down here to live, I want you to live. To do that, we must remain as quiet as possible, and kill only when necessary. Most of all we must pray, and we must trust in our God to protect us."

Sarah shook her head. "I do not believe God is watching out for us. He is gone somewhere else where he does not have to worry about the Jews. In the temple they told us we are the chosen people. Chosen for what, Ishmael? To die like pigs in a slaughterhouse? To be hunted like wild animals and left to die in that dark forest? No. I do not believe we are a chosen people. Not anymore."

Ishmael looked at Sarah somberly. "My heart burns for you, and I am saddened because of your anger, as you are just a child. Yes, I too am angry. I lost many family members, but my hate will not bring them back." As Ishmael cleaned out his pipe, he shook his head.

"Sarah, God has kept you and I alive, when so many others have died. You and I have a mission from our God. I do not know what it is, and neither do you. But we must live, Sarah. Sometimes when I kill, I feel God will turn his back on me, but he always gives me a new way to go. He is here, in this basement. You must help me and the others to survive now. But most importantly, you must avoid killing anyone, even though you feel it is your mission. Sarah, it will haunt you forever, no matter your reasons."

After checking the area where the car was parked, Ishmael looked at Sarah. "The border to Vichy is closed so tight we cannot get through right now. So, we must survive here until a new plan can be created. Trust me, trust God, and trust Baruch, our leader. He is a smart man. Most importantly, do not do anything you are not instructed to do. That will threaten all of us."

Sarah did not like being closed up inside the basement tunnels. She longed to be outside in the fresh air where she could walk and feel the warmth of the sun. Each day the desire to sneak past the guards and run up the ramp toward the daylight festered in her soul. She was not created to live like a hermit in an underground prison. After searching the caverns, Sarah found an abandoned storm drain just the right size for her to crawl though. Reaching the end of the pipe, Sarah found herself on a small street that was overgrown with weeds and cluttered with debris from a wall that had collapsed long ago. It was good to feel free and let the sun beat down on her face.

Day by day Sarah explored more of the ruins from the abandoned factory and had fun playing her own little games. After a month she became bored with the old factory and decided to go for a walk down the street to see where it went, disregarding everything Ishmael had explained to her about venturing out on her own.

Coming to a street corner, Sarah felt as if she were being watched, but she could not see anyone. Feeling somewhat fearful, she turned and began walking briskly back toward the factory. Before she could realize what was happening, a black Mercedes came up behind her. Turning to look at the car, it was evident she had alerted the Gestapo.

Sarah stood frozen in place as the two men exited the vehicle and walked up to her. The oldest of the men called out. "Girl, what are you doing in this neighborhood? Where are your parents?"

Unable to speak, and knowing she had just placed everyone in the basement at risk, tears began rolling down her cheeks."

"I shall only ask you one more time. What are you doing here and who do you belong to? Are you a Jew hiding from us?" The man smiled slightly as he asked, knowing he had possibly uncovered a Jewish hide out.

"No. I am not a Jew. I went for a walk and got lost," Sarah replied, knowing they would see right through her explanation.

"Out for a walk? From where, child? There are no homes or apartments for several miles. I think you are a Jew, and I think there are more of you in this old factory. Grabbing Sarah by the arm he led her back through the doorway she had used when she left the factory. "Now, tell me where they are, and I will go easy on you, I promise. Now tell me!"

As the younger of the two agents looked around, he became dangerously close to the drain pipe Sarah had used to crawl up from the tunnel. If he found it, everyone in the community was going to die. Pulling loose from the Gestapo agent, Sarah backed up and kicked the man as hard as she could in the leg. As he stumbled forward, Sarah ran in the opposite direction of the pipe, as the agent yelled out. "Stop her, shoot her, don't let her get away!"

The younger man chased after her through the factory ruins, but Sarah knew the place well, and was not about to be captured. She began climbing up onto a walkway that had led to the roof at one time. Nearing what was left of the roof, she watched the Gestapo agent climbing up another walkway that was going to cut her off from an escape route. Not sure what to do, she picked up a broken piece of concrete block and hurled it toward the man as hard as she could.

The agent yelled out as the heavy block struck him in the forehead. He swayed back and forth on the ladder for several seconds as blood gushed from the large ragged cut above his right eye. As if in slow motion, he fell backward without a sound until he crashed into the wreckage below. Sarah shook in fear, not knowing where the other man had gone, and now she knew he would kill her the first chance he got.

Looking over the walkway, Sarah could see the young agent below. She knew he was dead because he had fallen onto a broken steel water pipe that had pierced him clean through.

Just as she was about to move to another section of the walkway, she heard Ishmael's voice. "Sarah, are you alright, come down from there."

She closed her eyes for a moment, attempting to calm her nerves before climbing back down the rickety ladder. Reaching the main floor, she observed Ishmael and another man from the basement standing near the body of the young agent.

"I don't want to look at him," Sarah said, with a nervous voice.

"Look at him, Sarah. You killed him. You must see what your actions have created. Did I not warn you what killing a person would be like? Especially one of our enemies."

Sarah looked down at the man's dark blue eyes as they gazed up into the late morning sky. Although he was trying to capture her and kill everyone in the tunnels, she felt pity for the young man. He wore a wedding band on his left hand and probably had small children at home. Tears rolled down her cheeks as she turned toward Ishmael.

"Where is the other man? What will happen to his body?"

"We killed the other man before he could get back to the car and radio for help. He is in the trunk, where this man will join him. They will be burned along with the car outside the city. But now you must show us how you got out here, before the Germans find it one day." Ishmael spoke with a direct tone of voice Sarah had never heard from him before.

After showing them the location of the drainage pipe, Ishmael took Sarah back down into the tunnels where Baruch was waiting for her. "You have caused us much trouble today, Sarah. Luckily, one of our roving guards caught sight of what was going on. If he had not, we would all be on our way to a death camp by now. Have you forgotten who rescued you from the Germans? Have you forgotten what it is like to live in exile? We took a vote and decided to give you one more chance, but next time you will be sent out of here, even though you are just nine years old. You would have to be on your own, and would not last very long in this city. Do you understand?"

Sarah nodded her head as she replied, "Yes, I do. I will behave myself as you want me to do."

For the next week Sarah could not sleep or eat, as the dark blue eyes of the Gestapo Agent kept looking at her from every corner of the basement. Ishmael talked with her every day, attempting to sooth the anger and fear that now haunted Sarah, but nothing appeared to be working.

After writing a goodbye letter to Ishmael, Sarah crept quietly out of the factory one last time, not knowing where she was going or what she was going to do for food. But it was better to be hiding day by day, than living inside the factory where the spirit of the man she had killed roamed freely.

Desperate for food, Sarah began walking alleys behind restaurants and cafes looking for food that was tossed out. Even though every type of food was rationed in Paris, the eating establishments were given ample supplies to feed visiting German dignitaries as well as German officers and their mistresses.

One evening as she dug through a garbage can, she heard a restaurant owner yelling at a young boy for not getting the dishes clean enough for his guests. As the boy walked away, Sarah approached the angry shop owner. "I can wash your dishes cleaner than anyone. Give me a chance and you will be happy with my work, I promise you."

The shop owner sneered at Sarah. "You are not old enough, I will get in trouble for hiring someone so young. Be on your way."

Sarah stepped forward. "My name is Helga, I am thirteen and old enough to work for you."

The man laughed. "You are no more than eight, maybe nine. I have a daughter your age, I am no fool. Now go."

Not ready to walk away from the possibility of a job, Sarah continued. "Would you not want someone to help your daughter if she was in need?"

Shaking his head, the owner had to smile. "Yes, I would want someone to help my child if necessary, of course." After a moment of thought he stepped closer to Sarah. "Are you a Jew?"

"No, I am not Jewish. I just need to find a job to help my family. I would appreciate it very much if you could help us," Sarah replied nervously.

Looking at Sarah's ragged condition, the restaurant owner inquired. "I am sure you are going to tell me you have no identification papers to prove who you really are. What shall I do if the Gestapo comes to my place asking to see the papers of my employees? Tell me Helga, what will I do?"

Feeling defeated, Sarah just nodded her head and turned to leave without saying a word. After a moment of thought, the man called out.

"Alright Helga, I will give you one chance. There is a stack of dishes that need to be done right now. Go to work and we will see how things go. My name is Jocko. If you need anything just call for me. If you see the Gestapo talking to me, get out the back door as quickly as you can," Jocko stated, as he held open the back door to the kitchen.

Throughout the evening, Sarah kept to herself and washed dishes as fast as she could, inspecting each dish and utensil to make sure they were spotless. After closing the restaurant for the evening, Jocko walked up to Sarah. You did well tonight. If you want the job it is yours. So, tell me where you live, and I will make sure you get home alright."

Before Sarah could say a word, one of the waitresses spoke up in perfect German. "I know her, she and her family live across the hall from my apartment. I will walk home with her."

"Fair enough." Jocko replied with a smile as he walked out of the kitchen.

Sarah turned to the young woman. "Thank you, I don't know what to say. My name is Helga."

The woman smiled at her. "I am Rochelle, come on, let's get out of here."

After walking three blocks, Rochelle took Sarah to a small third floor apartment on a busy street. "I know it's small, but you can sleep on the sofa. It is very comfortable. Will that suit you?"

Sarah nodded her head. "It will be just fine and I will pay you rent each week from my wages. We can work out a payment." Sitting down on the sofa, Sarah looked up at the woman. "Jocko was right. I am just nine years old. Why did you help me?"

Rochelle sat down beside Sarah. "You reminded me of my little sister. She was killed when the Nazi's invaded Paris. She was in the wrong place at the wrong time. My family then moved to Stuttgart, and I came here to attend art school. I still go there in the mornings and work in the evening. You had a look of fear in your eye, and I did not want Jocko to fire you. So, here you are. We will get along just fine."

Sarah enjoyed living out in the open, and Jocko had a worker's document created so there were never any problems with soldiers when she was stopped for an identity check. During their free time, Rochelle gave Sarah walking tours of Paris and they enjoyed sitting in the parks while sampling different cheeses and crackers that were still available to the public.

Two months after she had moved in with Rochelle, Sarah was walking toward the restaurant when Ishmael walked up to her. She did not recognize him at first, as his hair was now completely gray, and he was walking with a heavy wooden cane.

"Good afternoon, my sweet Helga, I see you are living the high life here in Paris. Have you forgotten who you are and the problems you caused us before you left?" Ishmael inquired, as he gave Sarah a disapproving glance.

"Your disguise is good, Ishmael, I did not recognize you at first. How did you know where I was? I explained in the letter why I was leaving, and I don't want any trouble with you." Sarah replied, feeling very intimidated.

Ishmael took her by the hand, leading her to a bench that sat along the road. After sitting down, he looked at her sternly. "Things were tense for a while after you left, for none of us felt safe. We didn't know what was going to happen if you were captured. But now you live better than any of us in this city. And have way more to eat. I feel you owe us a debt of gratitude for all we did to save you. Twice."

Sarah shook as Ishmael glared sternly at her. "You would not turn me in to the Gestapo, would you? That would not be right of you to do that, we are both Jews!"

"Turn you into the Gestapo? No, that would get you killed and possibly me as well. But what do you think would happen if Jocko and your roommate found out you are a Jew? Do you trust them enough to know they would not throw you out, and turn you over for lying to them. How do you think this Rochelle would feel after treating you like a sister?" Ishmael inquired as he took out his pipe, waiting for her to speak.

"I need to get to work, I can't be late. What do you want from me?" Sarah asked, angrily.

"Ah, it is not so good for you to lose your temper with an old man on the streets of Paris, Sarah. You could attract the Gestapo without even realizing what you are doing. Temper, temper, my little flower." After lighting his pipe, he continued. "Meet me tomorrow morning near the fountain by your apartment after your roommate goes to school. I will have an assignment for you, the first of many. Consider it your debt for all the pain you have caused us. It must be paid in full." Slowly standing up, Ishmael walked down the street smoking his pipe.

Sarah felt sick. She had made friends, and Jocko liked having her around the restaurant. Now she would have to operate behind their backs and put them in serious trouble if she were caught. Fighting back tears and the urge to run from Paris, Sarah stood up and walked slowly down the street, knowing she was going to be watched by Ishmael and the underground where ever she went.

The following morning, she met Ishmael at the fountain as he requested. He handed her a blank envelope. "This needs to be delivered to a Mr. Green. He lives in the suburb of Clichy. You can take the bus there for a small fare. Walk toward the downtown area when you get off the bus. He will find you. Wait for him to hand you another letter for me, and then get on the return bus. I will meet you on your way to work, and give you your next assignment."

Everything went as Ishmael had explained, although Sarah was terrified the entire time. No matter how hard Sarah tried to convince Ishmael that she wanted out of the Jewish underground, he just laughed at her and said, "A debt needs to be paid, my child. You scared a lot of people."

Just before Christmas, Sarah was sent to the suburb of Perret where she had gone many times. However, there was no holiday spirit in the air when she stepped from the bus, just the feeling of dread when she observed six black Gestapo cars and a truck for prisoners parked just a block away. The woman she usually made contact with was nowhere in sight. Trying not to stand out, Sarah walked into a small candy shop where she could browse for a short time without being questioned by the owners. Smiling at the elderly woman behind the counter, Sarah pointed toward two small chocolate candies in a festive wrap.

"I think my sister and I would enjoy these tonight as a treat. They look ever so good."

The woman smiled, wrapped them carefully, and placed them in a bag as Sarah handed her the money. As she turned to leave, the woman called out. "Maybe you should leave through the back door, it might be safer."

Nodding her head, Sarah turned and walked through the store exiting into an alley, where several delivery trucks were being loaded. As she passed the second truck, the woman she was supposed to meet stepped out of the cab. Grabbing Sarah by the arm, the woman pushed her up against the wall.

"Never do anything other than meet me, once again, you put us all at risk! Give me the envelope!"

Sarah handed the woman the envelope and watched her walk quickly down the alley as if the devil himself were chasing her. After composing herself, Sarah walked down the opposite end of the alley. Just as she turned to walk back toward the bus station, a Gestapo man stepped out in front of her.

"Papers, please!" he demanded, as he held out his hand.

Removing the identity papers from her coat pocket, she handed them to the impatient man as she called out, "Heil Hitler!"

The man looked at her while mumbling, "Ja, Ja, Heil Hitler."

After checking them over twice, he handed them back to Sarah. "What are you doing in this neighborhood, and what do you have in the bag? I need to see it, Fraulein Helga."

Sarah nodded. "I have two small chocolate cakes. One for me and one for my sister. I came here to this candy store as they make the best candies in all of Paris. I wanted to surprise my sister."

The agent pulled the candy from the bag and tossed them on the ground before smashing them with his foot. "Move on," he yelled, as he pushed her away.

Sarah shook with rage, being only nine years old, she had not the slightest idea how to handle the situation. When the agent pushed her again, she turned and kicked him in the leg as she punched him in the arm.

Before she realized what was happening, the agent had pushed her up against the wall and pulled his Luger, pointing it directly at her head. He called out for his lieutenant as he glared at Sarah.

By the time the lieutenant arrived, Sarah was crying like any child who had just had a treasure taken away. Although the officer told her to shut up, she cried all the more.

"What is going on here?" the lieutenant called out.

"She kicked me and punched me in the arm. I have placed her under arrest. We will take her in and deal with her parents," the angry officer called out as he held Sarah against the wall by her throat.

"My cakes, my cakes, he smashed the cakes I bought for my sickly sister. I didn't do anything wrong, he smashed my cakes, and I don't have any more money to buy her another. It's her birthday, and now I have no gift for her," Sarah blurted out as she began to cry harder.

As nearly a dozen Parisians gathered to see what was going on with the little girl, the lieutenant shook his head. "Release her, she is just a child! We are looking for Jews and law breakers. Have you checked her papers?"

"Yes, they all appeared to be in order Herr Lieutenant," the officer replied, as his anger began turning into complete embarrassment.

Stepping forward, the lieutenant placed his hand on Sarah's shoulder. "Stop crying child. I will walk you back to the store and replace your cakes. In fact, I will buy two for you also. That way you and your sister can have a party together. How does that sound."

Continuing to sniffle Sarah partially smiled. "That would be nice Herr Lieutenant."

As they turned to walk back to the chocolate shop, the officer looked at his officer. "We will talk about this later. Get back to the car."

Leaving the shop, Sarah looked at the S.S. officer. "Danka Herr Lieutenant. You have made my sister and me very happy. Heil Hitler."

As Sarah collapsed into her seat on the bus, she was close to crying again, but fought back the tears. She felt she had paid the debt to Ishmael and the others in the factory basement, and was not going to do any more missions.

That evening after returning to the apartment from work, Sarah handed Rochelle two of the ornately wrapped cakes. "A little gift for all you have done for me." Sarah said, with a broad smile on her face.

Before opening the chocolate treat, Rochelle examined the wrapper. "These came from a shop in Perret. I had an apartment just down the street from it before I moved here. What were you doing in Perret? That is a good hour bus trip from here."

Sarah suddenly felt trapped by the one person that had helped her without conditions. As Rochelle stood quietly waiting for an answer, Sarah walked toward the window to watch the traffic on the street below. After a brief moment, she turned back to Rochelle.

"I'm sorry, I cannot tell you."

Rochelle stood stiff as a statue as she looked at Sarah. "Does it have anything to do with the man that meets you near the fountain?" After taking in a deep breath she asked the question that terrified her the most. "Helga, are you a Jew?"

As tears began to roll down her cheeks, Sarah sat down on the sofa. She looked up at Rochelle who had not moved an inch since the conversation began. "My real name is Sarah, I am a Jew. The man that talks to me is also a Jew, he is a leader in the Jewish underground. I made a bad mistake when I was living with the group, so now he has me delivering letters until the debt is paid off. I am so sorry for misleading you all this time. You have been the best person I have met since I have been on the run, and now I have destroyed everything. I will pack my things and get out, I do not wish to bring the Gestapo down on you."

Rochelle walked over to the sofa, placing her hand on Sarah's shoulder. "I have had a feeling for a while that you were holding back on me about who you were, and I suspected you were a Jew. But I like you as a sister, and I do not wish to have anything bad happen to you. We can continue on as we have been and you need not fear me. Just promise me you will stop going out on the missions. Eventually you will get caught, and that will mean death for me also."

Sarah smiled as she nodded her head. "I decided today that this was the last mission. I shall tell him tomorrow it is over."

Feeling relieved, Rochelle placed her hand on Sarah's cheek. "Sarah or Helga, whoever you want to be is fine with me. Now, let's eat these chocolates, they smell heavenly."

As Sarah laid on the sofa after Rochelle went into her room, she wondered what would have happened if she had totally lost her composure today, and admitted to the Gestapo agent she was a Jew. The thought of it shook her to the core, knowing it would probably mean certain death.

The next day as she sat near the fountain, Ishmael approached her. "I have your next mission ready to go. Let me tell you—"

Before he could finish, Sarah interrupted. "No. There will be no more missions. I am finished. Everything went wrong yesterday, and I was almost arrested by the Gestapo. I cannot risk being seen by them again. This debt you talk about so arrogantly is now paid. Goodbye, Ishmael."

Instantly, Sarah stood up from the bench and walked as fast as she could toward the restaurant, although her shift did not begin for hours.

A very real sense of calm came over Sarah and Rochelle as everything was out in the open, and the missions had come to an end. Unfortunately, the new year of 1942 did not give Parisians much more to hope for, as the German government continued tightening the noose around the necks of everyone. Shops and restaurants began closing at a rapid rate, as their merchandise was now being sent into Germany to keep everyone on the home front contented. Arrests went up as the Gestapo began cracking down on black marketing and underground activities.

Luckily, Jocko's business continued to operate, as many German officers loved his cuisine, and selection of liquor. Little did they know that the underground supplied most of the liquor, as officers talked openly when they were drunk, allowing underground agents to pick up important information.

By now, Sarah had become accustomed to having no real celebrations for her birthdays, but this one she would remember for the rest of her life. As she walked near the fountain, an all too familiar voice came from behind her.

"Happy birthday, Sarah. It is good to see you looking so happy and healthy," Ishmael said quietly, so no one nearby could hear him.

Sarah spun around and glared at him. "Go away, I do not wish to see you or talk to you. My life is safe, and I have friends I can trust. I do not need you destroying it all. Go away, please!"

Ishmael glared at Sarah. "Have you forgotten you are still one of us? Have you forgotten that while you live comfortably, many more do not. We must all help or we will certainly all perish as one. It is your turn to step up, my child. I have no one else to turn to, we have had so many of our people captured or killed in the name of freedom."

"No! That is why I will not help. I do not want to become one of those captured or killed. It gets me nothing," Sarah replied angrily.

"So, you will not help Isaac? You have turned your back on him also!" Ishmael stated coldly.

"I loved him like a brother, but he left me in the forest to be killed or captured. He turned his back on me, why should I go out on a limb for him. Explain that to me, Ishmael!" Sarah replied, fearing that Ishmael could now hurt her as surely as he had saved her before.

Walking up very close to Sarah, Ishmael looked around to see who might be listening.

"Because Isaac is in the hands of the Gestapo and is going to be executed in three days with five other Jewish underground people. We need your help to save him, and as many of the others as possible."

"You are asking me to throw everything I have built for a mission that may not work. The Allies are coming one day, and I want to be alive and safe when they get here. Do not ask me to throw this all away," Sarah replied, as she brushed past Ishmael and returned to the apartment.

That night Sarah tossed and turned as she thought about Isaac being slaughtered in a public display. It made her sick, although she still was angry at him for abandoning her in the forest.

Early the next morning, Sarah carefully peered out the window at the fountain where she enjoyed feeding pigeons. Sitting alone on a bench with a newspaper was Ishmael. He looked forlorn, and ragged. It was evident that the underground activities were taking a toll on him. Dressing quickly, Sarah walked down to the bench.

Tossing bread crumbs for the pigeons from the small bag she was carrying, Sarah sat down next to Ishmael. "You figured I would change my mind last night, did you not?"

Ishmael smiled slightly. In a calm voice he replied. "Yes, I have prayed all night that you would decide to help us. And God must have heard me, because here you are."

Sarah shook her head. "God did not send me here. As I have said, he no longer exists. I know that for a fact. I came here because I cannot let Isaac hang in a public square. Tell me what you want me to do, and I will help, although it will kill Rochelle and destroy everything I have tried to build."

"Whatever your reasons, we appreciate your willingness to help us. We will pick you up near your restaurant around midnight. I cannot tell you the mission right now for safety reasons. We will tell you everything tonight. Sadly, I am guessing you will not be able to come back here when this is over," Ishmael explained.

Entering the apartment, Rochelle stared intently at Sarah. "I saw you with that man. He has convinced you to go on another mission, hasn't he. Sarah, he will get you killed, you know that. Honey, we all know the Allies are coming to free us, it's just a matter of time. You can stay here and wait and be free when they come. Why must you do this thing?"

Sarah dropped down on the sofa. "In just two days, a young man that saved my life several times is going to be hung by the Gestapo. His name is Isaac, if it were not for him, I would not be alive right now. How can I turn my back on him in his time of need? I must do something to help him, so I must go. I am so sorry and I love you very much, but I must do this. They will pick me up at midnight."

Rochelle walked slowly around the small apartment, contemplating everything Sarah had explained. "Fine, then I must do something to help you. I will go with you to save this man named Isaac. That is final, Sarah. "If you go, I must go."

Slightly irritated with Rochelle's response, Sarah shook her head. "This is not your fight, Rochelle! You are not Jewish, so no, you cannot go with us. I do not want your blood on my hands."

Rochelle folded her arms as she glared at Sarah. "Best my blood be on your hands than that of the Germans. To truly live, I might have to die. I have played it safe since this war began, never putting myself on the line for anyone. It is time I make a stand. We will die together if need be."

As Ishmael approached Sarah in the alley behind the restaurant, he looked at Rochelle. "She cannot come with us."

Sarah walked up to Ishmael. "We have made a promise to one another. She goes!"

Realizing Sarah was adamant regarding Rochelle, he nodded his head. "Fine, another hand may be a good thing. Let's go."

The driver took a familiar route back to the old factory where several more men waited to load weapons and ammunition on the truck. Once all the preparations were made, Ishmael walked up to Sarah and Rochelle.

"We are headed to Orleans. Klaus Barbie, who is the chief of the Gestapo in Lyon, is planning a hanging to enlighten the French people as to his determination to eradicate the Jews and punish anyone who gets in the way. He is also planning to execute French citizens as a stiff warning. We either act now, or forever sit back and wish we had. This mission is dangerous, and there is no doubt some of us will die, and some of us may end up being hunted until this war is over. But act we must."

Chapter Eight
Klaus Barbie

A stiff wind-driven rain washed down on the city of Lyon, France as a sharp crack of thunder rattled the windows in Hauptsturmfuhrer Nicholas 'Klaus' Barbie's bedroom. Exactly at 0600, as usual, Sgt. Wilhelm Schiffel entered the darkened ornate bedroom to awaken his commander. However, on this morning he found the usually angry officer already sitting on the edge of his bed.

"Good morning Herr Captain, I see you are awake early today. Is there anything I can get you right now?" the sergeant inquired with a smile on his face.

"Yes, I am awake, how can anyone sleep with all this God-forsaken noise." After rising from his bed, the captain slipped a robe over his silk pajamas and walked toward the window. "Ya, draw my bath and set out my shaving materials. Then get a hold of Lt. Rouchmann and tell him I want him in the conference room no later than 0730. And tell that damn baker I want cherry danish this morning, I am tired of the apple."

Bowing, Sgt. Schiffel replied, "Jawohl, Herr Captain. I will see to it right away."

As the sergeant left the room, Captain Barbie shook his head, "Damn piss ant, is that what our Reich is coming to!"

After shaving and a hot bath, the captain put on a perfectly tailored black S.S. uniform that fit him like a glove. Examining himself in a full-length mirror, he smiled. "Klaus, you are still a perfect example of what a leader in the Fuhrer's army should look like."

After slapping the side of his leg with his black leather gloves, he walked out of the bedroom with his cocky strut. Entering the staff office outside the conference room, everyone immediately jumped up from their desks, raised their right arms, and in unison called out, "Heil Hitler, Herr Captain!"

Raising his right arm halfway, he responded, "Ja Heil Hitler." Entering the conference room, once again everyone around the large oak table stood up and raised their arms while yelling out, "Heil Hitler, Captain Barbie."

This time the captain responded more officially. "Guten Morgen, Heil Hitler! I'm happy everyone braved this foul weather this morning and is ready to work."

After carefully placing his hat and leather gloves on the mantel above the fireplace, Barbie took his place at the head of the gleaming conference table. Sgt. Schiffel stepped forward, placing a steaming cup of coffee and a plate containing two cherry danish in front of him. Smiling at the men at the table, he called out. "Please have a danish. I ordered them special this morning."

Quickly the large platter was passed around the table. Not one person considered refusing Barbie's invitation to take a danish. They all completely understood that their arrogant commander would take it as a personal insult if they refused. As the officers consumed their pastry, everyone agreed it was the best danish they had eaten in a long time.

With a broad smile on his face, the captain took another sip of coffee. "Now let us get down to business. Lt. Rouchmann, how many Jews did we capture this past week."

The lieutenant stood erect. "Herr Captain, the numbers have continued to drop as we figured they would. We picked up and transported three hundred and twenty. Fifteen were killed attempting to escape. We know there are many more hiding we have not found yet, so we are setting up more raids. Plus, as you know, some are still getting into Vichy country, so we cannot capture them."

Captain Barbie stood up from the table and walked over to a large map of France that sat on an easel. After studying it for a moment he pointed at the city of Dijon. "We did not do well there. We must go back with force and tear the city apart. We will find Jews in every nook and cranny. Set it up Lieutenant, I want to go along, our Fuhrer feels we must do better, and we will."

After sitting down again he looked over at Lt. Miller. "And how have we been dealing with the underground. We need to cut off the head and kill the body. Tell me what you know!"

Lt. Miller stood up clearing his throat. "Herr Captain, we arrested twenty and killed five more. Unfortunately, the pigs we arrested have told us nothing, and seven of them did not survive the questioning. However, we have heard about a new group near Orleans, and we have sent a large contingent of Gestapo to the area. I expect excellent results."

Barbie half smiled at the report, understanding the need to eliminate the French Resistance. They would never get full control of the people as long as they had a rallying point.

Looking next at Lt. Meyer, who was new on his staff, he inquired. "Tell me Lieutenant Meyer, how are we doing with rounding up French Army deserters?"

Quickly, the man jumped from his chair and snapped to attention. "Herr Hauptsturmfuhrer, In the past week we arrested just ten. But we have found several caches of weapons and explosives. My intelligence tells me there are warehouses full of weapons near Toulouse in the south. We could send commandos there to destroy them if you give us the order, sir."

Once more, Barbie stood up to find exactly where Toulouse was located on the map. Scowling, he walked to a window and looked down at the rain-soaked streets. "I will make some calls and see what can be done. We need to get them out of circulation so they do not fall into the hands of the damn resistance." Walking back toward the table, Barbie looked at Lt. Meyer. "Although Hauptsturmfuhrer is my official title, you may address me as Captain."

Turning red, the Lieutenant nodded his head. "Jawohl mine Captain."

As the rain continued over most of France the next two days, the weather inside Barbie's command center was not fit for man or beast.

With each day that operations were being hampered, Barbie became more agitated, and the staff took the brunt of his hostility.

When the storm front broke, Lt. Rouchmann immediately set up a raid on the city of St. Etienne, a short drive from Lyon. The raid using Gestapo agents, S.S. soldiers, and regular Wehrmacht troops, began at 0500 when a good part of the city was still asleep.

Doors were kicked in, people were pulled from their beds, attics were torn apart and basements were searched with dogs. Captain Barbie walked impatiently on a street as he listened to the screams of the citizenry, and the demands of his men. It did not take long before soldiers were bringing Jews and the people that hid them to the waiting trucks.

One particular young attractive French woman screamed as a soldier pulled her toward a truck by her long red hair. "Let her go!" Barbie called out, as he walked over to the crying woman. "Tell me, why are you being arrested!"

Attempting to speak her best German she looked up at Barbie. "My girlfriend that lives with me is a Jew. She works with me for the government and does a good job. She is loyal to the Third Reich, and will do the Fuhrer no harm. Please do not take us away."

Nodding his head, he held out his hand to her. "Get up, Mademoiselle. Show me who your friend is."

Smiling, the woman stood up and pointed toward her friend who was standing by one of the trucks. "You can see she will not be of any harm, and neither will I."

"Go get her and bring her to me." Barbie called out to one of his men, as he patted the woman on the shoulder. When the escorting soldier was about half way back to him, he pulled out his pistol firing two shots, striking both women in the forehead. "I dare say you were right, Fraulein. Neither of you will ever cause the Third Reich any problems."

By days end, they had arrested one hundred fifty Jews and nearly that many French citizens accused of hiding them. Turning to Lt. Rouchmann, Barbie smiled. "A job well done. Take the Jews to the rail yard at Lyon and send them off. Take the French to the old Fort, we will have to let the French deal with them I am afraid. Find a place to bed down our men. We will hit part of Dijon in the morning.

By the end of the third day, Barbie was happy with the results.

As he walked toward his Mercedes staff car, Lt. Rouchmann came running. "Herr Captain, we arrested a French officer and his wife. They had two Jew servants working for them. What do you want us to do with them?"

After a moment of thought he looked at Lt. Rouchmann. "Are there any children?"

Jawohl, Herr Captain, a girl and a boy, both about fifteen or sixteen."

"Ja, it is too bad the parents did not think of the welfare of their children. Drive them to the city dump and execute all of them. They have proven they cannot be loyal to the Third Reich. Have gas poured on their bodies and burn them, then cover the remains."

"It will be done, Herr Captain!" the lieutenant replied, before running back toward his men.

Returning to his office, Captain Barbie was in a jovial mood after watching his men in action over the last three days. But he was still bothered regarding the number of Jews hiding in southern France. The following day he made a phone call to Vichy to speak with Marshall Phillippe Petain, the leader of the Vichy Government. However, Petain was not willing to make any agreements or changes to the original armistice.

Angered, Barbie attempted to find Pierre Laval, who was assisting the Germans in the occupation of France. However it soon became evident the crusty old politician was not going to turn against Petain or his countrymen on this issue, at least for right now. With both doors slammed in his face, he realized the only solution was to fly to Berlin to see Heinrich Himmler, head of the S.S.

Arriving at Tempelhof Airport in Berlin, it was clear to see that Germany was doing very well. Shops and stores were overflowing with goods confiscated by the military from the occupied lands, while restaurants had cheeses and other fine foods and wines, the Wehrmacht shipped home for German consumption. The night life in Berlin was happy and exciting with plenty of liquor, dancing, and young women looking for a good time, since their men were off fighting on the Russian front.

Barbie enjoyed walking the safe busy streets of Berlin, without having to deal with the Jewish human refuse that other countries in

Europe had still not cleaned up. He was proud of what Hitler and his Third Reich was attempting to accomplish.

The following day he was able to meet with Himmler. As they walked through the Reichstag, Barbie explained his dilemma, while asking Himmler if he could intercede with Hitler, allowing them to clean out southern France.

"Sir, you have to understand, even though we are not allowing travel into the south, Jews are still finding ways to avoid our road blocks and take refuge there. It is time we get permission to end this problem once and for all," Barbie insisted as they sipped French Cognac in a sitting room.

"Herr Captain, you have to understand that there are times when certain niceties need to be adopted in negotiations, even in the midst of war. We cannot fight a protracted ground war in France while fighting is so tough on the Russian front. Once we destroy the Russian Army, we will be able to throw out the armistice with France and do as we choose. They will have no choice but to follow our directives at that point. The Fuhrer has already made plans to follow through with occupying all of France, right down to the Spanish border. Franco will then allow us to operate freely, cleaning up the Jewish problem in Spain, as he owes us for getting him into power during their civil war. When we are finished, not one Jew will remain on the continent. You need to be patient right now, Klaus. You are doing an excellent job, and the Fuhrer trusts you and appreciates all you have accomplished. He also likes the name Jews have given you. The butcher of Lyon suits you well my friend. Be proud of it."

Realizing he was not going to get permission at this time, though a promise was on the table, Barbie flew back to France somewhat satisfied. Arriving at his headquarters, he was told about a major problem at Orleans, where a small disorganized band of Jewish underground had attempted to set prisoners free and killed one S.S. soldier. This was purely a slap in the face to everything he was attempting to do, and he could not allow such violence to take place again.

The following morning, he called his lieutenants together. "We are going to make the people of Orleans and all of France take notice that no such uprisings will be allowed. We are going to send a detachment of our best S.S. soldiers to Orleans. We will hang the seven Jews we captured during the uprising, and the ten French civilians that were hiding them, or attempting to help the resistance. I will attend the hanging to give credence to its validity. Gentlemen, make it happen!"

Driving south from Paris, Ishmael was still nervous about taking Rochelle along on the trip. He did not know her, nor did he totally trust her, but he was sure he could find a mission for her.

Sitting quietly in the back of the truck, Sarah felt an overwhelming sense of loss. Jocko had been very good to her, and Rochelle had treated her like a sister, opening her home, not only to a stranger, but a Jew. Risking a certain death sentence had she been found out. Even worse, Rochelle had no idea what she was getting into, and there was no doubt there would be bloodshed before it was over.

Driving north from Lyon, Barbie was excited about what he and his men were going to do. He was finally going to teach the French people that being uncooperative came with a huge cost and it had to stop. What was about to happen, would no doubt make it tougher for Jews to hide and evade capture in France, thus making the job of his soldiers much easier and safer.

Early in the morning, Ishmael drove the truck off the highway into a small secluded farmyard. They were greeted by ten well-armed Jewish underground operatives. They made their way into the cellar of the farmhouse where several maps of the city of Orleans were laid out on a table. A man named Elazar approached the table, pulling out one special map.

"This is the Place du Martroi. As you can see, it is the largest square in all of Orleans. Here is where the Nazis are planning to execute seven Jewish men and ten French civilians they feel have been harboring Jews." He pointed to a drawing someone had made on the map. "This is where the platform has been built to conduct the hangings." Moving his finger along the map, he stopped at a building about one hundred feet from the platform. "Here in the basement of this building is where all the condemned are spending the night. It is heavily guarded by S.S. soldiers, and is too formidable for us to attack. But tomorrow will be a different story." Elazar carefully explained.

Over the next hour, he laid out the plan his men had created to disrupt the entire operation and escape with the Jewish prisoners as they were walked toward the gallows. Turning toward Sarah, Elazar looked very intense.

"I hear you are a strong girl, so what is going to be asked of you will take much courage. There is a man in the group old enough to be your father. As he nears the wooden stairs, you must run forward from the crowd yelling, 'Papa, Papa' as loud as you can."

Turning to Rochelle, he continued. "As Sarah is yelling and causing a commotion, you will light this long string of fire crackers and toss them on the ground, then run toward the gallows dropping this smoke grenade. Can you do that?"

Rochelle suddenly realized they were asking far more from her than she ever intended to do, but she understood how important this was to Sarah and everyone in this basement.

"Yes, I can do it."Rochelle replied nervously

It was nearly midnight when Ishmael and Elazar were satisfied everyone knew their assignments, and they were confident they could pull off their plan.

Early the following morning as a crowd began to gather in and around Place du Martroi, no one recognized the eight Jewish partisans walking among them.

Klaus Barbie stood on the small balcony outside his sitting room, enjoying the crisp morning air and the elegant buildings in Orleans. As he sipped his coffee, he looked at Sgt. Schiffel, "Have Lt. Meyer and his team left yet?"

"Jawohl, Herr Captain, they left about forty-five minutes ago. Lieutenant Meyer said they had information there could be some partisan activity and they wanted to infiltrate the crowd early to make sure nothing happens," the Sergeant responded quickly.

"Good, that is good. Get me Lt. Rouchmann on the phone. We need to talk," Barbie instructed as he tugged at his collar which appeared to be much too tight this morning.

A few moments later Sgt. Schiffel returned. "I have the lieutenant on the phone, Herr Captain."

Walking briskly to the phone, Barbie picked up the receiver. "Good morning, Lieutenant. Tell me what is happening."

"Good morning, Herr Captain. Everything is set for the hanging. We tested everything during the night so we know it works. Lt. Miller has gone over all the security details with his men and they are ready to go. I cannot think of anything we have missed." Lt. Rouchmann replied calmly.

"Ya, ya. That all sounds good, Lt. Rouchmann, and butterflies are beautiful, but I am nervous that things will go wrong. You know these French people as well as I do, they will risk their lives to stop this, and they just don't give a damn. I tell you, if this goes awry, heads will roll, and I am not playing games. You best make sure these people are doing their jobs." With that said, Barbie slammed the receiver back down on the phone and shook his head. "Ja, everything is under control, no, I think not," Barbie mumbled as he picked up his coffee cup.

Not a cloud in the sky obscured the dazzling sun that warmed the Place du Martroi, as a large crowd had now filled the square. Sarah and Rochelle were now about four rows deep into the crowd, exactly where Elazar had wanted them. Ishmael was wearing a French Gendarme uniform, and was patrolling west of the gallows like a good police officer. However, under that uniform he was sweating immensely, hoping no one in authority would question his presence in the area.

Elazar was deeper into the crowd to Sarah's right, holding tight to a sawed-off shotgun under his coat. Four other men from the team were stationed in locations that would allow them to move in quickly to grab the prisoners and get them to the trucks. Sarah's heart was pounding so hard and fast, her chest almost hurt. She watched closely as activity was beginning to take place near the door where the men would exit into the square.

Klaus Barbie and his entourage sat on the second floor of the building directly behind the gallows. He smiled as he watched the nervous crowd shuffling back and forth. "Ya, they will all learn a valuable lesson this day. They will understand dictates from the Fuhrer are meant to be taken seriously. There shall be no more hiding of Jews, not in my area of responsibility."

All the officers in the room adamantly agreed that time had come to let the French people know exactly who was in charge. Barbie loved the sound of all the officers giving him adulation.

A hush came over the crowd as the Jewish prisoners exited the building in single file, walking toward the large wooden platform. Suddenly, someone grabbed Sarah by the right arm.

The Gestapo officer she had problems with in Perret near the candy shop, stood beside her, smiling.

"Good morning, miss chocolate cakes. I was hoping we would run into one another again. We have a definite score to settle, and now I can prove you are a Jew. Come with me!"

As Sarah attempted to pull away, the officer drew his Luger. He was about to point it at her when she spun around, landing her left fist into the man's face. Grabbing hold of his hand, she pushed the Luger into his chest, pulling the trigger. Everyone nearby screamed and began pushing and shoving, attempting to get away from the shooting. As the officer staggered, Sarah fired a second shot into his chest before turning to run. Gestapo agents and S.S. soldiers descended on the scene looking for the person who had just killed their comrade. Fearing for their lives, several people in the crowd described Sarah while pointing out which direction she had gone. One of the women pointed toward Rochelle yelling, "She was with the other girl, I saw them talking several times!"

As a Gestapo agent turned toward her, Rochelle jumped forward, clawing the man's face with her long fingernails before tuning to run in the opposite direction of Sarah. As she ran, she lit the fuse on the fire crackers dropping them on the ground. The crowd turned into a panicked mob yelling and creating confusion for the soldiers who were in pursuit.

Ishmael and Elazar immediately realized all their planning had gone bad, and they would need to act quickly. As both S.S. soldiers left their post on the east side of the platform, Ilan, another of Elazar's men, dashed between the platform and the building jamming a long knife into one of the guards on the west side. Sparing no time, Elazar raced forward out of the crowd, pulling out a Luger. Taking quick aim, he shot an S.S. soldier that stood on the wooden platform holding a machine gun. Grabbing hold of the first Jewish prisoner, he pointed at Ishmael. In a split second, all seven men were running into the panicked crowd, as two more or Elazar's men began firing at S.S. soldiers and Gestapo agents from inside the fast-moving crowd.

Up on the second floor, Barbie jumped from his chair spilling a full glass of cognac. "Stop this, stop this!" He screamed at his men as his face turned a dark shade of red. Pulling his Luger from its holster, Barbie ran for the stairwell to join in the chase for the Jewish criminals and escaped prisoners that were now on the run. However, Lt. Rouchmann grabbed hold of him at the bottom of the stairs.

"Sir, you can't go out there. People are shooting in every direction and you may get killed. You need to stay inside!" the lieutenant yelled, just as a bullet struck him in the shoulder.

Seeing his trusted aid bleeding and falling back onto the stairs, Barbie yelled. "I want all of these people dead, do you hear me. I want them dead."

Sgt. Schiffel lunged forward, pulling Barbie down onto the stairs near Lt. Rouchmann, as several bullets slammed into the door frame sending sharp splinters flying about.

Sarah had broken through the crowd and was running as fast as she could toward the west. Turning into an alley about six blocks from the square, she took cover behind a parked car. She was surprised to see that not one S.S. soldier or Gestapo agent was chasing her. It was evident her spinning back and forth through the crowd had helped her break free of the ensuing enemy. After catching her breath, she looked down at the pistol in her right hand. Both the pistol and her hand were covered in blood from the agent she had killed. Seeing a rain barrel aside of the garage, Sarah washed her hands and the gun, before placing it into the large pocket of her jacket. After waiting fifteen more minutes, Sarah continued walking toward the rendezvous point slowly, not sure if anyone would be there to pick her up or not.

On the east side of the courtyard, Rochelle was also struggling to break through the crowd. After setting off the smoke grenade, she weaved back and forth through terrified onlookers, searching for a safe place to hide. She knew full well it made no difference anymore whether or not she was Jewish. She had attacked a Gestapo officer and that carried an automatic death sentence. Reaching the east side of the square, Rochelle turned toward the south, attempting to push her way through the crowd that was now scattering for their own safety. Reaching a side street that continued heading east, she slowed to a walk, tossing her jacket into the back of a truck that was parked nearby. Arriving at the end of the block, a black Mercedes screeched to a stop as it neared the intersection. Two men carrying sub-machine guns jumped from the rear doors, aiming their weapons at her.

"Hands up!" one of the men called out, as he walked toward her.

"Slowly raising her hands, she called out, "Heil Hitler! Why are you stopping me, I have done nothing wrong. I just came here today because the Gauleiter in my neighborhood told me I should attend, if I was loyal to the Fuhrer. What are you arresting me for?" Rochelle asked as calmly as she could, while staring down the barrel of an automatic weapon.

Before she could say anything else, the front door of the car opened. The face of the man that got out was covered with scratches and blood.

"Do you call this nothing?" the man screamed, as he approached her with a pistol in his hand. "You are a criminal, and were helping that other woman we are looking for. Where did she go and where were you going?"

Rochelle totally understood her life was over, and there was nothing she could do to change it. She was angry at herself for leaving her comfortable apartment and safe job to join Sarah, but at the same time, she was happy she had made some attempt to save the lives of those innocent men.

Looking at the angry Gestapo man in front of her, she calmly replied. "I think I am about ready to meet my father in heaven. Do what you need to do."

The agent grabbed her by the throat, pushing her to the ground. "Woman, do you not realize I have the power to execute you right here and now, or offer lenience and let you walk away. Why are you being so foolish?"

Rochelle looked down for a moment before looking back up into the cold gray eyes of the angry officer. "I do not believe you will let me walk away after what I did to you. But if you choose to do so, I will return to my home and continue living as a loyal citizen of the Third Reich."

"Loyal member of the Third Reich? I saw what you did back there. You were helping a Jewess and her companions to kill soldiers and allow more filthy Jews to escape the punishment they deserved. You are guilty of the worst crimes," the man shouted as he glared back at her.

"Then let it be done, do as you must, I know that—" Rochelle could not finish the sentence before a bullet pierced her chest.

"There. Now you got what you asked for!" the agent replied, as he turned and walked back toward his car.

Rochelle struggled hard to breathe as she lay dying in the alley. As blood poured from the bullet wound she opened her eyes, hoping to look up toward the white puffy clouds that drifted lazily across the heavens one more time. Instead, she saw the face of a German soldier standing over her as he pointed his sub-machine gun toward her body. For a brief moment she looked at his dark blue eyes that glared down at her from under the black S.S. helmet, before looking away toward a nearby garden. A second later, a short blast from a German Schmeisser echoed off the buildings.

Ishmael pushed people out of his way as he made a hole for the escaping prisoners to follow. As Isaac ran close behind, he knocked down a real French Gendarme and stole his pistol. He knew it would come in handy before the day was over.

Elazar brought up the rear of the escaping prisoners, firing his shotgun at several S.S. soldiers caught off guard by what was happening. Ilan attempted to join Elazar in the race out of the square, but was cut down by a Gestapo lieutenant that came running up behind him.

After bouncing off the building, Ilan dropped to the ground, gasping for air after one of the bullets had torn a large hole in his left lung. As the Gestapo officer looked down at him, Ilan smiled, held his hands upward toward him and said with his last breath, "Shalom, my brother."

Simcha, who had been firing from the crowd when the disturbance began, dropped his rifle and ran toward the side street with the screaming crowd. He continued yelling, "Run, they will kill us all, run for your lives!"

When he saw Elazar cut down the two S.S. soldiers with his shotgun, he quickly picked up one of their machine pistols, joining Elazar as he covered the escape.

Elazar's brother Moshe had been stationed on the east side of the square where most of the German vehicles were going to be parked. When the commotion started, he immediately began running from one vehicle to the next, sticking his bayonet into tires. He had taken care of nine vehicles when a bullet slammed into the door of the vehicle he was attacking. Throwing himself to the ground, he crawled under a truck and waited to see who was going to come after him. Slowly a Wehrmacht corporal walked from vehicle to vehicle searching for him. Moshe crawled out from under the truck, standing motionless at the rear by the tailgate, waiting for the soldier to appear around the far side. With superior speed, Moshe grabbed the man around the head, thrusting his bayonet into the soldier's throat twice, before letting the body slide to the ground.

After taking a good look around, Moshe realized he was trapped. Soldiers were running from every direction to get their cars started. Pulling out his pistol, he began firing at any soldier that came within range. After dropping his third man, Moshe began running back toward the screaming crowd. Just as he approached the platform, two S.S. soldiers fired at him. One bullet struck his upper left leg shattering the femur, while the second struck the platform. Knowing he was going to die, he decided not to go down without a fight. Leaning back against the platform he returned fire with his pistol striking one of the soldiers in the chest. Three more soldiers returned fire hitting Moshe several times, ending his valiant fight.

Having everyone on board the old Mercedes truck Elazar had stolen from a farmer weeks ago, Ishmael drove slowly toward the rendezvous point. Driving into an orchard, Elazar, Simcha and Ishmael grabbed their weapons and prepared for battle as they waited fifteen minutes for the others to arrive. With five minutes to spare, Sarah came running into the orchard, totally out of breath. Leaning against the truck she gasped for air as she looked at Ishmael.

"Rochelle is lost, I am sure of it. She had so many S.S soldiers after her there was no way she could get free."

Seconds later Ben, Elazar's good friend, arrived in the orchard carrying a Schmeisser. Shaking his head, he reported, "Ilan and Moshe are dead, we need to go now before they get a chance to close down the city."

Elazar nodded his head. "Yes, we must go, everyone, get on the truck." As he closed the tailgate, he looked up at Sarah, "You are sure Rochelle is lost?"

She nodded her head without saying a word as she looked sadly at Elazar.

Arriving back at the farm where they started, Isaac walked up to

Sarah. "You were very brave, and I have missed you. I never thought I would see you again after that day in the forest."

Without saying a word, Sarah slapped him across the face as hard as she could, before pulling the pistol from her pocket and aiming it at his head.

"You left me to die, you simply ran off and left me to the soldiers! How could you do that to me, how could you leave a little girl. I was so tired and so scared, and you just left me. What kind of a man does that?"

Isaac looked at the ground for a minute before looking straight into Sarah's eyes. "I was scared and young, too. You laid down and refused to get up no matter what I said. I didn't know what to do, and I could see the soldiers coming. I only had a shot gun, and they had machine guns and rifles. I knew there was no way I could fight them." Isaac was quiet for a moment as he leaned back against the truck. "I have wondered many times what happened to you. Mostly, I just thought you must be dead. I had to find a way to justify it so I could go on, but I never really did. I'm sorry."

"Sorry," she scoffed. "I have come to wonder what that word truly means. We are all sorry for one thing or another, but in the end what difference does it ever make? We are still hunted, and we are still dying just because we are Jews. Can you tell me how I am to forgive you for leaving me to the soldiers?"

Ishmael walked up behind Sarah. "Daughter, we all have to make choices we will someday regret if we live long enough. But we each must always find a way to survive, as you did today, knowing that decision might very well end up sacrificing a friend. Regrettably, those decisions seldom work out the way we wanted them to." Looking down at her blood splattered blouse, he continued. "Did you ever think when you left your home with your family that day when you were just seven, that you would kill two men by the time you were ten?"

Shaking her head, Sarah began to tremble. "I am not sorry, but I may have to kill more and it scares me. Working with you I have learned how to hate, something I never thought was possible. But now my soul is darkened, our God has turned his back on us and my heart aches, and nothing you can say or do will change any of it."

Tossing the Luger into the back of the truck, Sarah walked slowly to the old barn to lay down on the bed she had made the night before.

As Isaac reached out to grab Sarah's arm, Ishmael pushed it away. "Although she saved your life today, she sacrificed the life of a dear friend who was not even one of us. Plus, as I said, since you left her in the forest, she has killed two men. Many things have gone wrong for her and she is still just a child. Her soul is in turmoil right now, Isaac. Give her some time and she will see the light of day."

Captain Barbie stomped his feet as he paced back and forth in his temporary office. Slamming his fist against the large map of France hanging on the wall, he shouted. "I want them all dead! I want them captured and killed one way or the other. We will clean out this nest of Jewish vermin one way or the other. They will never humiliate me like this again! Do I make myself clear, Lt. Rouchmann?"

With his shoulder wrapped in a battle dressing, but not yet treated by a doctor, Rouchmann replied.

"Jawohl, Herr Captain. I have men scouring the city right now looking for the perpetrators and our prisoners. We did kill three of them in the process so far, but we will get the rest, as we have road blocks on all the roads around the city. In the morning we will start covering a ten-mile circle around Orleans. We will find them, I assure you. They cannot go far."

"And Lt. Miller, have you located him yet?" Barbie called out, as he glared at his chief aid.

"His men are involved with the search all over the city, and it is dark, Herr Captain. We have not been able to locate the lieutenant yet, but we are trying, sir."

Barbie folded his arms across the small of his back as he paced back and forth for several minutes, before looking over at Lts. Rouchmann and Meyer. "I have spoken to Himmler in Berlin within the last hour. Miller is to be executed on sight for allowing this to happen. FIND HIM!" Barbie yelled, as he stomped his foot.

Around midnight, Elazar and his group of partisans shook hands with Ishmael as they left the farm, heading west toward Brittany and the English Channel.

Quietly, at one o'clock in the morning, Ishmael, Sarah, Isaac and two of the escaped prisoners named Shlomo and Menachem, climbed aboard the truck Ishmael had driven from Paris to Orleans.

Their intention was to rejoin the Jewish underground organization that still lived in the old factory. Sarah knew she could never return to the restaurant to work for Jocko, or to Rochelle's apartment where all her belongings were, as the Gestapo would be keeping a keen eye out for anyone associated with Rochelle.

Throughout the long drive, Sarah's stomach was tied in knots as she feared the Gestapo might very well arrest Jocko for aiding the underground, even though he was innocent. With the Gestapo, you could be arrested and shot simply of being guilty by association. What made matters worse was that she had no way of warning him of what might be coming his way. In the end it would just be more blood on her hands, the type you could never wash off.

Just south of Orleans near the small town of Beaugency, Lt. Miller and one of his trusted platoon leaders. Sgt. Becker, were parked in a Kubelwagon, a small German military staff car, near a stack of straw.

"Lieutenant, you know it's suicide for us to return to Orleans. Barbie will hold all of us responsible for everything that happened today, as we were supposed to be on the lookout for underground activity. He will have you shot or hung as a traitor to the Reich. We must find a way to get into southern France and work our way down into Spain. I am sorry to say sir, it's our only chance to survive," Sgt. Becker explained, as he kept a close watch on the road.

"Ja, I am well aware of what that butcher will do to me if I show my face. It was not all my fault, our intelligence people could not give us any solid information regarding the Jewish underground that we could use. Plus, their plan was very well thought out. With all the people Barbie herded into Place du Martroi, it was a perfect set up for them to operate. We killed way too many civilians today for no good reason. I can no longer serve that man or Himmler. Since I am not married, I have no wife or children to worry about. But you Becker, you have a young wife. They will kill her when you go missing. You must try and save her." Lt. Miller stated as he looked over at his long time friend.

Becker nodded his head. "Herr Lieutenant, do not get angry with me, but I have been thinking of going to Spain for a while. What we are doing is wrong, and I can no longer condone killing innocent people. I had my wife leave for Bordeaux on a train three days ago, with false papers. She knows some people close by we can hide with until we can work out a plan."

"Gut, that is gut, Sergeant. I do not think less of you, in fact I am proud of you for being so brave. Defecting is an automatic death penalty for any soldier and his family. You were bold, Becker,"

Lt. Miller responded, as he drove the Kubelwagon back out onto the road heading southwest, following the Loire River that flows into the Bay of Biscay at Nantes. "It will take time for Lt. Rouchmann to get a good search organized and then get it moving. It's only 335 kilometers to Nantes, we can safely be there before sun up. Then we will figure out how to get to Bordeaux."

Everything in Paris appeared to be normal as Ishmael parked the small truck in a parking lot about three miles from the old factory. Under the guidance of Elazar and Simcha, the small band worked their way through back alleys and side streets until they came to a man hole about three blocks from the factory. Kneeling down Simcha carefully removed the cover. "We go down here. Stay in a group until Elazar gets the cover back on. Then stay close, if you make a wrong turn, you could wander down there for a long time before anyone could ever find you. The sewers of Paris are treacherous."

As the sun rose over Paris, the eight partisans were safely back under the factory. Sarah sat by herself on a makeshift bed she was given. Tears ran down her face as she thought about killing the Gestapo agent. He must have been married and had children. Now she had taken him away from his family, although he was doing the same to Jews day after day. One life for another. It made no sense to a ten-year-old girl. But she understood she was far tougher than the seven-year-old that had gone to the train station in Munich three years ago. What was a birthday cake now that her hands had killed two human beings and her family was dead? What was the value of life at all when you had to hide underground in the sewers of Paris.

As the sun rose over Nantes, Sgt. Becker parked the Kubelwagon near the bridge over the Loire River and walked toward a check point where two privates were standing guard. "Heil Hitler!" Becker yelled out, startling the two soldiers. Seeing the black S.S. uniform, both men called out, "Heil Hitler, Herr Sergeant, is there anything we can do for you?"

Both men appeared to be very willing to answer questions, than ask anything relevant to their jobs. Anything, if it meant the S.S sergeant would leave them alone.

"What new orders do you have this morning?" Becker called out, using his sternest S.S. voice.

Handing a clip board to Becker, one of the soldiers replied. "Nothing new, Sergeant. These are the same orders we had yesterday. Are we missing anything, Herr Sergeant?" The soldier responded in a shaky voice.

After looking over the clipboard, Sgt. Becker nodded his head. "No. All appears to be in order. My Lieutenant and I are doing a security inspection for Himmler, and we are to report any improprieties directly to him. It is good to see you are complying with all directives. We will be on our way now. Heil Hitler!" Becker called out before walking back to the staff car.

The soldiers could not raise the stop arm fast enough, allowing the staff car to pass on through. When the car had passed over the bridge, one of the soldiers stated. "The only thing that scares me more than an S.S. officer is my mother-in-law, and she is sixty years old."

The other soldier laughed heartily in agreement as he once again lowered the stop arm.

It became quickly apparent that Lt. Rouchmann's arrest order had either not arrived this far west, or they weren't being sought this far from Orleans. They cleared every checkpoint along the way to Bordeaux without incident. Of course, the S.S. uniform and powerful intimidation kept all of the young soldiers they met at the various check points along the way from ever asking for their identification papers.

By six o'clock that evening the men had pushed the Kubelwagon off a cliff into the Gironde Estuary near Libourne, and stolen civilian clothing from unattended wash lines, before walking the last few miles to Bordeaux and the home where Sgt. Becker's wife was staying under an assumed name.

There was much to work out, but from Bordeaux to Baztan, Spain, was only 147 kms., and freedom from the Third Reich. They both knew that the French underground would be very nervous about helping two former S.S soldiers from escaping into Spain. Doing so could put their entire operation at risk, on both sides of the border.

Back in his headquarters in Lyon, Klaus Barbie ordered all the French prisoners they were holding be transported to camps in Germany, along with the Jews they were capturing. However, now Barbie was taking a more active role during the searches, and was quick to shoot any French man or woman he felt was being uncooperative. Everyone in France was quickly beginning to understand exactly why Klaus Barbie was called the butcher of Lyon.

However, at night, he studied every security report on the ever-widening search regarding sightings of Lt. Miller or Sgt. Becker west of Lyon to the English Channel, or east toward Switzerland. He would find them and they would be made to suffer along with their families. No one played Klaus Barbie for a fool.

Chapter Nine
French Underground

If there was one thing the Germans were never going to be able to control in France, it was the underground movement known as the Maquis. Although the organization operated all over France, most of the command centers were located in rural areas. Members of the Maquis were commonly called Maquisards. At first. leaders were nervous about accepting Jews into their tightly knit organizations, but after observing the abilities and determination of the Jewish freedom fighters, many groups were asked to join the French resistance.

Within days of returning to Paris, the Gestapo arrested and tortured Jocko. They had learned from papers they took from Rochelle's purse, that she had worked for him. Quickly, they put out a dragnet throughout Paris, hoping to find the woman by the name of Helga who was living with Rochelle. Jocko died about a week later, after he was injected with a supposed truth serum the Gestapo used on many detainees, that never really gave them the results they desired.

As the dragnet widened, and more Gestapo agents arrived in Paris, it became clear to Ishmael and Elazar, that the group would have to leave the basement of the old factory. Elazar learned of an underground unit near Beauvais that was hurting for members, and willing to let them join.

However, not everyone in the old factory wanted to make the move, as they had become quite comfortable where they were. So, Elazar left it to each person to decide on who would stay, and who was willing to take the chance of relocating. The night they were to move, just fifteen residents decided to go. Once more, Ishmael pleaded with the others to get out of Paris, but no one took heed of his appeals or warnings.

The move was a big relief for Sarah, as many of the women in the factory had treated her badly, arguing her lack of respect for the rules last time had nearly spelled disaster for all of them. Now they trusted her even less, feeling she was responsible for the deaths of Rochelle and Jocko. Sarah had felt like an outcast from her own people and it hurt tremendously. There were many days she was served only half the food ration everyone else was given, or overlooked completely.

Regardless of the risk in moving, Sarah was much happier being out of the dark wet basement, and could breathe fresh air, and pick fruit from an orchard nearby. Over a period of weeks, she had finally been able to forgive Isaac, and they once more became good friends, although Sarah had come to realize that making friends could be very painful and dangerous, the way they were now forced to live.

It did not take long for Ishmael and Elazar to move up the ranks in this new organization, as it was clearly evident they had the skills and daring that could make the group a real thorn in the side of the Germans.

Three weeks after Elazar and his followers made the move to Beauvais, a large contingent of S.S. soldiers and Gestapo officials descended upon the factory, along with tanks and armored vehicles. For three days, battles raged in the tunnels, as the determined partisans worked desperately to open new passages, allowing them a chance to escape through the massive sewer system.

However, the equally determined Germans attempted to block every avenue of escape, using explosives to collapse sewer lines and adjacent tunnels. On the evening of the third day, partisans and soldiers fought in hand to hand combat to control the main entrance to the underground enclave. As shells from a Panther tank crushed the last remaining supports, the roof collapsed. Baruch and fifteen survivors sat in darkness in what had been the kitchen as they contemplated their fate. There was one last possible escape route the Germans most likely did not know about, but they would surely be watching all the rubble for signs of life. Everyone realized surrender meant certain death, but they also understood the Germans might now gas them right where they were, and it would be over. At midnight, Baruch led the survivors up a decrepit stairwell that led to a partially buried ventilation shaft. After quietly clearing debris from the damaged shaft, they could see stars twinkling overhead in the clear night sky. Baruch exited first, taking cover behind a pile of fallen concrete. Seeing no one in sight, he motioned for the rest to follow him. Without any warning, two machine guns opened fire cutting down several of the survivors, as children screamed. One of Baruch's trusted aids threw up his hands, yelling for the Germans to cease fire.

Instantly, several large search lights illuminated the area, as soldiers streamed into what had been a blacksmith shop when the factory was operating. Baruch dropped to the ground, rolling under several huge timbers, holding his Schmeisser at the ready so he could fight to the death.

After the Germans had climbed down into the tunnel one more time to be assured there was no one left alive inside the factory, the fourteen remaining Jews were lined up against a wall. Klaus Barbie walked down into the shop and smiled.

"You have caused me much pain, though I fear some of those we are looking for are not here, but we will catch them later." Walking up to an S.S. sergeant, Barbie said calmly, "Sergeant, let me see your weapon." Taking it in his hand, Barbie looked over the machine pistol. "You keep it in good shape Sergeant, that is very good. One never knows when it will have to be used." In a split-second, Barbie turned, firing the weapon at the remaining survivors. Handing the machine gun back to the sergeant, he pulled his sidearm. Without checking the bodies, he walked up to each one, firing a bullet into their heads.

Smiling, he turned back to the S.S. major behind him. "We are finished here, gather up your equipment and move back to your headquarters."

Baruch remained under the timbers until the following day.

About mid-morning, after the last of the Germans drove off, Baruch departed the ruins for Beauvais.

Everyone along the coast of France became increasingly nervous as the German military began building camps for soldiers that were keeping a close eye on the slave laborers that were building the Atlantic Wall, Hitler's dream fortification to keep the Allies from invading the continent. The massive fortifications ran from Spain all the way to Norway. It was a tremendous undertaking, being supervised by Field Marshall Erwin Rommel. Using false names and identification papers, Ishmael and Isaac went to an office in Ruen that was hiring locals interested in working on the project. They were hired easily and told to report for work the next day. They worked hard, digging foundations and pouring concrete for large gun emplacements that would cover what later became known as Omaha and Utah beaches.

All the while, as they worked, they collected information on German combat units in the area, visiting officers and officials from Berlin, Gestapo agents, and the lay outs of the massive bunkers. All of this information was passed to local underground members that were sending it all to England.

Sarah, who was now going by the name of Elsa outside the compound, went daily to the construction sites with another young girl named Yvonne, to sell homemade muffins to the soldiers and engineers. They were treated very well, and from time to time sang folk songs for the soldiers to earn a few extra cents. However, each day when they reported back to their farm, they were able to relate who they spoke to, what patches they had seen on uniforms, and occasionally, handed over documents they had the chance to pick up.

During the early morning hours of August 10, 1942, it was clear to any French person living near the coast that something was happening far to the north. Trucks loaded with troops left their compounds, while artillery pieces that had been dug in as beach defenses were quickly pulled out, attached to trucks and driven away.

Construction crews were banned from going to work as the remaining German security forces became tense as they watched the rough waters of the channel, and the activities of the citizens behind the beach head. It was not until late in the afternoon that the underground passed on a message stating that Canadian and British forces had attempted a cross channel raid near the city of Dieppe, just 104 kms. northwest of Beauvais. Sarah was excited knowing Allied forces had come so close to where they were living.

However, over the next few days it became evident that the nine-hour attack was a complete disaster. Canadian forces had 907 men killed and 2,460 wounded, while German forces had captured 1,946 British and Canadian soldiers. Still, the attack gave Sarah a feeling of hope, knowing the Allies had come that close to where she was. They had to be planning something big, or they would not have attempted the raid in the first place.

A week after the raid at Dieppe, civilians were once more allowed back to the beach head. As before, Yvonne and Sarah delivered muffins and other baked goods to the hungry soldiers that enjoyed the delicacies, and the company of the young girls. Little did any of them ever know, the one known as Elsa was really Sarah, who always carried a French commando knife inside the lining of her jacket. She was determined never to be captured without putting up a fight.

Several weeks later as they arrived near the beach, they could see something different was taking place. All the soldiers were standing on the sand dunes and bunkers yelling their approval and taking photographs. A lieutenant the girls knew well ran up to them. "Come quickly, this is your chance to meet our boss, he is here for an inspection. I know he would love one of your pastries."

Soldiers pushed the girls forward until they were standing by a black Mercedes. Near the back door stood Field Marshall Erwin Rommel. The lieutenant bowed as he stepped up to Rommel. "Herr Field Marshall, you really must sample one of the pastries these young girls bring us every day, they are wonderful"

Looking down toward the basket, he smiled. "Ah, apple muffins, my very favorite. How much do you need for one of them."

Sarah shook her head. "For you, Herr Field Marshall, there is no price, help yourself."

"Nonsense, Rommel replied, as he removed his billfold from under his coat. "Your parents need to purchase ingredients for these wonderful treats. Will five Francs be enough?"

Yvonne beamed with delight when she took the money from Rommel. "Danka, Herr Field Marshall, my mother will be very happy with this."

After patting both girls on the head, Rommel picked up a muffin from the basket. All the while, Sarah had her hand just above the small opening she had made in her jacket, so she could pull the knife in a hurry. She stared at Rommel, wondering how much of a loss it would be to the German war effort if she killed him. Her pulse quickened and it became hard to breathe as her hand neared the knife, maybe this was what she was meant to do for the Jews that were being slaughtered.

After finishing the muffin, Rommel smiled at the girls. "You know, I will be here about this same time tomorrow for one more check. Bring me another apple muffin and you will earn another five francs." All the men surrounding the staff car cheered, knowing their Field Marshall would remember his visit here, and it would reflect well upon them.

Arriving back at the farm with an empty basket and more money than normal, the girls excitedly related what had happened. After Sarah explained her thought about killing Rommel, Baruch jumped up from the log he was sitting on.

"Never attempt anything like that, Sarah. If you should kill him, the S.S. will come down on us like the wind on a house of cards. They will move everyone away from the beachhead and kill those of us they feel are Jews. That would be a disaster for hundreds of people. Feed him, take his money and smile a lot. That will help our cause more than killing one Field Marshall. We knew he was coming here last week. Our intelligence is good and getting better, we can't let anything stop that."

Ishmael walked up to Sarah, removing the knife from her jacket. "You may have this back after Rommel leaves. I know you, Sarah, you act out of emotion. I am doing this for all of us."

The following day, Sarah and Yvonne went back to the beach with more muffins than normal, knowing all the soldiers would buy them, along with their Field Marshall.

Rommel was clearly not in the same frame of mind he had been the day before, although he treated the girls very well. It was clear he was more concerned about the massive wall they were constructing between two gun mounts. On a piece of paper, he drew out a plan for the placement of walkways and phone lines to be dug into the sand to connect gun emplacements. As the men turned to walk down toward the beach, a sergeant tossed the paper on the front seat of the car near the door. With everyone headed back to work or following Rommel, Sarah reached into the car, grabbed the paper and shoved it under her blouse. She began slowly walking back to their camp as she yelled goodbye to the soldiers that were guarding the slave laborers.

Baruch was excited with the drawing when Sarah laid it on the table. "This, this is what we need more of. England will be very happy when they see this." Standing up from his chair he gave Sarah and Yvonne a big hug before carefully folding the map for transport.

In early November, several trucks arrived, bringing more slave laborers to the beach. Some of them were wearing the yellow Star of David on their coats, identifying them as Jews. Sarah was intrigued by these people as they spoke Czechoslovakian and another language she did not understand.

One of the men in his forties was assigned to mix concrete behind one of the new bunkers. He watched the girls closely every day, especially when they walked back home. About a week later, Isaac brought the man to the camp blindfolded, with his hands tied behind his back. Walking up to Baruch, Isaac whispered. "I found him walking along a hedgerow near Gisors. I thought it was best to jump him before he wandered into our camp. He is wearing the Star of David on his coat, and he was trying to speak with me in very good Yiddish."

The camp directors, along with Isaac and Sarah stood quietly as Ismael removed the blindfold from the very scared man. Seeing Sarah, he relaxed a bit, but was terrified of the machete Baruch was holding. Shaking his head, he bowed toward Baruch. After taking a deep breath, he began speaking slowly in Yiddish. "My name is Malachi, I come from Ushgorod, right by the Russian, Czech border. I was a carpenter by trade. When the Germans raided our village, my wife and I, along with our two children were taken to a camp in Poland called Auschwitz – Birkenau. When we jumped off the cars, we were in the Auschwitz camp. We were put in a very long line. A man in an S.S. uniform stood on the platform looking at each person. If you were a man and looked healthy, you went to the right without your families, everyone else, the women, children and old people, went to the left. Dogs barked, soldiers shot people, everyone was screaming and calling out for family, it was awful. I was put in a barracks with other men that were in good shape. There were some from Czechoslovakia like me, others were from Russia and Romania. The next day we were all transferred to the Birkenau camp.

I asked one of the Jewish workers in the camp how I could see my family. He pointed toward the smoke rising from the large smoke stacks and said, 'Say goodbye to them, there they go.' He then explained the process they were using to kill us, it was ghastly."

Baruch and the other men asked questions about the process, turning white as Malachi provided the answers. Sarah turned pale as she listened intently, understanding what had become of her family, and knowing she would never see them again. Isaac placed his arm around her as Malachi continued.

"After three days of beatings and other physical abuse, we were loaded back onto a train and delivered to Rouen, France. From there we were trucked to the beach as you are aware. The soldiers here are much better than in the camps. They know all this work has to be done by someone, so if they kill us, they have to answer to Rommel's staff, and no one wants to do that. But I know when the work is done, the S.S. will kill us all. Each day I've seen the girls bringing pastries for the soldiers, but in my heart, I knew they were from the underground. So, last night as they took us to the cage, I dove behind a pile of sand and pulled a bunch down on me. The guards looked for hours before a sergeant told them they would find me in the morning. That was when I slipped away, and walked until your man caught me. So, what are you going to do with me now?"

Ishmael looked at Baruch and Elazar. "We can't set him free, he knows too much, and it won't take long for the Germans to find him. I think we can use a man of his skills and determination."

All the men agreed as Isaac cut the yellow stars from his clothing and placed them in the fire.

Awakening to the shrill cries of the hungry sea gulls on May 10, 1943, Sarah felt sad. Today was her eleventh birthday, and she had no family to celebrate with. She thought back to that last day in Straubing, Germany, when all that was important to her was eating a piece of the birthday cake her mother had made for her. She longed to have her childhood back, when she had not a care in the world. When cake was her biggest concern, and she had a loving family around her to share it. But the world had turned over several times since then, and there was no going back to such a peaceful time.

Laying on her simple bed of straw, Sarah wondered what most eleven-year-old girls around the world were doing these days. Certainly not spying against one of the most dangerous armies in the world, or having to live with the fact that they had killed two men just to stay alive, and gotten her friends killed as well. This was not the life she had dreamed of so long ago, nor the life she ever wanted, but it was the hand she was dealt, and she was well aware that the joker was still in the deck, just waiting to be played.

With Baruch now in full command of the group, discussions took place on a daily basis regarding attacks on German operations that could cripple or slow down the building of the shore batteries. Although they had accumulated several cases of explosives and machine guns, no attacks had been carried out.

Secret conversations regarding the Allies coming to liberate them flowed like water, especially when American or British photography planes flew low passes over the beach construction areas. Sarah would watch the planes passing over at high rates of speed, wishing she could jump on board and fly back to England, and a new life free from fear. But as always, the plane was soon nothing more than a black dot disappearing into the clouds over the English Channel.

Going to feed the soldiers on the beach was now more dangerous than ever before. As many gun emplacements and communication centers were complete, the gestapo and S.S. units moved in to maintain security. The girls were no longer allowed in certain areas, and all too often the Gestapo sent them back home without making a sale.

One afternoon as the girls were returning home, Sarah had an idea. Pulling Yvonne down behind a sand dune, Sarah covered her mouth. "Shhh, listen to me. You keep going home, I'm going to sneak into the area over by the new bunker and see what's going on. Do not tell anyone where I went, we need to get information for the British. Do you understand?"

Yvonne stared at Sarah. "If they catch you, they will kill you, no questions asked. You cannot do this, Baruch will be angry for sure."

Sarah smiled at her good friend. "Go now, and do as I said. Everything will be fine."

After Yvonne departed, Sarah climbed over the sand dune and ran head long toward the beach. Ducking down into an unfinished trench that would eventually connect several bunkers, Sarah slowly made her way toward the new bunker that was nearly completed. No one was around as they were allowing the concrete to harden before continuing. Finding a small tablet and pencil in a tool box, Sarah quickly drew out a floor plan of the bunker. She stepped off the distances from corner to corner and drew a sketch of a control panel near the gun port.

When she was finished, she ran down the trench to another bunker that had been completed a few weeks earlier. Her jaw dropped down to her chest as she stood face to face with an eighty-eight-millimeter artillery piece, bolted to a steel frame work, allowing it to traverse left to right about ninety degrees. She immediately went to work sketching out the bunker as best she could. Before leaving, she walked up to a spotting scope that stood on a tripod by the gun port. Smiling, she pulled out the pin that attached the scope to the tripod and tossed it out the window. Taking the scope, she ran out of the bunker and began to head home. But moments later, she heard a voice yelling at her to halt. Looking over her shoulder, she noticed a soldier running toward her with a rifle.

Sarah ran in between the dunes, keeping slightly ahead of the soldier as he continued yelling at her. After he fired a shot at her, Sarah ducked down behind an old collapsed barn, crawling under some of the debris. She laid quietly, holding her breath, as she watched the man walk back and forth looking for her. As he approached the debris pile, Sarah knew she was about to be discovered. The soldier stopped about fifteen feet from the pile and called out. "I know you are there. If you do not come out, I will start shooting into the pile."

Knowing she was caught, Sarah called out. "Do not shoot, I'll come out."

After pushing an old door aside, Sarah climbed out of the rubble, still holding the spotting scope. There was no doubt the soldier was more fixated on the scope than he was with her. Letting go of the front of the rifle, he held out his hand. "Give that to me, you are in big trouble!"

Realizing the barrel of the gun was beginning to point toward the ground, Sarah tossed the heavy scope as hard as she could, striking the man in the face. The soldier stumbled backward for a moment before falling to his knees. Blood gushed from his shattered nose and mouth as he cried out in pain. Sarah charged forward grabbing the heavy Mauser away from the half-conscious soldier. Raising the rifle as high as she could, she slammed the butt of the weapon down on to the scope, shattering it. Then swinging it like a baseball bat she drove the butt of the rifle against the soldier's shoulder. Sarah could hear the bones snap as the soldier fell to the ground where he rolled in pain.

After tossing the rifle into the sand dune, Sarah removed the soldier's bayonet from its scabbard, and began running through the dunes, keeping an eye out for other German guards roaming the area. Baruch and Ishmael had all but given up on Sarah when she came walking into the camp as the sun was setting.

Handing the note book to Baruch, Sarah said. "I think the people in England might be interested in these sketches. It took me most of the afternoon to draw them."

The men were delighted with the sketches and other information Sarah was able to tell them, as she devoured a plate of food one of the women handed her.

When Baruch was finished, Ishmael sat down next to her. "Child, tell me what else happened while you were out there."

Sarah shook her head. "Everything went well. I had to hide sometimes to avoid the guards, but they never caught me."

Ishmael nodded his head as he took hold of her arm. "Are you injured, or does this blood belong to someone else I should know about?"

Sarah looked at the blood on her pants for a moment before replying. "He is alive, he will fight another day, but not for a while. I did not kill him if that is what you are wondering. But I could have easily done it." Sarah said, as she held up the captured bayonet.

Ishmael gazed at Sarah for a moment before standing up.

"I believe you could have, Sarah. I believe you could have."

As Ishmael walked away, his words kept flowing through her mind. She wasn't sure why she hadn't killed the soldier, but the thought of how easily it would have been to end his life bothered her intensely. This was not what eleven-year-old girls were supposed to be thinking about.

Chapter Ten
Border Race

Lt. Miller and Sgt. Becker worked for weeks attempting to find a safe route from Bordeaux to the Spanish border, but every plan ran into serious errors. Finding people you could trust was just not possible in Southern France. Although Germany had agreed to leave Vichy France alone, the Gestapo operated openly in many areas, and had undercover agents posted anywhere local governments allowed them. Plus, they paid huge sums of money to civilians or government officials for information on Jews and German military deserters.

The woman named Katherine that had put up Mrs. Becker when she first arrived walked up to Lt. Miller. I know a man that can set up a crossing for you. But you must take me with you as your wife, I no longer feel safe around here. Please, do not let them get their hands on me, I will do as you say, and never complain. I helped you this far, now you must help me, plus I have a sizable amount of money we can use to pay our way. Just do not ask where the money came from."

After discussing the situation, with the Beckers, the decision was made to take the woman along as Lt. Miller's wife.

The problem Katherine spoke about was very true. To find reliable French and Spanish underground agents was dangerous, and they demanded large sums of money to safely transport people across the Franco/Spanish border. They quickly realized the safest place to cross into Spain was over the Pyrenees Mountains near the town of Bagneres-de-Luchon, 280kms. east of Baztan, their original planned crossing point. The cost would be nearly double, and they would have to walk over the 11,169ft. mountain peak. However, this plan looked to be much more secure, as it appeared the French underground in that area was completely trustworthy and had no time for the Gestapo or the dreaded S.S. The problem was, they had to cross over the mountain by mid-October, or wait until the spring of 1944, and they knew they could not hide out in Bordeaux much longer, as the Gestapo was becoming relentless and more ruthless in hunting down Jews, traitors, and deserters.

On September 15, the men packed their gear into the old Renault Sgt. Becker's wife had purchased when she first arrived in Bordeaux. Avoiding most of the main highways and only travelling during daylight when the Gestapo was less curious, it took them three days to travel the 385kms.

Arriving in Bagneres-de-Luchon, Sgt. Becker walked into a small cafe. Looking at the old woman that came over to wait on him he said. "I hear it was not a good year for the roses around here."

The woman nodded her head. "One cannot predict the future."

Sgt. Becker smiled, "Surely your grandchildren will have more luck next year."

The woman grabbed him by the arm pulling him into a supply room. "I was told to expect four, where are the others?"

"Walking in the small park waiting for me to report back," Sgt. Becker explained.

"Get them and all you want to carry along with you. You will need to start tomorrow, there is a big change in the weather coming. It is now or never, and if you don't go, you cannot stay here, that would draw attention from the Gestapo. Drive your car into the garage behind the cafe, we will dispose of it.

With everyone safely in the garage, a young woman named Elise, her husband, and two Jewish men entered the shed. Looking over the two couples Elise began.

"Normally, we would not have started for two more days, but the weather is getting worse." Taking the hand of one of the men, she continued. "This is my husband, Phillipe. He is a crack shot and a good cook, and he knows the Spanish people we need to contact at the border. Cooperate with us and you will be in Spain in two days, maybe three, depending on the snow fall. Get some sleep now, it will be a very long cold night.

At eleven o'clock that evening, Elise and Phillipe arrived back in the garage bundled up in heavy hiking clothing. "Everything is quiet in town and it is starting to snow, and that is good. We will not leave any tracks and it will be impossible for anyone to see us as we begin moving up into the foothills. Come now, we must go." Phillipe explained very seriously.

A half hour later they left the garage heading up into the mountains. The incline was very mild as they began, allowing them to make good time, but that began to change in the next hour.

By one o'clock in the morning the trail had become more vertical and treacherous as everything was wet and icy. Sometimes the snow blew so hard it was nearly impossible to see the person in front of them, and then there were times when a few stars were visible through the broken clouds between the mountain peaks. Either way, the torturous biting wind made the long night bitterly cold.

Around noon the following day, they came upon a rough looking cabin set back about fifty feet from the trail, with smoke coming out of the chimney. Entering the small cabin, everyone let out a sigh of relief as they all nearly collapsed on the floor.

Elise looked at the older man that lived in the cabin. "Have the supplies arrived as planned?"

Smiling, the man kissed Elise on the cheek. "Yes, my daughter. Everything arrived two days ago, and the carriers left right away. They saw German mountain troops about three kilometers from here heading south, so they wanted to get out of here quickly."

"Mountain troops? Are there more of them around?" One of the other Jewish men asked as he looked sternly at Elise. "How often does that happen? How safe are we?"

Elise walked up to the man. "Herman, we are not safe now, nor will we be safe until we are several miles into Spain, at least. The Germans patrol that far across the border, and the Spanish government does not care to stop them. Once we get to Pica-de-Anelo you will be safe."

Angered by Elise's response, Herman and his friend Iman stood up and paced the cabin for several minutes as Phillipe began preparing food for everyone. Looking down at Lt. Miller, Herman spoke up. "You and your people don't look Jewish. Who are you? Why are you here?"

"Like you, we are seeking safety, that's all that matters." Lt. Miller responded calmly.

"Well, it matters to me and my friend!" Herman called out. "I want to know! If you are not a Jew who are you? Are you going to turn us over to the German patrols? Tell me or I'll kill you right now!"

Elise walked up placing her hand on Herman's chest. "Everyone we take across here has a story, and it does not matter to us as long as they can pay. So, sit down and leave them alone please."

As Elise turned back to help her husband, Iman pulled a German bayonet from under his coat and pulled Sgt. Becker from the floor. Pushing the knife up against his throat, Iman called out. "Are you a damn German attempting to run from your Fuhrer? Because if you are, I'm going to kill you and your friends right here and now, and leave your carcasses for the wolves."

Hearing the sound of a hammer being pulled back on a pistol, he looked over toward Phillipe. "Put the knife down or you will die right here and go no farther. I do not care about your problems, your anger, or your political beliefs. I agreed to take you and your friend to Spain and we will. Then you are free to do as you choose, but for now put the knife down."

After pushing Becker to the floor, Iman placed the knife back under his coat. "Don't turn your back on me Kraut. Like I said, I'll gut you and leave you for the wolves and I mean it."

It was a very uncomfortable night for everyone, as there was no doubt there would be trouble before they reached Spain.

After scouting the following morning, Elise took the lead, moving toward the summit of the mountain. Phillipe attempted to keep Iman and Herman separated from Becker, Miller and the women as best he could. When they stopped about midday, Phillipe walked forward to speak with his wife. As soon as he had walked a short distance away, Iman jumped up, pulled his knife, and lunged at Sgt. Becker.

Both men rolled in the snow, screaming at each other, as they both attempted to avoid the blade of the whirling bayonet. Phillipe immediately turned and came running back to stop them. Before he could reach the fight, he was tripped by Herman, who held him to the ground.

Pulling a knife of his own and holding firm to Phillipe, he called out, "Let them end it. Then we can move on and let the rest of them freeze to death up here. They need to die for what they have done to our people."

Before another word could be said, a gun shot rang out across the frozen snow-covered mountainside. Blood from a bullet wound in Iman's throat turned the snow crimson red as the dying man gasped one last time. Lt. Miller quickly pulled Sgt. Becker to his feet before spinning around to face an outraged Herman.

"Put down the knife or you'll be next, and don't play the fool. We're not that far away from freedom," Lt. Miller yelled to the friend of the dead man. 'This is not what I wanted, but you two could not leave well enough alone. I am sorry, but we want to live as badly as you do. Drop the knife or you will die also."

Slowly the man lowered the knife, apologizing to Phillipe. "My friend watched his family get killed in Leon by Klaus Barbie. He has been filled with rage ever since. I am sorry it ended this way. Please, let's end this here, and I will cause you no more grief. I also want to live."

After dragging the body off the trail, Phillipe said a short prayer before continuing on toward Spain. Just after midnight, they arrived near another old hunting cabin that was unoccupied this time of year. Phillip and Elise made a meal while everyone else rested.

With near blizzard conditions the following day, Phillipe felt it was best to lay low. It wasn't until about eleven in the morning that he felt it was safe to move on. Around six in the afternoon, a lone man came walking toward them. His dark skin made Lt. Miller feel comfortable that they were finally in Spain. Walking up to the young man he called out. "Spain?"

The man smiled, "Espana yes, welcome my friend."

It was well after midnight when they walked out of the mountains toward a small lodge. Elise looked at the five survivors. "We did what you paid us to do. You can stay here the rest of the night or you are free to go on your own. You can catch a train from here that will take you to Bilbao on the coast at noon tomorrow, or one that will take you to Madrid at seven in the morning. We will help you get tickets to where ever you want to go as we promised."

Lt. Miller approached Elise while shaking hands with her. We should have enough money left to purchase tickets to Portugal, where there is a German community not too far from Lisbon. If you can help us with that, we will be in your debt."

Elise smiled. "You paid us what we asked for, and we will finish the job. I will meet you at the train station at six-thirty."

As planned, Elise met Lt. Miller at the station, handing him the four sets of documents they needed to travel to Lisbon. After shaking hands with everyone she said, "The world is in a sad place, with many people caught up where they do not want to be. What is happening to the Jews is beyond wrong, and I am afraid we can save very few of them. Phillipe and I wish you the best of luck in your new lives."

Arriving in Lisbon the following day, Katherine contacted a man she had heard about while living in Bordeaux. By late afternoon he had supplied them with the tickets they required. At six o'clock they boarded the train, and were traveling north toward a small community near the Atlantic Ocean, where about a hundred German families had set up a productive farming community.

Lt. Miller and Sgt. Becker never let their guard down, constantly keeping a keen eye out for anyone that looked suspicious, or was asking too many questions of the residents. During the war years, they were always concerned that Barbie might find out where they went and send an assassin to kill them. Immediately after the war ended, they worried more about the secret Nazi organization named Odessa, that might hunt them down for failing their responsibilities to the Third Reich. Despite the serious concerns, they were still very happy to be far removed from the horrors of war, and the evil operations conducted by Klaus Barbie and the S.S.

By 1947, they were sure their permanent safety was secured. Neither of them ever looked back or even considered returning to Germany. Lt. Miller, had married Katherine, and the community had accepted them all with open arms, held nothing against them, and asked no questions. Although haunted by their relationships with the S.S., both men were able to slowly move on, gradually finding peace in their lives. Neither of them could have ever guessed as to what their fates may be.

Chapter Eleven
Capture

It was obvious to everyone living near the French Coast that the Germans were expecting something big to happen in the near future. The pressure on the workers to complete the projects was pushed in to high gear, and the soldiers no longer had time for the pastry carrying girls they had enjoyed so much in the past.

Areas of the sand dunes that local inhabitants had always enjoyed were no longer accessible to them. Rows and rows of barbed wire entanglements were now strung on fence posts for miles, while hundreds of land mines had been buried up and down the coast. All bridges and causeways were now guarded by no nonsense soldiers who had orders saying shoot to kill. Heavy pieces of artillery were dug into the sand, while heavy camouflage kept photography planes from discovering their positions.

The Wehrmacht began moving French citizens from their homes and farms if they were considered too close to the beach. Everyone was now suspect inside the invasion perimeter, which extended nearly ten kilometers to the east. It didn't take long for Baruch to realize they would have to pick up their operation and move before they were discovered. Over a period of three days the camp was torn down and moved southwest into the hills of Normandy, near Alencon and

Mayenne. This allowed them to send good information to England on what was coming and going from the beaches on a daily basis.

As the cold winter winds of January, 1944 whipped up the surf in the English Channel, Sarah was more convinced than ever that the Allies were coming to France soon. She was well aware that the Germans would never be this nervous if they were not expecting something to happen soon. Flights of Allied photography planes increased over the beaches while large cargo planes dropped more and more bundles of military equipment for the underground.

However, the Gestapo and S.S. were increasing their patrols each time they were notified that cargo planes had made another drop. Picking up the sacred bundles became a very dangerous job, as each night underground members were captured or killed in the process. One night, a man by the name of Seth was captured after being hit in the leg by a bullet. He was not only an underground member, but he was of Jewish descent. There was little doubt in the underground community that he would be horribly tortured. It was always impossible to know how much a man could take before he was broken. Many men over the last year had caved in with the promise that the torture would cease, if they just handed over the information they possessed. Of course, once they did, it was a bullet to the head that ended the torture as promised.

Seth endured severe torture until dawn, before he finally told them where one of the base camps was hidden. Immediately, a platoon of S.S. soldiers backed up by two squads of Wehrmacht Infantry, descended on the camp near Mayenne. The partisans fought with tenacity, refusing to give ground while allowing some of the women and children time to escape to the east.

Sarah was terrified as the battle raged on, driving the partisans back inch by inch. Isaac ran up to Sarah, grabbing her by the arm.

"It's time Sarah, we must leave. Ishmael has already made his way out, and Baruch, Elazar, Ben and Simcha are all dead. Everything will collapse shortly."

Taking Isaac by the hand, they ran along the field side of a hedgerow, heading south, as a German half-track filled with soldiers rumbled along the dirt road on the far side of the hedgerow. Coming to a crossroad, Isaac pushed Sarah into the overgrown hedgerow. He crawled toward the road just as another half-track rumbled past.

He laid perfectly still, hoping the dust would conceal his position from the soldiers. As soon as the steel monster was out of sight, Isaac jumped up, grabbing Sarah once more by the arm. They continued running south in the hope of finding safety near the town of Ernee.

As evening fell, Isaac and Sarah found a small wooded area where they could sit and relax for a few minutes. Sarah's mouth was parched from the dust and her feet hurt from running over the uneven ground. Isaac closed his eyes for a moment before looking at Sarah. "Stay here, I'll be back in a couple of minutes."

Sarah did not argue, she was too tired to run anymore today. Breathing heavily, Sarah leaned back against a large tree pondering what must have happened to the remaining partisans in the camp. She knew all too well that the Gestapo and the S.S. would never take pity on women and children.

If only the Americans had come to save them. What was taking so long? Why were they not coming across the channel to save the suffering French people. Since the Germans appeared to be scared of them, they should come right now and win the war.

Several minutes later, Isaac came back. "There's a small stream right near the edge of the woods. It's cold and clean, come on, you can get a drink."

Without arguing, Sarah followed Isaac back to the stream. After washing off her face, she took in some of the cold water. She felt it wash down all the dust she had sucked in and made her feel somewhat alive. After several more sips, she looked at Isaac.

"Where do we go from here? Once again, we are lost and everyone is against us. Tell me, where are the American's and the British? Why aren't they coming to rescue us?" Sarah pleaded, as she looked at her best friend.

Unable to answer her questions, he smiled. "Come on, there's an old barn a little ways down the road. We can spend the night there, and then decide in the morning where we want to go."

Crossing the road quickly, Isaac and Sarah ran toward the old barn. It was good to get out of the wind and away from all the prying eyes of those that wanted to hurt them. They walked over to the far corner of the barn where they laid down, pulling several empty grain sacks over them.

They had been sleeping only a short time when a bright light came down upon them. Shielding her eyes from the brightness, Sarah gasped. Four S.S. soldiers stood merely feet away from them, holding their weapons ready to fire. Isaac raised his hands, shaking his head.

"No shoot, do not shoot!"

The sergeant in charge of the squad stepped forward. "Papers, please!"

Both Sarah and Isaac knew it was finally over for them. Slowly standing up, Sarah replied.

"We have lost our papers. We don't have any and we are lost."

Shaking his head, the sergeant replied, "Every good German or Frenchman has their papers. That makes you either Jewish, or part of the underground group we broke up earlier today. Which is it? No matter which you choose, the penalty will be death."

Isaac looked at Sarah for a quick moment. "We are Jews, we were not members of any underground group."

As the soldiers walked them out of the barn past a Mercedes staff car, a voice called out from the back seat. "Bring the girl to me!"

As Sarah approached the car, a captain slid out to look at her. Calling out to his sergeant he said, "I don't know what this tramp has told you, but she was delivering pastries and muffins to our men on the beach all last summer. She is a member of the underground and a spy. Send her to headquarters in Paris. They will have questions for her."

The sergeant nodded his head before speaking. "Herr Captain, she also admitted to being a Jew."

Filled with rage, the captain stepped forward, slapping her across the face with his leather gloves. As she fell back against Isaac, he spit on her face. "I guarantee you will pay for your crimes, Tramp. I should shoot you now, but I want you to suffer for the problems you have caused, and your insults against the Third Reich. Get her on the truck!"

Just as the soldiers pushed Isaac into a cargo truck, several low flying British bombers streaked over head from the channel. As the soldiers stopped to look up, Sarah pulled lose from the soldier that had her arm, and bolted into the night. The men yelled for help as they swung their flashlights in every direction, trying to see where she went.

The sergeant in charge of the squad was outraged. He stood face to face screaming at the corporal. "You let a Jewess get the best of you and escape? Find her or you will find yourself on the Russian front within a week!"

Sarah ran along a hedgerow, not knowing which direction she was going. Ahead of her, massive explosions from the bombers shook the ground and illuminated the night sky. Realizing the glare from the massive fires and continued explosion would allow the pursuing Germans to see her, Sarah ducked into the hedgerow, pulling branches on top of her for concealment. After several hours of hiding, Sarah jumped as a small bird landed nearby and began singing. She realized she had fallen asleep, and daylight was now beginning to filter through the low hanging clouds. On the far side of the hedgerow, German trucks were continually driving back and forth. Just twenty yards out from where she laid, ten soldiers were finishing up the task of camouflaging two small artillery pieces they had dug into the field the day before. Several other soldiers were stringing barbed wire and attaching small mines to fence posts that had been pounded into the field in various positions. Sarah felt trapped, knowing all she could do now was lay still and hope none of the soldiers came in her direction.

About midday, a man walked out into the field blowing a whistle as he called out "Imbisswagon, Imbisswagon." All the men dropped what they were doing and walked off to her left to get a meal from the mobile kitchen. When Sarah could no longer see anyone, she threw off the branches and ran back in the direction she had come the night before. Coming to the edge of the hedgerow near the barn, Sarah dropped to the ground, scanning the area. Everything appeared to be quiet except for the trucks that continued driving back and forth from the beach.

There it was again, the beach. The gateway to freedom. If only she could find a boat and paddle it across the channel to England, she would be free. There would be people more than willing to take care of her and feed her, and all her fears would be put to rest. She knew attempting to cross the wicked channel in a small boat was sure suicide, but now it appeared that it may be her only chance at survival.

Throughout the next several nights, she cautiously made her way north to the beach side town of Arromanches that she had heard so much about from the Germans. It was about midnight when Sarah laid on a small hill looking down over the town. German sentries walked the streets as soldiers with large binoculars stood on the concrete pier scanning the channel. However, there didn't appear to be any signs of a boat anywhere. As dawn began to wash away the darkness, Sarah crept carefully to a small two-story barn near the edge of town. From the second-floor loft, she was able to see three over turned boats tied up to a heavy timber near a house about twenty yards up from the seawall. It would be a struggle for one person to maneuver such a big heavy boat, much less a young girl who had not eaten in several days. Throughout the day Sarah slept and kept an eye on the Germans and the citizens that still remained in the small town. It also became evident the people that had lived in the house with the boats had been moved out. There hadn't been a soul anywhere near the house all day long.

As nightfall settled in over the town, Sarah climbed down from the loft, and stealthily made her way to the boats. It was clear the boat farthest from the house was the smallest, and would be easiest to handle. Since the boat was leaning up against a tree, Sarah had little problem pushing it over onto its bottom. However, sliding the heavy wooden boat toward the sea wall was a major task due to its weight. It took Sarah just over an hour to get the boat to the seawall. Since it was high tide, the water was only about two and a half feet below the wall. Giving the boat a good push, it quickly slid down over the rocks into the water. Holding tightly to the bow rope, Sarah hid behind a large tree to see if the noise had attracted any attention.

After seeing no one moving along the sea wall for several minutes, she slid into the boat taking hold of the large wooden oars. Sarah struggled to row the heavy boat toward the south, so she wouldn't be seen by the men with binoculars when she turned out into the channel. When she was sure she had gone far enough, she turned the bow out into the deeper water. The strong current pulled the small craft out into the channel at a good rate of speed. Sarah pulled at the oars with all her strength as she began hitting larger waves that tossed the small boat like a cork.

In short order, the boat was being pushed by the large waves up one side and then down into the trough before riding up on the next wave. The boat spun around, crashing into wave after wave as the howling wind in the channel now had full command of the small craft. Sarah sat on the floor screaming, as she held tightly to a rope that had been tied around the middle seat. As the next big wave caught the boat, the bow rode straight up on the dark green monstrous wave and began tipping backward. Not wanting to be caught under the boat when it tipped over, Sarah let go of the rope and jumped clear.

In mere seconds, Sarah was sucked under the large wave. She held her breath until it felt like her eyes were going to pop out of her head. Moments later she popped to the surface in the trough directly between two massive waves. She had no idea which way to swim back to France, but she knew she had to either swim or die. But the small amount of swimming she did made no difference, as the wind and tall waves pushed her wherever they wanted. As she gasped for air, something large struck her leg and side. Turning over, she noticed a large wooden door just a few feet away. Grabbing hold of the hinges, Sarah pulled herself on top of it and laid down, gripping tightly to a large handle that went the width of the door. The thunderous waves tossed the door about as if it were a tooth pick, slamming it down into the troughs with a terrific force, before forcing it up once more into the raging surf.

Sarah had no idea how long she floated on the door, but she was glad it had come along. It made the difference between life and death throughout the long dark night.

Awakened by the sound of voices, Sarah looked about to get her bearings. She was terrified to see the door had washed up on a beach filled with German barbed wire and mines, and was solidly entangled. The voices she heard were three German sentries that kept yelling at her to lie still. About a half hour later, two soldiers had worked their way to her and cut her out of the entanglement.

Taking her farther inland, the soldiers handed her over to a German S.S. officer. The lieutenant placed a blanket over her shoulders and said. "Come on, we will take you to headquarters and get you some dry clothes and something warm to eat. Then we can find out where you came from."

Sarah was terrified, realizing her long battle with the monstrous waves of the English Channel had delivered her once more into the hands of the dreaded S.S. In a way she wished she would have drowned in the channel instead of being recaptured by the German Army.

After she had eaten a plate full of scrambled eggs and a hard biscuit, the lieutenant sat down across from her. "So. Tell me, where have you come from? We do not know of any boats or ships going down in the channel last night, so what is your name and where is your family?

Sarah looked down at her plate for a moment before responding. "My name is Helga Brown. My parents and I sailed out of Norway yesterday on a fishing trip. We collided with a large ship that smashed our boat to pieces. I was able to find the door, but my mother and father must have been killed, I never saw them again. I was drifting on the waves all day and all night until I came ashore here, where ever we are."

The lieutenant looked at her skeptically. "Do you mean to tell me none of our patrol boats or search aircraft would have seen you during all that time?"

Looking at the officer, Sarah replied. "It was not that big of a door, Herr Lieutenant. With all the waves, maybe they just couldn't see me?"

"Or, maybe you are the girl that escaped from the Gestapo yesterday during that British bombing raid. What do you have to say about that?" The lieutenant replied, clearly angry with Sarah's responses.

Sarah knew the Gestapo could easily recognize her, but she also realized it was in her best interest to convince the lieutenant she was telling the truth. "Sir, you must believe me, I am telling the truth. I know nothing about a bombing raid or what happened with the Gestapo yesterday. How could I, I was in Norway yesterday, that is until the accident."

Standing up, the Lieutenant walked slowly toward a small stove where he picked up a large coffee pot, and poured himself a cup of the steaming hot liquid. Leaning back against the iron stove, the lieutenant asked. "So, what kind of a ship did you collide with? Was it one of our naval ships, because if it was, we can clear this up very quickly."

Sarah shook her head. "No, it was a transport of some type, it was painted black and red. It never slowed down, it kept right on going. I don 't think they even saw our boat."

Walking slowly back toward the table, the lieutenant asked. "What kind of flag was it flying? What colors were on it? You must have seen something as it sailed away!"

"Sir, as our boat was smashed, I was tossed in the water. I was sucked under and kept fighting my way to the surface time after time. When I finally came up the last time, I was struggling hard to breathe. I was disorientated and all I wanted to do was find my parents, you must realize that!" Sarah pleaded, as tears rolled down her cheeks. "Now I have no family and here you are trying to make me a criminal." Sarah continued, as she wiped her face with her arm.

Smiling slightly, the lieutenant walked around the table. When he was once more across from her, he slammed his fist down hard on the metal table. Sarah jumped as the lieutenant glared at her. "I think you are a good liar and that you are a Jew. I also think you are the girl the Gestapo is looking for. I shall give Herr Walters a call to see if he can come and identify you. If he says you are not the girl, then we will send you back to Norway and find your grandparents for you.

About two hours later the lieutenant returned with a Gestapo man Sarah easily recognized.

"Ya, this is her, no doubt about it, Lieutenant. We will take her off your hands and make sure she is dealt with properly," Herr Walters exclaimed with a broad smile on his face. Motioning towards one of his men, Sarah was pulled from her chair and dragged out to a small troop transport with four soldiers sitting inside. The drive to the local Gestapo headquarters in Caen took about forty-five minutes. She was stuffed into a small cell overnight with another girl several years older than her. They traded just a bit of small talk, but kept mostly quiet since they knew the female officer outside the door was writing down everything they said.

Early in the morning, a secured box truck rolled up to the rear door of the Gestapo headquarters. After placing handcuffs and leg irons on the girls, they were tossed like bags of potatoes into the filthy truck. About three hours later the truck arrived in Paris, where the driver drove straight into a dark alley behind S.S. Headquarters, near the center of the city.

As the doors were pulled open, the soldiers literally dragged

Sarah into an interrogation room where they threw her on the floor. After catching her breath, she stood up and walked over to a chair. She wondered how many Jews and political prisoners had spent time in this room, then were never heard from again. She shivered as she looked up at the chains hanging from the ceiling and the scratches on the wall. She was positive many people had been scourged here over the years. She wondered what fate awaited her now.

About an hour later, two S.S. soldiers entered the room, one of them being a woman who was a captain. She sat directly across from Sarah and glared at her.

"My name is S.S. Captain Herald. We can make this easy or you can make it very hard. So, let us begin. What is your name, girl, and where have you come from?"

Sarah remained quiet and trembled as she looked down at the table for a moment before looking directly at the captain. "As I told the lieutenant, I came from Norway, where our fishing boat was sunk by a freighter. Have you no compassion?"

Captain Herald looked at the soldier that was standing near Sarah and nodded her head. He immediately slapped Sarah across the face with his gloves and pulled her head back by her long hair.

The captain leaned forward in her chair. "Let's try this again. What is your name and where have you come from? What were you doing near the beach yesterday? What have you been telling the British, and where is your radio set? We can shoot you or hang you as a spy. Which do you prefer?"

The soldier let go of her hair, allowing Sarah to once again look into the anger filled eyes of the determined woman sitting across the table from her.

"No matter what I say, I am going to be dead so it makes no difference anymore," Sarah replied, fighting back tears not wanting to show any emotion to the hateful woman. "You will hear nothing from me."

Captain Herald sat back and shook her head. "So, where did your family live in Norway? What did your father do for a living?"

Sarah was not sure where Captain Herald was going with this line of questioning, but she was ready to play along, hoping she could work her way out of this mess.

"We lived in Bergen, my father worked for a lumber company. My parents moved there when I was a little girl." Sarah replied.

Captain Herald laughed as she held up a sheet of paper. "Have you forgotten Germany has controlled Norway since 1940. Since you told Lieutenant Mueller when you were captured that your boat was sunk by a freighter, I had a list of all the ships sailing or arriving from all Norwegian ports compiled. I am sorry to tell you, no ships sailed or arrived in the port of Bergen yesterday. You are a liar and I think a dirty Jewess as well. Did you think I would not believe Herr Walters, a highly decorated Gestapo agent, when he recognized you? I just wanted to give you enough rope to hang yourself, and you have."

The captain looked at Sarah with a nasty grin on her face.

"So, tell me, how do you want your brother to die? He can live if you tell me what I want to know, and he will die if you do not."

"My brother is dead. You killed him several years ago. I do not know what boy you are talking about, but it does not matter who he is, because his fate like mine rests in your hands," Sarah replied angrily.

"Not your brother you say. Well you appeared to be very close to him according to the Gestapo. Maybe then your boy friend as you were sleeping with him." Captain Herald stated angrily.

"He is not my boyfriend, but at least I could have a man that cares for me unlike you." Sarah replied with a sarcastic smile on her face.

The soldier standing beside Sarah swung his gloves with all his strength, striking Sarah in the face, knocking her off the chair.

"Is this how you address my captain?" he yelled.

Laying on the floor Sarah replied, "Forgive me, Captain. I was wrong."

"Get off the floor, bitch," the soldier screamed as he kicked Sarah in the head.

With her left eye nearly swollen shut, and blood running from her top lip, Sarah picked up the chair and sat down.

"You don't look so pretty anymore, young lady. So, we'll begin again and try one thing at a time. Tell me your name." When she was slow to answer, the captain slammed her fist down hard against the steel table.

"It is Helga, Helga Greenman. I come from Straubing, Germany," Sarah replied, as she watched the male solder leave the room.

"So, Helga, tell me about the group you belonged to. What were your activities?" the determined S.S. captain inquired, smiling as if speaking to a friend.

Before Sarah could answer, the soldier walked back into the room, striking her across the side of her head with the back of his hand, knocking her to the floor once more.

"There were no Greenman families in Straubing," he yelled, as he kicked her in the back.

"So, you want it this way?" Captain Herald yelled as she stood up. "Get up off the floor and sit down. We will try this just one more time!"

Completely overtaken by fear, Sarah shook uncontrollably as she set the chair in place before sitting down. Her head was throbbing from being struck so often, but she was determined not to tell them anything.

After breathing heavily several times, Captain Herald stood up and walked back and forth, collecting her thoughts. "So, who was in charge of your underground network? And I want you to know that I will find out even if I have to personally beat it out of you, and leave you a bloody corpse."

Sarah shook her head. "I never knew who was in charge of anything. I had nothing to do with any of that."

Looking over at Sarah, the woman replied, "So, you did belong to a partisan group. Now I can begin to believe you, Helga, if that is actually your name. But this is good, it is a start. Now tell me, who was in charge of your little partisan team?"

Sarah was angry with herself for being caught off guard and admitting she was in a partisan group. She closed her eyes, knowing what was coming next. "I don't know his name, I never saw him, I had nothing to do with the meetings."

Instantly, a powerful blow from the soldier's hand sent her tumbling across the concrete floor. "Do you expect us to believe that? You all know who is in charge and who gives the orders."

The angry Captain Herald walked over to Sarah, looking down at her. "I am finished with you. By the end of this day you will wish you had cooperated with me, I promise you that." Looking at the soldier she continued. "Get Rolf, and take her away!"

As the captain exited the room, a second soldier arrived to help pull Sarah from the floor. The two men dragged her down the hall to another room. Sarah was horrified when she saw Malachi, the man that had escaped from the work crew at Normandy, hanging by his wrists from a hook in the ceiling. He wore no shirt, and it was apparent he had been scourged as his skin was sliced open and bleeding from his neck to his waist.

One of the soldiers placed a pistol in Sarah's right hand. "Shoot him bitch, he gave you up."

Sarah dropped the gun on the floor, replying. "No, I will not take his life!"

Once more the soldier picked up the gun, pushing it into her hand as he attempted to force her finger inside the trigger guard. Sarah struggled with all her strength, as the soldier tried to force her finger against the trigger. After several seconds of struggling, the gun discharged. The bullet was wide to the right, just creasing the side of Malachi's chest.

Pulling the gun up once more, the soldier tried to aim it as he pushed against Sarah's index finger. After a few seconds of intense struggling, the weapon fired. Malachi screamed as the bullet slammed into his left shoulder, tearing the bones apart. Sarah screamed all the more as she fought with the powerful soldier. Moments later, Captain Herald walked into the room. Walking directly up to Malachi she pulled her Luger from its holster, firing a round into his head. Malachi's tortured body shook for a few seconds before falling limp on the chains.

Placing her weapon back in the holster, she walked up to Sarah. "Are you ready to tell us what we want to know now? You know you are responsible for his death, you could have saved him if you had just told us what we wanted."

Before she could say another word, Sarah spit on her. Enraged, Captain Herald swung her left arm as hard as possible, striking Sarah across the face. "You evil pig! Take her next door!"

Entering the room, Sarah was pushed down into a metal chair. They snapped metal bands around her wrist and ankle that were connected by wires to the chair. Moments later a tall slender man with thick glasses entered the room and sat down across from her by a black box.

After turning some controls, he looked at Sarah. "They call me Professor Felix. I understand pain better than most doctors do, and I understand how to use it to our advantage. So, I'm going to be your worst nightmare if you do not cooperate. Now then, you can start by telling me who was in charge of the underground unit you were in, and where he is now. Answer please!"

Sarah sat quietly as she looked up toward the ceiling with her one good eye. Instantly, she tensed up and shook as a charge of electricity flowed through her body. Sarah screamed louder than she ever thought possible. When the power was turned off, she dropped back in the chair, gasping for air.

"One more time, Helga. Who ran your little partisan group, and what were you up to?" the professor inquired as he readied his hand on the power dial.

Sarah shook her head as she drooled. "Don't know, go ahead and kill me."

Once again, voltage ripped through her body as she screamed until she passed out. Turning off the power, he looked at the soldier standing next to Sarah. "Wake her please!"

The soldier picked up a bucket of water, tossing it over her. Slowly, Sarah began to open her eye as her body still shook, nearly uncontrollably.

"Now we will have some fun, Helga. I am going to count to ten, and then give you a quick blast of electricity. Then we will do it again and again and again until you say stop, and tell me what I want to know. Now remember, you are on a metal chair and you are very wet."

As the professor gave the knob a quick turn, Sarah stiffened and attempted to scream, but nothing came out of her mouth. Waiting several seconds, the professor turned the knob a bit farther. Sarah felt like her eyes were going to burst out of her head as her heart raced out of control. As the smiling professor turned the knob off, Sarah dropped back onto the chair, slumping forward on the table.

"Is she dead?" he asked the soldier.

After checking her quickly, he replied. "She is breathing and has a very weak pulse."

"Gut, now we will see what she is made of," the professor replied as he stood up and walked out of the room.

Returning, he had Isaac with him. After pushing Isaac down into the chair he had just occupied, a soldier attached a harness to Isaac's wrist, before strapping it to the control knob on the box.

"Wake her again, please," the professor replied with a wide perverted grin on his face.

After tossing a second bucket of water on Sarah, the soldier slapped her across the face until she responded. Opening her good eye, she was stunned to see a beaten and battered Isaac sitting across from her.

"Now Helga, this is the boy you told Captain Herald you know nothing about. But by now you surely know Herr Walters has stated he arrested both of you at the same time so don't act stupid. Just so you know, your friend here has told us what he knows, and he certainly expects you to do the same so we can quit torturing both of you. So, if you do not tell us who the leader of your unit is, where we can find him, and to whom you were sending your information, he is going to hurt you much more than I have. So, I suggest that you tell us," the professor explained as he folded his arms across his chest.

Sarah sat silently as she gazed at Isaac, who appeared to be in as much pain as she was. Her first attempt to talk did not work well, as her tongue was severely swollen. After several short breaths, she nodded her head and smiled at Isaac, "Just kill me."

The soldier next to Isaac twisted his wrist, causing the control knob to move all the way up into the red zone on the power scale. Sarah went stiff, bouncing off the wet steel chair as pain raced through every inch of her tortured body.

As the soldier turned the knob back down, Sarah collapsed onto the chair with her head slamming down hard on the metal table. Her arms and legs continued to twitch for several more moments as her body lay on the table.

"Sarah! Sarah!" Isaac screamed, as tears rolled down his face.

Once again, the S.S. soldier poured a bucket of water over Sarah's head and yelled, "Sit up!"

With his arms folded across his chest, the professor said, "Well, well, now we know your real first name. Speak Sarah, we are listening."

Sarah shook her head as she waited for what was coming.

"Again, again!" the professor yelled, as he stomped his foot on the floor.

Immediately, the soldier beside Isaac turned his wrist, sending the power scale back up into the red zone.

Sarah screamed out in pain as her body shook worse than it had the first time. When the power was turned off, Sarah dropped down like a beaten rag doll.

The professor shook his head as he called out to the guards. "What stupidity this is! Check her pulse, and if she is still alive get them out of my sight. There is nothing more I can do here. I am finished with these two. I do not want to kill them here there would be too many questions. Tell the captain this is useless and send them to an extermination camp where their kind of vermin belong."

Several officers dragged Sarah down the corridor to a dark cell. After throwing threw her on the cold damp floor, they slammed the steel door shut. She made no attempt to move as the cold concrete appeared to soothe the pain in her body.

When she awakened, there was no way of knowing how long she had been unconscious, as not one shred of light permeated any part of the cell. Slowly, she crawled toward a corner so she could lean up against the wall. Suddenly her hand touched something strange and she pulled back. Carefully, she allowed her hand to feel its way over the obstacle.

Screaming, Sarah rolled back across the floor after realizing it was the corpse of someone that had died in the cell. She shuddered and attempted to hide her face, as she could feel the cold dead eyes of the corpse staring at her through the dark, telling her it wanted to be left alone and warning her to stay away.

Checking out the corner nearest the door, she found it to be safe. She crawled into a fetal position and wept, wishing she would have stayed with her mother and avoided all this torture.

Two days later, Sarah was awakened by the sound of the door being opened. A bright beam of light from a large flash light burned her eyes as a soldier called out.

"Yeah, she is alive." Before closing the door, he dropped a metal pan and a spoon in front of her. Picking up the somewhat warm pan, she held it to her nose and sniffed. The aroma of cooked celery and chicken was a Godsend. While slowly sipping the weak chicken broth and chewing on a small dumpling, she looked over into the far corner of the room. "They didn't leave a pan for you I'm afraid, and no matter how much you beg, I'm not sharing. Besides, I think we're beyond helping you anymore. So, tell me, how long have you been in here?"

Sarah almost giggled when she thought of what her reaction might be if the corpse actually responded to her questions.

Time came to mean nothing to Sarah, as the only light she saw was the few seconds as the guard dropped the pan in front of her twice a day. To keep her sanity, she would hold regular conversations with the corpse, as if they had known each other from Straubing. She was not sure if it was a man or a woman, but she named it Ingrid, since she did not want to be accused of sleeping with a man. She counted the days by how many pans she had been given. By the sixth day she had given up hope of getting out of the cell. Crawling to the left rear corner of the cell she found it vacant. Smiling she called out. "Well Ingrid, I have decided to quit eating their drool. I have found my spot where I shall join you in death. The next occupants will have to claim the front corners. That's what they get for arriving so late." After two days of not eating her broth, the soldiers quit bringing it to her, so now she was certain starvation was going to claim her as it most likely did Ingrid.

After twelve days in darkness, two S.S. guards walked into the room, picked up Sarah, and carried her over to a room where an older woman wearing a rubber apron awaited her. Turning the hose on, the woman sprayed her over and over for several minutes washing away the filth that covered her body. Before giving Sarah a semi-clean set of striped coveralls, the woman cut her hair very short and uneven. When she was finished, the guards walked in and stood Sarah upright. Pain shot threw her legs as they had not been used since she had been repeatedly electrified. She screamed in torment as the soldiers kept yelling at her to walk. Arriving at a stair well at the back of the building, the soldiers finally decided to carry her up the stairs, as Sarah could not make her legs work as they should.

Arriving in the same alley behind the building as before, Sarah inhaled the clean fresh air, something she used to take for granted. Moments later, Isaac was brought to the alley by several other soldiers. He looked much better than he had the last time Sarah had seen him, but now he had a deep long cut on his right cheek that was still in the process of healing. After being tossed into a German weapons carrier, they were hand-cuffed and had their legs shackled before chaining them to their wooden seat. After the three guards were seated across from them, the driver left Paris heading north.

Arriving at Reims several hours later, they were taken from the truck into what appeared to be a Gestapo office. Isaac helped Sarah stand in the outer office, as her legs were still not strong enough to stand on her own. Several minutes later, a man Isaac and Sarah recognized from photographs walked up to them.

A smiling Klaus Barbie looked at the pair as he shook his head. "I said that day in Orleans, I would find everyone responsible for what happened." Stepping in front of Sarah, he slapped her across the face with his leather gloves. "You, a mere child, killed one of my men right inside the Place du Martroi, then thought you could escape. I am not as stupid as you seem to think, but you will never forget me, Fraulein. I assure you, the memory of me will be with you always. You see Fraulein, you will scrape the ground under my boots for a morsel to eat, and still you will starve."

Looking at Isaac, he shook his head. "You could have escaped all the torture had you hung that day in Orleans. Fools like you are responsible for the downfall of your Jewish race." Stepping back, he pulled out his Luger placing the barrel tightly up against Sarah's forehead. "So now tell me, where may I find Ishmael? Oh yes, I know who he is, and I know who all died in the raid on your camp, including Baruch and Elazar. Trouble. Far more trouble than they were worth."

Smiling at Isaac, Barbie continued. "So, I shall make you a deal, Isaac. If you tell me where that piece of crap is, I can assure you that you will live. Do not tell me, and I pull the trigger on your friend."

"Quiet Isaac!" Sarah yelled. "Let him kill me, what am I worth to the Nazis anyway? Do not help this bastard."

Angered by Sarah's comment, Barbie yelled, "Then we shall seal your wish." With that, he pulled the trigger.

Sarah jumped as she heard the trigger snap, but the weapon did not discharge. While Barbie and all the other soldiers laughed heartily, he placed his Luger back in its holster. "No child, you will not get off that easy. You need to suffer much more than that. So, one last time, whoever tells me where Ishmael is can go to a work camp. Whoever does not tell me will go straight to a death camp. Speak up, children."

As neither Sarah or Isaac knew where Ishmael could possibly be, there was no way for them to answer the question. They also knew that if they gave Barbie wrong information, it meant continued torture and eventual death. There was simply nothing they could say that could change the outcome of this situation. Shaking his head, Barbie looked at the S.S. soldiers.

"Ya, Ya, what can you do with these Jews? Take them to Dachau and let them die slow miserable deaths. They will wish they had talked, and there, they will remember Klaus Barbie until they draw their last miserable breaths."

As one of the soldiers took hold of Sarah, she looked sternly at Captain Barbie, yelling out. "Your day will come, your day will come. I shall haunt you and you will fear me like no other. Never forget me!"

A strange chill ran down the spine of Klaus Barbie as he stared into Sarah's cold determined eyes. "Remove her, remove her now!"

Arriving at the train station, Sarah and Isaac were placed in a rail car with about seventy other Jews that stared at them with fear in their eyes. If they had not already wondered what could happen to them, they certainly did at the moment they laid their eyes on Sarah.

Ishmael watched helplessly from a coal bunker, where he and several other men worked shoveling coal into hoppers that fed the coal cars on the trains. There were several other underground members working in the station, but there were far too many soldiers around for them to attempt a rescue. Ishmael's heart broke as he saw the terrible condition his young people were in. He could only imagine the horrors they must have already faced. As the train for Germany rolled out of the station, Ishmael walked back behind the depot and sobbed. He had come to love Sarah as a daughter, despite her strong will and her lack of control at times. Now, there was nothing more he could do for her but pray for her soul.

Sarah leaned against the back wall of the car looking at Isaac. "Well, I guess we have come to the end of the line. No more running, no more lying, no more anything. I think it will be good to die since there is nothing left to live for. I want to be with my family again."

Isaac looked intently at Sarah. "You sound so old for your years, Sarah. But you must never stop trying to live. Keep fighting, so we can survive and see one another again. Believe Sarah, believe in the mercy of our God."

Sarah shook her head. "I quit believing long ago, and after what we've been through, I know he does not exist or he would have swooped down and crushed the Nazis in that place. No Isaac, he has turned his head away from the Jews, and we are no longer the chosen people. No one knows where he has gone."

Throughout the long trip, Sarah listened to the people reciting scripture and praying out loud asking God to spare their lives. She remembered all the hours she had spent reading and memorizing passages from the Torah and the Talmud. But now, none of those words made sense to her, and she chose not to recite anything she remembered. Death was her next stop, and she welcomed it. From now on, she would no longer beg for her life.

As the train screeched to a final stop, they could hear the guards yelling at the workers to prepare to open the heavy doors, while anxious dogs barked and snarled.

Isaac took Sarah by the hands and kissed her on the forehead. In a desperate voice filled with fear, he pleaded. "Listen to me, Sarah. You must live. No matter what happens, you must live for all of us. Live, my little one, you have not come this far to perish in the fires of hell. Please choose life, do it for me, do it for your family where ever they are. Live Sarah, you must!"

Chapter Twelve
Dachau

Dachau in itself was a horrid world that offered nothing, gave nothing, and took away a person's dignity, along with all their dreams and hopes, and in thousands of cases, life itself. It was a drab, colorless world, devoid of the sense of time, where any form of humanity had long ago ceased to exist. It could be said that here is where souls waited for glorified redemption or cursed damnation from the abyss of unquestionable tragedy. To survive, to dream of another life, was nothing short of insanity. After you passed through the iron gates of hell, there was no turning back, and there was no one there to offer a reprieve. Only the souls of the persecuted were finally set free, in a holocaust of fire and smoke.

The problem of over-crowding in the box car had been alleviated for several days now, as so many people had died. Some of the stronger men in the car helped pile the corpses up on one side of the car, allowing more space for the living. At least now people were able to get off their feet and sit down, even if it meant their chair was the body of a family member or friend that had passed away. Sarah tried to remember what it had been like to take a breath of fresh air where the sky was blue, the grass was green, and busy honey bees glided from flower to flower. Now all she could smell was the scent of death and human waste that was several inches deep on the floor of the converted cattle car. Where were they going? When would this train ride to hell ever stop? Could life still exist wherever the Nazi's were taking them? Did it still make sense to wonder, or worse to even care?

Suddenly, the train began to slow and everyone left alive in the car began to murmur and wonder what awaited them when the steel door opened. Sarah remained seated on the old man that had tried to treat her so nicely before they boarded the train. He told her he would never survive and asked her to live on for him no matter what happened. Now, like everyone else on board, she waited to see what her future would be.

A beam of sunlight fell upon Sarah, nearly blinding her as the heavy door was slid open by camp workers called kapos. The S.S. soldiers yelled for everyone to get off the cars as they pulled at the people nearest the door. Sarah nervously waited in line as the older people in front of her climbed down onto the platform, where snarling dogs and soldiers with clubs and whips attacked them. Seeing her chance to get off the car, Sarah bolted toward the door, jumping over the top of an old woman that had fallen, and was being beaten by several soldiers as they laughed.

She was outside, but where was the fresh air? All she could smell was an acrid choking smoke that made her nauseous. It was like nothing she had ever inhaled before.

Before she realized what was happening, a soldier grabbed her by the arm, pushing her into a line of women and children that was being forced into a building. She knew better than to inquire where she was going, as the soldier looked at her with contempt as he shook his whip at her. Somewhere behind her, Isaac was lost in the shuffle of bodies. She longed to stay with him, but knew better than to turn around and look for him.

Entering the building, a female S.S. officer standing on a wooden platform told them to drop all of their belongings, strip off all their clothing, and move into the next room and be quiet. Many of the women were slow to comply as they took care of the crying children that clung to them in fear.

Not wanting to catch the wrath of the S.S. soldiers for taking too long, Sarah quickly dropped her clothing and walked into the next room where women waited to cut off their hair. Since Sarah's hair was already short, she quickly followed a line of women into a filthy shower. After being sprayed down with cold water, she was given a well-worn back and white striped jump suit. Moving out of the room, she walked up to a desk where a soldier took down her name and age before assigning her to the barracks.

Walking from the building toward the barracks area, Sarah was shocked to see the people. No more than skin and bones, as they stood and watched the procession of new people, knowing they would soon look just like them, if they survived the daily horrors of this maddening place.

Arriving at her assigned barracks, a soldier pulled her from the group. "Where is your mother, girl, you must stay with her!"

Sarah glared back at the soldier. "You tell me, you took her from me a long time ago."

Before Sarah realized what was happening, the soldier backhanded her, sending her rolling across the ground. When she came to a stop, the man stood over her, pointing a wooden baton in her face. "That is not how you address a soldier in the Third Reich, you filthy tramp. If you haven't learned by now, you will learn shortly how to address a soldier of the master race! Your life and those in the barracks may depend upon it. Learn well, Jew!" the soldier explained, as he kicked her in the abdomen.

Nodding her head, Sarah looked up at the soldier. "I apologize, I was out of line, please forgive me for my failure. I will try harder in the future."

After grunting, the soldier backed away, allowing Sarah to get back up. "My parents are dead, I am alone. The people that were looking after me are also dead, but I can take care of myself."

"Fine, this is your barracks. Get inside. They will explain the rules to you. Make sure you learn them or next time things will be a lot worse!" the soldier exclaimed as he stared angrily at her.

Entering the barracks with three other women, Sarah was taken back by the odor and filthy conditions the residents were living in and had become accustomed to. An older woman walked Sarah to a triple decked bunk.

"Here on the bottom is your mat. This is where you will live while you are here. It is no better or no worse than any other mat in the barracks."

After looking over the filthy mat, Sarah looked at the woman.

"What happened to the person that slept here before me? Where is she now?"

"She is gone, she has moved on. Only the smoke knows where her soul has gone, as it will for all of us in time," she replied. "Eat your meals, cooperate with the guards and you shall live a while. That is all any of us can hope for."

For days, Sarah laid on her lice infested mat, waiting for the sweet death that would allow her to finally escape to wherever troubled souls went once they were set free. She was angered by the women that offered her parts of their meager rations so she could keep her strength. It was almost laughable to toss small pieces of vegetables or dumplings on the floor, to watch women and children dive on them like vultures. Sometimes women would slap the children and take the morsels away from them, as it had become all to true, only the strong were going to survive here.

But it was in the dark of the night that Sarah resented the women of her barracks the most. The constant praying and reciting lines from the Torah angered her beyond words. How could they still pray or believe in a God that had most certainly forsaken them. How could they watch women or their children dying, day after day, and still believe that some higher power, some person called God, still cared for them. No, this is where the insanity of Dachau affected Sarah the most. On several occasions, she screamed at them to stop, and threatened to tell the guards what they were doing. But these women never stopped, they never faltered in their belief that the God of Abraham and Moses would come to their rescue, if only they just believed and waited a little while longer.

But each day, no one parted the sharp electrified wire fence, as Moses had parted the Red Sea. There was no manna on the ground to be picked up each morning to be eaten, and most of all, no one turned off the crematorium that consumed their very existence in this world.

Sarah would laugh each night and make fun of the faithful women praying Kaddish for the dead, because who was going to pray Kaddish for them when they were carried to the fires of hell.

But most of all, Sarah wondered what had happened to Isaac. It was clear when she stood outside for daily roll call, that there were very few fit young men living in Dachau. Only hunched over old men picked up the bodies each day and took them to the crematorium on carts. Like most camps, they were called kapos, and were hated by the prisoners for helping the Nazis for extra rations or a clean mat, or maybe even a better blanket when temperatures fell. What Sarah hated most about them, was that they actually turned in other Jews for breaking regulations like praying, or sneaking a bread crust. They were despicable traitors to their faith, that even the camp rats appeared to stay away from.

Her curiosity was answered one day when she spoke with a kapo named Yitzhak, that was a bit more caring than the rest. He explained that Isaac and several other young men were sent north to work in a granite quarry near a camp called Mauthausen. He explained to her that it was hard dangerous work that took the lives of many young Jewish men every day. She had desperately hoped that Isaac was still in Dachau or a small satellite camp nearby called Allach. Now her hopes of at least catching a glimpse of him were dashed, and it hurt badly.

One evening after final roll call, Sarah returned to her mat to find a woman sitting there. "This is my mat you are sitting on, and I would appreciate it very much if you would get off of it so I can lay down," Sarah stated boldly, knowing that this woman was usually the one who began evening prayers in the barracks.

Smiling up at Sarah, the woman responded. "My name is Galenka, my husband and I came from Stuttgart. He is long dead now, and I have no idea what has happened to my grown children and their families. I am sure they have all been killed by the Nazis. I'm guessing I am the only one left of my beloved family, and who knows how long I shall survive. I grow weaker every day but pray I shall yet see the shores of Israel before I die." After a moment of silence, she looked up at Sarah. "So, you look like you need a friend, and I think it's time we become acquainted with one another. Sit and talk with me, and you will see that talking is not so bad for you."

Sarah shook her head in disgust. "I know who you are, you are the prayer leader, the one who quotes readings from the Torah and Talmud. I never had time for those books when I was a child, and I have no time for them now. It's all lies. There is no God who cares for the Jews, there never has been, and all those old worn out stories we were taught are false. None of it existed, and none of it ever happened.

Now please get up and leave me alone. Go tell your stories to those who still believe in fables."

The tired old woman stood up, placing her hand on Sarah's cheek. "Oh, my dear, the God of Israel does exist, as did Moses and Abraham, and you will learn the Torah from me in due time."

Sarah threw herself down on her mat, closing her eyes as Galenka walked away to meet with her older friends in the barracks.

About a week later as they stood morning count, one of the soldiers pulled Sarah from the ranks. Pushing her with his rifle, he led her away toward the kitchen.

Arriving in the foul-smelling structure they called the kitchen, the soldier pushed Sarah over to a large German woman with a triple chin. "This is your replacement for the woman you lost yesterday. She is young and can carry heavy pots," the soldier explained before leaving.

After eyeing up Sarah the woman glared at her. "My name is S.S. Corporal Messers. I run this kitchen with an iron hand and will not tolerate, theft, waste, tardiness or insubordination. Although you are a Jew and are used to a soft life of luxury, you will learn what it's like to work and work hard. You will not complain or beg for a different job, ever. Each morning after roll call, you will come here prepared to work, and you will stay here until I tell you to go in the evening. If you are caught stealing one morsel of food you will pay a heavy price. You have no name here, you will simply be called number 22. When I call number 22, you will respond to me immediately. Now get over by that counter and cut up those rutabagas for tonight's soup."

For the next week, Sarah did as she was told without saying a word. However, it became evident to her, that stealing small pieces of bread was easier than she imagined. So, each day after they served the morning and evening soup, she would shove a piece of bread in her mouth and quickly chew it as she washed kettles all by herself. A few evenings, she even took a crust of bread back to the barracks that she would eat once the lights were turned out.

The worst part of the job was working with women who had lost respect for themselves and certainly for their fellow prisoners. They constantly watched each other hoping to find a worker doing something wrong so they could be reported to Cpl. Messers. When the Corporal struck the troublemaker, or called the guards to punish the woman, the snitches would laugh and enjoy every minute of it. When a woman was removed from the kitchen, the spies would instantly begin to search out their next victim. Nobody was exempt from their constant cruelty.

One morning as Sarah chopped rutabagas, she watched one of the spies named Bina keeping a close eye on a Polish woman named Leticia, who had defended the last woman they turned in. As Leticia turned to pour the chopped vegetables into the simmering broth, Bina pushed her, causing her to spill some of the food onto the floor. Instantly, the second spy named Nava pointed at the mess, yelling for Cpl. Messers.

Angered by the mess on the floor and wasted food, Cpl. Messers slapped Leticia on the face. "Can you not do the job I have assigned you, or are you just a filthy Jewish swine?"

Leticia bowed to the Corporal, "It was not my fault, Corporal. That woman, Bina, pushed me just as I was dumping it into the pot. There was nothing I could do. Please, I'm telling you the truth."

The Corporal turned to Bina, knowing full well what she was all about and asked. "Did you push this woman causing the mess?"

Bina threw her hands up in the air and yelled, "She is always trying to get me in trouble, she is a mean person and does not care for the rest of us. I did not push her, ask Tikva what she saw."

Tikva was also one of the problems in the kitchen, and was always conniving with Bina and Nava. "Corporal, I was standing right here and I can tell you for a fact that Bina never pushed that woman, she is lying."

Nodding her head, Cpl. Messers grabbed Leticia by the arm. I cannot have a worker like you in my kitchen, you will have to go with the guards."

But Leticia pulled away, pointing at Sarah. "Ask her, she saw everything. She was standing right across from me, ask her!"

It was obvious that Cpl. Messers did not like the fact that this argument was getting out of control, but she looked over at Sarah anyway. "Did this woman called Bina push her?"

The last thing Sarah wanted was to get in the middle of an argument involving the spies. She knew if she told the truth, she would have to watch her back the rest of the time she was in the kitchen. If she lied, it was clear that Leticia was going to be horribly punished for something she was not guilty of.

After a moment, Cpl. Messers pointed at Sarah with the heavy steel rod she always carried.

"Well, tell me, 22. What did you see? If you refuse to tell me you are just as guilty."

By now, several soldiers had arrived in the kitchen, ready to take away the trouble makers. After taking a deep breath she looked at Leticia and closed her eyes. "Yes, she spilled the rutabagas on the floor, it was her fault."

Bina and Nava smiled confidently, as Tikva placed her arm around Sarah as she whispered in her ear. "You are a smart girl, if you want to survive, do not mess with us!"

Before anyone could say another word, the soldiers pulled Leticia from the kitchen as she screamed and resisted. As the last soldier was about to leave the kitchen, Cpl. Messers placed her hand on his shoulder and whispered something. The soldier nodded his head and continued following the others."

Corporal Messers turned to her crew, waving her rod in the air. "Now, get back to work unless you want to be punished the same as number 19. And shut your mouths or I will crack you a good one!"

The women had barely returned to their assigned tasks, when a volley of gun fire cracked near the rear of the building.

Bina yelled out, "Woo-hoo, Leticia won't cause us a problem again, she's on her way to the ovens. I knew she would not last long around here."

Nava and Tikva openly laughed as they did a little dance. Nava pushed up against Sarah and said, "What, are you not going to join in our fun? You feel sorry for that bitch?"

Sarah was unsure how to respond, knowing her life could easily be on the line if she said the wrong thing.

"No. I don't feel like celebrating when someone dies. It's not who I am," Sarah replied nervously, waiting for some type of snide remark. Instead, Nava walked back to her work station without saying a word.

That evening Sarah was physically sick, knowing that by not standing up for Leticia, she had cost the woman her life. She could not believe the women in the camp could turn on their fellow Jews in order to make their suffering worse, or get them killed. But now,

Sarah understood what she was up against, and she would have to find a way to deal with it.

For the next several weeks, everything in the kitchen appeared to be normal. The three snitches were minding their own business and leaving everyone alone, but there were times they would huddle in the rear corner and whisper back and forth, as if they were plotting something.

The following week a new arrival in the camp named Alona was assigned to the kitchen. She was in her mid-twenties and very attractive. As she had just arrived, she still had meat on her bones and displayed a good figure. Everyone knew she was going to be an instant target for the snitches. While scrubbing floors with Alona, Sarah did her best to give her the lay out of the kitchen, and told her about Bina and her friends. Alona smiled and thanked Sarah, but replied coldly.

"Let them kill me, the guards already killed my baby and shot my husband, so I do not care if I live. I don't want to look like the rest of the women in this camp. I will welcome death no matter how it comes. Just let them do as they must!"

Sarah was angry with herself for telling Alona about the snitches, as she was sure Alona would now seek them out in the worst way.

Two days later, as Tikva was carrying a basket of bread toward the front of the kitchen, Alona intentionally tripped her. About half the bread fell out of the basket before Tikva was able to regain her balance. Corporal Messers walked over toward Tikva, waving her infamous steel rod. Before she could strike, Bina called out.

"It was her, it was 25 that tripped Tikva, it was all her fault, she should go to the box."

Alona turned to face Bina, "Why don't you take me to the box since you have such a big mouth. It will save the guards some work."

As Cpl. Messers attempted to grab Alona, she pulled lose and ran toward the back of the kitchen, where she punched Bina in the face, knocking her to the floor. Nava picked up a knife and charged at Alona, plunging the blade deep into her shoulder. Before Nava could stab Alona again, another woman Sarah knew as just 15, slammed Nava across the back of the head with a heavy cutting board, splitting the back of her head open, causing her to drop the knife.

As Bina attempted to get up off the floor, Alona began kicking her in the ribs and chest. Scraping the knife up from the floor, Bina plunged it deep into Alona's thigh. Shrieking in pain, Alona pulled the knife from the wound, allowing blood to flow like water down her leg. After staggering for a moment Alona dropped down on top of Bina, stabbing her several times in the chest.

Angered at what was happening to her friends, Tikva attempted to grab another knife from the table, but Sarah pulled it away. Enraged, Tikva doubled up her fist and swung at Sarah but missed, as she was pushed from behind by several other women.

Moments later, five soldiers charged into the kitchen led by an S.S. Lieutenant who had drawn his pistol. Seeing Alona standing up with the knife still in her hand, he fired two shots into her chest. As Tikva was still attempting to grab Sarah, one of the soldiers fired several shots in her direction, killing her instantly.

Sarah, along with the other workers, fell to the floor with their hands in the air, hoping to avoid being shot.

Corporal Messers walked to the back of the kitchen, grabbing hold of number 15. "You can take her and shoot her. I saw her strike this woman on the floor with a cutting board." Spinning around, the Corporal scanned the other women before her eyes fell on worker 17. Take her too, I saw her attack several other women, she is guilty."

After dragging the women from the kitchen, they were forced down on their knees in the yard and shot in the back of the head. Under supervision by the lieutenant, several kapos came into the kitchen to remove the bodies of Alona, Bina and Tikva. After dropping the bodies at the crematorium, they came back to the kitchen and hosed down the floor.

Nava was taken over to a bench near the door by Cpl. Messers, so another kapo could bandage the back of her head. Looking over the rest of her crew, Cpl. Messers yelled. "Get to work, you need to make up for the food that was wasted and you will not have any additional help!"

As Sarah tore up loaves of bread, Cpl. Messers struck her across the back of the legs with her steel rod, causing Sarah to drop to the floor. After quickly crawling into a fetal position, Sarah covered her head as she awaited the next blow. Instead, the Corporal yelled at her to get up. Once Sarah was standing. Cpl. Messers pushed her up against the large heavy table. "I know you were guilty of something today, 22. If I find out what, I can still have you shot, so you best understand I will be watching you."

Sarah bowed slightly. "Yes Corporal, I will be on my best behavior. I will not cause you any problems, I promise."

The Corporal sneered as she took the end of the rod pushing it up against the bottom of Sarah's jaw, forcing her head back. "You were born trouble and you will always be trouble. It will be my pleasure to rid the world of your kind."

After releasing Sarah's jaw, the Corporal walked off, striking each of the remaining workers with her steel rod.

That night, Sarah recounted everything that had taken place in the kitchen. Although Bina and Tikva were dead, she knew Nava would be worse than ever, trying to cause problems wherever she could to get even.

Several days later as Sarah was tearing up bread, Nava walked over, attempting to dump one of the full baskets onto the floor. Before it could go off the table, Sarah was able to grab it and push it away from Nava's hand.

"Leave me alone, bitch!" Sarah called out, as she doubled up her fist. "I will not put up with you, and now you have no friends to back you anymore. Get away from me!"

That was all Cpl. Messers needed. Instantly, she grabbed her rod and walked over to Sarah with a look of death in her eyes. Swinging the rod with all her strength, she struck the table with a loud crash as Sarah ducked out of the way. Angered, the corporal called out for Nava to hold Sarah against the table. However, being much younger, Sarah pulled away from Nava and grabbed a broom.

Cpl. Messers laughed loudly. "If it's a duel you want, 22, it's a duel you will have." As if possessed, the Corporal came at her, swinging the heavy rod in every direction. Several times, Sarah blocked the rod with the broom handle, until it finally snapped. Sarah looked quickly at the sharpened end of the handle, but knew that killing a guard meant instant death. Throwing the handle to the floor, Sarah called out.

"I quit, I quit, please do not hurt me. I'm sorry for causing you trouble."

Corporal Messers laughed, "You have no idea how sorry you are going to be, girl. I am going to break every bone in your body one at a time. Let's see how much pain you can endure before you beg to be sent to the ovens."

Sarah kept backing away from the corporal as she continued swinging the heavy rod closer and closer to her head as she laughed cruelly. Approaching the front door, Sarah heard Cpl. Messers gasp and stop in her tracks. As blood began to drip down the side of her mouth, she dropped the rod and turned around slowly to see who was standing behind her. As she turned, Sarah could see the broken broom handle protruding out of her back. The Corporal made a few steps before falling onto the stove, tipping over a large kettle of boiling water that scalded her face and chest. She shook violently for several seconds before falling dead to the floor.

Seeing her protector dead, Nava ran straight toward the back door, swinging Cpl. Messers steel rod at any one that came close to her. Hearing the commotion in the kitchen, several soldiers were already running toward the back door with their rifles at the ready. When they saw Nava exiting the building swinging the rod, they both fired several shots toward her. Dropping the rod, Nava shook her head as she stared at the soldiers in disbelief before falling over.

Moments later the lieutenant arrived with several more men. Seeing one of his staff dead on the floor, killed by a Jew, he was outraged.

"I shall shoot each and every one of you for what you have done. No one will escape punishment this time. Now file out the front door and kneel on the ground." Before the women could leave, one of the soldiers spoke up.

"Herr Lieutenant, the woman we shot coming out the back door came at us with the Corporal's rod. You could see she was angry and out of control. I'm sure we have the killer!"

A woman with the number 16 bowed toward the angry officer. "Herr Lieutenant, that woman has been causing problems for Cpl. Messers for a long time, and today it just exploded. We are sorry the corporal is dead, but your men killed the right person. Please do not kill us all, we know our jobs and will do them, please spare us today."

The lieutenant looked at number 16 for a moment before replying. "You are a Jew, why should I believe a filthy rodent like you?"

Scared to the bone, Sarah stepped forward. "Herr Lieutenant, she is telling you the truth. None of us had anything to do with what happened, several of us tried to stop it, but were not able to. Please believe us, sir."

"You are a child, what are you doing in this kitchen?" the lieutenant inquired, while still pointing his pistol at number 16.

"I am number 22, I was sent here right after I arrived. I like working here and I'm strong enough to lift some of the heavy things the rest of the women can no longer manage," Sarah replied slowly.

Looking down at his watch, the lieutenant shook his head. "We are supposed to feed everyone in an hour. If you can do that, you will all live. If you fail the job, you will all be shot before evening count. Now, get to work!"

One of the soldiers stayed in the kitchen to supervise the women as they worked. When the meal was finished, a female S.S. private walked into the kitchen. After looking around, she called everyone over to her desk. "Call off your numbers, so I know who you are."

When they had finished calling out their numbers, she looked at them. "I will not use the rod Cpl. Messers did. If you get the work done and do not create problems, we will get along fine. If you cause me problems, believe me, I will start using the rod and will not put up with you. There is always room in the crematorium, I'm afraid. Do we have an understanding?"

All of the women agreed as they counted off their numbers once more, as the private asked them to do.

Although the three spies were gone, Sarah knew full well someone else would fill that role in short order, so she kept her mind on her job, and cooperated without question.

Over the next month, everything was going well in the kitchen and everyone appeared to be getting along. Feeling much more comfortable, Sarah forgot the camp was filled with spies that would turn you over to a kapo or a soldier for an extra cup of watery soup. One afternoon, as she walked back to the barracks with the others, a soldier pulled her out of line. Pulling her pants down he found a piece of bread tied around Sarah's calf with a length of string. After knocking her to the ground with his rifle butt, Sarah was placed in a dark wooden box that stood out in the middle of the camp. It was so small, no one could stand up or sit up straight, and it was too short to lay totally flat. All you could do was lay in a fetal position on the dirt floor until your muscles began to spasm and tighten up.

By the seventh day, Sarah's legs were cramping so badly she wailed in pain, but no one was going to come to her aid. Ants and other insects chewed on her skin as if she were one of the corpses waiting to be burned outside the crematorium.

On the ninth day, two soldiers opened the door and slid her out into mud as it had been raining for several days. "Get up!" one of the soldiers yelled out as he kicked her.

Sarah struggled to straighten her legs, but her cramped up muscles would not allow them to respond. Once again, the soldier called out, "Get up or you go back in the box for another week!"

Trying to cooperate, Sarah rolled on to her knees and began to force her left leg to straighten, but it was just not going to happen.

Angered, the soldiers pushed her over onto her side and rolled her back into the box. Sarah screamed, "No, please no! I'm sorry for taking the bread, I'm sorry I could not stand up, please don't put me back in there, I can't do that anymore!"

Sergeant Wilhelm, the leader of the camp guards, looked down at her. "And I suppose you are also sorry for being a Jew."

Nodding her head, she said calmly. "Yes, yes I'm sorry I am a Jew. We count for nothing, we are nothing, we will never be anything!"

Laughing the huge sergeant replied, "You are beginning to understand what our Fuhrer has said for years, but a zebra cannot change its stripes, and you will learn what can happen to a Jew that does not cooperate." With that, the door was slammed shut.

Sarah wept as she laid in total agony, just wishing she could die. She thought of Isaac's words to her so long ago. "Live Sarah, you must live." Now she wondered why. What was there to live for, to care about? What reason did she have left to care if she ever saw another sunrise? But that night she made herself a promise if she lived. No longer would she cry in front of the Germans. No longer would she allow the S.S. to break her mind or spirit. From now on, she would look them in the eye and make them kill her. She would show them no emotion, she would not give them that satisfaction.

After the fourth day, the door was once again opened. Like last time, the soldiers dragged her out across the ground and threw her off to the side. But this time, the soldiers had a reason for removing her from the box. As Sarah struggled to straighten her legs, she watched in horror as the soldiers beat a woman in her forties unmercifully with rubber blackjacks as she continued struggling with them. When she finally gave up, the soldiers pushed her into the box and spit upon her. Sarah knew the woman would be in agony much sooner, as she was several inches taller.

"No, don't do that to her, please, please stop!" Sarah screamed, as she saw the desperate fear in the woman's eyes.

As they prepared to close the door, the woman looked at Sarah. "Pray for me child, pray for me."

With the door closed, Sarah shook her head as she yelled back to the woman. "I'm sorry, there is no one left to pray to. I'm sorry, I know no more prayers. We shall all die here."

The soldiers laughed as they dragged Sarah back to her barracks, throwing her on her filthy mat. Before the last soldier walked off, he struck Sarah on the forehead with his blackjack. "You had no right to talk to the woman. Learn to keep your mouth shut! I can put you back there when we are through with her if you cannot cooperate."

"Please no, I will not cause you any more problems. Please, do not put me back in there," Sarah pleaded, as she shook in fear. After the soldier left, Sarah was angry with herself for showing fear, something she had promised she would never do again. But the thought of being placed back in the box seriously frightened her.

Knowing Sarah had been placed in the box for stealing food, none of the women in the barracks had any pity for her. They would pass by her and say. "The little you stole you could not even share with us, not even with our children. What are you to us!"

Around midnight, Sarah was finally able to straighten her legs but she was in pure agony as she was covered in her own waste. In extreme pain, Sarah rolled off her mat and crawled to the wretched bathing area. After several minutes she saw two women standing against the wall. In fear that she was going to be turned in to the guards, she fell to the floor and cursed at them. "Go ahead, do as you will. I'm nothing to you as you are nothing to me. Kill me yourselves and be through with it. Is that not why you are here? Were you not voted in by the women in the barracks to finish the job the German did not complete. If you choose not to bloody your hands, get a kapo to do your dirty work."

Without responding, the two women came toward her, knelt down and began to bath her as best they could. Galenka laid Sarah's head on her lap as she washed her face and hair.

"Peace child, be at peace." She continued whispering as her friend Raizel rinsed out Sarah's coveralls.

Prior to morning count, Galenka walked up to Sarah. "You must make count, or you will be right back in the box. If we carry you out, that means you are too weak to live, and you will get a bullet and a free ride to the crematorium. You must stand and walk on your own, child."

Staring up into those deep dark brown eyes Sarah nodded her head. "I will try."

When the whistle was blown for count, Sarah sat up on her bunk and swung her legs down to the floor. With the help of Galenka and Raizel, she slowly stood up, but the pain was intolerable. Sarah cried out in pain, falling face first to the floor. Although time was running out, the two women once more pulled Sarah from the floor.

"You must walk from here child, or this shall be your last day. They will have no pity on you!" Galenka insisted, before walking out to make count.

The S.S. soldier was just finishing count when Sarah walked up into the last row of women. He glared at her for a moment before walking forward to announce his count was correct.

Although in complete misery, Sarah slowly walked over in line to get her morning soup. She had not eaten anything since she had been tossed into the box. She had lost so much weight now, she couldn't believe what her body looked like. She had barely picked up the bowl handed to her, before another woman knocked it out of her shaking hands.

"Steal food and you don't share it, maybe you don't need that food either, bitch." The woman called out, as she and her friends laughed.

Quickly, Sarah crawled over to her bowl and picked up the bits of celery and carrots from the dirt, placing them in her mouth. Watching a soldier walking toward her, she stuffed the small crust of bread into her mouth, swallowing it without chewing."

"Get up!" the soldier called out. "Do you want another week in the box? I can arrange that if you cannot behave."

Sarah held up her hand and shook her head. "Sorry, I'm sorry. It will not happen again."

Picking up her bowl, Sarah set it on the table before walking back to the barracks, where she laid down and fell into a fitful sleep. After evening count, Sarah was careful, safely guarding her bowl so no one could knock it out of her hands again. She sipped the dark broth slowly and chewed each small bit of soggy rutabaga as if it was the most delicious food on earth. When she finished and was about to return her bowl, several friends of Galenka's came by, pouring some of their soup into her bowl. Before long, she had more soup than what her original ration was.

As the door to the barracks was shuttered for the night, Galenka walked over to Sarah. "How are you feeling child? Any better now?"

Sarah nodded her head. "My name is Sarah, Sarah Rosenbaum. I will be twelve years old shortly, although I feel like I have lived a hundred years. I came from Straubing near the Bohemian Forest. I believe everyone in my family is dead. Only I have survived, I am sure of it."

Galenka sat down next to her. "You have been through too much for such a young child. On the other hand, I have experienced the best of life in many ways. I was married, raised three children, had a nice home and was about to have my third grandchild when Hitler came into power. As you, I believe they are all gone now. It's almost funny, I do not understand why I have survived all of this, when so many younger have perished. So, tell me your story, Sarah."

Shaking her head, Sarah looked over at Galenka. "There is no story to tell. Just death and pain, but everyone here has that story to tell. I'm nothing special, just a German girl that was born Jewish, so I have no life, no hope and no family. I will welcome death when it arrives."

Galenka was quiet for a moment. "Ah, but we all have stories, Sarah. We must share them because no one knows who will survive. The survivors can then tell the world who we were."

Sarah lowered her head as she laughed. "We shall not survive, no one will. We are already dead, we just don't realize it yet. No, none of us will survive."

Galenka placed her hand down on top of Sarah's. "God Sarah,

God will not let us all die here. He will look out for us as he did when our ancestors were captive in Egypt."

Sarah pulled her hand away as she looked coldly at Galenka. "God! You still believe in this God! If he ever did exist, he does not anymore. And all those stories in the Torah, they are make-believe. Like I said before, they never happened, those people did not exist. Look Galenka, look where we are. There is no rescue, no help, just death. Please leave me alone."

After a moment of silence, Galenka stood up. "As you wish, Sarah."

Days passed and Sarah's loneliness and anger only grew, until she was ready to test her fate one last time. She decided she would slap the soldier at morning count, earning her a severe beating, and maybe even a bullet. At the least, she would get one final trip to the box where she would surely die. Exiting the barracks the following morning, Galenka grabbed her by the arm.

"Whatever you are planning to do, don't do it. Please Sarah, do not die this way."

Sarah stopped and stared at Galenka and Raizel. "What are you talking about? I just want count to be over so I can have my soup. I'm hungry."

Raizel stepped in front of Sarah. "We can see what you are up to, we have seen it many times. You have that look of determined death in your eyes this morning. Don't give in to it."

Pulling away, Sarah began walking toward the assembled women. She had made about four steps before Galenka hit her on the side of the head, knocking her to the ground. Seeing the commotion, Corporal Barnard came running over.

"Back away, back away! What's wrong with the girl!" he screamed, as he looked at Galenka.

"She is feeling sick this morning. I think she should lay down, we will bring her a bowl after count, Herr Corporal, if that's fine with you."

"If she's so sick she cannot stand, she must be taken to the hospital, those are the Commandant's orders, she must go!"

As he was about to call for help, Galenka realized she had made a serious mistake. As Sarah moaned, Galenka pulled her by the arm into a sitting position. "See, she's not so bad, she can stand now, let us take her to her mat. After she eats and rests, she will be able to stand tonight. Please Corporal, she is just a child. A trip to the hospital means death for her. Please Corporal!"

After looking at Galenka and Raizel, he nodded his head. "Put her on her mat. If she's worse tonight, she will need to go to the hospital. Do I make myself clear!"

"Yes, Herr Corporal!" Galenka replied, as she and Raizel pulled Sarah from the ground.

Raizel sat with Sarah as Galenka and another woman named Hadar brought bowls of soup and bread rations. Before allowing her to take the bowl, Galenka looked fiercely at Sarah. "Tell me, are we wasting a food ration, or are you eating this to stay strong. You see, we stole extra bread for you. Which way do you want it, girl. Do we dump it on the floor and distribute the bread to others, or do you wish to survive. You must decide now, or you are making fools of us all!"

Sarah felt embarrassed by her actions and was not sure how to respond, as she understood each of the women could be punished severely for stealing the bread. Reaching up for the bowl, she realized the struggle between life and death in the camp was becoming a more serious matter each passing day. Much different from anything she had experienced since running from her mother, and this time neither Ishmael or Isaac were going to come forward to save her.

After drinking some of the broth, Sarah passed out much of the bread to other women, knowing what a precious commodity it was. After finishing her soup, she walked over to the serving table with Galenka to get some air. She looked at the procession of carts filled with bodies being pushed by the kapos toward the crematorium.

"Galenka, I'm sorry for my behavior. I thank you for saving me, but I'm not sure I can handle this as long as you have. My mother use to tell me my stubbornness, impatience and lack of discipline would someday get me in trouble. Now I know she was right, but I'm not sure how to control it. Tell me, how do you and the others survive? I cannot understand all of this, and I fear I may get someone hurt or killed. What do I do?"

After they walked back toward the barracks, Galenka led Sarah toward an outdoor bench. "I know you will argue with me, so I fear bringing this up as it will just cause problems. But without what we memorized from the Torah and Talmud as children, we would have nothing to cling to. Yes, we believe that God is watching, and knows what is best for us. Certainly, we do not understand why this is all happening, but we trust in him, we must trust, Sarah. Without that, you will remain angry and have nothing in your soul. You will strike out in vengeance, and your soul will truly die along with your mortal body."

Sarah looked up toward the cloudless azure blue sky. "Why is the sky as blue in here as it is out there beyond the wire. I want to run through the fields of clover, I want to smell fresh air, not this stench of death. When can I do that again, Galenka?"

Shaking her head, Galenka smiled. "Only God knows, my child. We must wait, and pray for him to set us free. Join us tonight in prayer, it will sooth your tormented soul. Please give it a try."

That evening as the doors and windows were secured, Sarah walked down to the gathering of women in the middle of the barracks. Sitting down beside Galenka, she listened to Hadar recite several passages from the Torah, followed by each of the other women. Sarah felt ashamed she was not able to add to the prayers, as she had never actually memorized the passages as other children her age had.

Laying on her mat that evening she thought about the woman that had replaced her in the box. She remembered the woman's plea for prayer, when all she could do was tell her there was no God. She wondered if the woman had survived, or if her soul had gone up in smoke. Knowing she had turned her back on the woman during her darkest time hurt terribly.

Laying on her mat, Sarah began to think how her selfishness and demanding nature had caused problems with the people in the forest. How her carelessness had endangered the people under the old factory in Paris. Worst of all, she had used Rochelle to the point of death, and she was not even a Jew. Then she allowed herself to become far too comfortable around the soldiers on the construction project in Normandy, which led to the destruction of the partisans and her capture.

Now Isaac was in a forced labor camp, and she had no way of knowing what happened to Ishmael, but she feared he must also be dead. As she listened to the sobs from the new women that entered their barracks today, Sarah felt more ashamed of herself than she ever thought possible. How many deaths was she responsible for? How many people suffered tremendous torture because of her actions or inaction? And most of all, those men. She herself had taken the lives of two men. True, they were the enemy, but their deaths led to more suffering by people that had placed their trust in her.

Several weeks later at morning roll call, Sarah became frightened as she observed Klaus Barbie standing next to the camp commandant. She wondered if he remembered the threat she had made toward him. He was the last person she wanted to see again. After count had officially been secured, Cpl. Barnard approached Sarah, grabbing her by the upper arm.

"You are to come with me. It's best you comply and do not cause us any problems today. The people that wish to see you will not put up with bad behavior, I promise you."

Sarah walked with Cpl. Barnard to an interrogation building. He pushed her down into the seat and cuffed her hands to the chair. Grabbing Sarah by the hair he pulled her head back. Admit to whatever they ask, odds are that way you may go back to the barracks tonight."

Just a dim light bulb illuminated the dark smelly room. It reminded Sarah of the rooms in the basement of the S.S. building in Paris. Several minutes after Cpl. Barnard left, an S.S. captain and major walked into the room. The major leaned up against the wall in the corner of the room as the captain leaned across the table facing Sarah.

"So, you were a member of the underground in France located near Beauvais. Tell us who was in charge of your unit, and where can we find him?" the captain asked angrily.

Sarah glared right back at him. "He's dead, your men killed him along with his second in command. They were named Baruch and Elazar."

Almost surprised by Sarah's response, the captain stood up straight. "Who did Baruch report to, and how did they communicate?"

Shaking her head, Sarah responded. "I never knew any of that. I was just a runner."

Walking around the table, the captain slapped Sarah across the face. "I don't believe you. Either tell me what I need to know, or we'll have to try other methods."

Sarah glared at the captain's face that was just inches from hers. "Then do as you must!"

Using his foot, the captain tipped over the chair. Sarah's head slammed down hard on the concrete floor as he kicked her solidly in the abdomen. "So, who was the person Baruch spoke with?"

Sarah turned her head slightly so she could see the officers face and replied, "Eat shit!"

The major stepped forward, "Enough! Take her out back!"

Corporal Barnard and one other S.S. soldier entered the room and dragged her behind the building where they tied her to a post.

Five soldiers were standing about ten yards away, holding rifles. The captain ordered them to aim their weapons at her. Looking toward the sky he yelled, "Fire!"

Sarah jumped as all the rifles clicked, but not one shot was fired. "I guess we have a problem, reload!" The captain called out as the soldiers ran their bolts, slamming an actual round into the chamber of their rifles.

Sweat poured down Sarah's face as the captain nodded his head. "Fire!"

Sarah jumped as all five weapons fired, striking her in the face and chest with wadding that is stuffed into the end of a blank round.

Sarah slumped forward on the post, wetting her pants as the soldiers laughed. Taking a deep breath she yelled out, "None of you have the guts to shoot a girl. You are all a bunch of cowards!"

"Reload!" The captain called out as he shook in anger. "Aim, Fire!"

Once again, all five rifles discharged, but this time a bullet slightly creased her left arm. After letting out a scream, Sarah stood tall against the post. As blood ran down her arm, she called out, "Here, let me make a better target for you so you will not miss next time, since you are all piss poor shots."

Angered by Sarah's perseverance, the captain yelled at Cpl. Barnard. "Bring her to the yard. We will see what she's really made of."

As soon as Sarah was delivered to the yard, a roll call was called for. Once everyone was assembled outside their barracks, Klaus Barbie and one of his aides walked past the groups of women, selecting a woman here and there randomly, and pulling them to the center of the yard. After they had six women standing in the center of the yard, Barbie walked up to Sarah.

"Well, well we meet again, but not as you expected, since it is not on your terms. So you see I still have the right to decide who lives and dies, no matter the situation. Either you tell me what we want to know about your partisan group, or these women will die. So, how did your leader communicate with the British?" Barbie screamed, as he pushed Sarah to the ground.

Coming up to her knees, Sarah shook her head, "As I've said so many times, I don't know, I'm telling you the truth."

Immediately, Barbie turned to his left and drew his side arm, shooting one of the women in the head. Turning back toward Sarah, he continued. "How many more do you want to die? They live or die because of you. Who led your group and how did you communicate?"

Sarah cried out, "Stop it, stop it. Please do not hurt these women." Shaking her head Sarah pleaded. "How can I make you understand, I never knew how the group operated, I was just a runner. You must understand me, please don't do this."

Barbie laughed. "Believe you? You are just a filthy Jew." Once again, pulling his side arm, Barbie fired two shots into the next woman. "You see, you are responsible for their deaths. Do you now want to tell us what you know so the others may live?"

Sarah screamed all the louder. "No! Please stop, don't do this, those women did nothing wrong. If you want to shoot someone, shoot me! Please don't do this, please stop!" Sarah screamed, as she looked up at her tormentor. "Sir, I realize the power you have, and I know you are an important man. But I cannot help you with what you want to know. I don't know who communicated with who or how they did it. I never knew any of that, honestly I did not."

After a moment of silence Barbie placed his sidearm in its holster as he looked down at Sarah. "I do believe you, I now think you are telling me the truth." As he turned to walk away, he nodded at his aide who was standing in front of the remaining women holding a Schmeisser.

Instantly, a long blast of bullets flew from the sub-machine gun, killing the rest of the women. Sarah screamed in agony as she fell to the ground, holding her abdomen as she yelled. "No, no, no! Oh my God, what have I done!"

Sergeant Wilhelm yelled at Cpl. Barnard, "Take her to the box! Maybe this time she will learn her lesson."

Sarah was quiet while they marched her to the box. After binding her wrists and ankles they slid her into the familiar container. As they closed the door she whispered, "Goodbye Galenka." Although she had promised never to cry again, the thought of the six women being killed was more than she could handle. Tears flowed as an overwhelming grief ripped at Sarah's heart.

On the evening of the sixth day, two S.S. soldiers opened the door and dragged her out as Klaus Barbie's Captain peered down at her.

"I have come back to see if you are ready to talk now that you have had a chance to understand what your silence has cost those poor women. Now, so no one else has to suffer, what can you tell us?"

It was impossible to speak as Sarah's mouth was dry and filled with dust. No matter how hard she tried, nothing came out. Finally, one of the soldiers knelt down holding a canteen to her mouth. After swallowing the water, she looked at the soldier and said. "Danka." Looking up at the captain, she said, "Put me back in!"

After kicking her twice, the captain and the soldiers walked off, leaving her on the ground beside the box. About midnight, Cpl. Barnard came over and cut off the ropes binding Sarah's hands and feet. He dragged her over to the bench outside the barracks. "Lay down and sleep here. The women will find you in the morning. Barbie's officers have left the camp, but I don't think they are through with you yet. I feel they will be back one day and he will finish it for sure."

As the women exited the barracks the following morning for count, Galenka and Raizel gently pulled Sarah to her feet so she could be counted. After once again cleaning her in the shower room, they placed Sarah down on her mat. Within moments, she passed out.

After evening count Sarah sipped slowly on her soup and slowly chewed the small pieces of bread several women had given her. As the women held their nightly prayer session, Sarah laid on her mat wondering why she was still alive. Why did Barbie kill the rest of the women and not her? She laid on her mat with her arms tightly wrapped around her chest. Her heart ached for the women that had died, and wondered if the rest of the women in the camp would forgive her for what had happened.

There was no way of knowing what Klaus Barbie was capable of, so she feared he would go to Mauthausen and torture Isaac, searching for the same information. She realized there was no earthly reason she had survived everything she had been put through. It just made no sense to a twelve-year-old girl. Slowly, she stood up and walked to Galenka's bunk to join the other women in prayer.

Chapter Thirteen
Galenka's Wisdom

Although Sarah had survived Klaus Barbie and the box, she began to believe there must be a reason she was still alive, but honestly, she had given up all hope of surviving Dachau. If Barbie returned, there was no doubt he would kill her.

Right before evening count one day, she watched a woman from another barracks turn and run into the wire fence before the tower guard could shoot her. Sparks flew as her body was thrown back twenty feet before dropping to the ground. It was evident that no one need check the smoking body for a pulse to see if she was alive. The kapos simply loaded her onto a cart and delivered her charred remains to the crematorium. Watching that episode, Sarah was intrigued. How many times had she thought about how easy it would be to run into the fence, and have it over with in a heartbeat. Several mornings after count had been completed, she stood, silently staring at the buzzing monster, knowing death would be instant and her suffering ended.

Each time, Galenka would take hold of her hand and whisper, "That is not the way, child. Be strong, and do not let them take away all you have left. Our God of Israel has a plan for you, be brave."

Returning to the barracks one morning, she looked at Galenka.

"What do I have left? There is nothing, and none of us will get out of here alive. You have seen the death around here longer than I have. There is nothing to live for anymore, so what plan could this God have for me?"

Galenka smiled, "Ah, but you are wrong, Sarah. See the children huddled in the corner around the sick woman. They would love to have you take their minds away from death and fill them with fun. Go to them, Sarah, it will also save you. You are young enough, they will follow you, and enjoy being with you."

Unsure of how to handle the situation, Sarah slowly walked over to the eight children and sat down on the floor next to them. Immediately, a child of about three climbed into her lap, laying her head against Sarah's shoulder. A severely undernourished boy about six years old looked up into Sarah's eyes.

"I'm hungry, my mother died and I have no one to help me get food. The ladies push me away." After speaking, he sat down next to Sarah, taking hold of her arm.

By now, all the children had gathered around Sarah, looking up at her with wide empty eyes. Taking in a deep breath, she began to sing a song her mother sang to her when she was a little girl. After each verse, she repeated the words, trying to get the children to sing with her.

From that day forward, each day at meal time she made sure each child was given the proper ration of food, and would swipe an extra scrap of bread for them when no one was watching closely. If any of the women would mistreat the children, they would catch the wrath of Sarah before they could walk away. After a week, even the guards referred to the little ones as Sarah's children.

She helped them bathe as best she could, and made sure each of them received a kiss on the cheek before they went to sleep each night.

When the mother of the little girl died a week later, she was surprised how the child never cried or reached out to touch her mother before her body was taken away by the kapos. She just stood still by her mother's bunk, refusing to move for about an hour, as her bottom lip quivered from time to time. The next morning, Sarah found her dead, laying on the filthy mat her mother had died on. Although it was tragic, Sarah was happy the child had willed herself to die, so she could be at peace with her mother. Galenka and several other women stood together near the child, reciting Kaddish as the kapos removed the tiny emaciated body from the barracks. Sarah knew the tiny spirit would now be free and allowed to leave the camp forever in the thick smoke that rose towards the heavens.

The following day was tough as the children all wanted to know what had happened to their little friend. As Sarah was trying to find a way to explain it to them, another girl of about four stood on a bunk looking out the window. She pointed toward the black smoke rising from the crematorium chimney. "She is there, she is in the smoke, she is gone now."

The rest of the children turned to look at the smoke and appeared sad, but not one of them asked again about their missing friend, they had all come to understand what the smoke meant.

What Sarah loved most, was when they were able to go outside in the afternoons. She played games with them and required that they exercise so they would not wither away. Galenka and many of the older women found it music to their ears as they listened to the little voices squeal with fun and laughter at Sarah's games and jokes.

There were times Galenka had to pull Sarah aside and cool her down after the guards mistreated one of the children. By now Sarah knew which guards abused the children the most so she treated them with contempt. They had no qualms about kicking or striking the children if they came close to them. One afternoon as the children were playing outside, Sarah watched several kapos remove a dead woman from barracks building nearby. On top of her was a small child that also appeared to be dead. As they pushed the cart toward the crematorium, she noticed the child raise its arm.

Quickly Sarah ran toward the cart, screaming at the kapos to stop. Looking down at the child it was evident she was not in good shape. "I'll take her, she is still alive. I will not let you crush her skull with your jack boots," Sarah called out as she reached down to pick up the child that could not have been older than three.

An S.S. soldier walked up to Sarah. "Put her down, she is as good as dead, she is not one of yours. Do it or you will end up in the box along with her."

Sarah looked angrily at the soldier. Before she realized what she was saying, the words were out of her mouth. "She is mine, they are all mine, God has given them to me. Who are you to tell me she is not mine. Who are you to decide when or how she will die. As long as she is alive, she belongs to me, and God has willed it to be so!"

Galenka and the other women looked on in horror as the soldier began dragging Sarah toward the box. When the sergeant of the guard arrived at the box, he looked at Sarah. "I didn't think I would have a problem with you again. But if it's what you desire, I will accommodate you and that bastard child."

Sarah looked angrily at Sergeant Wilhelm. "What would you know about bastard children? Are you not a clean Aryan man that would have nothing to do with a Jewess?"

Seething with anger, the Sergeant slapped Sarah hard enough across the face to knock her to the ground. "Maybe I should just shoot you both and send your corpse to the crematorium, then I would be finished with you."

"That's your choice, but will it change anything?" Sarah responded, as she looked at an approaching soldier that had helped place her in the box on the other occasions.

"Go take the child and get out of my sight. It will surely die soon anyway." Sergeant Wilhelm yelled as he stormed off toward the guard's quarters.

With the help of Galenka and Raizel, they nursed the child back to better health, although she remained sickly and weaker than the other children.

Galenka was most proud of Sarah in the evenings before putting the children to bed, when she told them stories from the Torah she remembered from her childhood. There was little doubt in her mind that the children had softened Sarah's soul, and she now felt an obligation to teach the children about the Jewish faith as best she could.

Although Sarah loved the children, she was not ready to take on three more little ones that arrived in camp a few months later. However, she understood if someone did not adopt them, they would become fuel for the furnaces. As several women objected to having more children, they were allowed to move to another barracks in order to make room for them. That made it all the easier for Sarah to steal scraps of bread without anyone in the barracks reporting her to the guards.

The biggest problem with taking on more children was that Sarah soon began to wear out from tending to her little flock, and it was beginning to show. Women would give her extra bread, but it always ended up in the mouths of the hungry children.

However, her loss of strength was put to the test when Galenka became very ill. Sarah temporarily turned over much of the work with the children to a woman of about thirty named Levana, who admired Sarah's work, but did not get around well due to a broken leg that had not mended properly.

Day and night Sarah held Galenka and made compresses from pieces of material she had gathered from old coveralls that were being disposed of. Throughout many of the long nights, Galenka would recite prayers and verses from the Torah, and ask Sarah and Raizel to join her.

No matter how hard Sarah worked, Galenka slipped into a coma as her temperature rose. Sarah continued placing compresses on her forehead and wiping down her body, attempting to control the fever.

After missing count for three days, Cpl. Bernard told the women he could no longer cover for her, and ordered Galenka be moved to the infirmary where she could get better care. When two kapos arrived to pick up Galenka, Sarah stopped them. "You will leave her here. If you take her, she will surely die from lack of care and you both know it."

One of the kapos, a bent over old man nodded his head. "Yes, you are right, Miss. But orders are orders so we must take her, they need another empty bunk."

Raizel laughed, "They need an empty bunk? You tell us about bunk space? We already have twenty more women in here than this place was made for. You will have Galenka's bunk if she should die, we'll not give it to you while she still breathes."

The youngest kapo pushed Raizel to the floor as he reached for Galenka.

Before he could make another move, Sarah grabbed him around the throat. "Touch her and I will kill you, I promise you that."

Being in rather good shape from the food the guards gave him, he quickly tossed Sarah off his back, slamming her against the wall. She rebounded like an athlete, ripping at his face with her fingernails. He screamed as blood flowed down his face. As soon as he took control of one of Sarah's hands, she attacked with the other, pulling wads of hair from his head or scratching his forehead.

With all his might he tossed her to the floor, kicking her in the chest. Pulling out a leather blackjack he swung for her head, but did not get good aim as blood blurred his eyesight. Sarah pulled her left leg back and kicked the man with all her might at the side of his left knee. He howled as his leg collapsed, causing him to drop to the floor.

Sarah grabbed hold of the blackjack, pulling it from his hand. Shaking with anger she pointed it at the older kapo. "Get him out of here before I kill him! Get him out of here!"

The man grabbed his younger partner and pulled him to his one good leg. Before leaving the barracks, the younger man yelled. "I'll see you in the box before this day is over, bitch!"

Hadar took hold of Sarah, "What have you done, my child? You will pay for this with your life, they will kill you for sure!"

Sarah looked at the blood on her hands and arms. "I have done what I needed to do."

After washing her hands and face she returned to Galenka's side, changing the compress on her forehead. Within minutes the door to the barracks flew open. Sergeant Wilhelm walked up to Sarah, staring at the blackjack she was holding in her right hand. "Throw it down, bitch!"

Sarah tossed it on the floor as she stared at Sgt. Wilhelm, knowing she was going to get the worse punishment possible. Two soldiers grabbed her by the arms, pulling her out to the box. After slapping Sarah across the face, Sgt. Wilhelm pushed her to the ground. "Take your clothes off," the burly Sergeant ordered as he kicked her in the abdomen.

"No. I will not undress in front of you. Not now, not ever!" Sarah screamed.

Nodding to his soldiers, he called out, "Do it!"

The men pulled Sarah's coveralls off, throwing them on the ground. After spitting on her he ordered his men to push her into the box.

Each night she was in the box, Sgt. Wilhelm would come by and urinate on her through the cracks in the box. During the night of the fifth day, two soldiers pulled her from the box. Sgt. Wilhelm knelt down beside her and smiled. "Today we have something special for you."

Quickly the two guards descended upon her, holding her to the ground so she could not move or scream. Several minutes later, breathing heavily, Sgt. Wilhelm stood back up, pulling his trousers up in place. While adjusting his uniform tunic and tightening his belt, he looked down at Sarah. "Now you have something you can always remember me for. And just so you know, these men have seen nothing, so crying to the commandant will just get you worse. Throw her back in the box."

Sarah laid in the box, trying to put out of her mind everything that had just taken place, but that was not going to happen anytime soon. She could smell the Sergeants breath and the stale urine from his nightly visits. Closing her eyes, she once again prayed for death.

The following morning, Cpl. Barnard opened the box and looked angry when he saw Sarah's condition. "I will be back in a moment, stay where you're at."

Returning with a soiled blanket, he stated. "Wrap this around you as I walk you back to the barracks. You should not be seen like this with everyone out in the yard for morning count."

Sarah appreciated what the corporal was doing for her, but this humiliation was nothing compared to what she had gone through during the past night.

After washing herself, Raizel handed her a set of worn but rather clean coveralls. "Here, eat this bread, I stole it for you this morning. Eat it slow."

After eating the bread and drinking some water Sarah, looked up at Raizel. "Galenka, and the children, how are they?"

Raizel smiled. "The night you went to the box, the fever broke. Galenka woke up the following morning and is doing quite well. She wants to see you. The children have missed you badly. They are looking forward to playing with you again."

Sarah shuddered inside. How could she play with those sweet children when she felt so dirty and sinful. How could she face Galenka after what she had gone through. After much thought she made a decision. Today after she took the children back inside from exercise, she would run for the fence. They would never hurt her again.

That evening after count, Galenka was sitting on her mat as Sarah approached. "My child, what have you been through? What did they do to you? I can see the pain in your eyes."

Sarah took hold of Galenka's hand. "I have seen hell and it's ugly. The fence looks better tonight than it ever has before. But something powerful stood between me and the fence, it kept driving me back inside, despite my desire to end it all. It was all so strange. So, I'm back here to take care of you, that's all that matters."

Galenka smiled as she placed her hand on Sarah's cheek. "It was God my daughter, it was God. He is not ready for you yet, you must live. Now, will you pray with me?"

As Sarah held back the tears that welled up inside of her she whispered, "Give me strength, I need your strength and your blessing. Yes, I will pray with you."

Holding hands, Sarah knelt down beside Galenka's bunk and began to pray. After a few minutes, one by one the children walked up to Sarah, giving her a hug, or placing their little hands on her back and arms. Amazingly, after all she had gone through, Sarah never felt more loved, and she knew there was no way she could take her life this night.

Every day Galenka recovered a bit more, until she was once again able to walk to roll call unassisted, and get her own rations. Each day during count as she passed the kapos that had come for her body she would smile and say, "Does it bother you to have a ghost stand for count?"

A few weeks later a large black Mercedes sedan and a small cargo truck entered the camp. After looking over the camp, a middle-aged S.S. officer and his aides entered the commandant's office. Visitors like this always caught the attention of the prisoners as it never amounted to anything good.

Camp Commander Sturmbahnfuhrer Wilhelm Witteler sat in his office working on supply requisitions as Obersturmbahnfuhrer Fritz Hintermayer entered his office.

Witteler jumped up from his desk, extending his hand. "My dear Fritz, it's good to see you again. I was excited to hear you were coming for an official visit. I hope we will have time to reminisce before you are forced to leave. We have so much to catch up on."

Hintermayer shook hands as he smiled at his old friend. "If all goes well, we will have much time to talk and swap lies." Pulling an envelope from inside his jacket pocket, he handed it to Witteler.

"You will see that our boss Heinrich Himmler himself has sent me here to become the camp doctor, and continue on with some experiments I have been working on, that is if the lab is still in operating order."

After reading the letter, Witteler nodded his head. "Ja, Ja, the lab is fine, although it might be a bit dusty. It has not been used for quite some time. But I can get it cleaned for you very quickly. There are a few ladies from town that are more than willing to help out with office work and such. They will have it ready to go in no time."

"Gut, that is gut. Do you also still have connections to that wonderful Cognac you served me last time I was here. It was quite remarkable," Hintermayer asked with a broad smile.

"Oh Ja, I can still get it, and I have an ample supply on hand right now. Don't fret my dear Fritzy, I will take care of you while you are my guest."

The two men laughed as they once again shook hands. "So, tell me Fritz, how were things up at Auschwitz when you left? Are they continuing on with the program as they were six months ago? Our small crematoriums cannot keep up with the bodies we need to dispose of. You will see we have many of them piled here in the camp, we just cannot keep up. If we could get a crematorium the size that Auschwitz has, we would be in better shape. I keep asking for construction money, but Berlin will not give me what I need. Maybe with you here now they will send me more funds."

Hintermayer shook his head. "Willy, I am positive that will not happen. The war in the east is sucking up a tremendous amount of men and equipment. In fact, I was told that the Fuhrer wants all the camps destroyed before the Russians get a chance to over run them. I don't know that for a fact, but that is what I heard some S.S. officers talk about when I was in Chelmno a few weeks back. I suggest you just try and get by with what you have for the time being."

Witteler paced back and forth across his office for a moment before looking back at his good friend. "So, tell me, is the war going so badly on all the fronts. I see Allied bombers overhead every day now. How long can we last with this kind of force against us?"

Hintermayer laughed as he placed his hand on Witteler's

shoulder. "Do not worry, Willy. Just last week Himmler was telling me that Hitler has several new secret wonder weapons he is going to spring on the enemy in the next few months, and that will turn the tide back in our favor. If the Fuhrer still believes in ultimate victory, who are we to question it."

Several days later Witteler walked over to the medical facility with Hintermayer. Opening the door to the lab, Witteler smiled. "You see, good as new and ready for you to conduct all your tests. As I promised, the laboratory and surgical rooms were cleaned and sterilized by women from the local community, right after our conversation in my office. So Fritzy, what will you be working on now? Your experiments on the effects of extreme cold and heat on the human body were magnificent. Our pilots owe so much to you."

"Ja, it was good we had so many people to experiment with. What was losing a few Jews for the betterment of the German Luftwaffe. Someday the entire world will be using my testing results to make flight better for all people. But, to answer your question, I am still looking into sterilization issues we have never really answered. Doctor Mengele has let me read his files, so I think I have a few ideas that might take his results one step further," Hintermayer responded.

The kapos that ran the hospital were excited to see a real doctor making rounds again. What they did not realize, was that Hintermayer was selecting young to middle aged women for tests and surgical experiments on their reproductive organs. If they survived the doctor's experiments, they would be euthanized and sent directly to the crematoriums.

One afternoon as the women were out in the yard for exercise, Sarah observed Hintermayer playing with a few small girls from another barracks. When everyone was sent back inside, those girls were taken by the guards to the hospital.

Several days later, Sarah observed kapos removing the bodies of the girls from the hospital on carts. When the doctor walked over to the girls Sarah was playing with, the line was drawn. She walked up to Hintermayer and pushed him away from the girl he was talking to.

"You'll not touch the girls from this barracks in any way. I do not know what you are doing to them, but I know they are all dying. Keep away from these children, they belong to me," Sarah yelled, as she shoved the doctor backwards a second time.

Immediately, Sgt. Wilhelm and two of his men pushed Sarah to the ground. Before the doctor could say a word, they dragged Sarah away toward the box. After stripping off her clothing, she was tossed back into the box after a severe beating. As dark settled over the camp once again, Sgt. Wilhelm visited the yard, urinating on the box as he laughed. On the second night he arrived with three soldiers. Once the door was opened, she knew full well what was going to happen to her. Within seconds, the soldiers held her down and covered her mouth as Sgt. Wilhelm smiled and loosened his belt. Looking down at Sarah he smiled, "I have a special treat for you tonight."

Up to this point Sarah had experienced true evil at the hands of the Germans, but what she was going to experience tonight would be the most painful and humiliating experience of her lifetime.

After kicking Sarah several times, Sgt Wilhelm dropped down on top of her as he had before raping her. Sarah closed her eyes, refusing to look at her attacker although he ordered her to look at him several times. When he had finished adjusting his uniform, he picked up a circular metal rod that was attached to several wires that led to a small control box. After placing the circular rod inside of Sarah, he turned on the box. Sarah's body jumped and contorted as the electrical current flowed through her body. No matter how hard she attempted to scream, the huge leather glove held under her jaw by one of the guards forced her mouth shut. When the box was turned off, Sarah collapsed to the ground as the guards laughed. Looking down at Sarah, Sgt. Wilhelm whispered, "I could have just put a bullet in your head, but now you will think of me forever if you survive. I will be in your nightmares, I will be in your dreams, I shall haunt you forever."

As he laughed, he once again turned on the power. Sarah jerked violently for several seconds before passing out. After removing his tool of torture, he motioned for the guards, "Toss her back in the box, I am through with her."

One of the guards stood up, looking at Sgt. Wilhelm, "I think she's dead, Herr Sergeant, should we take her to the crematorium?"

"There is not enough current in that battery to kill her. Throw her back in the box, if she's dead in the morning we'll take her to be cremated then. Now toss her back in!"

Sarah awoke several minutes after the door to the box had been secured. No matter how much she tried, she could not stop shaking, her abdomen throbbed and her head felt like it was going to blow apart. Nothing that professor Felix had done to her had ever hurt so badly. Closing her eyes, she prayed that she would die before morning. The last thing she wanted was to face another day in this man made hell.

As dawn broke over the camp, the doors to the box were opened. The guards from the night before had two kapos pull her out onto the damp ground, laying her beside one of their carts.

"Ah, you have decided to join us after all. We thought for sure we would be taking you to the ovens this morning on one of our carts. You see we came prepared." The older of the two kapos commented, as he looked with anger at her ravaged body.

"Go ahead, crush my skull as you have done to others. Then you can take me to the ovens as you wish. I prefer you end this for me." Sarah replied hoarsely.

From the distance she could hear the voice of Sgt. Wilhelm. "No, we will let you live, we will not give you what you want!" Looking at one of the soldiers, he continued. "Have the kapos carry her back to the barracks." Grabbing Sarah by the throat he looked sternly at her. "Mention one word of this and I will slit your miserable Jew throat, and there is no man on earth that can protect you if I decide to come after you. Never turn your back on me, slut!"

Just as the women were walking out into the cool morning for count, the kapos dragged Sarah into the barracks, tossing her like a sack of potatoes toward her bunk.

After count, Galenka and several other women rushed into the barracks. Kneeling down beside the bunk, Galenka shook her head. "Child, what have they done to you?"

Sarah shook her head as she looked up at Galenka. "I want to die, I cannot take any more!"

Raizel and Hadar carefully washed off the blood that had caked on Sarah's legs overnight, uncovering severe burns. Although they continued asking what had happened to her, Sarah refused to answer. What really bothered Sarah was that she knew that no matter how much she loved little children, there was no way she would ever get pregnant if she survived. Sergeant Wilhelm had not only destroyed her innocence, but he had taken away her ability to create another human being, a chance to hold and nurture a little life she would have created out of love. She knew the day would come if she survived, that she would be able to work through the humiliation and depravity that had been dumped upon her, but to never have a baby would haunt her forever.

The following day as Sarah followed the women out for morning count, she realized there were no little children scurrying around the barracks.

After count was completed, she walked over to Galenka. "The children, what has happened to the children? Where is Levana? Have they been moved to another barracks? I would like to see the children again, I miss them very much."

Galenka began to weep as she placed her arms around Sarah. "You had been in the box just a short time when the guards came for the children. Levana desperately fought for them and was beaten to a bloody pulp. After the guards and kapos removed the children, Levana was taken to the crematorium.

We saw some of the girls taken into the hospital over the next few days, but none of them came out alive. The kapos were kept busy taking their bodies to the ovens. Kapo Philip told us they took the little boys behind the hospital and crushed their skulls with their rifle butts, as they were not needed for tests. I am so sorry my dear, but there was nothing any of us could do."

Sarah closed her eyes as she held Galenka tight, but tears would not come. All she felt now was hate and the overwhelming desire to kill Sgt. Wilhelm, along with the doctor and the men that did his dirty work.

After evening count, Galenka and Raizel sat next to Sarah on her bunk. "I know what's going through your mind right now child, but you must pray, you must pray hard. Our God will punish those people in time, you must let go of your rage," Galenka stated, as she held Sarah's hand.

Shaking her head, she looked at the two women. "They never did anything wrong, all they wanted to do was live and play. Why? Why does our God allow innocent little children to be murdered?"

Raizel smiled at Sarah. "We can never know what God has in mind for us. As Galenka said, we must pray. We must pray." Taking hold of Sarah's other hand, she began to recite from the Torah.

The following morning as Sarah prepared to walk out for count, she heard Galenka weeping as she sat on the floor. Walking up to the bunk where Galenka was seated, she observed Raizel laying on her mat with her eyes wide open, but she no longer breathed.

Hadar walked up to Galenka, taking her by the arm. "Come, you must come, if you do not the guards will kill you also. Please my friend, do not abandon us."

With the help of Sarah and Hadar, Galenka stood up as she nodded her head in agreement. Before heading toward the door, she took her hand and gently closed Raizel's eyes. "Be at peace my friend. I will watch for you in the smoke. Prepare a place for me as I shall not be far behind you."

As the kapos placed Raizel's lifeless body on one of the dreaded carts, a newer woman in the barracks by the name of Penina began reciting Kaddish as she took Sarah by the hand. Although somewhat concerned about the reaction of the guards, Sarah now openly joined in the prayers for the dead. She didn't care if they shot her or placed her back in the box, for she felt dead inside and no longer cared what they did to her.

Although death had been around her since arriving in Dachau, now it was coming closer to home. A virus seemed to be taking out many of the women that had been in the camp for a long time. A week after Raizel passed, Hadar was taken to the hospital after becoming so sick she missed count for two days. Philip the kapo informed the women of her death the next day.

Now all that was left of the small prayer group was Galenka, Freida, Penina and Sarah. However, it was obvious to Sarah that Galenka was going to die soon as well. She no longer ate her rations, and the cough that had started right after Raizel's death, had now became very deep and produced blood from time to time. The light that always radiated from her eyes had been snuffed out and they became dull and dry. Frieda fought every day to keep her friend motivated with questions about the Torah or the Talmud, but now Galenka would just respond, "Why ask me, my friend, you know them well, teach the others."

Several days later as the women stood for count, Sarah noticed a nervousness about the guards she had never witnessed before. Trucks parked near the hospital and the administration building were being filled with boxes and other things at a rapid pace. The usually calm Commandant Witteler paced back and forth between his office and the hospital, smoking one cigarette after another, saying very little to the soldiers he would pass along the way. Something was going on and clearly it affected the German soldiers in a very negative way.

All day long Sarah continued telling Galenka that their days in the camp were numbered. She prayed over and over that Galenka would survive just a few more days. That evening at count, Galenka's hand slipped from Sarah's grasp, as she fell to the ground.

Kneeling down next to her best friend, Sarah could see Galenka was about to pass. After a moment of silence, Galenka opened her eyes and looked up at Sarah. "You have learned much, you are strong willed, you will survive. Remember what I have tried to teach you. Remember that hate accomplishes nothing. Do not seek revenge as it will destroy you, my child. God will find you a way to punish the guilty that tried to destroy us, I fear it must be done. But first you must seek out the God of Israel, the God of Moses and Abraham, he shall give you the strength you need. Pray for me, my dear."

As Galenka took her last breaths, the women from the barracks knelt down around her. Tears flowed freely as the words of Kaddish sprang forth from the lips of the grief-stricken women.

Sarah held the tired, worn out, starved body of this woman she had come to love so much, as her spirit passed. "I shall remember you always, Galenka. I promise I will try to live as you have taught me. I will pray for you, but you need to pray for me, also. May the God of Israel welcome you home."

Suddenly, there was a hand on Sarah's shoulder. Looking up, she saw the face of Philip the kapo looking down at her. "Daughter, I need to take your friend or the guards will beat me again, they have become savages. Please let me do what I need to do."

Nodding her head, Sarah responded. "You can have her as you must. But I need for you to cut off a lock of her hair for me."

Without question, Philip removed a small knife from his pocket, cutting of a section of Galenka's gray hair and handing it to Sarah. After wrapping it inside of a piece of paper that was blowing by, Sarah gently laid Galenka on the ground and stood up.

"Do what you must do, although I do not respect what you have done against your people. But that is for our God to sort out."

Penina took ahold of Sarah as they watched Philip place Galenka's emaciated body onto the transport cart. After bowing slightly toward Sarah, Philip rolled the cart from the yard. What hurt Sarah most right now, was that Galenka's body would be stacked near the crematorium along with all the others that had died over the past week and were still awaiting cremation. It was one last humiliation from the Third Reich that could never be undone.

Laying on her mat after the barracks had been shuttered, Sarah heard the voices of Galenka and Isaac repeating over and over, "You must survive, Sarah, you must live." But how much more abuse could her body take and how long would it take for her redemption from hell.

But now as kapo Philip had pointed out, the S.S. guards were more brutal than usual, and they were definitely nervous about something. As she listened intently to the sounds of trucks coming and going, and commands being yelled out by officers, she feared the end was near. Sarah was sure any moment the doors would fly open, and soldiers carrying machine guns would walk through the barracks, killing every last soul. Finding peace in her heart, Sarah closed her eyes as she waited for the inevitable death she always knew would find her.

Chapter Fourteen
A Strange World

It was hard to believe any person could somehow adjust to the brutality, torture, hate and dehumanization that was inflicted on the Jewish population inside Dachau. Yet somehow there were survivors. What made them special? What made them stronger or tougher? That would be the question they would ask themselves the rest of their lives, "Why me, why me?"

Every day now since the Americans had arrived, Sarah became a little stronger. Every day her memory became a little clearer, and her heart mourned deeper for those that were not able to survive. This was not just a camp, it had become a home, it had become a place where souls searched for peace and left the earth forever in a cloud of smoke. It became a place where all reason and all forms of humanity were never allowed in.

Free from the ever-watching guards, snarling dogs and humming fence of death, Sarah wandered throughout the camp, scared and confused as to what was going to happen to her now. Most of the very sick prisoners had already been taken from the camp to be treated elsewhere. She wanted to get out of this manmade hell, but the new American guards had received orders no longer allowing anyone to leave until the top officials decided what should be done with them.

Over and over, the American's used the new term, displaced persons camp, but no one could explain what it was, or exactly how it was going to work.

Nearly six weeks after the camp was liberated, Sarah and four other teenage girls were called to the camp commanders office. Several women in tan military coveralls greeted them. The leader of the group took charge.

"My name is Angeline. As you can tell by my accent, I am from England. We are taking you to a displaced person's camp for young Jewish children. There you will be able to get better clothing, more food since your health has improved, and a good medical check-up. And of course, we will attempt to find your families and reunite all of you. We have been doing an outstanding job of gathering up the Nazis record system. Does anyone have any questions?"

For a moment, the five girls stood silent, not sure whether to believe Angeline. Was she telling them the truth, or was she lying to them as the Germans had for so many years. Finally, Sarah spoke up.

"What happens if we have no families left alive? What will you do to us then, put us in another camp? When will we be free, when will we be allowed to go off on our own? Can you tell us these things?"

Angeline nodded her head. "Those are all very good questions. We realize that most of you will no longer have surviving families. So, you may end up staying in the displaced persons camp for a while. You are all very young, we cannot just turn you loose to wander around Europe on your own. We have staff from every European nation along with the United States, working on plans for each person. You must be patient and understand exactly how many displaced people there are. Believe me, the Allied government will do its best for each of you."

Sarah shook her head. "I have no family left, and I want to be free to do as I choose. I will not sit in another camp and let someone else decide what to do with me. We have already done that here at Dachau and we will not let anyone dictate to us again!"

By this time, the other girls were yelling their approval and backing away from the women as they closed in tight around Sarah.

Smiling, Sarah continued. "Set us free, that is all we want. We will stay together until we decide what we want to do. If what you said is true, that we will just end up in another camp, we will stay here, where we already know what is expected of us."

Slowly, Angeline stepped forward looking compassionately at the girls. "Believe me if I could set you free I would, but that simply is not possible right now." Taking one more step toward Sarah, she attempted to reach out for her hand.

Quickly, Sarah stepped back, pushing Angelina's hand off to the side. "I do not trust you, we do not trust you. We want our freedom and that is all we want. You have no reason to hold us."

Before Angeline could reply, the camp commander entered the room. "Alright, there will be no more discussion regarding this matter. I have my orders and we will do as we are told. There is a truck outside waiting to take you to Munich, and you will be on it in the next five minutes, or I will have soldiers place you on the truck one way or the other. Do I make myself clear!"

Sarah glared at the commandant. "So, you are just like the German's. Get on the truck, get on the train car, do as you are told, we are just looking out for your welfare. After all, you are just following orders. Is that not accurate, Herr Commandant?"

The captain could feel his face turn red with embarrassment after Sarah quit speaking. He silently looked over at the faces of the frightened girls that were staring back at him, as they all clutched one another and began to cry.

Feeling ashamed for the way he had approached the situation, he looked down at the floor for a moment before clearing his throat. "Look, I am very sorry for what I just said to you. My job has been very tough, sending people where they do not want to go in many cases. You were lied to and abused by the Germans and I understand—"

Before he could finish, Sarah cut him off. "You understand nothing, Herr Commandant. You do not know what it was like to be loaded on to filthy cattle cars and watching people die. You do not know what it has been like to live in this camp and be starved and tortured just because we are Jews. The five of us were just little children when we were separated from our families because of grand promises that were all lies. We no longer trust you or other people in uniform, we just want to go home!"

Once more, Angeline stepped up beside the commandant. "Sarah, we mean you no harm, honestly we do not. All we want is a chance to help you as best we can. To feed you, to give you medical care, to help you find families, and yes, return home if that is possible. But we have thousands of girls just like you from all across Europe who are in need. You must realize it would be too dangerous to just set you free, there are many people that would take advantage of you and hurt you. Please work with us."

Sarah took the girls to the corner of the office where they whispered back and forth for several minutes. Returning to the center of the office, Sarah looked at Angeline. "We will go, we will not cause you any more problems. We all want to feel safe and find a way to go home, we hope you can find a way to help us. We will give you one chance."

When Sarah had finished speaking, they were led to a truck that stood outside the office. As Sarah climbed on board, she stopped for a moment on the tailgate, looking back at the horrid camp she had called home. No matter what the Americans had done to clean the place, it still contained the putrid smell of death. The buildings foretold the brutality that took place, that no human should ever have to experience. She knew Galenka's spirit would linger here forever, it could never be cleansed or destroyed. Before crawling into the truck, she whispered, "I shall come back, Galenka!"

In a little over an hour they arrived at a hospital in Munich where they were given showers, clean clothes and a hot meal. Over the next few days, doctors ran batteries of tests, took x-rays and prescribed medications or nutritional supplements.

They were housed on the third floor of what had been a Catholic Nuns Convent before the Nazis came to power. There were good beds, three meals a day, and continued follow up health care.

Like all the children in the building, Sarah was finally called into the displaced persons tracking office. The women in the office took down all the pertinent information survivors could give about their families, in hopes of matching them up with a relative.

There was little doubt in Sarah's mind that there wasn't anyone left in her family. After being in the center for five weeks, she was called back to the office. The woman that had completed the original interview was waiting for her.

"Sarah, we have worked over all the records we have. I'm sorry to say, your father died in Dachau right after he was arrested. Your mother, sister and brother all perished in Buchenwald. We cannot find any record of your mother's parents or your relatives that lived in Augsburg. We know your uncle on your father's side also perished in Buchenwald. Again, we have no record of your father's parents. It would be obvious that none of your grandparents survived, or maybe even made it to a camp to begin with. I'm so sorry."

Sarah sat still for a moment before replying. "Although it saddens me, I knew in my heart they were all gone, and I will never have graves to visit. But what about Galenka, did you find any family of hers? Did you find the Isaac Levin from Penzburg I told you about?"

The woman shook her head. "We found two other Galenka's registered at Dachau, and it appears both died about a year apart before you arrived. The woman you knew, we could find no living relatives from any camp with the records we have right now. We did find an Isaac Levin registered into Flossenburg about the time you were sent to Dachau. However, there is nothing after that. We do not know if he died in the camp or was killed in the quarry, or whether he in fact survived the war. There just are no records."

Nodding her head, Sarah glanced down at the floor for a minute. Looking back at the counselor she began. "I am ready to leave this place, I want to go home now. How do I get released from here?"

The woman shook her head. "Sarah, you have no home to go back to. Odds are after you left your home was given to an Aryan family that was resettled in Straubing. We cannot return the home to you, it's theirs under German law, and the agreement the Allies have signed."

"That is not right, it was our home, my father and mother purchased it. It does not belong to someone else. It belongs to me now," Sarah replied angrily.

"I'm sorry, Sarah. The house, if it was not destroyed in the fighting, belongs to another family now, and you cannot go there and attempt to throw them out. You must understand, some of the rules and laws created under the Third Reich still exist and probably will for a long time. The Allied Military Government has a strict plan of deNazification, but it does not include all the laws right now. So, we need to find some sort of plan for you. Would you like to go to the United States, Israel, or Great Britain? We are giving children first chance at resettlement. As you are thirteen, we would find a nice

Jewish family to take you in. It would not be a problem in the United States or Israel, but it could take a bit longer if you chose Great Britain." The woman informed her with a warm smile.

"No, no, I belong here. Here is where I grew up. Here is where my ancestors are buried and here is where I want to rebuild my life. I shall remain in Germany," Sarah replied confidently.

Leaning back in her chair, the counselor frowned. "Sarah, you do not understand the bigger picture here. All across Europe, thousands of people are attempting to return to their homes from prisoner of war camps, or internment camps such as yourself, or slave labor camps. None of them know if their homes are going to exist when they arrive, or what they are going to do when they get there. Europe today is a huge displaced persons continent, with literally millions of people going every direction under the stars, unsure of what will happen to them. We cannot just throw a thirteen-year-old girl into that mess without any plans, or anyone to take care of you. It simply can't be done."

Sarah was about to explode when the thought of Galenka's words came into her heart. After a moment of thought Sarah replied. "Then we must find a way. Let me go to Straubing and see what happened to our home. If it's gone, then we will come up with another plan. But I must at least see my home. Please let me do that."

Shaking her head, the counselor looked at Sarah. "I do understand why you want to do that, but it may just pile hurt on top of hurt. Give me a few days, and let me see what I can do."

A week later, Sarah was called back to the office. The counselor she had worked with was standing beside two military police officers. "Sarah, these officers are patrolling the roads between here and Regensburg. I worked it out so you can ride with them to check out your home. Now I have jumped through a lot of hoops to make this work, so please cooperate with them."

Sarah felt like crying as she realized her wish had come true, but refused to let down her guard. Once they passed through Landshut, everything began to look familiar, and there was little battle damage. Reaching the outskirts of Straubing, Sarah began having a hard time breathing as her pulse quickened. She directed the police officers to the street where her family home had stood. To her amazement, everything appeared to be just as they left it, with the exception of two little children playing in the front yard.

Getting out of the jeep, Sarah and the two police officers slowly walked up to the house. As they approached, a well-dressed, thirty something woman walked out the front door.

"Can I help you, is there a problem?" she inquired, as she gathered her two children close.

Sarah shook, unsure of what to say as she just stared at the house. One of the military police officers touched her shoulder and said. "Go ahead, Sarah."

"This house, this place is where I grew up. I lived here until the S.S. soldiers took us away. I am a Jew, my family was Jewish," Sarah explained.

The woman stood motionless for a moment as she looked at Sarah. "I have been afraid since the war ended that this might happen. But this is our home now, the government gave it to us when they moved us here. It is where we are raising our children. It is our home, and you must go."

Before Sarah could reply, a tall man drove up in a beat-up Mercedes. "Becky, what is going on? Why is the American Army here?" The man yelled out angrily.

"Donald, this girl says this was her house before they were deported, she is a Jew. I think she wants it back," Becky responded in a nervous voice.

"No, that will not happen. The government gave us the house when I was assigned as the gauleiter for Straubing. According to the surrender plan as I understand it, we cannot be thrown out. I am asking you to leave our home," the irritated husband replied as he glared at Sarah.

Sarah's cheeks began to turn red and burn with anger after listening to the husband rant. Taking a deep breath, Sarah responded. "No, I do not want the house back, it is yours. I had to see if anyone was living in it. But before I go, can I walk through it one more time?"

"No, I do not want you in my home! Officers, please remove her and let us live our lives. It is not right that a Jewess comes here and makes life miserable for us. We lost the war and now our country is suffering. Have we not paid a large enough price already?" The husband screamed as he glared at Sarah.

Not wanting the confrontation, Sarah turned to leave with the officers. Before she could reach the road, the woman called out. "Stop!"

Walking up to Sarah, she continued. "What is your name? How old are you?"

"I am Sarah Rosenbaum, I am thirteen years old. I was just seven when they took us away. It was on my birthday."

The woman placed her hands over her face as tears ran down her cheeks. "The cake in the upper cupboard, that was your birthday cake?"

Nodding her head, Sarah fought back tears. "Yes, I wanted to see it so badly, but my mother told me to wait until my father came home. But he never came. He had been arrested and taken to Dachau, and we never ate another meal here. By the end of the day we were on a filthy train headed north, and my father was already dead."

Before Sarah could say another word, the woman threw her arms around her tightly as she wept. After a moment, the woman pulled away, wiping tears from her face. "If you wish to see the house you may. Come with me."

Before they entered the house, her husband blocked the doorway. "I will not allow a Jew into my home. Becky, this is against the law."

One of the military police officers stepped forward, looking angry and ready for a fight. "Sir, those laws of ethnic purity went out the window when you lost the war. Part of my job is to report government officials that are not working to denatzify the country. If you persist, I may have to place you under arrest and take you to Munich."

Swallowing hard, the man glared angrily at the officer as he stepped aside. "No, that will not be necessary. She may walk through the house if she would like. It's fine with me."

Sarah slowly followed Becky into the living room. Although the position of some of the furniture was changed, everything else was the same, including the large paintings on the walls. She gasped slightly when she saw her mother standing by the door to the kitchen, wearing her bloody striped uniform from Buchenwald. On the second floor, Sarah was caught off guard as Rose's frozen spirit came out of her bedroom and gazed at her with hollow eyes. Jonathon sat on the bed in his room with a book in his hands. He motioned for her to come and join him, but she could not as she gazed at his shaved head and bloody clothing. Looking down into the backyard, she saw her father tending to the rose bushes he loved so much, with a noose still tied around his neck. He smiled and waved before returning to the roses. Feeling very sick, she turned toward Becky and said, "I have seen enough I must go, it's time to leave."

Sarah felt very weak and nauseated as they walked out of the house. Becky took her by the arm, looking intently into her eyes, "Are you alright? You look very pale."

After gulping in several breaths of fresh air, Sarah replied. "No, I will never be alright, nor will my family, nor will this house, nor will the world as the ghosts of my past seek peace and a place to rest. Everything has been turned upside down and there is no bringing it back. I hope you enjoy the house. Teach your children well and know that you have made me come to grips with my future, I will never forget that." Turning to Becky's husband, Sarah continued. "I hope you can find peace in your life. That is all we ever wanted here, and we lost it all, you and your government took it all from us."

After smiling once more at Becky, Sarah quickly turned and walked back to the jeep with the officers. As she sat down, she was forced by a strange power to look back. In the windows, she could see the blank faces of her family staring back at her, void of any emotion. Questioning, forever questioning.

Throughout the long night, Sarah's mind was a whirlwind of thoughts as she contemplated everything that had happened to her over the last few days. Her family was gone, her home now belonged to an anti-Semite who clearly hated her, and there was no word as to what had happened to Isaac. She considered the idea of going to the countries the counselor told her about, but she would be a stranger to everything in England and the United States. At least in Israel, she would know the language and the religion, and would surely be accepted with open arms. But no matter what had happened in Straubing today, all she really wanted was to go back to her childhood home, and live with the ghosts and memories that would forever haunt it.

About six in the morning, Sarah waited for the sentries to begin changing the guard. She knew they always left a gate close to the convent open for several minutes. Taking advantage of the mistake,

Sarah rushed out the gate while running past the hospital as fast as she could.

Finding the railyard, it took her just a few minutes to figure out which train was headed west toward France. She climbed into an empty box car and laid on the small blanket she had brought with her. In short order, the train began leaving Munich, bound for Reims, France.

During the trip, Sarah ate several cookies and a couple pieces of fruit she had gathered in her room for just such an occasion. Although the train made several stops along the way, no one checked the empty cars or bothered her.

Arriving in Reims, Sarah jumped off the car just as the train came to a stop. She dashed across several sets of rails before arriving near a former passenger depot, now under control of the United States Army. A sentry near the depot spotted her instantly, calling out for her to stop or he would shoot. Realizing the nervous soldier might very well carry out his threat, Sarah stopped and raised her hands.

In seconds, several other soldiers arrived taking Sarah into custody, walking her to the office of their commander. In the waiting room, clerks pounded on typewriters and answered ringing phones that never seemed to stop. Shortly, a young woman in an Army uniform walked up to her.

"Miss Rosenbaum, will you please come with me. We are going to meet Colonel Watson, the resettlement officer here in Reims."

Walking into the large office, Sarah felt like she had been in this situation way too many times over the past few years, and it made her physically sick.

Colonel Watson pointed to a chair as he sat down behind his large wooden desk. "Well, Miss Rosenbaum, according to your paperwork you have been assigned to a displaced persons camp for young children in Munich. You seem to be completely lost. What are you doing here in Reims?"

Sarah stood up and walked slowly over to the window overlooking a small courtyard. After a moment of thought she turned to face the colonel. "We are not displaced persons, we are Jews, we are human beings. We went from one death camp to another, and now we are herded like animals into your so-called displaced persons camps. What happens if you cannot find a place for us? What happens when nobody wants us around? You will not let us go back to our homes the government took from us, I found that out first hand. What will you do with us in the end when there is no place for us to go? Will you just finish Hitler's work?"

Colonel Watson jumped up from his chair totally enraged. "Miss Rosenbaum, I could have sent you back the minute you were caught. Instead, I brought you here so we could discuss your case firsthand. If you want to compare the American Army to Hitler's forces, then I can still send you back today. I'm here to help you, not take away your dignity or freedom."

Sarah looked up at the ceiling, fighting back tears she had vowed never to shed again. But this time there was just no holding them back. As they forced their way down Sarah's soft cheeks, she turned to look at the colonel. "You speak English and German, I speak German and Hebrew. What makes us so different? Tell me Herr Colonel. Someone needs to tell me why I'm so different!"

"We aren't different, Sarah. We are each people made by God. I cannot even come close to understanding what you and your people went through. All I can say is that those that did this are not my people, or those of my fellow Americans. So, let us start over please. Why are you in Reims?" The colonel inquired, as he attempted to regain his composure.

Sitting down, Sarah looked at the Colonel. "When I was finally captured by the Nazis, we had been hiding in Paris for a long period of time, before we moved south to Marmande with plans to cross the Spanish border to freedom. I was with four other people, one was a woman named Anna who had a very young daughter Isabelle. They tried to run but were shot while Isaac Levin and I were captured. Records indicate he entered Flossenburg, but there is no record if he survived. The other young man was named Ishmael, he is about thirty but looks much younger. He was able to get away that day. I came here to look for him, but I don't know his last name. Maybe he made it to Spain."

Colonel Watson shook his head. "I think I have nearly one hundred Ishmael's in my records. Most of them have already been sent back to resettlement camps in Germany, or he may have wandered off, as we were not able to hold everyone properly at first. But honestly, Sarah, he may not have made it through the war. He may have been killed a long time ago, and we would have no record of that. Without a last name there is just no way to help you. Plus, I cannot allow you to wander around France looking for a ghost. I know there are countless thousands of people wandering around Europe. Sadly, some of them will be lost forever. But no matter how you look at things, you are one of the lucky ones. Your age brought you to a camp in Munich where we can help you. We can find you a home, we can send you away from here to a better place. It's all your decision. Just let us know what you want."

Sarah was quiet for a few minutes as she thought over everything the colonel had explained. "Send me back to Munich, I want to go back there to start over."

The following morning, Sarah was driven back to the train station along with a female military police officer. They took a seat in the terminal as they were about forty-five minutes early. Near the ticketing counter, several men became involved in a shoving match. Quickly, the female MP jumped up, looking at Sarah. "Stay put, I'll be right back!"

As Sarah watched her attempt to break up the escalating disturbance, a hand came down on her shoulder from behind. A familiar voice said, "Child, you survived!"

Spinning around quickly, she saw Ishmael, now with a short haircut, and the beginning of a nice beard. For a moment she was not sure what to say or do, as she knew the officer would be back in a few minutes.

Ishmael nodded his head toward the side door, "Run like the wind, daughter, I will catch you. Run Sarah, I have a plan."

Just as Sarah stood up to run, the officer ran back yelling, "HALT! HALT DAMN IT!"

The angry officer quickly gave chase as she blew on her whistle for back up. As she neared the door, catching up with Sarah, Ishmael pushed a janitor's cart in front of her, causing her to lose her balance and fall. Turning, he swiftly charged out the door following Sarah through a parking lot filled with military vehicles, and into a commercial area where they slowed to a walk to blend in with the crowd. After reaching a park, they sat on a bench to catch their breath.

Sarah looked intently at Ishmael. "You also thankfully survived.

Where did you go when we were captured? I thought I would never see you or Isaac ever again."

Ishmael smiled. "I left Paris and came as far as here. I found some people that were hiding Jews. They took me in, dressed my wounds, and kept me safe until the Americans passed through. Since then, I have been doing odd jobs while securing and passing information between French, German and American people, and even several from Israel. It pays very, very well indeed. Last night I was told of this young girl who arrived alone on a train from Munich and was now in custody. The description and age matched you rather closely. This morning, I paid a French police officer to get me the name of this girl and where she was going. He told me the girls name was Sarah Rosenbaum and that you were going back to Munich this morning under U.S. Army guard. I thought it must be you, so I needed to find out, and see if that was what you really wanted."

After giving Ishmael a hug, she smiled. "Actually, yes and no. I thought I would go back and take the offer to go to Israel, and be placed with a Jewish family. But the other part of me wanted to find you and Isaac, but I'm afraid Isaac never made it out of Flossenburg. So now at least I have found you. Tell me Ishmael, what is your plan?"

Smiling, Ishmael placed his arm around Sarah's shoulder. "By the hand of God there is a ship leaving Le Havre supposedly for Alexandria, Egypt in two weeks. But in all honesty, it will dock at Beirut, Lebanon, from where we can get into Israel. I have already booked passage for myself, but I can get you on board to share my stateroom if you should desire to join me. I will list you as my little sister on the manifest, and no one will question it. Once we are there, I know a man that will put us up and get us real documents. He was a business man from Israel that was here doing business in France when the Germans came. He was not able to leave, but survived under Vichy government protection. The night I ran from Paris, the Germans were closing in on him. I killed one Gestapo agent helping him avoid capture, and then took him to safety with me, and found a way to get him to southern France. He is now home in Jerusalem, and he will help us anyway he can. So, either way you can get to Israel, but with me you will be safe, and always have a friend. Your choice, Sarah," Ishmael explained slowly.

Without hesitation, Sarah nodded her head. "I will go with you,

I trust you as you saved my life more than once. Can you hide me until then?"

Ishmael laughed, that loud confident laugh Sarah had been used to so long ago. "Yes, my child, you can stay in my small place until we go. It's not much, and I will need to keep working, so I will be in and out, but you will be safe, dry, and have food to eat."

For the first time since leaving Dachau, Sarah slept well that night, knowing she was safe, and with a good friend that would die for her if that's what it took.

Nine days later with newly forged paperwork, Sarah and Ishmael boarded a train for Le Havre. Ishmael needed to comfort Sarah when she realized the car they would be on was filled mostly with American and British Army staff, and a few military police officers. Ishmael kept telling her, "You cleared the document check before we walked on this train, no one here will suspect you or question you, just relax and try not to look so scared, little sister."

Arriving at Le Havre, Sarah was relieved when they were able to get right on board the ship, and not have to be around military people from all over the allied world. As she sat outside their cabin, she wondered what kind of trouble had befallen the M.P. that was supposed to accompany her on the train to Munich. Even more, she wondered how angry Col. Watson must have been after all he went through with her. But now her future was beginning to look brighter, and she was back with Ishmael and that was all that mattered.

As the ropes holding the old steamer to its pier fell away, Sarah leaned against the railing watching Le Havre and all of Europe begin to disappear into the morning fog. She felt like she was still in the middle of a bad dream and not quite awake yet, as it appeared the spirits of her family were standing on the pier, quietly watching her sail away. Everything she ever loved was slipping away in the heavy mist, never to be seen again. The true evil of what she had experienced was always just a thought away, always attempting to pull her back into a fear like no other on earth. But now she had escaped the bonds of her homeland, along with the ghosts of her family and friends. What was to come could only be better, and she found herself praying to Galenka to help her find a new path.

The seas were calm as the steamer made its turn into the straights of Gibraltar. She was surprised to see so many ships sailing single file in both directions. Most of them were warships from various nations, painted different shades of a dull gray.

Sailing across the aqua-blue Mediterranean, the temperatures were rather warm and comfortable. But at times the strong southerly winds created larger waves that crashed up against the bow, rolling the ship from side to side. Ishmael nervously attempted to keep track of where they were every day, as there was always a chance that British warships would stop the freighter to inspect the cargo and passenger manifest. If undocumented Jews were found on board, the ship would be forced back to where it came from. The British were doing everything they could to stop the flow of Jews from Europe into Palestine, so as not to upset the population majority in the British mandated area. London knew full well there was already a movement in place for the creation of the Jewish state of Israel, and they understood the negative impact that would have on the Arab population in Palestine.

Ishmael became somewhat calmer as they sailed past Algeria and Libya, but once again became noticeably nervous as they neared Egypt. This was where British warships operated day and night, stopping freighters heading for Tel Aviv, Haifa or Beirut. It was evident they had been busy as six old steamers were either floating at anchor, or were slowly sailing in circles as they awaited a decision as to whether they could enter one of the ports, or be sent back to where they came from.

Observing the situation and not wishing to deal with the British Navy, the captain turned the freighter hard to the north. He kept the ship on that course throughout the night before turning back toward the southeast and the port of Beirut, Lebanon.

At noon on the final day of the trip, the old steamer tied up against a pier in Beirut. Sarah took in the view with awe and wonder as she had never seen a country such as this. All along the pier, dark skinned men wearing turbans or headscarves worked with antiquated equipment to unload the ship, while teams of men used camels and horse drawn wagons to move cargo through the dusty streets. Far off in the distance, she could hear a man chanting over a loud speaker as strange music played in the background. Near the pier, women dressed in bright colored clothing wearing veils, sat at tables selling their wares to ship passengers that were coming and going. Sarah was fascinated as she took in this new culture she was seeing for the first time.

Later in the afternoon, Ishmael and another man Sarah had seen quite often since they boarded the ship approached. Smiling, Ishmael looked intently at Sarah. "So, little sister, what do you think of this new world."

"I'm not sure, Ishmael. I certainly did not know what to expect, but this is so different from France and Germany. As you say, it's a new world," Sarah replied, as she continued watching everything that was taking place around the ship.

Placing his hand on Sarah's shoulder, Ishmael began. "Sarah, this is Micah, he belongs to a group in Palestine known as the Haganah. It's one of three underground groups fighting the British in Palestine. They control a sector of the border you are going to cross tonight. Once across the border in Palestine, you will go to the city of Nahariya. There you will get the proper papers you need to stay and live in Palestine, so the British will leave you alone." Turning Sarah to face him, he continued. "And here child, our relationship shall probably end forever. Micah and some other Jewish refugees will travel with you to start your new life. I have been offered a new job I cannot tell you about, as it is very much a special secret. So, I'll be leaving you and Beirut the moment you are safely on your way. Micah has lined up a nice Jewish family for you to live with. They are good people, and will treat you well. I shall miss you my child, and hope you find the peace and love you deserve. Now that I have delivered you to the land of our people, I can feel great peace, and my mission is over."

Grabbing Sarah, the two hugged each other as tears rolled down their cheeks. Shaking her head, Sarah half-smiled. "I keep telling myself I have cried an ocean of tears and must stop, but at times like this I cannot help myself. I shall miss you, Ishmael. You have always been so strong, so smart, and never let me down, no matter how foolish I was. I will do everything I can to make a good life for myself, but I shall never forget you or what we have been through. Still, I believe our paths will cross again someday, and I hope that is true."

Ishmael hugged Sarah once more as he gave her a kiss on the forehead. "Little one, it's alright to cry, to share your pain or your happiness. It's a human emotion that is cleansing to the soul. No matter how many tears you have cried, there will always be one more reason to add to that ocean. You must trust me on that. Do not be afraid to share your emotions ever."

Leaving the ship, Sarah waved back to Ishmael before following Micah and ten other people to a run-down bus that sat just off the pier. In minutes, the rattling, smoke belching wreck was on the road driving out of Beirut. As they neared the Palestinian border, the driver left the main road, driving several miles into the desert where the road ended. After pulling out a rifle from behind his seat, Micah led the group about a mile on foot where they came to a barbwire fence that had been cut in several places. After taking a good look around, Micah directed them toward a path leading them deeper into Palestine, where several of his armed men waited with a truck.

About an hour later the lights of Nahariya lit up the dark night sky. Sarah thought the lights of the city shimmering off the calm waters of the Mediterranean a beautiful sight, as they drove along the coast road. Finally, the truck drove into a small orchard where everyone disembarked. Micah led them into a small warehouse where fruit was being packed in crates. In a back room, several men and women wasted no time preparing the documents each person would need. When it was Sarah's turn, a kindly looking woman smiled at her.

"So, you are Sarah. You can keep your first name as it is very appropriately Jewish. The family that is taking you in has the last name of Pearlman. So, you will be known as Sarah Pearlman from now on. You will have a younger brother by the name of Matthias, who really is the child of the Pearlman family. You will be attending a good Jewish school, where you can catch up with the education you have lost over the years. Do you have questions for me?"

Sarah was overwhelmed with everything that was happening, and was having a hard time realizing this all could be for real. Smiling at the woman, Sarah shook her head. "No, I'm just so tired. Is there somewhere I can sleep?"

"We can fix that also," the woman replied as she led Sarah into a storage room next door, where other women and girls were sleeping. You will spend the rest of the night here, and meet your family in the morning. If you have any questions, please ask one of us," the woman said, as she led Sarah to a bunk in the corner of the room.

The following morning, Micah drove Sarah to a nice home on a bluff overlooking the Mediterranean. As the car came to a stop, a young couple and a small boy walked from the home. As Sarah exited the vehicle, Micah said, "Sarah, this is Yoram, Sariya and Matthias Pearlman, your new family."

Sariya hugged Sarah right away, dispelling some of the worries Sarah had considered throughout the long night. As Yoram worked for British Petroleum, it was evident the family lived a higher class of life than Sarah had ever been accustomed to. They took her shopping for a completely new wardrobe, since the little clothing she had was badly worn. They purchased her a wrist watch, a black coral necklace and several other necklaces to go with her new clothing. But what interested Sarah most, was the amount of food they had in the house. She had never seen so much food in one house in her life time.

As Sarah laid in her own comfortable bed one night, Matthias walked into her room. Approaching the bed, he looked at Sarah with interest. "Father says you were in a place called Dachau and that you were tortured. Why did they do that to you?"

Sarah smiled at Matthias as she reached out to take his hand. After kissing him on the forehead, she slid over in bed allowing him to climb up next to her. "Matthias, you are too young to understand what all happened, and I am glad you never experienced it. But those were bad times, and the people that kept us there were very bad people. They are all gone now, so you never have to worry about them. Some day when you get older, we can have a long talk, and I will tell you the entire story. Is that alright with you?"

Matthias smiled. "Yes, as long as you will continue being my sister, I really like you."

Sarah smiled, while giving Matthias a hug. "And I love you very much. Now, go back to bed and get some sleep, and don't worry, I will always be your big sister no matter what. I promise."

With that, Matthias slid out from the covers and dashed away. But Sarah knew what she had told him was not true. Most of the people that had run the camps were not gone, they were still out there hating Jews, and would do it all over again if given the chance. Just the thought of that made her shiver. Many nights like tonight when she closed her eyes, the faces of Klaus Barbie, Corporal Barnard, Lt. Rouchmann and Professor Felix sneered back at her. The dreams she hated the most were those involving Sgt. Wilhelm. She could smell him, remembering the way his rough beard scratched her cheek. She could still feel the excruciating pain he had caused her. Throughout everything she endured by the Nazis, he was the most evil and despicable of them all, and she wanted him to pay for what he had done to her, understanding Galenka would disapprove of her desire for vengeance.

When she was but a little girl, her mother had told her many times that revenge is the sweetest morsel to the mouth that was ever cooked in hell. That probably was accurate, but regrettably, most nights Sarah laid awake thinking about how she could get revenge for all they had done to her and to countless others. She had been to hell, she had seen evil beyond evil, and understood hate better than most people on earth. Somehow, someway she would get revenge, no matter how much more it destroyed her soul. There had to be a way to bring those people to justice for her family, Galenka, Raizel, Hadar and everyone who had paid such a horrible price.

Still, on the other hand, she heard the words of Galenka over and over, telling her to forgive, and that living would be the biggest slap in the face to every S.S. soldier that had worked in the camps, because now they would have to fear a child forever. It was times like this that Sarah understood what the women of barracks fifteen had tried to teach her. She could see Galenka smiling at her, as she whispered, "Peace, my child, walk with God, he will show you what needs to be done and when. Let him strike down the enemies of Israel on his own time."

Chapter Fifteen
Constant Reminders

Ishmael had been right, the Pearlman family was good to Sarah in every way possible. They loved her and provided everything a growing teenage girl in Palestine could want. However, the problems between the Palestinians and the Jewish people bothered her immensely. She had seen firsthand what was possible when people let anger and mistrust boil over. She had come to know and like several Palestinian girls, and found no differences that would cause her to mistrust or despise them.

By 1948, Sarah was doing well in school and had totally adjusted to her new life. She had no second thoughts regarding her move to Palestine or becoming part of the Pearlman family.

It also was a special time in the lives of the Jewish people, as they were about to declare their independence and become the sovereign nation of Israel. Sarah's sixteenth birthday on May 10th, was overshadowed by the declaration of independence on May 14 by their new Prime Minister, David Ben-Gurion. Sarah joined in the celebration and was proud to see their new national flag flying from poles and buildings all over her adopted home land of Israel.

However, the joy of independence and the feeling of freedom was short lived for Sarah when all the memories of the Nazi S.S. troops and Dachau were brought back to life.

During the month of June on a school outing to Jerusalem, their bus was hijacked by two Egyptian terrorists. They shoved the driver off the bus and told the teacher to stay seated where she was in the front seat, before they secured the door. There was little doubt in Sarah's mind that these brutal terrorists were no different than the S.S. soldiers she had come to know and hate in Germany. One of the terrorists walked down the center aisle of the bus, slapping or striking each child as he laughed. As the children huddled against each other crying, Sarah sat erect in her seat, glaring at the terrorist, refusing to be intimidated.

The man walked back toward the front of the bus, removing a hand grenade from the bag they had placed on the driver's seat. Walking back a few rows, he looked directly at Sarah as he pulled the pin, tossing it onto the floor where it bounced down onto the steps. Holding the grenade just inches from Sarah's face, he yelled, "How brave are you now, you Jewish bitch!"

Without blinking an eye, Sarah grabbed the man's hand with her right hand, while thrusting a newly sharpened pencil deep into his throat with her left. Blood gushed from the wound, splattering Sarah across her arms, face and chest. Using both hands, Sarah pulled the grenade free from the dying man, while jumping from her seat.

She rushed forward to the front of the bus, just as the second terrorist was attempting to pull his pistol from its holster. Using all her body weight she pushed the grenade tight against the man's chest. Staring into the terrorist's frightened eyes, Sarah spoke calmly.

"I have died a thousand times, but each time I was reborn as me. Each time I visited death, it became clear that there is nothing to fear, it is a natural part of life. I fear nothing, as the God of Israel is watching over me. Tell me, who is watching over you? Has he told you to do this, has he prepared you to die with a grenade to your chest? Think about that for a moment. Are you ready to die here with me today? Shall we let the grenade explode, and then see if the doctors can tell who was Jewish and who was an Arab. I think they will just shove us in a box and bury our remains, maybe even together. Would you like spending eternity with a Jewish bitch?"

The man shook almost uncontrollably, allowing his pistol to drop to the floor. Sweat ran down his dark brown unshaven face. His eyes widened as he stared at Sarah's cold dull eyes and her blood covered facial features.

"I do not wish to die, please spare me, have you no fear of dying this day?" He mumbled as his breathing became more labored.

Sarah pushed her hands harder against the terrorist's chest. "Spare you? Were you and your friend going to spare a bus load of Jewish children? No, I do not think so, I think you meant to kill us all with the bomb you have in that bag. You are so brave around children, but now when you face death, you cry like the coward you are. No, I am not afraid to die, this day or any day. As I said, I have died many times and the God of Israel will be there for me if it must be so today."

Outside the bus, soldiers from the Israeli Defense Force stared through the windows in the door, helplessly unsure of what to make of the situation. One of the officers called toward Sarah several times, but she continued to ignore him.

She shook her head. "A brave woman named Galenka once told me that I need to forgive, that I need to let the God of Israel give me strength to do the right thing. I need to stop the hate, but did you see what I did to your friend? I did not stop the hate, I did not stop the hate with him, does it stop here with you?"

Giving a quick glance to her teacher, Sarah called out, "Free up the door!"

In an instant, the woman was out of her seat prying out the wooden shim the men had used to secure the door. Grabbing hold of the control arm, she pulled the door open and jumped out.

As two soldiers prepared to enter the bus, Sarah yelled at them. "Stay away, get out. This is not finished!"

Removing her left hand from the grenade, she took hold of the terrorist's shirt. "Turn and back down the stairs one step at a time and do not attempt to pull free."

"Yes, yes, whatever you say," the man mumbled, as he continued keeping eye contact with Sarah.

When they had cleared the bottom step, Sarah pushed the terrified man to the ground. "Galenka has won this battle for you, and it is she that allows you to live today. I don't know why, but she does."

Turning to face a soldier, she motioned to the steps with her left hand. "Please get the pin."

Seconds later, the soldier returned, carefully placing the pin back into the handle of the grenade, while spreading the ends of the pin apart, so it could not fall back out by accident.

Quickly, more soldiers rushed onto the bus, removing the body of the dead Egyptian and helping the children off. Sarah was escorted over to a military ambulance, where a medic washed the blood from her face and arms. When he was finished, he reached into a small duffel bag, withdrawing a neatly folded Israeli military shirt.

"Go into the cab of my truck, wash your chest and shoulder and change your blouse. The shirt may be a bit big, but it is all that I have for you."

When Sarah returned, she threw the bloody garment onto the ground. As she kicked sand over it, she watched the children climb onto another bus that had just arrived. When she began to walk toward the bus, the medic took hold of her arm.

"I'm sorry, Sarah, but you will have to stay here until our officers debrief you. We will then get you home to your family. They will be told where you are," the kindly medic explained.

Nodding her head, Sarah sat down on the rear of the truck by the soldier. As the last child boarded the bus, the man placed his hand on her shoulder. "You know it's okay to cry after what you have been through."

Turning toward the young soldier, Sarah explained. "I've cried enough tears to fill the Red Sea over its banks. Even Moses could not get to the bottom of the tears I have wept in my lifetime, to part them like he did the sea. But today they did drown one more of Pharaoh's soldiers, and that is enough for me. No tears from me will change anything that happened today."

Quickly picking up on Sarah's German accent, the medic leaned over and kissed her on the cheek. "Welcome home, child. Our land is your land, your pain is our pain, may we live as one."

Dusk was just settling over Nahariya, when a small black van pulled up to the front of the Pearlman home. Sariya and Yoram ran to the van, grabbing hold of Sarah as she stepped out. Walking into the house, Sarah went straight to her room where she sat on her bed.

Sariya placed her hand on Sarah's cheek. "My love, you still have some blood in your hair. Why don't you go bathe, I will toss this shirt and you can put on one of your new blouses, then we can have something to eat."

Removing the uniform shirt, she held it to her chest. "Mother, I do not want this shirt thrown away. I wish to keep it forever."

Nodding her head, Sariya smiled. "As you wish, Sarah."

That evening, as Sarah lay in bed, something did not feel right. Sitting up, she gazed at what appeared to be an apparition in the corner of the room. Without hesitating, she whispered, "Galenka, is that you?"

Very slowly the apparition disappeared, as a strange feeling of calm came over her. Smiling, she folded her arms across her chest. "I am not afraid, Galenka, I know it's you. I'm sorry I killed that man today, it's not what you tried to teach me. But I could find no other way, I had to save the children. I could not let more children be killed as in Dachau. Forgive me, and help me find the strength that I know is inside of me."

After several moments of quiet thought, Sarah opened up her copy of the Torah she now kept by her bed, and began reading the book of Shemot, more commonly known as Exodus.

When time allowed, Sarah loved swimming in the Mediterranean with Mathias or her friends. The water was so clear and warm it soothed every nerve in her body. When school let out in the summer of 1949, Sarah was given a late birthday gift, allowing her to stay with the family of her friend Hila, who lived right on the coast for two weeks. Another girl by the name of Rina was also there. From sun up to sun set the girls swam, snorkeled, played on the beach, and talked about the boys they had met in school that year.

Late one evening as Sarah and Hila strolled the beach, they noticed a young man who had been watching them for quite some time. Feeling nervous, Hila decided to go home, but for some reason Sarah was captivated by the way he played cat and mouse with them along the shore.

After Hila had left, Sarah picked up a broken boat oar and hid among several over turned fishing boats. As the young man crept past looking for her, Sarah slid out from under one of the boats, tripping him with the oar. As he tumbled to the sand, Sarah pounced on his back, raising the heavy section of the oar over her head.

"What do you want with us?" Sarah screamed, as she held the oar ready to strike.

Holding his arms out to the side the man said calmly. "I am not armed, I will not hurt you. Sarah, is it really you?"

Sarah gasped as she shook her head. "Isaac? I was told he never made it out of Flossenburg. Who are you really?"

"Sarah, get off my back and allow me to roll over so you can see my face. It's me, Sarah!" the young man spoke softly

After thinking it over for a moment, Sarah got off the man's back and moved away several feet, keeping the oar ready to swing if she felt threatened.

Slowly rising up from the sand, the man kept his arms straight out so she could see he was unarmed. Before turning to face Sarah, he said, "Do not be afraid."

Sarah gasped when she looked at his face. A long scar ran from his left ear almost to his mouth. His nose had been broken so badly it was now crooked and pushed off to the right. His right eye looked out from an eye socket that had been broken and mended badly without surgery, making him appear to have a continuous squint. His forehead had several large scars running back up to his scalp.

Dropping the oar, Sarah stepped forward, placing her hand on the long scar on his cheek.

"Isaac, it is you. I looked for you, they told me you died in Flossenburg."

Isaac nodded his head. "I was in Mauthausen working in the quarries. It was tough hard work, but it did not bother me. As the war came closer to the end, the few safety measures we had went by the wayside. I was hit in the face when a large section of granite broke lose. When the doctor at Mauthausen decided he could do no more for me, I was sent to Flossenburg. But everything was in total confusion as the Germans were trying to get out, and no one was keeping accurate records. I ran from the infirmary as fast as I could, my face still covered in bandages. After hiding behind a truck for several minutes, I ran toward a gate several guards had left open. Before I knew it, I was out of the camp. Over the next few days, I killed several German soldiers with a pitch fork I found in an old barn, before I was captured by the Russians. After they heard my story, they felt sorry for me. They sent me to a hospital where they did what they could, but their resources were bleak and their doctors totally untrained. However, it was still a good deal, because after spending several weeks there I was getting my strength back. Then one day the hospital was going to move farther west. The doctor gave me some pain medication, food and a pistol, and wished me the best of luck. So, I headed back toward southern Germany, hoping to get behind the American or British lines before the war ended.

Sarah took Isaac into her arms and gave him a hug. "How did you get here? Did Ishmael help you? He was the one that saved me."

Isaac shook his head. "I have not seen Ishmael since the night we were captured. When I arrived in Berlin nearly a month after starting my trip south, I was arrested after sneaking into the American Zone. Since I was a displaced person from a concentration camp, they wanted to hear my story. So, I sat with American investigators for several days, telling them all about what we went through and who was involved, in trade for a free trip to Israel. So, here I am. I found a job working here in the Marina once I arrived. The owner's son died in Dachau, so he was most gracious to me. I have seen you and your friends several times over the past few weeks, but I was afraid to walk up to you. I was afraid you would still be angry with me for everything that happened when we were captured."

Sarah smiled as she shook her head. "My dear Isaac, all that happened in another life time in another place, where all we wanted was survival, and we made many mistakes. No, I could never be angry with you. I'm just so happy we both survived."

Before returning home, Sarah visited Isaac several more times, discussing their pasts, their future plans, and dreams that they had placed on hold for so long.

The next year went by so fast, Sarah could hardly believe it when she prepared to graduate from school. Like so many other children in her class, Sarah had no doubts about what she wanted to do. She immediately signed up to join the Israeli Defense Force to defend her home land. Although she still harbored a strong anger for the German military establishment, she knew that serving in the Defense Force would be for the good of her country, and not to spread death and tyranny as the German war machine had done.

The day before she left for her training, Sarah walked with her adopted family to a large olive grove just outside of town. Kneeling down, Sarah dug a deep hole with a trowel she had carried with her. When she was satisfied with the hole, she placed a small metal box into it, containing the lock of hair and piece of clothing she had taken from Galenka. Smiling, she looked down at the box. "The dream you had to be buried in Israel is now complete, sweet Galenka. Rest well here knowing you are surrounded by people who love you. As you always wished for fresh olives when we were in the camp, now you have thousands to pick from all around you."

After closing the hole, they held hands, sang songs and prayed the prayers of Kaddish.

About eight months into her enlistment, she was ordered to attend a special training event in Tel Aviv. She was taken to a small conference room where she was told to have a seat and wait. About twenty minutes later, two men and a woman walked into the room. After taking their seats, the woman spoke.

"We are Mossad operatives investigating Nazi war crimes. I am sorry but we cannot give you our identities as of now, but we would like you to look at photos of some war criminals to see if you can identify them." Opening a large manila folder, she pulled out a stack of photos. Removing the top photo, the woman slid it across the table.

"Do you know this man?" she asked, watching Sarah's facial expressions.

Sarah nodded her head. "That is Klaus Barbie, I met him in Paris and in Dachau."

Sliding over a photograph of a man in a business suit, the woman said, "And him?"

After staring at the photo for several minutes, she replied. "No, I do not know him. Who is he? Was he also a concentration camp guard?"

The woman smiled slightly, "I cannot tell you his identity. If you do not know him, that is perfectly fine. But how about this man, do you know him?"

As she slid the photo across the table, Sarah stiffened and let out a shriek. She began to tremble as she stared into the man's evil eyes.

"I know him. He called himself Professor Felix."

The woman watched Sarah intently. "What did he do to you, Sarah?"

Shaking her head, Sarah pushed her chair back from the table. "No, I will not relive it. How dare you show me that photo and ask me to do that. No, I will not talk about him!"

The woman nodded her head as she picked up the photo, placing it face down on the table. Pulling out the next photo, she continued. "Sarah, do you know this woman?"

Sliding her chair back toward the table, she nodded her head. "She is pure evil, her name is S.S. Captain Herald. She was involved with torturing prisoners in Paris. I watched her shoot a man named Malachi in the head as if he was a pig ready for slaughter. They tortured him, hung him from the ceiling by his wrists, and tried to make me shoot him. When I would not, she finished the job. Both her and Professor Felix need to burn in hell!"

After giving Sarah a chance to collect herself, the woman slid a small stack of photos over to her. "Do you know any of these men?"

Slowly, Sarah looked at each photo. Stopping at the third photo she handed it back to the woman. "He ran Dachau when I was there, I shall never forget the monster." Stopping at the sixth photo, her hands began to shake as sweat poured down her face. Biting her bottom lip, Sarah fought hard to hold back her tears as she pounded her fists on the photo.

"You bastard, you bastard," she continued to scream, until she could no longer hold back the tears. Leaning forward onto the table, she continued to cry uncontrollably.

Quickly, the woman rose from her chair and knelt down beside Sarah. "Shhh, it's alright, Sarah, he will never hurt you again. Tell us where you know him from."

Looking up toward the ceiling, Sarah called out, "I am sorry, Galenka, but I want him dead!"

Sarah leaned sideways, placing her head on the woman's shoulder as she called out, "I want him dead, I want him dead!"

One of the male officers stood up and leaned across the table, looking intently at Sarah.

"What did he do to you?"

Continuing to shake, Sarah stared back at the officer. "He was an S.S. Sergeant in charge of the torture box in the camp. He put me in there several times. At night, he would come around the box to urinate and spit on me. Twice while I was in there, he came with two other men. They dragged me out of the box. One man held me down while the other covered my mouth so no one could hear me scream while he raped me. When he was done the last time, he shoved something inside of me, and then turned on a black box he was holding. The electrical current racing through my body was nothing like I have ever felt before, it was unbearable and they laughed. I must have passed out, because when I came too, I was back in the box again, and everything inside of me hurt terribly. The pain was much worse than anything I felt when Professor Felix tortured me. I bled from my vagina for two days. The guards were surprised the next morning that I was still alive. The day they released me from the box, he told me if I ever whispered a word about the rape, he would make me watch as he killed every woman and child in the barracks. Then I would really have something to remember him for. I never said a word to any of the women, not even Galenka. I have never been more terrified of a person then I was of him. He loved torturing people, especially women, like no one else I have ever met before or since."

After sitting up, she looked intently at the three officers. "So, now that I have shared all of that, I think I should tell you about Professor Felix after all." She explained in detail everything the professor had done to her before turning her over to Capt. Herald. After taking a deep breath, she looked at the Mossad investigators. "Where did the Germans find these people and how could anyone do the things they did? They were monsters!"

Once more, sitting down across from Sarah, the woman handed her the next photo. "And this man, do you know of him?"

Nodding her head, Sarah explained. "That is Corporal Bernard. There were times when he was nice, almost sympathetic. But when the other soldiers were around, he was nearly just as nasty. I think he had to play the game as best he could. I believe he might have wanted to run away if it had been possible. But yes, he was an S.S. Guard at Dachau.

Nodding her head in understanding, the woman smiled slightly. "Sarah, I have just a few more photos for you to look at, then we will discuss something else. Do you know any of these men?"

Within seconds, Sarah identified two more S.S. soldiers from Dachau but was unsure of their names. The last photo she held in her hands for the longest time without speaking, but once more she began to shake.

Immediately, the woman walked over and sat down beside Sarah. "Who is he, Sarah. Tell me who he is and what he did to you."

Sarah bit down hard on her bottom lip. "This is S.S. Capt. Muellor. He forced us out of our home on my seventh birthday. He was very cruel to my mother. When the train broke down and we were laying in the ditch, I watched him shoot two old men in the back of the head for no reason. He and several of his men chased some of us into the forest. When we were hiding in a hole made by a downed tree, I watched him pick up a woman from the ground and shoot her in the face, then stomp on her throat with his boot heel," Sarah said, before looking back at the agents. "Now that you know all of this, what difference does it make all these years later. Look what you have done to me. Was it worth it? Did you enjoy it?"

The woman placed her hand on Sarah's shoulder. "Enjoy? Hardly, Sarah. But there are people that are looking for these animals. We need to have first-hand evidence to the crimes they have committed. And to be totally honest, we were told you might be of big help in identifying some of them, as very few young people survived in Dachau. We were also thinking you might be a great person to be on one of the teams that will hunt them down, if you would be interested."

Sarah frowned, as she looked at the woman. "Please tell me your name, and who told you about me? I need to know these things."

Standing up, the woman walked back to the other side of the table. After placing the photos into a briefcase, she smiled. "As I told you earlier, we cannot tell you our names. You must never know, for your safety and ours. But the man that spoke to us about you is an old friend of yours. You knew him just as Ishmael, but now he is known as Capt. Ishmael Stein of the Mossad Special Operations Department, and he is waiting to talk with you."

Sarah shook her head as she stared at the woman. "Your Hebrew is good, but I detect an accent that would appear to be English. Are you British or American?"

"I cannot tell you any of what you want to know, Sarah, and if you join Mossad you will understand more than I can explain here today."

"So, you are either American CIA, or British MI-5 I presume." After a moment of thought, Sarah looked up at the woman. "Alright, take me to Capt. Stein, I would like to see him." Sarah replied, feeling like a mouse caught in a big trap.

After taking an elevator down two floors below ground level, Sarah was escorted into a dark paneled waiting room where a very stiff woman sat behind a desk wearing an Israeli Army Sergeants uniform. Without saying a word, she pointed to a leather covered chair that sat directly across from her desk. After about a ten-minute wait, the woman stood up and motioned for Sarah to follow her into a brightly lit conference room. The sergeant glared at her. "Sit down, and stay there!"

The woman had barely left when a door on the opposite side of the room opened. Sarah was stunned to see Ishmael standing there in what appeared to be a very expensive suit. What silver hair remained on his head was cut down to about a half inch length. He walked forward toward Sarah with a concerned look on his face. After sitting down next to her, he smiled slightly.

"Much has changed since we parted. What I do now is the most important work I have ever done. I take it seriously, and I demand that from everyone that works within my section. Sarah, I have been tasked with finding German war criminals all across the world. We work with the CIA, MI-5, and several other organizations involved with the same task. We share everything we learn, and we do not care who takes the bastards down. You will have a partner, maybe several partners, and you will never work alone. To be honest, I looked into Isaac, but he turned me down, and I understood his reasons. So, is this a job you would like to be involved in, Sarah?"

Sarah nodded her head. "Yes, Captain, I would like to hunt down these criminals. I will start anywhere you want me to go, and do whatever you feel is best."

That evening, as Sarah tried to sleep, she had terrible nightmares reliving the horrors she had fought so hard to forget since leaving Dachau. But now, every wound was reopened, as if she had been cut with a sharp knife. She was sure that taking this job and bringing these people to justice would help give her closure, but more importantly, it would help capture some of the most evil people on earth.

For the next year, Sarah worked diligently, sorting documents, clipping stories from newspapers from all over the world, while compiling questionnaires and investigative notes from field agents. What she enjoyed most, was being able to walk up to a wall containing photos of German suspects, and marking either captured or dead across their forehead in red.

In the summer of 1950, Ishmael called her into the conference room. "Sarah, we have located Professor Felix and have him under surveillance. He is living in Calcutta, India, and going by the name of Dr. Frank Wilson. He is employed as a neurologist in an Italian operated medical clinic. He arrived in India in 1946, by way of a refugee resettlement program. His false documents were prepared by Odessa in Algeria. He lives with his wife and three children that were also sent to India by Odessa via false British papers. We have no problem with his family, and prefer they not be harmed. However, we want the professor captured and brought back to Germany for trial, however, if that is not possible, his death has been sanctioned by the highest authority, but we will need positive proof he is dead. We have been looking at bringing you up for investigative work, are you willing to start with this case?"

Sarah thought for a moment as she looked over the file Ishmael handed her. Looking into the evil eyes of the professor, the pain she endured returned, as if he had just finished torturing her.

"Yes, I would like to see him brought to justice. Who will I be working with?" Sarah inquired, hoping to capture Professor Felix herself.

Ishmael smiled slightly as he stood up. "Your partner from now on will be an agent named Josiah. He has been a good operative for the last two years. After you take the professor down, a transportation team will package him for delivery. Then you and Josiah will return here to help prepare documents for his trial.

Josiah had grown up in Palestine, and was about ten years older than Sarah. He was a dedicated Mossad officer who had worked with now Prime Minister David Ben-Gurion during the struggle for independence. There was no doubt in Sarah's mind he would be totally professional and could be completely trusted, and ruthless if the job required it.

After boarding an Israeli military plane, Josiah removed a folder from his back pack. He passed several photos to Sarah. "These are the latest photos we have of the professor and his family. They were taken about three months ago during the Easter season." Handing her three more photos, he continued. "This is the home they live in near Howrali, just a short drive to Calcutta. These next photos are of the office building where he has his practice, and the last is the blue French Peugeot he drives to work every day. We would like to grab him at home, but we will do what we need to do. Any questions?"

Sarah shook her head. "I will sleep much better knowing he is in our custody and that he will pay for what he has done."

Arriving in Calcutta, they were greeted by a young woman named Mari, that drove them to a small run-down apartment building several blocks from Professor Felix's home. Two men from the transport team were also there to firm up the operational plan.

Over the next several days, Sarah and Josiah surveilled the home without seeing any signs of life. On the third day, Mari took their neighbors dog for a walk right past the front of the house. She reported back that neither the newspapers or mail had been picked up, and the shades in the windows had not moved since they had started observing.

At ten o'clock that evening, Josiah and two other team members Ishmael decided to send along, named Ira and Caleb, carefully entered the house from a rear deck door. After realizing the house was empty and all the closets had been cleared out, Sarah and Mari joined them looking for any clues as to where they might have gone. Around midnight, Mari walked into the small living room carrying a small piece of paper she had found behind a night stand in the largest bedroom.

"Does anyone know where Diu is located?" she inquired.

Nodding his head, Ira replied. "It's a city on the western coast of India, right off the Gulf of Cambay. It has a rather large sea port. Why?"

"This paper says Diu, with tomorrows date, Midnight Sun, Pakistan. Any ideas?" Mari asked, as she looked around the room.

Caleb jumped up from the floor where he was sorting through documents. "It means a Pakistani registered ship called the Midnight Sun will be sailing from the port of Diu tomorrow. They are running, they caught on to us!"

Josiah looked over at Sarah. "That makes sense. Mari, contact the airfield in Calcutta. Tell them to get the plane ready right away. Tell them we will be there in about an hour, and that we are heading to Diu.

In a little over an hour they were flying west toward Diu. Josiah studied a small map of India's west coast cities provided by one of the pilots. Unfortunately, it was evident the ship could be at any of ten loading terminals inside the busy harbor. Around three in the morning, Mari drove the small van they were able to commandeer from a parking lot at the airport, to a road just outside the port. Sarah scanned all the ships that were either loading or were berthed in the port with her binoculars.

"There it is, the black ship with the white stripes sitting at anchor about fifty feet from shore. The crew on board appears to be very busy, so I'm guessing they're preparing to sail. We need to find out what time that ship sails, and fast." Sarah called out desperately, as her pulse raced.

"Go back toward the small bridge we crossed, there was a small grocery store there. They might have a local newspaper, and they always publish which ships are coming and going over the next day or so," Josiah explained to Mari as she spun the van around.

Returning from the store with a copy of the local paper, Ira smiled, "The Midnight Sun is scheduled to leave at eleven o'clock tomorrow night. Thank goodness we will have some time to put a plan together and hit right after dusk settles in."

During the next day, Sarah and Mari stayed in a small park along the waterfront, watching the ship with binoculars, as the men went about setting up their plan to gain access to the ship. It was about noon when Sarah finally observed Professor Felix exit the superstructure of the ship onto the cat walk. Instantly, she tossed the binoculars to Mari, as she ran behind a tree and vomited.

In all reality, she never expected to see that despicable man again, and now she was nearly face to face with him. As the anger within her built, her hands shook as rivers of sweat ran down her face. She once again became physically sick as she watched the professor lean over and kiss his daughter on the cheek. How could he touch an innocent child? How could he act like he had never been anything more than a loving father and husband? The more she watched Felix, the angrier she became. Pulling a pistol from her waist band, she walked up to the shoreline and prepared to shoot, although the ship was a good two hundred yards away.

Mari grabbed Sarah by the arm, pulling her back toward several trees that lined the shore. "If you shoot now we will lose him forever. You must wait, Sarah. You cannot act out of vengeance or he will go underground forever. You must wait for the others, that is the way we do things!"

With pure hatred in her eyes, Sarah turned toward Mari. "No, I will kill him now, let go of me, I must do what needs to be done!"

Mari fought with all her strength to hold Sarah back, as she cried out, "No! This is not the way. Wait for Josiah, he will have a better plan!"

As Professor Felix walked back inside the ship, Sarah dropped down to her knees. It felt like her heart was going to jump out of her chest as the rage inside her continued to boil.

The deep voice of Josiah behind her brought her back to the present. "Sarah, is everything alright? I hope you can do better and cooperate with us, as we have a very good plan, but we need you to be part of this crew. Can I count on you, or must I send you back to Ishmael and tell him he was wrong about you."

Those words struck her like a sword. To be sent back to Ishmael was a fate worse than death. After that, she might as well leave Israel and wander the globe, never to find a home again.

Looking up at Josiah, she replied. "I'll be fine, let's do what we came here to do."

About nine-thirty that evening, everyone loaded onto a twenty-foot boat Caleb had arranged to use from a fisherman in a small marina nearby. Using oars, he and Ira pushed the boat out into the current. When they were about fifty yards from the Marina, Mari fired up the engine, setting course for the Midnight Sun. Nearing the back of the ship, Caleb tossed a grappling hook they had stolen from a work barge up toward the railing. With a sharp clang, it was solidly hooked. Everyone sat quietly for a second to make sure the crew members would not come running to investigate the noise, but Josiah figured the noise from the tug boats working nearby would cover the sound.

Mari stayed in the boat as the other four scampered up the rope onto the ship. With everyone set, Ira led the way up the steel stairway to the third deck. After carefully peering down the catwalk to make sure it was clear, he signaled Josiah, Sarah and Caleb to move forward. Just as Josiah was about to open the door to the superstructure, several bullets were fired from the bridge deck overhead.

Knowing everyone was now alerted, Ira jumped out toward the railing and fired a short blast from the German Schmeisser machine gun he was carrying. He heard a solid thump on the upper catwalk as a pistol fell past him into the water below.

Inside the ship, people were now frantically yelling and running. Josiah pulled the heavy steel door open as Sarah knelt on the deck, aiming her pistol down the dark passage. "The passage goes clear over to the far side of the ship. They are getting away!" Sarah screamed, as Josiah and Ira rushed past her.

As Sarah jumped up to follow them, she heard noise in a room to her left. Not wanting to have someone shoot her in the back, ever so slowly she backed up, placing her hand on the door knob. After taking a deep breath, she turned the knob and pushed the door open as she yelled, "Israeli Mossad, I'm coming in!"

Standing up against the back wall of the room were the wife and children of Professor Felix. All of them were focused on the pistol in Sarah's hand as they trembled. Lowering the weapon, Sarah shook her head. It was a pitiful sight as the children cried and their mother tried desperately to protect them as she fought back her own tears.

"Please don't hurt us," the mother pleaded, as her soft eyes burned into Sarah's heart. "We mean you no harm, please leave us alone."

Looking back at the woman in disgust, Sarah replied, "My mother did the same thing for me, my sister and brother, as you are doing for your children now. Yet the Nazi's took us away and stuck us in a filthy rail car after they murdered my father. I escaped, but my family did not. They are all dead. You cry out in fear, but you have no idea what real fear is. You have no idea what it's like to live in fear for years when you are just a child with no family. I'm sorry, but you make me sick, you know what your husband did to me and other people all those years, they were my people, innocent people. And now here you stand acting so innocent, like you never did anything wrong. Well, you are wrong, you are not innocent, you never tried to stop him, you lived the life of a good Nazi Officer's wife with all the privileges, food and luxuries that came with it, and you never asked him to quit what he was doing, did you? So, don't stand there and tell me you never knew. Worst of all, you stayed with him and raised his children, and now you run with him when the world wants him brought to justice."

Sarah desperately wanted to strike the woman with the pistol, but instead turned to leave. As she opened the door, she turned back to face the frightened woman. "All the while you knew what kind of a monster he was and you turned your back on it. If you want to see what he did, take a look at the burns on my wrist and ankle, but it's impossible for you to see the scars on my soul," Sarah explained, as several gun shots rang out on the back of the ship.

Exiting the room, Sarah dashed back outside. She ran toward the gangways on the back of the superstructure. As she rounded the corner where they had come up from their boat, she observed one body lying on the catwalk, while a second one was draped over the railing. Josiah came down the stairway from above, as Ira stood near a life boat on the far side of the ship.

Sarah removed a small flashlight from her pocket, pointing the brilliant beam of light onto the body that was draped over the railing. "It's not him!" Sarah yelled out in anger.

Josiah shook his head, "Ira and Caleb killed two of Felix's body guards on the far side of the ship, I got the guy on the railing, kind of hard to say which one of us killed this guy."

Sarah walked over to the body of the man on the catwalk and rolled him over. After placing the beam of her flashlight on the man's face, she called out, "This isn't him, either."

Josiah stared at Sarah as she turned to face him. "How is the family, what did you do to them, Sarah?"

Placing her pistol back into the waist band of her jeans, Sarah shook her head. "They are scared, they were alone, but they are fine. But now we need to go back and talk to them again, and this time we need to be tough on them, or Professor Felix will surely disappear."

Before Josiah could say a word, Sarah rushed back to the cabin, throwing open the door. Pulling out her pistol, she aimed it at the youngest child. "I saw men like your husband shoot children this age for fun. So, if you want to save his life, tell me where your husband is!"

Caleb stood behind Sarah, not sure what to do as he realized this situation could go either way in the beat of a heart.

Kneeling down, the woman wrapped her arms around the boy. "He has left the ship, he went to see a man about a change in plans for our trip. I do not know where the meeting was to take place."

Caleb stepped forward toward the woman. "What was the change in plans?"

The woman shook her head as she peered up at Caleb. "I don't know. All I can tell you is that it was a last-minute decision for our safety. This was not supposed to happen!"

"That's crap!" Sarah yelled out, as she glared at the woman. Tell us what the changes are or one of your children will die. Decide right now!"

The woman screamed as Sarah fired a shot that crashed against the bulkhead, inches from her eldest daughter's head. "Alright, alright, please don't hurt us. We were going to Guadalajara, Mexico. My husband knows several other men that have gone there before moving on to other locations. Please, that is all that I know."

Just as Sarah was lowering her pistol, she observed the woman's purse sitting on the bed behind several suit cases. Walking over to the bed, she dumped out the contents of the purse. Picking up several documents, she smiled. "I know where the bastard has gone, and I have their plans here in case anything went wrong."

The woman cried out in agony, as tears rolled down her face. Reaching up to Sarah, she begged, "He is all we have left, please do not take him from us. What will become of us?"

Sarah stared at the distraught woman for a moment before replying. "What happens to your husband now will depend on him. He can surrender or die, it matters not to me. As far as you and your children are concerned, the world owes you nothing, you have made your bed and now you must lay in it. But be assured, we will leave you unharmed to fend for yourselves. Galenka would be proud."

Running toward the back of the ship, Sarah handed Josiah the documents. After reading them he smiled, "Now we will catch him."

Arriving back at the van, Mari drove into Diu at a rapid pace. Arriving near the German Consulate, Ira and Caleb jumped out of the van, entering a small coffee shop across the street with a good view of the consulate's doors. Sarah and Josiah stayed in the van taking photos of everyone coming and going from the large brick building, while Mari sat on a bench reading a newspaper. About a half hour later, Sarah perked up as she pointed toward a small rotund man leaving the consulate through a side door. "He was with Felix, he brought the buckets of water into the room to be poured on me."

After alerting Mari, they watched him walk up to a car where he opened the back door and spoke to someone. A moment later, he crawled in behind the steering wheel and started the motor.

Mari was returning from the coffee shop with Caleb and Ira as the man began to drive off. "We should have jumped him right here, we just missed our chance!" Sarah yelled, as she shook her head.

"Not here in front of the consulate. They would have had the police all over us in seconds and he would be gone. No, we have to be smart about this, Sarah. He is ours tonight," Josiah replied smugly.

Mari followed the car for several miles as it wound its way along the waterfront. Suddenly, Felix's driver realized they were being followed and took off at high speed. Mari drove the van like a pro, keeping close to the car as they skidded through curves and threw rocks up from the shoulder of the road. As the car headed down a hill, the driver lost control, side swiping a guard rail and bouncing back into the oncoming lane of traffic, where they brushed against the side of a delivery truck, which sent them back across the road and into the ditch near the end of the guard rail, where the car came to a stop.

Mari slammed on the brakes, coming to a stop just a few yards from the smoking car as the passengers began jumping out. They began firing at the van breaking several windows. Ira and Caleb exited the van returning fire, taking down a man fleeing from the front seat, as Sarah and Josiah ran toward the guard rail for cover.

Quickly a game of cat and mouse broke out on the hill above the coast, as Felix, his driver and another body guard attempted to evade the inevitable. It did not take long for Ira to capture the driver as he had been wounded during the initial gun fight. Josiah caught the bodyguard circling around toward the van and shot him, sending his body tumbling down the steep bank into the ocean.

Now, Felix was caught up between Sarah, Caleb and Josiah, and there was no way out. Sarah desperately worked her way through the tall grass as a light rain began to fall. Out of the dark, a tree branch struck her on the side of the head. As she rolled backward, she heard the sound of rushing feet, before a forceful hand attempted to pull the gun away from her. Kicking up with her left leg, she struck her assailant a sharp blow against his right ankle, sending him backward onto the ground.

After wiping blood away from her eyes, Sarah rolled to her right before regaining her feet. Standing up, she was looking down into the face of Prof. Felix, who was trembling in fear. As the rest of the team arrived, Sarah smiled. "Gentlemen, meet Professor Felix."

"Look, I was just doing a job, the job Himler hired me to do. You cannot blame me, you cannot take me back, I have a family to look out for. Please, let me go," Felix begged over and over.

As Josiah reached down to pull the man to his feet, Felix began to struggle. He grabbed hold of Josiah's arm, attempting to toss him over the cliff. Sarah and Ira fired several shots into Felix as Caleb dove forward, grabbing onto Josiah. Slowly, Felix rolled up onto his knees as blood poured from two abdominal wounds. He clutched his midsection as he glared at Sarah, "Tell me what you have gained, Jew girl! Go ahead and shoot me, I will not make it back to stand trial in Germany in this condition. I would rather die for my Fuhrer right here!"

Before Sarah could respond, a scream echoed through the night as Felix's body flew over the cliff to the rocky shore line below. Stunned, Sarah turned immediately toward Ira, who had kicked Felix in the ribs, sending him over the cliff. "Did we win, Ira? Does that make us any better than who he was, and what he did to our people?"

Josiah walked up to Sarah. "He would have never made it, he was in bad shape. It might have been for the best." Turning toward Ira, he continued. "However, I do not condone what you did, as we cannot allow our emotions to control us. I will overlook this once, but never again or you will be off the team. Let the report show he fell over the cliff after being shot. Any questions?"

Everyone was silent, understanding Josiah was right. They needed to perform their jobs professionally so they could be respected by their peers, and not turn Mossad into a dreaded killing machine.

The team slowly drove down to a parking spot near the shore. Walking about two hundred yards along the shoreline they found Felix's body draped over several large rocks. After Ira took photos and cut off two fingers for identification, they tossed the body into the surf where it was quickly pulled out into the ocean. With the job completed, they walked back toward the parking area where Mari and Caleb waited.

Being overwhelmed with fear for his life, Felix's driver began singing like a bird as they drove off. He identified himself as S.S. Corporal Carl Kolmar, a former guard at Auschwitz. He pleaded with Josiah and Sarah to look out for his wife and children, as they would also now be on their own. However, all his pleas and begging went unheeded, as they considered him nothing more than just another Nazi war criminal that deserved to be brought to justice.

Settling into her seat on the airplane at Diu, Sarah peered out the window as rain pelted the tarmac below. She had come a thousand miles to a city that meant nothing to her, to kill a German war criminal the world would never know about. The local press would simply report there had been a shooting along the coast that led to the deaths of several unidentified men. It would be a story that no one would care about, as things like this happened all too often in this part of the world. No doubt Odessa would spirit the family away to an undisclosed site, until either the US State Department or the British Government could decide what to do with them, that's just the way it worked.

Corporal Kolmar was a minor player, but would be tried for crimes against humanity and would go to prison for several years. But did anyone actually care?

The President of India would call the Israeli Prime Minister to complain about the actions of Mossad, and the Prime Minister would regretfully inform the President he knew nothing about the incident, and a clerk at the Mossad office would write 'deceased' across the forehead of Professor Felix's photo, and the world would continue to spin.

Chapter Sixteen
End of the Beginning

Night after night in Dachau, a determined Galenka would counsel Sarah saying, "Violence begat violence, and hatred begat hatred, and only true forgiveness of your fellow man can ever reclaim your very soul. You must learn to forgive, you must know our God is alive, you must leave vengeance to God. If you don't, it will destroy you."

Although Sarah truly believed everything Galenka had taught her, trying to find that separation was a constant struggle. With more study, Sarah began to understood the words of the Torah, but it did not stop her from becoming an ardent Nazi hunter. She also believed that the wicked of this world needed to be brought to justice for the sins they had committed against the multitudes of innocent humanity that could no longer speak for themselves. Believing in that wisdom and the vision of a better world, she never turned down an assignment that might just lead to the capture of another high-ranking Nazi official.

There were successful missions and there were failures. Intel went bad, spies disappeared, Governments interfered, and worst of all, some informants worked both sides of the fence, collecting huge sums of money from both the Mossad and Odessa. Throughout every corner of the world, Odessa worked unceasingly to care for and hide former high-ranking Nazi officials, members of the S.S., and concentration camp guards.

While on leave May 10, 1952, Sarah celebrated her twentieth birthday with the Pearlman's at their home in Nahariya. She loved listening to Matthias recount his latest sports stories and helping Sariya in the kitchen. The one thing that broke her heart, was that Isaac had quit his job and disappeared about a year ago. Neither Hila or Rina had any idea of what had happened to him.

She thought if anyone would know where he might be it would be Micah, who still ran illegal border operations out of Lebanon. However, being a Mossad operative, there was no way she could get permission to go into Lebanon for any reason. So, she left word down at the marina that she would like to speak with Micah as soon as possible.

The day before she was to leave for Tel Aviv, Micah arrived at the Pearlman home. After exchanging pleasantries, he looked intently at Sarah. "I am so sorry to tell you that Isaac has been killed. He decided to go after S.S. Captain Herald by himself for what she did to him. I tried to talk him out of it, but he would not listen. He sailed from Beirut to Genova, Italy. There was rumor she was hiding out somewhere in the Bergamasque Alps near Sondrio, but it was never substantiated. With the injury he had to his leg from the mining accident, he was not in the best of shape to be crawling around the mountains."

Sarah nodded her head in agreement. "Do you know how he died? Who told you all of this?"

Micah looked seriously at Sarah. "Isaac hired a young Lebanese man named Torya that worked on the docks in Genova to go with him, as a pack carrier to be honest. The man told me Isaac had found where Capt. Herald was living. There was a shoot-out and Isaac was killed. Torya told me he ran and hid for three days before he was finally able to escape from his pursuers and make his way back to Lebanon. He did not feel safe staying in Italy, and has no idea what happened to Isaac's body."

Sarah was haunted by what Micah had told her about Isaac. True, he had abandoned her that one day in the forest, but he had worked hard to earn her forgiveness. It was only right that she paid back the debt she owed him.

Arriving back at Mossad headquarters, Sarah was disappointed to find there were no missions scheduled. Settling down to work in the archives, Sarah, Josiah, Mari, Caleb and Ira began digging under every rock, boulder or tree branch. They checked and rechecked every name, town or rumor that had anything to do with S.S. Captain Herald. Two weeks into the project, Mari found that the name of an Italian town called Riva, came up way too often. Checking maps, she found it on the extreme north end of Garda Lake, just 170 miles from Sondrio. Sarah immediately called for a conference with Ishmael to discuss a possible operation.

However, Ishmael was nervous about authorizing the mission on such scant intelligence, knowing how much the Italian Government would object to having Mossad operatives on their soil once again. The Italian police had already killed one Mossad operative, and jailed two others for several months before returning them to Israel. No matter how much the Italian Government denied still having ties to Nazi Germany, when it came to chasing down war criminals, their deeds spoke volumes.

After conferring with his superiors, it was decided to go after S.S. Captain Herald. The team was split up, allowing Sarah and Josiah to enter through the port of Trieste, while Mari, Caleb and Ira flew to Innsbruck, Austria and crossed over into Italy. The group finally met in the northern Italian city of Merano. Josiah was upset that their advance agents on the ground had not come up with any more positive information. The next day they drove south to Trento, just a few kilometers north of Riva.

Lake Garda is a large lake situated in a vividly beautiful valley, surrounded by many snow capped mountains. There are many fine resorts and ski chalets scattered throughout the picturesque region. For a week the team acted as tourists, checking out restaurants, shops and attractions with the hopes of catching a glimpse of the captain, or picking up some new information, but that was not to be. Ishmael was considering moving the operation to Sondrio when Mari was sure she had seen the captain taking a walk along the west side of the lake with a large German Shepherd.

For the next two days the team scoured the area intensely, hoping to catch a glimpse of her. As they were preparing to leave on the third day, Sarah observed a black Mercedes drive up to a grocery store.

The driver waited as a man and a woman fitting the description of Captain Herald and her husband entered the store. As the evening was cool, Sarah pulled a stocking cap down low over her ears, while pulling the collar from her jacket up as far as she could.

Walking into the store with Caleb, Sarah set her senses on high alert. As she looked at several magazines, she listened to the couple discussing fish. When the man made a small joke, the woman laughed, leaving no doubt it was indeed former S.S. Captain Herald. Walking around the counter, Sarah took a good look at the woman who paid no attention to her, as she was still examining packages of fish.

Caleb followed close behind Sarah, seriously hoping she would not go off the plan and just shoot her on site right there in the store. It was imperative they took her alive, so she could be interrogated while a complete sweep of her home was being conducted for documents and names.

Arriving back at the car, Sarah exhaled heavily. "It is her."

They followed the Mercedes carefully as it wound its way back up the mountainside and turned into a gated property. Ira shot photos of the car and house as they drove past. It was obvious that security was tight. Two armed guards strolled the compound, carrying German made machine guns.

Ishmael ordered a fly over, so one of their aerial teams could get an eagle's eye view of what they would be dealing with on the ground. After studying the photographs, it was evident that attempting to attack the compound would take a large contingency of troops, and that was just not possible.

Again, for the next week the team watched every time the car left the home, and followed it to find out where it went. Quickly, the team decided that the weekly grocery shopping trip would be the safest time to go after her. The following Thursday, as the driver pulled up to the same store, the crew was in place and ready. Sarah slowly walked into the store, looking at the magazines again, as Caleb walked slightly ahead, keeping a close eye on their prey. When Captain Herald began looking at steaks, Sarah stepped forward from the magazine rack.

Without thinking of the consequences, Sarah addressed Captain Herald. "Do you still want to know where a Jew girl like me is from, or are you going to have Professor Felix do your dirty work. By the way, have you seen him lately?"

A look of shear panic covered the woman's face as she rushed forward, pushing Sarah backwards into a shelf. Angered by Sarah's lack of control and refusal to stay on plan, Caleb instantly stuck his pistol into the bodyguards back, yelling, "Go for it and you die!"

However, before anyone could grasp what was happening, the clerk behind the cash register pulled a German Schmeisser from under the counter and began shooting. Sarah ducked as bullets began striking all around her, with one grazing her wrist. Caleb dove for cover behind a cooler, as the body guard spun around with a pistol in his hand, searching for a target. Having kept his eye on the large body guard, Caleb fired two shots, striking the man in the chest. Instantly, two more people came running out of a storage room, firing at Sarah as she ran toward the back of the store. Without hesitation, the man behind the service counter gave pursuit, only to run into a well-prepared Sarah, as she had dropped down behind a heavy ice cream freezer. In a split second, the man lay dead on the floor of his store.

Grabbing the captain by the arm, one of the men from the storage room pulled her through the double doors, as his partner sprayed bullets in every direction from a German machine gun.

Josiah and Ira came running into the store, guns in hand, as Caleb pointed toward the storage room. After firing two rounds from his shotgun into the storage room, Ira and Sarah entered. The delivery door to the storage room was wide open, allowing the sound of an escaping vehicle to echo off the walls.

Running out the front door of the store, Josiah climbed in behind the steering wheel of the van, preparing to give chase. Sarah sat in the back seat, angry at herself for trying to be cute. It had cost them the chance to arrest a known war criminal safely, and there was no doubt she would be seriously reprimanded by Ishmael for her actions.

The driver of the car Josiah was following was a pro at mountain driving. Instead of driving back to their house, he was heading due east toward the town of Roverto on the twisting narrow road. It did not take long for the driver to lose Josiah. Pulling into a scenic turnout, Josiah stopped the van. Looking over his shoulder he asked, "What happened back there, what went wrong?"

"It's all my fault, I did not think, I should have acted instead of trying to be cute with her," Sarah replied, knowing her career as a Nazi hunter probably just came to an end.

Caleb got out of the van and walked back toward the road as he kicked a rock in disgust. However, the sound of a car driving up a narrow mountain road on the hill to their left caught his attention. Turning toward the van, he yelled, "Sarah, Josiah come over here, now."

He told them what he had heard and roughly where the sound of the straining engine had stopped. Getting back into the van, Josiah back tracked until he came to a very narrow dirt road leading up the side of the hill. When they were about halfway up, Caleb and Ira exited the van and walked forward, keeping a close eye on the thick lilac hedge to their left.

Returning to the car sometime later, Ira smiled. "The car is parked by a house nearly two hundred yards above the turn out where we stopped. There is no other way down, but there is a foot path that continues east along the high bank. I did not see any guards outside the house."

They all understood they had no choice but to continue after her, or possibly lose the captain forever. After reloading his pistol, Josiah took the lead, keeping everyone tight up against the lilac hedge. Arriving at the driveway, Sarah and Mari quietly made their way toward the back of the house, as Caleb, Ira and Josiah ducked behind the warm car. After watching for any signs of movement near the house, Josiah and Ira cautiously began making their way toward a small porch about ten yards away.

Just as Caleb made his way around the rear of the car, two bullets struck the sheet metal just inches from his head. In seconds, gunfire erupted from several windows. Sarah and Mari had just ducked down behind an abandoned car that stood on wooden blocks, when the back door of the house burst open. From the light inside the house, it was clear to see it was Captain Herald and one of her bodyguards.

Mari jumped up quickly as she yelled, "Drop your weapons, you have no place to go," as she kept steady aim on the body guard. Sarah immediately stepped out to the left of Mari, knowing something wasn't right.

The body guard waved his pistol in the air as he called out, "Don't shoot, we are willing to surrender, we do not want to die."

But Sarah was not buying one word he said. "Then throw down your weapons and place your hands behind your heads and walk toward us."

Captain Herald called back, "Alright, we will cooperate." As she slowly began to bend forward to lay down her pistol, the body guard fired at Mari. As Mari ducked behind the car, Sarah fired several shots, striking the man in the shoulder. At the same time, Captain Herald spun around, fired several shots, while ducking down behind several large shrubs disappearing from sight. As her body guard fell to his knees, he fired several wild shots toward the old car before being cut down by Mari's accurate fire.

Sarah took off running toward the shrubs, with Mari close behind, as she kept a wary eye on the back door of the house. However, the captain was not there, she apparently escaped up the path leading away from the house. The climb up the hill was strenuous for Sarah, who was in excellent condition, so she knew the captain could not be far in front of her. Rounding a curve in the path, Sarah observed her prey no longer running, but walking briskly as she looked back over her shoulder. Coming to a stop by a large tree, Captain Herald struggled to catch her breath as she turned to face Sarah and Mari, who had now caught up with their dangerous fugitive.

Clutching dearly to her gun, Capt. Herald called out. "Stay back where you are or we will both die tonight. If you allow me to go free, we can both live."

Sarah could not control herself as she burst out laughing. "Let you go free? That will never happen, so you best drop your weapon and give up. You can hear there is no more shooting back at the house. That means your people are all dead, and my people are now coming this way to back me up. It is over, Captain. You will be standing trial for every disgusting thing you did during the war."

Mari attempted to step forward in front of Sarah, fearing she would shoot the Captain before the woman surrendered, but Sarah blocked her by holding out her left arm. "Understand, I will not allow you to kill yourself, you will stand trial. I am not like you, I will not kill just because I can."

The Captain looked to her right as Caleb and Ira approached with their weapons pointed in her direction. Seconds later, Josiah stood next to Mari as he called out. "They are all dead, no one is coming to your rescue, Captain, it's over. It's time for you to stand tall and admit your guilt to the world."

The next few seconds were as if time stood still. No one moved, and no one spoke, there was just the eerie silence that occurs when one is about ready to pass from life into death. Captain Herald suddenly let out a blood curdling scream as she raised her pistol toward her head. Before she could complete her fatal mission, Ira fired one shot, striking the Captain's right shoulder.

The Captain's arm fell uselessly to her side as her knees buckled. Sarah rushed forward as the Captain struggled to grab the pistol with her left hand. With a swift kick, the weapon slid across the ground toward Ira's feet.

Without hesitation, the crew rushed forward, knocking the Captain to the ground as they searched her vigorously. Within seconds, Caleb removed several small silver metal cyanide capsules from the lining of her jacket.

After applying a combat bandage to the wounded shoulder, Mari pulled the injured arm behind the Captain's back so she could be handcuffed.

As Mari was snapping the cuff shut on the left wrist, the captain yelled out. "Have you no concern for my shoulder, you may be damaging it more!"

Sarah smiled confidently. "I don't believe you will ever have much need for that shoulder, Captain. Plus, do you think we really care? You think I should care after what you did to me? Mercy has long been removed from my vocabulary, Captain. You should be able to understand that."

Arriving back at the van, they observed two police cars coming up the hill with their lights flashing. Ira and Mari stuffed the captain into the small rear seat while placing a gag on her. Caleb quickly turned the van around, as Josiah and Sarah stood in the road as the police officers exited their cars, not quite sure of what to make of the situation.

The lead officer held his weapon in his hand but did not point it in their direction. "My name is Lt. Benwha, tell me what is going on here, or we can do this very differently."

Sarah stepped forward. "We are Mossad. We just captured a Nazi war criminal that we intend to see stand trial at Nuremberg."

The officer glared at Sarah. "I expected so much after what happened at the market. How do I know the person you have is a war criminal? Who else was killed in all the shooting?"

Josiah stepped up to Sarah, "We have the dossier on the woman in the van, you can look it over if you wish."

"Woman! Even that does not seem proper for the Mossad. Maybe I should just take her into custody until we can have our headquarters in Rome verify this dossier you talk about," the lieutenant replied as he stepped toward the van.

Still carrying her weapon, Sarah stepped in front of the belligerent officer. "If you want to take her from us, you will have to shoot me first. You will find I do not die easily, and I will not allow you to take her, hide her out, or release her under a new name with the help of Odessa!"

Angered by Sarah's accusation, Lt. Benwha glared at her. "You have made a very serious allegation against our government, Signorina. Do you have evidence to back up such a charge?"

Sarah laughed. "Lieutenant, your country allowed the Germans a free hand to do whatever they wanted during the war, including transporting thousands of Jews to concentration camps to be put to death. Some of the Italian leaders that allowed it to happen still roam freely all over Europe, and you expect us to believe that Odessa does not wield some power over many of your politicians? If they do not, show us proof of that."

Clearing his throat, Lt. Benwha looked sternly at Sarah and Josiah. "I would like to see the woman, get her out of the van and bring her here."

Josiah shook his head. "You can see her photo in the dossier if you wish, but we are not getting her back out of the van. We will not allow you to try and take her from us, that's just the way it has to be."

Lieutenant Benwha realized he was in a no-win situation, and any attempt to take Capt. Herald was going to end in bloodshed that would have repercussions around the world. "So, tell me, how many did you kill back at the house, and do you know if they were Nazi's also?"

Reaching into his jacket pocket, Josiah tossed a passport at the feet of Lt. Benwha. "This man was from Algeria, where Odessa has one of their main headquarters. Do you wish to see the others?"

After Lt. Benwha looked over the passport, he tossed it back toward Josiah. "No, I do not wish to see the others. However, I can assure you my superiors in Rome will not appreciate what happened here tonight, and neither do I. Nevertheless, I believe it will be best if we permit you to leave Italy with your prisoner and return to Israel tonight. But be assured, if you and I find each other at odds again things will not go so easy for you. I will have no problem locking you up until everything can be rectified, and you could possibly spend a long time in our jails."

Sarah grinned at the lieutenant. "Mossad is not easily intimidated. Do what you must."

After the police cars cleared the hill, Caleb drove down the narrow trail to the main road. As they rounded the first bend, Josiah looked into the back seat. "How is our guest doing?"

Smiling, Mari replied. "That injection I gave her on the way to the van knocked her out within seconds, I think she will have a long nap all the way to the safe house."

Arriving back in Trento, a doctor removed the bullet from the Captain's wounded shoulder before stitching it up. "She will be fine to travel back to Israel, but make sure a surgeon looks at that shoulder, the bullet did a lot of damage."

Sarah nodded her head. "Like she did for everyone she tortured?"

The doctor walked up to Sarah. "I work with Mossad as do you, but I'm still a doctor that must do my best for each patient I see. I cannot separate that oath from the work I do for Mossad."

Feeling humbled by the doctors admonition, Sarah nodded her head. "I will see to it when we arrive in Israel where she will be held until her trial."

During questioning in Tel Aviv, Capt. Herald swore she had no information on the death of Isaac, and that if he had been killed, one of her guards would have handled it quietly, to keep her presence in the area a carefully protected secret.

A month later, Captain Herald was handed over to a contingent of American military police to be transferred to Nuremberg. Sarah stood near the exit of the building as the captain approached. Stopping the M.P.'s, Sarah stood directly in front of the captain. "I know you will not be hung which is a shame, you do not deserve to live. However, I shall pray for your soul."

Captain Herald glared at Sarah. "I should have let the professor kill you, as he wished. After all, what was one more dead Jewess to the Third Reich. Remember Sarah, this is not over. Germany shall arise again and we will finish what Hitler started. You are nothing but trash!"

Sarah smiled slightly. "What you will never understand is that no matter what I went through, Dachau taught me many things. It taught me to have faith, and it taught me how to be a better person in ways you will never realize. May the God of Israel watch over you."

Captain Herald laughed as she shook her head. "Your God of Israel didn't do much to protect your people, Sarah. I don't think you should count on him now."

Ishmael was upset with Sarah's lack of composure in the store, that could have led to the loss of Capt. Herald and the deaths of Mossad team members. Although a part of him wanted to ban Sarah from going on any more missions, another part of him realized she had much to offer Mossad. In the end, he told Sarah she would be confined to office work indefinitely, until he felt comfortable sending her back out on captures. Sarah was comfortable with the decision, fully realizing she had allowed her emotions to endanger an entire team.

Over the next several years, Sarah spent countless hours studying files, preparing documents to assist teams in capturing several high-ranking Nazis, and traveled to Washington to dig through the reams of captured documents taken from Germany. She was happy each time a high value target was captured and brought to justice. But the one person she wanted to capture most never appeared on the documents she studied. Of course, it was possible that Capt. Wilhelm could have been killed in the war or captured by the Russians, but there was always that underlying feeling that he was still out there hiding in plain sight, just waiting to be plucked, and she desperately wanted to be the one to take him down.

On a dark rainy fall day in 1955, Sarah sat at her desk paging through several files she had brought back from Washington on her last trip. The CIA agent that prepared one particular file had written a notation regarding a young woman's reference to a brutal Sergeant in Dachau. Picking up her coffee cup, Sarah leaned forward in her chair and began carefully reading every word the woman had said to the agent, just a little over a year earlier in Portugal. Throughout the next day, Sarah pulled up more files from the Portugal investigation written by the same investigator, as well as several files compiled by British Intelligence. Slowly, a pattern began falling into place. Rolling a large portable cork bulletin board over to the middle of the room, Mari and Ira began using push pins to attach notes, photos, newspaper clippings and listings of names. On the back side of the board, they attached a street map of Lisbon using corresponding numbers to the notes on the opposite side.

Over the next several days, the crew read through fifty more files, made countless phone calls to the CIA agent in Washington, spoke with agents from other Nazi tracking organizations, and tracked down the Jewish woman in Portugal who was most willing to speak with them. During the following weekend in her small apartment, Sarah studied maps of Portugal and Lisbon until she knew them almost as well as the streets of Tel Aviv.

On Monday morning, Sarah and Mari called Ishmael and the balance of the team over to Sarah's cubical to lay out everything they knew, along with names of people in Lisbon that needed to be questioned. No matter what Ishmael asked, either Sarah or Mari had an immediate answer or could hand him the appropriate document. After pacing the floor for several minutes, Ishmael looked at Sarah.

"We all know you want this man very badly and for good reason. However, you do not know where he is, and that's a problem if I'm going to send in a team. So, I will send just you and Josiah to complete the investigation, and see if you can locate Sgt. Wilhelm. If you find him, I will send the balance of the team to extract him. You will not do it by yourselves. Does that work for you, Sarah?"

Smiling, Sarah replied. "We will gather up all we need here and leave in the morning."

Nodding his head, Ishmael replied. "Do this right and you can return to active investigations. Allow your feelings to control your judgment as you did with Capt. Herald, and your career with Mossad will be over in a flash. Do well, young lady."

Arriving in Lisbon, Sarah and Josiah went straight to the Israeli Consulate to set up their center of operations. They spoke with the agents stationed at the consulate regarding any information they had obtained that would make the investigation go smoother. By mid-afternoon, they were at the door of the woman that was named in the file. After several hours, the woman took Sarah and Josiah on a driving tour of the areas where she had seen Sgt. Wilhelm, and then to the home of another Jewish woman that had actually confronted him.

Sarah was nearly shaking she was so excited, when they entered the home of Angela Cohen. "So, you actually confronted the sergeant about six months ago?" Sarah inquired.

"Yes, I was at the market when I saw him sitting outside the bistro across the street with two other men. At first, I thought it was my eyes playing tricks on me. But then when I went outside, I heard him laugh, and I knew it was that horrible monster. They were just getting up as I approached, so I gave him a push and yelled at him, something about being a murderer and burning in hell. Well, one of the men with him pushed me back as Sgt. Wilhelm glared at me. He said nothing, but his eyes made it perfectly clear he was afraid of me. I thought for a moment they might kill me right there, or follow me home and kill me. I was fearful for some time and was very careful where I went. I can tell you, I saw fear in his eyes that day."

Josiah looked at the woman, "Have you seen him in that area again?"

"No, I never saw him again, but I saw his two friends several times at a different market down the street. I followed them once as they left the market carrying several bags, but then I was approached by a woman that told me it was safer for me if I minded my own business. She scared me terribly, so I have never been near that market again, and have never seen them since. But a friend of mine that worked in the store told me where they would sometimes deliver orders the woman called in. I was surprised it was a small house next to a church just a few miles away."

That evening Sarah and Josiah drove by the small house next to the church of the Holy Cross. They watched several small children playing in the yard as a young woman watched them. After a second drive past the house, Sarah told Josiah to stop. Getting out of the car she walked over toward the woman.

"Hi, my name is Carla. My husband and I are looking for a small house in this area. Have you ever thought of selling your home, it would be perfect for us." Sarah explained.

The woman smiled back at Sarah. "Sorry, we don't own this house, it belongs to the church. The parish has been good to us, allowing us to live here until we get back on our feet. You would have to ask the priests if they would be interested in selling it, but I doubt if they will be. They usually use it as a temporary home for people in financial trouble, just like they did for the man that lived here before us. We were lucky when he and his daughter moved out of Lisbon about four months ago."

Not wanting to be pushy, Sarah smiled. "Well, thank you, we'll just have to keep looking."

As she walked back to the car, it was evident she was being watched from the front step of the church. A priest in his seventies was keeping a keen eye on every move she made. As they drove off, Sarah explained what the woman had told her.

Josiah nodded his head. "Sounds like it had been a safe house for Sgt. Wilhelm and his female friend until Mrs. Cohen called him out. I think we should go talk to the priest."

After circling the block, Josiah drove into the parking lot next to the old ornate church. He and Sarah had barely stepped from the car when the priest exited the church, walking up to them.

"I have seen you drive by several times now. I know you are Israeli agents and I know what you are attempting to do. That woman and her husband know nothing about who lived there before them. You must stop your search for the man and let him live in peace. He has asked for God's forgiveness, and I have given him absolution in the sacrament of confession. He came to Mass every morning and helped me around the church, until some woman came after him and would not let go of her anger. Yes, he made some terrible mistakes, but he has a good heart now, and is trying to make amends for all the evil he caused. He just wants to live in peace and continue to repent for his wrongs. Please leave him be and go back to Israel and live in peace yourselves."

Sarah glared at the priest. "Do you know what he did to people? Do you know what he did to me? He treated us like so much garbage and tortured us every day. I do not believe he is sorry, I believe he is scared, as he should be. We may be of different religions, Father, but we both have the same God. I am sorry, but I don't believe God has set that man's soul free. He must be brought to justice."

The priest looked at Sarah. "I'm sorry my daughter, but God surely has forgiven him. You must leave him in peace and go home. The God of Israel was forgiving when your people turned against him in the desert and decided to worship a golden calf. He took you all lovingly into his arms and delivered you back to your home of Israel, did he not?"

Sarah nodded her head. "But he also killed the evil Egyptians by drowning them in the Red Sea, and this man you protect is far more evil than all of them." They both stood quiet for a moment as they stared at one another. Finally, Sarah broke the silence. "I'm sorry, Father, but we will find him, and he will be brought to justice for his crimes against humanity. I will let you know when we find him, so you may give him council if you wish."

As they drove off, Sarah was angrier than she had been in quite some time, but she was also more determined to find Sgt. Wilhelm, knowing he was still alive.

Arriving back at the consulate, Sarah and Josiah laid out everything they had learned. After several weeks of searching, Sarah and Josiah returned to Israel empty handed.

In March of 1956, Sarah and her team went to Tunis to help capture two former S.S. officers. One of the men swallowed a cyanide capsule, but the second man was wounded in a gun battle before he could do the same. The house they lived in had also been used by Odessa at times to track and move Nazi war criminals throughout Africa. The team returned to Israel with one prisoner and twenty boxes of files they would need to sift through and study.

Several documents mentioned Leiria, Portugal. Sarah became interested when she realized the town is about a hundred miles north of Lisbon, and very near the coast with a large population of German immigrants.

Once again, Sarah and Josiah flew to Portugal hoping to get a lead on Sgt. Wilhelm or other Nazi war criminals that could be hiding in the area. Quickly, it became evident that the former German's living in and around the town of Leiria were a tight knit group that protected their own and did not trust outsiders. Many of them operated farms, while others worked in orchards, and some ran very profitable businesses, but they were all suspicious of any strangers that stopped in their town.

Walking through the shops and stores, Sarah did most of the talking, as her German was beyond reproach. As they strolled past a bench outside of a gift store, an old German man was sitting comfortably sipping on a bottle of wine. He looked up at Josiah. "You have a pretty girl there. I think you need to marry her to keep the other boys away."

Sarah smiled as she looked down at the kindly man. "You are very sweet, thank you for the compliment." After the man took another sip of the wine, Sarah smiled and said, "How long have you lived in Leiria?"

After wiping his mouth with the back of his hand, the old man replied. "My wife and I moved here back in 1930 when things were going bad in Germany. We were glad we were gone when Hitler came to power, we wanted nothing to do with him. We never questioned our decision to move here as that war was terrible. We own this gift shop and do rather well."

Not sure if he should push it or not, Josiah asked. "Do you still get a lot of German folk moving down here now that the war is over?"

The old man snorted. "Ya, we get those that are trying to escape the past. They are more trouble than they are worth. They take jobs down by the orchards so they can stay out of sight. But a nice young couple like you would be welcomed any day."

Sarah patted the man on the shoulder, before moving on down the sidewalk toward their car. After closing the door, Sarah looked at Josiah. "That was reckless, he might not be as drunk as you think. We may have just lost our chance to catch Sgt. Wilhelm!"

Arriving back in Lisbon, Sarah called Ishmael to inform him of their progress. He immediately placed Caleb and Ira and three members of an extraction team on an old British military aircraft they used for special missions.

The following day, Sarah, Josiah, Caleb and Ira drove to Marinha Grande near the coast where there are many orchards. Men were loading trucks with fruit from warehouses, while others were cleaning up branches and leaves that had fallen over the winter months. They were not sure how they were going to single out Sgt. Wilhelm, as many of the workers lived in old trailers right on the plantations and never wandered very far.

After looking around the warehouses, Caleb and Ira walked into a building nearest the road that had a sign advertising for employment. Caleb spoke with one of the foremen about a job for several minutes, as Ira cautiously looked out the windows at the workers. After agreeing with everything the foreman said, Caleb and Ira sat down to fill out the short applications they were handed.

As Ira walked them back to the foreman, the back door of the office opened. He was almost breathless as the large man carrying two boxes of fruit was in fact S.S. Capt. Wilhelm.

The foreman pointed to a table where he wanted the boxes placed before speaking. "Alfred, these men just applied for the jobs we have open. They will start in the morning, why don't you give them a quick tour."

Nodding his head in agreement, he motioned for Caleb and Ira to follow him back out of the office. Walking into the warehouse, the men stopped to see how the fruit was washed before placing it into boxes. Caleb smiled. "My wife would like to see this. She is waiting in the car, do you mind if I go get her. She really would enjoy watching this process."

Wilhelm nodded his head with a smirk on his face. "If you wish, we will wait here."

Caleb hustled back to the car, telling Sarah and Josiah the good news. Being extremely careful, Caleb and Sarah decided to enter the processing building from a side door, so Wilhelm would not catch a glimpse of her from a distance and decide to run.

However, Sarah was barely through the door when Sgt. Wilhelm turned. Even though it had been seven years since he had seen her, he recognized her immediately. Pulling a pistol from his waistband, he struck Ira across the side of his head. As Ira collapsed to the floor, several other workers pulled weapons and began firing at Sarah and Caleb. Josiah came running through one of the overhead truck doors returning fire, hitting the worker closest to Ira. Sarah dove to the floor for cover near Caleb, as Wilhelm ran deeper into the processing building. Pulling his pistol, Ira rolled to his right side, attempting to remove himself from the line of fire. Hearing a scuffing noise behind him, Ira quickly sat up, firing several shots into an approaching man carrying a large machete.

A forklift driver in the warehouse did everything possible to impede the chase, only to be knocked off the forklift by gunfire from the pursuing Mossad operatives. Sarah ran through an overhead door near the back of the building, where several more forklifts and tractors were parked. Scanning the area, she was sure the sergeant had exited the building just moments before her. Caleb ran out a service door on the east side of the building, only to be met by a large German Shepherd that clamped down on his left wrist. The dog pulled and twisted on the wrist, breaking bones with every move. Before Caleb could respond, Ira fired two rounds into the dog's chest, killing it instantly.

Caleb threw himself back up against the building in severe pain as Ira wrapped his shattered wrist with a handkerchief he carried in his pocket.

Meanwhile, Josiah dashed out the same door Sarah had used only to find her gone, and her pistol lying on the ground near a small pool of blood. He knew damn well either Wilhelm or another ex-Nazi had grabbed her.

As Josiah met up with Ira and Caleb, he explained to them what he had found. It was impossible to know where the men could have taken Sarah, as the orchard covered hundreds of acres. They had walked about fifty yards when they heard Sarah scream off to their left. Running through the orchard at full speed, Ira called out, "Look, over by that green truck!"

Quickly, the men split up, attempting to work their way around the truck and catch Wilhelm and his protectors off guard. Sliding under the back of the semi-trailer, Ira observed a man crouched down behind a forklift with a shot gun. Taking quick aim, he shot the man in the head. After watching the man drop, he continued on toward what appeared to be a pump house about ten yards away.

Although in severe pain, Caleb chased down a man carrying a large ax that had thrown a knife at him moments earlier. Once he had a clear field of fire, Caleb fired several shots into the man's back.

Josiah knew full well that Wilhelm was not far away with Sarah, as he watched the blood drops on the ground. Walking forward at a brisk pace, he observed Caleb and Ira catching up on his right. They all ducked for cover as a shot rang out just a short distance in front of them, followed by a shrill scream. Without hesitation, the three men charged forward to find Wilhelm bleeding from a gunshot wound in the shoulder, as he held a pitch fork just inches away from Sarah's throat.

With his eyes glazed over, Wilhelm glared at the three Mossad agents. "I'll kill her like I should have in Dachau, I swear I'll kill her. Drop your weapons, leave the orchard and go back to Israel and I will let her go free. I just want to live in peace. If you cannot agree to that, I'll kill her for sure."

Josiah stood firm as he glared right back. "She dies, you die. There is no way out of this for you. Drop the fork and we'll take you back to Germany to stand trial as it should be."

"Trial, there won't be any trial. I will be guilty no matter what is said. I will hang like all the rest of the S.S. There will be no jail time for me. I have come to far to give up now. She must die with me, that is the only way this can end."

Before he could say another word, another gunshot rang out, striking Wilhelm in the knee. As he stumbled for a second, Sarah was able to roll to her right, just as the fork came down next to her head.

As Wilhelm collapsed to the ground, a middle-aged man came walking forward with his hands in the air, still holding a pistol. "My name was S.S. Lt. Oscar Miller, I also fired the first round that hit Wilhelm in the shoulder. He is nothing but a pig, I should have killed him a long time ago. I have heard the stories about what he did in Dachau." After a moment of silence the man continued. "I was part of Klaus Barbie's command. I defected from Germany in 1944, along with a friend and our families. We could no longer be part of what Barbie was doing and what the Third Reich had become." Dropping the gun, he walked over toward Ira. "Take me in if you must, but I will not tell you the name of the man that escaped with me. He deserves his freedom, I will take whatever punishment the court deems necessary."

Standing up, Sarah walked up to Lt. Miller. After staring at him for a moment, Sarah shook her head. "Somehow, I feel our lives have crossed somewhere in the past, but I'm not going to question you about it. Today you saved my life when you did not need to get involved, and I thank you, that was very brave on your part. Now go, we are not hunting you or your friend. Live in peace."

After Lt. Miller had departed, Sarah walked over to Ira and Josiah as they bandaged Sgt. Wilhelm. Looking down at the wounded man, she said. "I have no pity for you. Be assured I will testify at your trial and tell everything to the jury that you did to me, and those poor children. I will make sure you die at the end of a short rope."

Wilhelm closed his eyes for a moment before looking back up at Sarah. "Take your weapon now and get your revenge, I do not wish to hang. Do what you must, you are Mossad."

Sarah walked over to Josiah to retrieve her pistol. While starring at Sgt. Wilhelm, she checked the magazine to see how many bullets were left in the gun. For several more moments, she stared at her tormentor in silence before slamming the magazine back into the weapon. Shaking her head, she slid the pistol into the waist band of her jeans where she always carried it. Turning toward the man she hated for so long, she replied. "It's not for me or for any single living soul to get revenge. Rather, it's up to the law of man that you will need to plead your case. I know Galenka would want it that way, no matter how I feel, and so it will be!"

Before they could lift Sgt. Wilhelm from the ground, a young woman came running toward them, carrying an old revolver.

"Get away from my father or I will shoot. I mean it, I will shoot. What are you doing to him?" the terrified woman called out in desperation.

Sarah slowly bent over, placing her weapon on the ground as she cautiously replied to the angry woman. "We are Israeli Mossad, we are here to arrest your father for war crimes."

Raising her hands in the air, Sarah kept a close eye on the frantic woman with the shaking pistol, hoping she would not fire her weapon.

Scowling, the woman looked harshly at Sarah. "War crimes? What kind of war crimes could a cook commit. You have the wrong man, look what you have done to him!"

With his hands also raised, Josiah knelt down beside Sgt. Wilhelm. "Sergeant, I think it's time to come clean with your daughter before anyone else gets hurt. The ball is in your court."

After taking a deep breath, Sgt. Wilhelm called out. "Helen, hand over that gun to one of the agents and come here. Please do not shoot anyone."

Totally unsure of what was happening, Helen slowly walked forward, handing the pistol to Ira, before giving each of the Mossad agents a cautious look. Sarah placed her hand on Helen's shoulder and whispered, "Now go to your father and hear what he has to say. Be strong."

Kneeling down next to her wounded father, Helen took his hand. "Father, tell me what is going on. Why is Mossad here, I am so confused."

Looking up into his daughter's eyes, Sgt. Wilhelm searched desperately for the words to answer the pleas of this young woman he loved so much. After closing his eyes for a moment, he began.

"I am so sorry, my dear. It has all been a lie. I was not a cook at the S.S. barracks as you were told, I was a guard in Dachau. I am not proud of the horrible things I did to the prisoners there."

Frowning in disbelief, Helen replied. "Like what? Did you kill them? Did you rape them? Did you torture them? Tell me father, what kind of a monster were you?"

"Daughter, you must forgive me, for yes, I am guilty of all those things. I tried to hide it all from your mother, but she realized everything I had told her was a lie when I said we had to escape from Germany or the Allies would hunt me down. She said she could never forgive me. Your mother did not die in an auto accident as I told you, she committed suicide with my side arm."

Helen shook her head in disbelief, as she pulled her hand out of her father's grip. After a moment of silence, she grabbed hold of her father's shirt and began to shake him.

"Did you kill children and send their innocent bodies to the crematorium? Did mother not treat you well enough that you needed to rape Jewish women for pleasure and torture? What kind of a beast are you?"

"Yes, yes all of that is true, I was a horrible man. I am so sorry my child, so sorry," Sgt. Wilhelm screamed as he watched tears roll down the face of his daughter.

Standing up, Helen wiped the tears from her face as she shook with anger. "Do not try and justify what you did. How could you father? How could you?" Looking toward Josiah, she mumbled, "Take him away, get him out of my sight. I never want to see this miserable man ever again."

As Helen walked away, Sgt. Wilhelm called out, "Child, you are all I have left. Please! I need your forgiveness!"

Sarah turned to see what Helen's reply was going to be, but she never responded. Everyone watched as she walked back to the trailer and closed the door. As Sarah and Josiah pulled the sergeant to his feet, a blast from a shotgun rang out from the trailer. Spinning around quickly, Sarah could see blood running down the large window next to the door.

As Ira and Josiah helped Wilhelm back toward the car, they were stopped by several police officers from Leiria that came to investigate what was happening. The police sergeant looked at Josiah.

"We shall take custody of that man and all of you. Put down your weapons and place your hands over your heads."

Sarah pulled the pistol from her jeans and walked over to Wilhelm. Placing the barrel up against his head, she looked at the police sergeant. "This man is a Nazi war criminal we have been tracking for some time. We are taking him back to Germany where he is going to stand trial for his sins. I do not wish to be judge, jury and executioner, but I will if you think you are going to take him from us. He will die right here by my hand."

As the sergeant stepped forward preparing to speak, Sarah pulled the hammer back on her pistol. "By the power of the God of Abraham and Isaac, and the nation of Israel, I condemn this man to death."

Josiah and Ira held their breath as they looked at the determined expression on Sarah's face. Holding up his injured hand, Caleb stepped closer to Sarah.

"Do not do this, Sarah, it is not what you are about. We will get him back to Israel one way or the other. You know Ishmael will never allow him to go free. I know your hatred for this man, but don't become him, do not let him win. Let Helen's death count for something."

After listening to Caleb, the sergeant lowered his pistol as he looked wide-eyed at Sarah. "I believe you would execute him as you said. Then we would have no choice but to have a shoot-out with you and your accomplices, and that would gain us nothing. So, I do not wish to do that, as there has been enough bloodshed here today. I knew some of these men you killed. I know their backgrounds are questionable, but I liked them. I also know many of these workers are war criminals being supported by Odessa, and I do not like it one bit. They are destroying the peaceful humble community we have been building here for many years. I have no problem with them being gone from our community. There was never a doubt in my mind that this day was going to come, and I have dreaded it. So go now, take him back to Israel and put him on trial for all the world to see, but do not come back here again. If your government sends you back, I will not be able to guarantee your safety as you are now marked people. Believe me, Odessa will not look favorably on what you have done here. In fact, I can promise you they will be putting out a vendetta on your heads. We do not want problems with Odessa, Mossad, the CIA or MI6. We are a peaceful community and we wish it to remain so. If there are any other war criminals here that you want, I insist you contact our government in Lisbon. However, they may just want to place you in our prison for the killings you were involved in today. I can tell you for a fact that Odessa will surely demand it as they pay many officials in our government. So, I recommend you leave immediately while I'm being so generous, and let these people live in peace. The war must finally be over."

Two days after returning to Tel Aviv, Sarah was told that Wilhelm wanted to see her before being transferred to Nuremberg. Arriving in an interrogation room, Sarah sat down across the table from the arrogant S.S. sergeant.

"I am here, what do you want?" Sarah asked coldly as she stared at the man that had so brutally tortured her.

"Do you know that I have been repenting for my sins? Do you not know that I was just following orders, so I am not guilty of anything? Was it worth torturing my daughter so that she killed herself?" Sgt. Wilhelm stated boldly, as he sneered at Sarah.

Sarah looked down at the table for a moment before responding. "The priest in Lisbon told me he had given you absolution for your sins. Do you honestly believe you can be forgiven for what you did to me and so many others? It is clear that neither your wife or daughter could ever forgive you."

Sgt. Wilhelm nodded his head. "Yes, the priest says it is possible if I went on to live a good life and repent. I have to believe it is true."

Sarah shook her head as she laughed. "Lead a good life? Have you forgotten you were just trying to kill me a few days ago? Did you believe in God when you were torturing me? Did you believe in God when you raped me? Or did you start believing in God when you knew Mossad was looking for you?"

"They were complicated times, we just followed orders," Sgt. Wilhelm replied sternly.

"No. I don't believe your orders were to rape and torture young girls. I believe you are a sadist, and I think you enjoyed it, even though you knew you could have been shot for having sex with a Jewess." Sarah replied, as the anger in her began to build.

Shaking his head, Sgt. Wilhelm replied. "I understand there is nothing I can say that will change the way you feel toward me. You want vengeance and your heart will not rest until you get it. Actually, I feel sorry for you, but what will you gain by putting me to death? What did you gain by watching my daughter kill herself? Are you happy now?"

Sarah stood up and walked slowly to the door of the interrogation room. "There is no reason to speak to you about any of this again. I will be at your trial to testify, and I will be at your hanging to represent all the peoples of Israel, along with your wife and daughter. I know you have been trying to see how angry you could get me, but a woman by the name of Galenka that died at Dachau taught me better than to allow someone like you to ever control me again. You see, I do not pity you, I do not believe the man I am looking at right now is any different than the man who tortured and raped me in Dachau. Whoever or whatever you feel you are now, concerns me not."

As she turned to walk out the door, she looked back at the broken trembling man sitting all alone at the table. "Shalom, Sgt. Wilhelm."

Several days later, Ishmael called the team together for a briefing. "I know you were threatened by the police in Marinha Grande, but I am afraid you will need to go back again. Arrest warrants have been issued for an S.S. Lt. Oscar Miller and an S.S. Sgt. Eugene Becker. They both served on Klaus Barbie's staff and are wanted for the deportation of Jews from France."

Josiah looked at Ishmael. "Lt. Miller helped us capture Wilhelm. He shot several of Wilhelm's associates and saved Sarah's life. We told him he was not wanted, so he should leave and stay quiet."

Leaning back in his leather chair, Ishmael looked at Sarah. "Will this be a problem?"

"No, we will get them and bring them in. At least we know where they live," Sarah replied, knowing it would be tough to capture someone that had saved her life."

Arriving in Portugal, the team felt like they were under constant surveillance, although they had not seen anyone suspicious. The following day they drove to Marinha Grande where they contacted an agent named Geoffrey, that Ishmael had sent there a week earlier to gather information.

Geoffrey laid out a map of the area, pointing to the house where Lt. Miller lived. "Miller is well respected among the German immigrants, and they will not be happy to have him arrested. Most of them are well armed, and I think would fight for him. Your Sgt. Becker lives right here in Marinha Grande and will be much easier to capture. He is bound to a wheel chair after a bad car accident several years ago. Every day he leaves his apartment at 0830 hrs., and rolls down the street to Columbus nursing home where his wife is a patient. He may be armed, but he keeps pretty much to himself."

For the next several days Ira and Ramo, a replacement for Caleb, kept an eye on Sgt. Beckers routine to decide when the best time to grab him would be.

Sarah, Josiah and Mari carefully surveilled the Miller residence and their movements, knowing this capture would be much tougher.

The plan was to make both captures in the evening, when Sgt. Becker returned from the nursing home, and Lt. Miller would be driving home from the plantation.

Parking their van around the corner from Sgt. Becker's small apartment building, Ramo and Ira could easily watch the road Sgt. Becker would use on his way home. Around 1800 hrs., they followed Becker's slow progress toward his mailbox, where they had planned to capture him.

As Becker arrived at the mailbox, he stopped and took a long look around in every direction. It was obvious he sensed something was not right. Reaching down into a canvass bag he always had with him, he pulled out a semi-automatic pistol. He rolled back away from the mailbox, looking toward the small hedge that circled the yard around the apartment building.

"Come out, I know you are there. If you want to rob me you are out of luck, I have no money or wealth that would do you any good. I know how to use this weapon so I suggest you leave!" Becker shouted, as his heart rate climbed and his hand shook.

Slowly, Ira stepped out of the shadows with his sidearm drawn. "S.S. Sgt. Eugene Becker, I am not here to rob you, I'm here to arrest you for crimes against humanity."

Becker laughed, as he glared at Ira. "I'm a crippled old man dying from cancer. What good would it do anyone to arrest me for things that happened in another world, that I could not prevent. There are bigger fish to fry than me, go after them. But I assure you, I cannot help you find any of them. What will my wife do now when I no longer come to see her. Think of her!"

Ramo walked up slowly from Becker's left side. "Sir, why don't you drop your weapon, it will do you no good. Just come quietly with us and let this be done."

Becker looked at both men for a moment before replying. "I feared this day for a long time, but eventually I decided there was no reason anyone would want one of Barbie's sergeants. What good would it do you. But I'm afraid things are as you said, let this be done." Before Ira or Ramo could move, Becker placed the muzzle of the gun under his jaw and pulled the trigger.

As the sound of the shot echoed off the buildings along the street, Ira and Ramo ducked back into the hedge. When no one appeared after several minutes, Ira ran forward, taking several photos as Ramos removed Becker's wallet and cut off his right index finger for identification.

The men quickly ran to their van and drove west out of town, passing two police cars heading into the town with flashing lights and sirens.

As Ramos sealed the finger in an evidence bag, he looked at Ira. "Coming with us or shooting himself the results are the same, his wife will still be alone. What did he gain?"

Ira looked over at Roma. "The obituary his wife and friends will see in the newspaper will say he was shot during a robbery. They will never see his name in the paper as a captured war criminal. I guess that was better for him all around. Odessa will clean it up."

Josiah watched Lt. Miller walk to his small car after leaving the packing plant. He could see the semi-automatic pistol tucked into his waist band. Miller spoke for a minute with a co-worker that

Sarah photographed for investigative reasons. After finishing the conversation, Miller slid into his car driving south out of the parking lot headed toward his home.

Mari sat in a car about two miles from the plant at an intersection the team called able-strike. She waited for a call from Sarah, who was following Miller in a van along with Josiah. Sarah would radio her when Miller was a half mile away. As Miller reached able-strike, Mari quickly pulled out directly in the path of his car. Attempting to avoid hitting Mari's car, Miller had no choice but to go down the steep water filled ditch on his left.

Immediately, Josiah jumped from the van, smashed the window on the driver's door, and thrust a hypodermic needle into Miller's neck. With Mari's help, Josiah pulled Miller from the car, dragging him to the van. Seconds later, Sarah slammed her foot down on the accelerator as Mari pulled the sliding door closed. For the next half hour, Sarah drove around on several different roads to make sure no one was following them.

Later that evening, Sarah and her team arrived at the safe house in Lisbon to meet Ira, Roma and Geoffrey. Josiah was upset to hear what had happened with Becker, but was happy they had captured Miller so quickly.

About an hour later, Miller awoke. He looked at Sarah for a moment and half smiled. "I remember you from the plantation. You did not keep your word. You came after me as if I were a criminal, though I did nothing wrong."

Sarah leaned forward in her chair. "If we had known that day you were wanted, we would have taken you then. We didn't know there was a warrant out for you and Sgt. Becker until we returned to Tel Aviv. Things change, and we do as we must to bring Nazis to justice."

"I never was a Nazi, I just was assigned to Barbie's operation and did as I was told. You do what you must to survive. My friend and I ran off well before the war ended." Stopping for a moment, Miller looked at Josiah. "And Becker?"

"He shot himself before we could take him into custody," Josiah responded coldly.

About midnight, Sarah gave Miller another injection to keep him under control and quiet as they drove to the Lisbon Airport. Arriving at a large freight hangar, Sarah drove the van straight through an open overhead door. Inside the hangar was an Israeli military C-130 being readied for takeoff. Once everyone was loaded, the pilots taxied to the runway and left for Tel Aviv.

As the C-130 was climbing into the dark night sky over the Atlantic Ocean, Detective Fernandez from the Leiria Police was in Lisbon tearing apart the safe house Geoffrey had left clearly scrubbed clean.

Walking toward the back door, he stared up into the night sky watching several aircraft leave the Lisbon Airport. Slamming his fist against the door frame, he yelled. "Damn Mossad! I told them last time if they returned, I would send them all to prison. Once again they have made a fool of me."

Chapter Seventeen
The Search Continues

Slowly, Sarah began to feel as if her life was finally beginning to take on real meaning. She was working toward closure, for Galenka, for her family, and for millions of her people by the long hard hours she spent digging through files and musty records. She searched diligently for information on horrific war criminals like Adolph Eichmann, the creator of the final solution; Dr. Joseph Mengele, the angel of death from Auschwitz; Klaus Barbie, the butcher of Lyon; and Walter Rauff, the creator of the mobile gas chamber. Though often times her work would lead to the arrest of lessor known war criminals, those victories were no less important.

In 1958, several women that had survived Auschwitz contacted Mossad regarding the sighting of Dr. Joseph Mengele near Miami, Florida. Feeling the information was credible, Ishmael sent Sarah and Josiah to the United States to question the women. After several days in Florida, spent questioning the women and studying enlargements of photographs the women had taken, there was no doubt they had in fact seen Doctor Mengele in several locations.

Ishmael immediately sent Caleb, Ira and their new team member Olga Armand, a Russian Jew that had survived Sobibor, to help the team in Miami. Looking over the photos, Olga identified two of the men with Mengele as S.S. soldiers she knew from when she had been in Treblinka.

Over the next two weeks, the team worked in shifts, patrolling the Marina and the apartment complex where the sightings had taken place, with no luck. Midway through the third week, Olga observed, followed and photographed two of the bodyguards talking with the crew of a large yacht in the marina. Ishmael sent information that Mengele was indeed in Florida and that he was planning a move to South America, so they should not let him get away. The team now turned all their attention to the Marina. On Sunday afternoon, a taxi drove onto the pier, stopping at the yacht they had been watching. They were stunned to see Doctor Joseph Mengele step from the taxi, along with a single bodyguard. The driver followed close behind them, carrying several suitcases onto the boat.

"He's running!" Ira called out, as he watched the doctor's henchmen welcome him on board.

As soon as the Dr. Mengele was taken below, the huge marine engines sprang to life. Realizing their quarry was slipping away, Sarah ran as fast as possible down the pier. Jumping onto the stern of the boat, she landed hard on her on her right ankle, causing it to snap. Confusion mounted quickly among the crew as Sarah rolled in pain on the aft deck of the yacht, and the boat slowly began to leave the slip.

Realizing that Sarah was injured and they could no longer stop the yacht from leaving, Ira ran back down the pier. Jumping into a rubber boat, he fired up the motor. Olga and Josiah cut the ropes tying it to the pier as they continued watching for any signs of Sarah. Slamming the throttle forward, the tiny boat leapt from the pier, heading straight toward the side of the escaping yacht. As Ira guided the small craft up against the yacht, Olga and Josiah attempted to climb on board, but were met by a hail of bullets coming from an open door of the pilot house.

Seeing the gunman attempting to get a better shot at the dingy, Sarah propped herself up against the side of the raised pool, firing several rounds. The man stumbled backward into the pilot house as blood sprayed from his wounded left leg.

Once again Ira brought the dingy alongside the yacht, preparing to let Josiah climb aboard, when a man on the front deck of the yacht leaned over the railing firing a blast from a small machine gun. Several rounds punctured the dingy, causing it to rapidly lose air and begin to slow, allowing the yacht to sail away from them.

Two men ran from the main cabin, firing their pistols toward Sarah as the boat began to gain speed. Rolling to her right, away from the protection of the pool, Sarah laid prone on the deck returning fire, cutting down one of the attackers. The second man returned to the cabin, yelling for assistance.

Josiah shook his head and swore as Ira ran the damaged dinghy into a nearby pier, allowing everyone to get clear of the sinking boat. Olga screamed as loud as humanly possible as she jumped up and down, "Sarah, jump off the boat!"

As several more men came walking from the main cabin carrying automatic weapons, Sarah realized she was well outnumbered and outgunned. Raising her right hand into the air, she pitched her pistol over the back of the yacht. As the men approached her, she heard a voice calling from the steps of the cabin.

"Don't shoot her!"

Seconds later, Sarah was looking up into the face of a grinning Joseph Mengele. After kneeling down on one knee, he grabbed Sarah's ankle and shook it.

Sarah screamed in pain as Mengele laughed with delight. Standing back up he looked at one of his men. "Ja, it's broken bad, there is no way for her to walk on it. Throw her over the side and let the sharks have her for lunch."

Sarah glared at Mengele as the body guards carried her to the railing. "You'll get what's coming to you someday, you bastard."

Mengele laughed as he motioned for the men to toss her over the railing.

Sarah tumbled several times as she hit the water, causing her ankle to twist as it slammed against the surface. After treading water for several moments, she finally attempted to swim toward the shore which was about two hundred yards away. When she was about halfway there, a Miami Dade County water patrol boat came screaming up to her with its siren blaring. As the boat came to a stop, several officers pointed their pistols at her as they screamed, "Show us your hands!"

"You idiots, Doctor Joseph Mengele is getting away on that yacht, you need to go after him."

But the officers just kept pointing their pistols at her until they could pull her out of the water.

As the officers placed handcuffs on Sarah, she continued screaming.

"Listen to me, the Nazi, Dr. Mengele is getting away. You need to go after that yacht!"

As the pilot of the patrol boat steered it back toward the north, a police lieutenant knelt down next to Sarah.

"Lady, you are under arrest for assault and murder. Just shut your damn mouth."

Within an hour, Sarah was taken into the Dade County jail, where she was photographed, fingerprinted, and booked on three counts of assault and one count of murder.

After she was allowed to change into an orange jump suit and a nurse had wrapped her ankle, she was taken to an interrogation room. About an hour later, a tall well-built man in an expensive suit walked in and sat down across the table.

"My name is U.S. Marshal Sam Swenson. You have been charged with three counts of assault, and one count of murder. We know you are a Mossad operative and we're looking for your friends. We will find them. The decision was made not to turn you over to the Israeli government, but instead to bring you to justice here. So, you can plan on spending at least the next thirty years of your young life here in the U.S. in our custody."

Sarah glared at the cocky marshal. "But it's just fine with you to let a Nazi war criminal like Dr. Mengele escape and do nothing about it."

The man scoffed as he looked at Sarah. "Dr. Mengele, my ass. You have no idea who was on that yacht, and you apparently had no qualms about killing an American citizen in cold blood. You think as a Mossad agent you can do whatever you want, wherever you want. But let me tell you, down here in Dade County we are tired of your kind."

Angered by the marshal's attitude, Sarah pounded her fist on the table. "Your people never even tried to stop that yacht to see who was on board or to look for dead or injured. What did they do, just phone in a complaint? Do you allow all your citizens to carry automatic weapons? Or just those protecting Nazi war criminals? And if there was a dead body on board, I would like to see it. Or, was it just tossed into the ocean for shark food so no one could ever recognize him? Exactly how much money does Odessa pass around Dade County to get you to turn your backs!" Sarah screamed, as she beat her fist against the table again.

"Now you wait just a damn minute, lady. Who the hell do you think you are talking to? I have a mind to come over and shut your mouth for you," The marshal shouted angrily.

Sarah laughed as she shook her head. "Well, you just let the world's foremost expert on closing people's mouths sail away, so I'm guessing he must have given you some valuable tips."

Before the angry marshal could respond, another man walked into the room. "Alright, that's enough of this crap. I am Ed Barimore, Federal Attorney for the District of Miami. First off, what Marshal Swenson said is accurate. You are all being charged with murder here in America, and there will be no bail since you would just go back to Israel and disappear. This time Mossad has bitten of more than it can chew, and you will pay the price. Now then, do you want to make a statement and get this over with quickly?"

"Not quite a statement, but a question, and believe me it will come up at the trial. The Miami police never searched that yacht, they never arrested anyone that was shooting at me, and they allowed the vessel to sail off with the supposed body on board that was the only evidence of the supposed crime. Like I asked before, exactly how much did Odessa pay officials here in Miami to hide Mengele while he was here. How much more to allow him to escape while they watched?"

Ed Barimore turned as red as an apple as he glared at Sarah. "Are you actually accusing me of taking payoffs from a Nazi war criminal? How dare you! I'm going to make you wish you had never said that or come to Dade County!"

Sarah smiled. "That's exactly what I'm saying. I'm accusing you and Dade County of taking payoffs, and I think Mossad and several other Nazi hunter organizations will want that question answered. In fact, I believe your President Eisenhower himself may also want an explanation. You may need to think about all of that before taking me to trial. Remember, I could recognize Mengele and I did. He was leaning directly over me exacerbating my injury and ordering me thrown overboard to a certain death. Where is your murder charge against him?"

Silence came over the room as everyone knew some serious questions would be asked down the road. Finally, Ed Barimore nodded his head. "I can take a little heat. It's the word of a long-term trusted law enforcement official against the word of a murdering rogue Mossad agent, after all. Marshal, take her to a cell where she can wait for arraignment in the morning. Then we can deal with that ankle. Welcome to the U.S., Miss Rosenbaum. Now you'll see how American justice works."

Sarah refused to talk to her appointed attorney or attend arraignment the next day. She refused to eat and tore off the splint the nurse had placed on her ankle, causing it to swell badly. When the nurse looked at her ankle the following morning, she told Marshal Swenson that Sarah needed surgery on the ankle to have it reset right away.

About an hour later, two deputies arrived to transport Sarah to the hospital. She struck both men in a wild fight while scratching their necks and faces, accusing them of taking her out to be killed because of what she knew. Realizing Sarah was not going to back down, the deputies left the cell, battered and bloodied.

After a full week of battling back and forth, Ed Barimore had Sarah delivered back to the interrogation room in a wheel chair. "You have proven to me that you are a dangerous Mossad agent capable of anything, with no regard for law enforcement. So, let me tell you the way this is going to be. In the morning, several U.S. Marshals are going to hog tie you if necessary, and take your sweet ass to the hospital, one way or the other. We will get that ankle taken care of whether you like it or not. When you get back you are going to appear in front of a Federal Magistrate for arraignment on the charges, even if we have to keep you hog tied in court. The federal attorney that has been assigned to you as council will do whatever he feels necessary, whether or not you like it or approve. And I don't give a damn if you accuse me of taking bribes or not. You are going to prison for thirty years and that's final!"

The following morning, two marshals arrived at Sarah's cell. After placing handcuffs, a waist chain and leg irons on her, they picked her up and set her down in a wheel chair, then rolled her out to a squad car where a female marshal sat behind the steering wheel. Arriving at the hospital, Sarah was placed in a treatment room where she slid herself up onto a gurney. Several minutes later, a nurse walked into the room telling the officers she needed to take a blood sample before taking Sarah over to the x-ray department.

The nurse smiled at Sarah. "I hear Israel is nice this time of year, I have always wanted to travel there. I'm sure you miss it. When do you think you will get back there?"

Nodding her head, Sarah replied, "Soon, very soon, I'm hoping, once this kangaroo court is finished with me. There is much work to do and I have come to realize how much I dislike your country and so many of your people."

One of the deputies scoffed and shook his head. "Dream on, sister. You'll be a gray-haired old lady when you get back to Israel, if you survive in prison, that is." Both deputies laughed before returning to a fishing story they were discussing from the past weekend.

Moments later, Caleb entered the room wearing a set of blue scrubs and holding a clip board. After saying good morning to the deputies, he looked over Sarah's ankle, carefully asking the usual questions an orthopedic specialist would ask regarding the severity of the injury and how it occurred. Realizing the deputies were not paying attention to anything that was happening in the treatment room, he looked across the gurney at the nurse, nodding his head.

Motioning for one of the marshal's to walk over to the gurney, the nurse smiled as she placed her hand on his shoulder.

"We're going to take her down the hall for x-rays now. We really would appreciate it if you could take off the ankle chains since they'll mess up our pictures. Do you think you could do that for me honey?" she asked, as she flirted and brushed up against him.

The deputy smiled back at the nurse as he began removing the shackles without saying a word. As he turned to walk away, the nurse quickly stuck a hypodermic needle into the side of his neck, while pressing the plunger. Before the second marshal could react, Caleb came up behind him performing the same procedure. In seconds, both men were out cold on the floor. After placing Sarah in a wheelchair, they cuffed the men together and used the set of leg shackles they had taken off Sarah to hook their legs together through the cross supports of the gurney. As they prepared to roll Sarah out the door, she kicked the older man in the back with her good leg.

"Don't ever call me your sister again, you son of a bitch!"

In seconds, Caleb and the nurse were rolling Sarah down the corridor at full speed, heading toward an emergency exit where Josiah and Olga waited in a van.

Marshal Swenson exploded when he heard what had happened in the hospital. He called in every off-duty police officer in Dade County to assist in the search for Sarah and her accomplices. Ed Barimore realized someone in the jail had informed Mossad about Sarah's trip to the hospital, and he was determined to find out who it had been at all cost.

Arriving in Fort Lauderdale, Sarah was taken directly to a private orthopedic clinic run by a Jewish doctor that had strong ties to Israel. By midnight, the doctor had finished operating on Sarah's ankle and put it in a cast. From there, she was taken to a large seaside home that had been rented by Ishmael under an assumed name. After getting some sleep, Sarah met with Ishmael, the Assistant Director of Mossad, Andrew Gabel, and the rest of the team. They spent several hours going over everything that had happened since they arrived in Miami. The Assistant Director was very interested in Marshall Swenson and Prosecutor Barimore, regarding their lack of effort or determination to stop the yacht. Gabel informed the team that the man they were chasing was in fact Dr. Mengele, and he was now in the wind, but they felt he was holed up somewhere in Cuba until things died down.

The following morning, the Assistant Director spoke with the U.S. State Department at length regarding all that had happened, including the fact that someone inside the Miami Police Department or U.S. Marshal's Office was on the Odessa payroll. By four in the afternoon, President Eisenhower had been informed of the situation and was beside himself. He could not believe that Dr. Joseph Mengele had been in the United States for nearly a year and had managed to stay under the radar all that time, and worse yet, had now been allowed to escape capture unchecked. However, the President was equally unhappy knowing Mossad had been operating on American soil without his knowledge or approval.

Several days later, at two in the morning, an Israeli C-130 rolled to a stop near an Air National Guard flight line. As the ramp on the back of the aircraft went down, Caleb, Ira, Josiah, Olga, Sarah and the Mossad nurse named Judith, exited a nearby van.

As they made their way to the aircraft under secret service guard, Ed Barimore stepped up to them out of the darkness. He was followed by a representative from the U.S. State Department. Barimore looked sternly at Sarah and Josiah.

"I asked the State Department to be here before you flew off. I want you to know I do not agree with the way this has turned out, or the way it was handled. We will find out who your informant was in the jail and deal with that person very harshly. Mossad will pay a price for infiltrating the Dade County justice system. We will not accept such treasonous behavior in our jail, or our legal system." Turning toward Judith, he continued. "Your photo and aliases are now part of the FBI's data base. You so much as come back here to visit Disney World and I'll have you arrested. Try me and you'll find out the hard way!"

Judith smiled as she nodded her head. "Sir, I am perfectly alright with that. Since I have been in Florida, I have seen enough rats to last me a lifetime. I certainly don't need to come back and see some damn mouse."

Just as Barimore was about to explode on Judith, Ishmael stepped forward, glaring at the angry attorney. "If I were you, I would be more interested in finding out who is on Odessa's payroll. You know we will find out, and that person or persons will be brought to justice properly under United States law. We have assurance from your President on that issue. As far as a Mossad agent or mole in the jail, I will neither confirm or deny any such person exists. But remember, for Israel to exist, those are the kind of things we must do. We have eyes and ears all around the world, including in the United States, and your precious Dade County is no different."

As Josiah began to roll Sarah up the ramp, Barimore stepped up to the wheelchair. "I assure you from the bottom of my heart, if any of you ever step foot in Florida again, I will make it my life s work to see you get tossed in jail. Nobody ever screws with Ed Barimore and gets away with it!"

Sarah stared up at the angry attorney. "And if I find out it was you or Swenson that was taking money from Odessa, I can guarantee there is no rock big enough that you'll be able to hide under. We will find you and your connections, and you will stand trial and rot in prison. Keep that in mind! Mossad will never rest until all Nazi war criminals and their supporters have gone straight to hell."

Before Barimore could say another word, one of the secret service agents ordered him off the plane.

After two months of recuperating in a Mossad safe house near the Mediterranean, Sarah returned to her cubicle to work. Ishmael desperately needed Sarah's expertise on a case that would once again send Mossad operatives halfway around the world on a major capture. One that would turn the world upside down.

In 1957, a German prosecutor working on war crime trials told Mossad officials that Adolph Eichmann was living in Argentina. However, attempting to nail down a location was not easy so the investigation came to a halt. By 1958, Mossad was once again hot on the trail of several major Nazi war criminals. Sarah was added to a hand-picked team to analyze, piece together, and eventually place a team on the ground to capture Eichmann. There appeared to be more dead ends than positive leads for the first year. Finally, a team of Mossad agents on the ground was able to come up with information that appeared to be promising.

Soon, it became evident that Eichmann was living in the San Fernando district of Buenos Aires, under the assumed name of Ricardo Klement. Since Argentina was celebrating their 150th anniversary celebration, thousands of people were visiting from all over the world. Mossad took advantage of the celebration to send more agents into the country using false travel documents.

After several tough days of nonstop work, the team notified Israeli Prime Minister David Ben-Gurion that they had nailed down Eichmann's home. After countless rehearsals, the team went after Eichmann on May 11, 1960. They attempted to capture him as he walked from a bus stop to his home, but all did not go well.

The team hid Eichmann in a safe house, where they interrogated him around the clock until they were positive beyond all doubt that they had the right man. Sarah spent many sleepless nights communicating with the team, verifying information and giving them clues they could use to bait him.

Sarah longed to be in Argentina to help take down the man that had created the extermination camps, but Ishmael was adamant that she was serving a better purpose working out of Mossad headquarters.

All the while, the Argentinian Government was protesting to the Allied Governments and the United Nations, regarding the kidnapping of Ricardo Klement by suspected Mossad agents. They argued extensively that he was not a Nazi war criminal and that Mossad had no right to be holding him, though they had no idea where Mossad was operating from. It became regrettably apparent that Argentina would not be willing to extradite Eichmann under any circumstances, as they continued to deny he had been living there under protection.

Everyone in Mossad headquarters understood they would need to come up with a plan to get Eichmann out of Argentina soon, before their hideout was compromised. Quickly, a daring plan was created to transport Eichmann out of Argentina. On May 20, 1960, Eichmann was drugged and taken to a waiting Israeli airliner wearing a disguise. When officials at the airport questioned the condition of the drugged man, they were informed that he was an airline employee that had suffered a fall and sustained severe head trauma. Although some Argentinian officials at the airport questioned the story, they had no proof the man in the disguise was Eichmann or Klement. Top well paid government officials in Buenos Aires worked desperately to stop the flight, however an eleventh-hour agreement was reached, allowing the airliner to leave for Israel.

In a world televised trial held in Jerusalem that began May 23, 1960, Eichmann was found guilty of several charges, including crimes against humanity. He was hanged on May 31, 1962, with his ashes being dumped into the Mediterranean.

It was during this trial that Sarah finally met the love of her life, a Mossad attorney by the name of Simon Waldmann. He had grown up in Haifa, Israel, but had lost an uncle and aunt that had moved to Germany for business prior to 1932, and eventually died in the holocaust. Angered by the world's indifference, he had made finding Nazi war criminals his life's work, enduring him to Sarah from the first time they met.

Although Sarah had traveled to Nuremberg several times for trials, she had refused to visit any of the concentration camps.

However, Simon had traveled to nearly all of the camps, looking for information and interviewing survivors that had come back to visit the camps they had been in. He stressed over and over that Sarah needed to return to Dachau to close the door on her past, but she always refused.

The happy couple were married in Tel Aviv on September 23, 1962, surrounded by her adopted family and a raucous gathering of Mossad employees. Although Sarah was nervous about ever returning to America after her problems in Miami, Simon convinced her everything would be fine if they honeymooned in New York City. Both of them were interested in visiting Time Square, Broadway, the Statue of Liberty, and many other sites.

Simon was well aware that Sarah would never be able to become pregnant after what Sgt. Wilhelm had done to her, but he felt it was important that they adopt a child. It took some convincing before Sarah finally agreed to adoption. Finally, on February 12, 1963, they were able to adopt a two-day old Jewish girl they named Simchah, which means gladness or joy in Hebrew.

Sarah continued working with Mossad at home by reading files, organizing records, or any other tasks Ishmael sent her way. One of the more massive projects she undertook was compiling records and studying the Nazi escape routes through Switzerland and down into Italy and Spain. There were many different routes that were used, depending on who was doing the funding. These escape routes became known by investigators as ratlines. However, there was one escape route that had haunted investigators since the end of the war. It had become known to investigators around the world as the monastery route. Nazi hierarchy and S.S. criminals were able to get false documents in Germany through Odessa, then travel south through Switzerland to Italy. They were then moved from one Franciscan monastery to the next, before finally arriving at the Monastery-Via Sicilia in Rome. There, they were outfitted with their final documents and travel arrangements to wherever they were planning to go. Investigators began referring to the monastery as the transit station. It became clear to the Mossad that the Monastery-Via Sicilia was operated by a Bishop from Graz named Alois Hudal. Throughout many interviews, it became clear that Hudal and the other Franciscans in the monastery felt that helping the fleeing Nazis was an act of Christian charity, but not so for Mossad.

As the investigative process wore on, it had become clear that Archbishop Carlo Romani of Graz, through cooperation of the Vatican, had helped move some of the worst and most dangerous Nazi war criminals to many parts of the world. Roughly four hundred fifty million dollars in German gold, most of it looted during the occupation years, was used to finance the operation.

Throughout hundreds of hours of work, Sarah began compiling a chilling list of information, linking names of Nazi war criminals, dates of transit, possible destinations, and who set each operation into motion. Finally, Sarah felt she had enough information to call for a meeting.

After the presentation, Ishmael decided to send Ira and Mari to Italy to seek out some of the people involved and attempt to question them. Ira was overwhelmed at the information they were collecting from many of the individuals they contacted. Each night Mari would type contact sheets and send them by Mossad courier to Sarah the following morning.

Upon returning to Rome after completing several interviews in the town of Viterbo, just north of Rome, they found their hotel room torn apart. The mattresses and pillows had been shredded, the carpet had been torn lose from the floor and even the bathroom cabinets had been removed from the walls. They wasted no time packing up their clothing and leaving the hotel as fast as possible. Mari was shaken by what happened, but Ira understood completely that there were people in Rome that wanted everything involving Nazi war criminals in Italy to remain buried forever, and they would do whatever was possible to stop Mossad from searching. Luckily, they had not left any records in the room that could be used by Odessa, or whoever was behind this attack.

Ira quickly left Rome, driving to the port city of Civitavecchia, about eighty kilometers northwest of Rome. He knew several men there that worked for an Israeli cargo company that would keep them safe overnight. After settling into the cramped quarters, Ira notified Ishmael as to what had happened. Ishmael was certain this incident would not be the last if the team stayed there, so he told them to return to Tel Aviv the following day. But Ira had lined up an interview with a retired priest that sounded very promising for the next afternoon, and he was not about to let it slip away. The man lived in Latino, about ten kilometers south of Rome. Sarah verified the name of the retired priest as being involved with the monastery line for some time, and was anxious to hear what he had to say.

Around four in the afternoon, Ira and Mari arrived near the park where they were to conduct the interview. They sat in their car for about twenty minutes, watching who came and went from the park, but the priest was nowhere in sight. Feeling their time had been wasted, Ira started the motor and began backing up. Quickly Mari pointed to an older man just arriving at the park from a taxi. As Ira once again parked the car, they watched the man walk over to a bench where he had said they could meet. Feeling relieved that the trip was about to pay off, Ira and Mari approached the man.

Ira smiled as he held out his hand. "I'm Ira, we talked on the phone yesterday."

Nodding his head, the old man shook hands with the two before asking them to be seated.

"Son, the war has been over for a long time, and not everything should have happened the way it did. I have felt guilty for a long time over my part in helping Nazi criminals to escape. It was not right, but there was nothing I could do to stop it."

Mari looked into the man's eyes. "Are there any records you might be aware of that no one else has seen? Can you give us information that might lead to the arrest of these criminals?"

Reaching into an inner pocket of his jacket, he pulled out a thick envelope. "I'm sure this is what you would be interested in. I have made notes along the edges and added a sheet near the end with some things I can recall. Take it, and let the chips fall where they may. You see, I'm dying, and I want my conscience to be clear when I pass on. But I warn you, there are powerful people that will stop at nothing to keep you from doing anything with this intelligence. Now leave, go back to Israel and do what must be done. But remember, no matter what people claim, Odessa does—"

Before he could finish his statement, a bullet struck him in the back of the head. A second bullet grazed Ira's upper left arm as he reached for his pistol. "Run, Mari! Get back to the car!" Ira called out, as he tossed her the envelope.

Several windows on the car exploded as Ira drove forward up over the curb, heading west across an unoccupied athletic field. He tore through a chain link fence and side swiped a concession building before bouncing over another curb back onto a street. Mari was screaming from the floor of the car where she had taken refuge. Shifting down into second gear, Ira stomped on the gas pedal. Smoke rolled from the spinning tires before Ira grabbed third gear. Instantly, the car screamed through several residential streets, knocking over four trash receptacles and breaking through one road barricade, before arriving back on the highway leading toward Rome.

When they were about two miles out of town, Mari brushed the glass off her seat and climbed up from the floor. "How is your arm? Where did the shots come from? Are we going to get out of here alive? How do we get back to Israel before—"

"Stop it!" Ira yelled out in Hebrew as he passed several slower cars. "I'm fine, Mari. I think the shots came from that stone building across the street, and in case you did not notice, we are alive. From this point forward we play it one step at a time until we get back to Tel Aviv."

As Ira was finishing his explanation, he observed a black Mercedes in the rear-view mirror, passing car after car as it was gaining on them at an incredible speed. He knew there was no way the rental car they were driving could outrun their pursuers. Without signaling, he turned sharply onto a smaller asphalt road that ran down toward the coastline. Looking back in the mirror, he saw the driver of the Mercedes slide past the turn with all four wheels locked up. Ira hoped that mistake would give them a slightly better chance to get away, but he knew his car was not made for driving curvy roads at high speeds like that of his pursuers. Within minutes, the Mercedes was once again gaining on them as the driver was caring little about the oncoming traffic, often forcing them off the road.

A man on the passenger side of the black car began leaning out the window firing his automatic weapon toward them. Ira attempted swerving back and forth trying to dodge the hail of bullets that were smashing into the rear of their car. As he began rounding the next curve in the road, a bullet struck his right rear tire. It took everything Ira had to keep the twisting car on the road as they were entering the next curve. He fought desperately to pull the car back to the right as a small delivery truck was now facing him head on. The two vehicles scraped sides, sending Ira's car into a chaotic spin he knew he could not overcome. Nosing toward the ditch at high speed, Ira yelled out. "Hold on, Mari, and pray we don't go over that cliff into the ocean."

As the left front wheel struck a boulder sticking out of the ground, the embattled car flipped over, rolling four times before coming to rest against a tree.

Three men exited the black Mercedes, cautiously approaching the car carrying automatic weapons. Knowing his right arm was completely shattered, Ira struggled to pull his weapon clear of its holster with his left hand. The man standing beside the door fired a quick blast from his machine gun into Ira's chest.

Reaching in through the passenger side door, a second man picked up the blood-stained envelope and tossed it across the car.

"We got what we came for, let's get out of here before the Polizia arrive. The woman was most likely thrown over the cliff when she was tossed out of the car. We must go!" The nervous gunman declared as he watched traffic on the narrow road.

The man holding the envelope was not ready to leave without knowing what happened to Mari. "Go look over the cliff and see if she is laying in the tall grass. We need to make sure she's dead or Major Rolph will make sure we are."

After scouring the tall grass for several minutes the nervous man called out. "I have blood here. She must have slid along the grass before going over into the sea. I don't see a body anywhere."

Convinced Mari was dead, the men climbed into the Mercedes and drove back toward the main highway.

It was dark when Mari came to. Every inch of her body was in pain from what she had gone through from the time she had been ejected from the car. She could hear the roar of the dark, cold forbidding ocean as the waves slammed into the shear rock cliff below her. The only way out of her predicament was back up through the slippery wet grass and small trees she had passed over on her way down to the narrow ledge she was laying on.

There was enough starlight for her to see a small inch wide three trunk sticking out of the ground about two feet above her head. It looked solid, but if she had loosened it when she slid over the top of it on the way down, there was no telling if it would be of much help.

After maneuvering her aching body a bit, she cautiously grabbed on to the little tree. Although it gave a little as she pulled, Mari was able to get a good foot hold and boost herself up several feet. Grabbing handfuls of sodden grass, Mari painfully worked her way up the slippery cliff until she reached the top. Everything was dead quiet except for the roar of the ocean below. The car remained up against the tree where it had stopped, with Ira's body still inside the mangled, bullet riddled wreckage. Reaching over Ira, Mari pulled her purse from under the seat. Removing a small flash light from a zippered compartment, she aimed the small beam of light at her partner. Realizing Ira was dead and the envelope was gone, she dropped to the ground and sat against the car.

About an hour later a police car came down the road and stopped. It was apparent they were in no hurry and were fully aware of what had happened. As they waited for an ambulance, one of the officers knelt down beside Mari. Leaning over by her ear he said quietly, "Once you are released from the hospital, go back to Israel. You have no idea what and who you are dealing with here."

Sarah grabbed hold of Mari as she stepped down from the Israeli military plane that had flown her back home along with Ira's remains. Holding Mari tight, Sarah whispered, "This should not have happened. I'm so sorry."

Mari looked up at Sarah with a frightened look on her face.

"They are coming after us here at home. It's not over yet. Mossad has become a huge target, I'm afraid."

Over the next few weeks, Sarah and Ishmael reviewed and changed many of the security protocols governing the operation of Mossad and its agents. However, Odessa was determined to shut down everything to do with investigating the monastery route.

Josiah was looking forward to the weekend as he drove his Toyota past his apartment building heading toward the parking lot, but something felt out of place. Parking the car about a block away, Josiah opened the trunk, taking out a small automatic rifle and several spare magazines which he had wrapped in an old jacket.

Being on high alert, he ducked behind a large garbage dumpster, allowing him to scan the usually quiet parking lot for anything out of place. Nothing out of the ordinary caught his attention, yet the nagging feeling was still haunting him. Slowly, he scanned the building itself from south to north, keeping a close eye on the edge of the roof. When his eyes came across the living room window of his own apartment, he knew something was amiss. The large flower pot with the cactus that normally sat by the window was missing, and it had been there when he left for work. He remembered his girlfriend Ruth was going to make dinner for him tonight, but there would be no need for her to move the huge plant. Backing away from the dumpster, Josiah feared for Ruth, but there was no way he could approach the building without being seen. Watching a delivery truck stop by a small grocery store across the street, he had an idea. Running to the truck he grabbed the drivers jacket off the seat and put it on. Picking up two small boxes from the back of the truck and an empty clipboard he made his way toward the front door of his building. Pulling his weapon to the ready, slowly he ascended the three flights of stairs leading to his apartment. Peering down the corridor, he noticed the door to a usually locked equipment room was partially open. He knew full well there was a set of eyes staring back in his direction through a rifle scope. Descending back down the stairs, Josiah exited the building, walking over to the east side where a maintenance ladder was built onto the side of the building. Although it was six feet above the ground, Josiah was able to jump up and grab the bottom rung. Quickly, he pulled himself up, making his way to the roof. He walked over to a trap door that would allow him to drop down at the end of the corridor behind the storage room, and out of sight of the rifle scope. After picking the lock, Josiah carefully pulled the steel door open and checked out the corridor to make sure it was empty. After lowering himself down, Josiah crouched in the corner for a moment, listening for any unusual noises. Laying his rifle on the floor, he pulled out his semi-automatic pistol and screwed on the silencer that all Mossad agents carried for times like this. Standing just outside the storage room, Josiah closed his eyes for a second before kicking in the door and turning to his right. A stunned man looking up in fear, fell to the floor still holding onto a sniper rifle. Before he could take a second breath, Josiah placed two rounds into his forehead.

The next door on the right was his apartment. Quietly moving forward, Josiah observed a trip wire affixed to the door frame, about three inches above the floor. He couldn't be sure there wasn't another contact switch on the door that would blow the bomb when he opened it. Backing up to the equipment room he found a phone on the wall. Quickly, he dialed the emergency number for the Mossad bomb squad. After explaining the situation, Josiah sat quietly in the supply room, all the while wondering about Ruth.

Within thirty minutes the crew arrived. They climbed to the roof as Josiah had done earlier, then made their way along the roof so they were directly above the window where the cactus normally sat. They swung over the roof, smashing through the window into the apartment, ready to fire on anyone that moved. All they found was Ruth's body, sitting in a chair near the door with her throat cut, and a large bomb on her lap that was wired to the door.

Josiah knelt down near her body. He had loved her for a long time and intended to marry her in the near future, but now Odessa had taken away their dreams.

Everyone at Mossad was now on high alert as they now knew for sure they were being hunted on their own turf. A week later, Caleb stopped by a grocery store on his way home from work. As he looked over some French bread, he saw the reflection of two men coming up behind him in the glass of a dairy cooler. He spun around in time to see one of the men pulling a sawed-off shot gun from under his coat. Caleb fired quickly striking the man in the chest and throat. As blood gushed from the dying man, the second assassin dove behind a counter, firing his pistol without making contact. Caleb attempted to run to the far side of the store, but was quickly chased back by two more Odessa agents that had just entered the store. Boxed in with no place to go, Caleb dropped to a knee, taking aim at his new assailants. A hail of bullets roared up and down the aisle for several moments as screaming customers ran out the doors. When it was over, Caleb lay dying in a pool of blood, as did one of the assassins from the front of the store. The other Odessa gunman gasped for air while holding his side where one of Caleb's bullets had ripped open his right lung. The original gunman walked by Caleb's body, firing two more rounds into him before picking up his wounded partner.

After identifying the two bodies from the market shooting, Mossad was able to come up with a fairly good idea who was behind the attacks. Over the next month in Israel, six members of the assassin group were killed and two more arrested.

Sarah took Simchah and moved temporarily back to Nahariya with her adopted family. They were happy to have Sarah and Simchah staying with them, although they did not understand the reason for the sudden trip. Sarah attempted to act as normal as possible, although she realized Odessa could have tracked her back home. After nearly six weeks of peace and quiet, Sarah was feeling much better, but never totally let her guard down.

One evening while the Pearlman's took Simchah to a gathering of friends down on the beach, Sarah walked about a mile to a small bar where many of her friends hung out. As she walked in the door, a blue Nissan caught her attention. She was sure she had seen it several times over the past few days, but decided it couldn't have been the same car. Inside the bar, she walked up to an American friend named Janet. After getting a drink, they sat down at an outside table with several other young people. The balmy Mediterranean breezes made for a rather relaxing and enjoyable evening. Sarah sipped her red wine as she laughed heartily at the stories her friends told her regarding their latest exploits.

About an hour later, Sarah and Janet walked up to the bar to order some appetizers. As Sarah was paying, she observed a large man standing near the bathroom that just did not fit into the mix of young people enjoying the evening. No matter how hard she tried to put the man out of her mind, she knew something was wrong. When Janet walked off with the first platter, Sarah pulled her pistol from her waist band and clicked off the safety. Looking down into her purse she carefully removed the two spare clips she always carried and put them in her jacket pocket.

Picking up the second plate of appetizers, Sarah noticed the man by the bathroom nod his head toward someone else in the bar. Now her survival skills were running in over drive. She knew if there were two, there probably were three. The last thing she wanted to do was take the plate back to her friends and place them in jeopardy. The bartender looked questioningly at Sarah. "Is there anything else I can get for you, young lady?"

Nodding her head, Sarah smiled. "Yes, I am Mossad, you can duck!"

Seeing Sarah bring up her pistol, the bartender dove for cover as he reached for a telephone under the bar.

The man by the bathroom quickly jumped off his stool and reached for a gun inside his jacket, but never made it. Sarah dropped him with two clean shots, just as a bar lamp next to her head exploded. Diving to the floor to avoid the second shooter, Sarah scrambled away from the bar, coming up behind a large jukebox. Peering around the tinted Plexiglas cover, she could see a man holding a pistol near the bar looking around for her. A third man with a shotgun was making his way toward the table where her friends were hiding.

Afraid for her friends, Sarah ran out from behind the jukebox, firing three rounds at the man with the shotgun, hitting him in the arm. He spun around just as the man by the bar fired in Sarah's direction. The bullets struck the jukebox as Sarah dove toward the floor again, rolling over toward a coat rack. Scrambling up to her feet, she wound her way through screaming customers as she struggled to reach the exit. Several more rounds struck the door post, as Sarah dropped back to the floor and rolled out of the building onto the sidewalk. Regaining her feet, Sarah began running toward the intersection where she observed a woman standing by the blue Nissan with a gun in her hand, while another man quickly slid out of the back seat. Sarah fired several shots at the woman as she dashed across the street toward an automobile repair shop.

Dropping to her knees behind a wrecked car, Sarah removed the empty clip from her pistol and slammed a fresh one into place. She watched the two men from the bar enter the street where the woman stood, pointing toward the parking lot behind the repair shop. Looking over her shoulder, Sarah observed an old Israeli Army armored personnel carrier parked along the back fence, with a wrecker right beside it. Running toward the carrier, she stopped to look inside the wrecker. The keys were hanging in the ignition. Without hesitation, Sarah jumped behind the wheel and fired up the rough sounding diesel engine. She knew that would slow her pursuers, giving her enough time to get in the carrier or hide somewhere else. Running quickly behind the wrecker, she hoped the back door of the carrier would open. Grabbing the large steel handle, she pulled down with all her strength. To her amazement, the handle worked smoothly and the door opened wide enough for her to get in.

With the hatch secured from the inside, Sarah made her way to the front of the carrier to get a look out of the periscope above the driver's seat. She could see the man with the shot gun just inside the gate, but was unaware where the other two could be. Removing a tiny flashlight from her purse, Sarah ran the narrow beam of light over the controls. Remembering her training at Mossad, she turned on the power switch. Happily, all the gauges instantly illuminated. Sarah giggled for a moment before placing her hand on the ignition switch. She closed her eyes for a second and prayed as she pushed in the starter button. The diesel engine rolled over several times before the old carrier shook and rattled as the power plant sprang to life. Looking back through the periscope she saw the man with the shotgun about ten feet in front of the carrier, with the other two assailants still standing near the gate. Confidently, Sarah slid the gearshift into the forward mode, then quickly released the hand controls for the tracks. The old beast leapt forward as if it had never been taken out of service. The man with the shotgun turned to run, but Sarah had slammed her foot down on the throttle overtaking him within seconds. She could feel a slight thump as he went under the left track.

The men at the gate fired several rounds at the approaching armored behemoth, as if it was possible to stop twenty-five tons of fury with a pistol. Sarah sideswiped the wrecker before striking a wrecked car near the gate, pushing it out of the way. She steered the carrier to the right, ripping out a compete section of chain link fence as she aimed for the Odessa assassins. She watched through the periscope as one of the men and the woman took cover behind a large dumpster sitting by the bar. Quickly, Sarah released the turret cover, allowing her to bring the seat up, so the upper half of her body was now out in the open. As she hit the dumpster with the carrier, the man jumped out in the open preparing to fire at Sarah, but the moving dumpster knocked him off balance. Slamming on the brake, Sarah brought her pistol up, firing at the man as he attempted to get up off the ground. He stumbled once before falling forward, dead.

As Sarah put the carrier in reverse, the engine quit and would not restart. Quickly, Sarah dropped back down inside, pulling the turret cover closed, and locked it. Peering through the periscope, she could not be sure, where the woman or the other man had gone, but there was no doubt they were close by.

For several moments Sarah pondered her decision as she

continued trying to restart the engine with no luck. The smell of gas caught Sarah's attention as she listened to a man's footsteps on top of the carrier. It was evident the man was pouring gas onto the carrier, attempting to turn the iron beast into her funeral pyre.

Gas began to drip in around the gunner's hatch on the far side of the carrier. If she did not escape in the next few seconds before the match was tossed, she would be blown to bits. Gathering all her strength, Sarah ran to the back door of the carrier, lifted the locking latch, pulled up the handle and pushed on the heavy door, just as a whoosh of flame roared past her. The explosion threw Sarah's body flying out the back door of the burning carrier where she bounced along the road, landing with a thump about fifteen yards from the blazing machine. A secondary explosion ripped a section of track lose from the carrier, sending it slicing through the air, nearly tearing an onlooker in front of the bar in half.

Shaken and sore, Sarah quickly realized she had lost her pistol in the process, and she could not be sure who else was still out there trying to kill her. As she staggered to her feet, she was suddenly pushed to the ground from behind by the woman she had seen by the car. After spinning away from the woman's foot, Sarah jumped up, grabbing a handful of long blonde hair and pulling with all her strength. The woman screamed as she struggled to break free of Sarah's grip. Wielding a bayonet with her left hand that Sarah had not seen, the woman swung it toward Sarah's neck with full force, seriously cutting her left shoulder. The pain was intense, but all she could think about now was Simchah and Simon. There was no way she was going to lose her family tonight. There was no way she was going to lose everything that was finally right in her life.

Still having the long blonde hair wrapped around her hand, Sarah swung the woman backwards with all her strength, pulling both of them to the ground. Pushing the screaming woman away from her, Sarah rolled to her right, picking up a three-foot metal bracket that had been torn from the top of the fence when she drove the carrier through it. Grabbing hold of it, Sarah jumped to her feet, just as the woman was coming back after her with the bloody bayonet. With a quick swing Sarah struck the woman across the arm before they collided. The bayonet fell to the ground as did the steel bracket Sarah was holding. The two women rolled across the road, striking one another over and over with massive blows. Glancing quickly to her right, Sarah realized her hand was just inches from the steel bracket. Grabbing hold of it, Sarah struck her determined assailant on the side of the head, causing her to drop to one knee. Scraping up the bayonet from the road, the woman regained her feet but appeared to be faltering.

Sarah held up her hand. "Let's end this now, no one else needs to die tonight, drop the bayonet and this can be over."

With fire raging in her eyes, the woman let out a primal scream, lunging at Sarah with the bayonet. Sarah stepped back one step, then thrust the jagged steel bracket forward as hard as she could at her lethal adversary. A moment later, Sarah watched one of Odessa's best female assassins fall to her knees, with both hands grasping the steel bracket that had penetrated clear through her body. Blood ran from her mouth as she tried to speak, but no words could be heard. Slowly, her eyes rolled back into her head as she tumbled forward. In the distance, the welcome sounds of sirens could be heard racing toward the bar. The raging fire in the carrier continued sending out eerie shadows over the macabre scene of death and destruction.

Exhausted, bloodied and mentally distressed, Sarah walked a few feet where she picked up her pistol from the road. She slowly scanned the area, knowing the man that had set the carrier on fire was still nearby, before dropping down on the curb, unaware of the large crowd that had gathered on the street corner across from the bar. Moments later, two fire trucks, several police cars and three armored Israeli Army vehicles arrived to secure the area.

As soldiers from the Israeli Defense Force exited their vehicles, Sarah called out. "Be careful, there is still one more man around here. I don't know where he went."

One of the medics ran up to Sarah and took her by the arm, leading her back toward the curb to begin working on her injuries. They had barely sat down when Sarah observed the man standing in the crowd near one of the fire trucks. Pushing the paramedic to the side, Sarah jumped to her feet and began walking down the road toward the last assailant. She was already about halfway there when he spotted her coming toward him. Before he could raise his pistol all the way, three shots rang out dropping him to the road. Sarah stopped walking and slowly turned to look behind her. The female medic that had attempted to treat Sarah was still on one knee preparing to holster her weapon.

Standing up, the young medic walked over to Sarah. Taking her by the arm, she led Sarah slowly back to the curb where her first aid pack was. "It's over now sister, it is over. You have done enough for one night. Let me patch you up before I take you to the hospital."

As another medic arrived to help, Sarah leaned her head against his shoulder. She closed her eyes and took a deep breath.

"I let Galenka down tonight. I killed, I killed four people this night. I have become what I never wanted to be. How do I come back from this, how do I hold my Simchah again and feel like a mother. Tell me, when does this end? When do we live in peace? Can you tell me that?"

The medic placed his arm around Sarah. "I do not know who Galenka is. But I feel that wherever she is, she would be proud of you tonight. Had you not fought as you did, how many more young people in the bar might have been killed, your daughter Simchah would no longer have her mother, and these assassins would still be alive to kill more Jews. I believe this Galenka would forgive you. You are a brave woman."

After being treated at the hospital, Sarah was sitting in a treatment room waiting to be discharged when a nurse walked in. Picking up the phone receiver she handed it to Sarah.

"You have an important call, you can take it here."

When the nurse had left the room, Sarah said, "Hello." She almost cried when she heard the voice of Ishmael on the other end.

"Sarah, my child, how are you? I heard you went through hell this evening."

Smiling, Sarah replied. "I did what I needed to do, Ishmael. I may not have avenged the deaths of Ira and Caleb completely, but Odessa now knows we may bend, but we will not break. I just hope Galenka can understand all of this."

Ishmael nodded his head. "I'm happy you survived this attempt, my child. We have secured your family and the Pearlman's, they are all safe. Take a few weeks to rest up and when you are ready, I have some work I would like you to get into. But know that Galenka and I are both proud of you tonight. You fought for your family and the life of Israel, you are a true hero. I have always thought of you that way, ever since we first met in that Godforsaken forest so long ago."

Sarah had to laugh when she thought about how Ishmael dressed and acted when they had first met. "I will be back in Tel Aviv in ten days, ready to go to work. I will leave Simchah here for a while more."

After hanging up the phone, Ishmael stood up and walked to the window of the conference room. He knew very well that with Mossad under attack, avenging the deaths of agents like Ira and Caleb may become a common thing, but if they were to survive, it was evident more agents would be lost along the way. He prayed his Sarah would never be one of them.

Chapter Eighteen
Major Victories

No matter how hard Sarah worked on solving cases and taking down former Nazi's, the escape of Doctor Mengele in Florida continued to haunt her. The Mossad and the Simon Wiesenthal Center had spent huge sums searching for the elusive doctor, but always coming up short. It was evident he was somewhere in South America and that he had a well-organized security system funded by Odessa working to keep him safe.

Sightings and eye witness testimony sent teams scrambling across Brazil from Rio de Janeiro to Sao Paula. Then word came that he was holed up in Montevideo, Uruguay, where a large German population lived that was very pro-Nazi. From there, Mossad teams searched Buenos Aires, Argentina, and up to Corrientes, then on to Villarrica, Paraguay, where again they found many former Germans in small communities that were anything but helpful or trustworthy.

By the end of 1978, Sarah was sure Mengele was spending more time in Sao Paula than he was in Paraguay. She knew there was a family in Sao Paula that was dedicated to helping Nazi criminals with money and escape materials to keep them free. With all that information in hand, Josiah, Mari and Olga made their way to Brazil, using the cover of oil executives. The problem was that many people from Brazil, Paraguay and the United States were flocking to the warm beaches of Sao Paula for a festive holiday. The crowds made it more difficult to track the people they were following.

By News Years Day, the team had positive proof the doctor was somewhere in the Sao Paula area having a holiday on one of the nearby beaches, but there were hundreds of resorts and private homes lining the pristine sandy coastline, where armed security guards worked diligently to protect the occupants.

On February fifth, an informant told Josiah that Mengele was in fact in Beritoga, a fashionable resort area south of Sao Paula. Late in the afternoon of February seventh, the team observed a large contingent of police vehicles and people running to a section of beach. Jumping from their car, they joined the throng of people being held back by the local police.

Olga walked up to an older man of about seventy that appeared to be upset with what was happening. Looking up at the crying man, she inquired. "I am from America, what is all this fuss about, did something bad happen?"

The man nodded his head. "Have you ever heard of Doctor Joseph Mengele? They just pulled him out of the water. He must have drowned!"

Being stunned by the man's explanation, she said. "Did you know this man?"

Nodding his head, the man replied. "He has come here often over the last few years. We have made him feel at home since so many people are trying to capture him. He was a very nice man, and a good doctor, he treated many of us for nothing when we were sick. I shall miss him."

Immediately Olga reported to Josiah what she had learned. Quickly, the team approached the police, identifying themselves. It was clear now that the man was dead, and no one really cared about what happened to him. Every police officer was taking photos with the corpse, and talking to the hastily assembled press, trying to act as if they were the one that discovered the body. Young boys were poking the body with sticks while many local residents took photos of the uncovered body lying on a blanket.

Josiah and Mari took finger prints and pulled one tooth for testing, as a team from the Wiesenthal Center compiled their own evidence.

With everything confirmed, Ishmael was happy to mark the photo on the wall as case closed. The family he was staying with claimed the body, along with help from Odessa. The official cause of death after a crude autopsy, was that Mengele had suffered a massive stroke while swimming and he drowned. Days later, the body of the sadistic doctor was taken to a cemetery in Embu das Artes, Brazil, where he was buried under the name of Wolfgang Gerhard.

Sarah was angry they had been so close and still hadn't been able to capture the infamous evil doctor. However, there was little doubt that getting the man out of Brazil alive would have been a hard-fought battle. Many judges and politicians had been paid very well over the years by Odessa to keep the doctor safe. Though frustrated, Sarah and the team were happy they were finally able to put an end to a search that had haunted them for so long.

Nevertheless, the search went on for other high-ranking Nazi war criminals, and Sarah and her team were still up to the challenge.

January 19, 1983, started out as a typical Wednesday in Mossad headquarters. Sarah sat in her cubical, sorting, reading and cataloging intercepts from the last twenty-four hours, compiled by agents working all around the world. Much of it had to do with top Arab leaders such as PLO leader Yasser Arafat, Egyptian President Ahmad Mohieddin, Syria's President Hafez al-Assad, Jordan's King Abdullah and the young militant, Colonel Muammar Gaddafi, that had become leader of the Revolutionary Command in Libya.

Whatever those men did, wherever they went, whoever they visited was always a concern for Israeli Prime Minister Menachem Begin. Couple that with the constant plotting of Russian President Yuri Andropov, and you had yourself a daily tinder box that threatened the very existence of Israel. Nothing could be overlooked, nothing could ever be taken for granted.

As Sarah analyzed an overnight intercept from an agent in Bulgaria, Ishmael walked into her cubicle. "Find anything that looks ominous this morning, Sarah?"

Shaking her head, she replied. "Andropov is talking about visiting Romania again. He sent some of his state department people there late last night. I wonder what he's up to?"

Ishmael couldn't help but smile, as Sarah never let anything slide. She was always looking for a conspiracy under every rock and all too often, she found one. Sitting down across from her, Ishmael leaned forward.

"Sarah, the Prime Minister received a message early this morning from Bolivian President Hernan Zuazo. The negotiations they have been having with the French have finally paid off. They have agreed to turn Klaus Barbie over to the French government today. He was living in LaPaz as we suspected, still using the assumed name of Klaus Altmann as he had been earlier. We have ordered several Mossad agents to be involved with his transfer to France to ensure nothing goes wrong."

Leaning back in her chair Sarah smiled. "So, when do I leave for France?"

"Always the eager one!" Ishmael replied, as he stood up. "It will take some time before his trial begins, perhaps even a couple of years. We expect his lawyers will pull every trick in the book to have all or some of the charges tossed out, although they are going to have a very tough uphill battle. Remember, he was already tried and found guilty in absentia back in 1954, so there is a very good precedent already set. So, for now, we want you to continue with what you are doing, and when we have some idea of a trial date, we will put you to work on the case full time."

Nodding her head, Sarah smiled. "Just the thought of finally bringing him to justice excites me. Keep me informed and I'll pull out the files soon so we have them ready."

With the trial for Barbie finally set to begin on May 12, 1987, Sarah and her investigative team flew to France in April to work with the attorneys. Each passing day Sarah found it harder and harder to concentrate as she thought about finally bringing the arrogant butcher of Lyon to justice. She would have felt better if she could have just stood him up against a wall and shot him herself.

On the morning of the twelfth, Sarah was unable to eat and was physically sick. Today, she would come face to face with the man who sent her to Dachau and caused her to endure such brutal torture. He was also responsible for the deaths of Rochelle, Moshe, and many other underground operatives.

As he entered the courtroom in handcuffs and leg irons, Sarah studied the despicable man from top to bottom. How small and inconsequential he looked now without his creased black S.S.

uniform and his gleaming medals. Gone were the glossy black hobnail boots he enjoyed using to kick his fearful prisoners. Gone were those heavy leather gloves he enjoyed using to slap helpless people relentlessly across the face. Gone was the stiff riding crop he used to beat women and old men into submission. But most of all, gone was the cocky smirk he always wore on his face, and the twinkle in his eye that appeared to glow brighter the more sadistic he became. And thankfully, gone were the leaders of the Third Reich that had given this sadistic man unbridled power.

Still, he was not a broken man by any means. In his arrogance, he would mock the judges, prosecutors and witnesses as if they were nothing more than sacrificial lambs he had yet to crush under his heavy hobnailed jack boots.

He would go off on tirades, regarding who had power over him and how he felt he was being mistreated. After all, he had just been following orders, and they were just making the world a better place.

During the last day of testimony after Sarah had passed some new documents to one of the prosecutors, she felt a pair of eyes burning into her, and she knew right where it was coming from. Looking over to defendant's dock, enclosed in bullet proof glass, it was clear that Barbie was glaring at her, as his bottom lip quivered. Was it anger? Fear? Was it disbelief that the very people he had tried to eliminate from the face of the earth now had power over him, and there was no way out? Or could he just not believe that someone with his prestige and social status was facing the possibility of hanging for his crimes.

After much deliberation, on the morning of July 4, 1987, Klaus Barbie was found guilty of 17 crimes against humanity. Sarah and Ishmael were angered by the verdict. He had originally been charged with 117 counts that included the execution of 4,000 Jews and the deportation of 7,500 more. The fact that he was sentenced to the balance of his life in prison helped somewhat, but Sarah had really hoped to see him swing from the gallows.

After much pleading and begging, Sarah was granted permission to speak with Barbie before he was transferred to prison.

Handcuffed and with leg irons on his ankles, Barbie sat quietly at a steel table looking straight ahead as Sarah entered the small interrogation room. Without saying a word, Sarah walked toward the far side of the table and sat down. She looked up at the red light that was attached to the camera in the corner of the room. She knew everything they said was going to be videotaped for the record.

As she turned to face Barbie who was showing zero emotion on his face, he began speaking. "So, did you cleanse your heart by testifying against me? Do you feel better now that you are sending a real monster to prison for good?"

Sarah shook her head. "No. I do not feel better. Those that were close to me are still just as dead. And those that you sent to the camps shall never return. To be honest, I wish you had been hung, I do not believe you should live out your life being taken care of by prison guards."

Before she could say another word, Barbie broke out in a large belly laugh. "You wanted me hanged, you wanted to watch me swing from the gallows, eh? Did you want a piece of the rope as a trophy? You Jews are all alike, all you want is your measly pound of flesh. Well, I shall tell you Miss Rosenbaum, your testimony in court was a joke. It was all for nothing and it got you nowhere. Worst of all, it didn't give you a single thing you could take home for a souvenir. You remain a pathetic Jewess, a clown, a flea that I can still crush with my boot. So now you can go home and tell your Mossad friends that you sat face to face with the barbaric and infamous Klaus Barbie. It will be nothing more than a simple war story, a bragging right. Tell me, what were you looking for coming in here with me? An apology, redemption maybe? What? Tell me what you are looking for? I'm guessing you can't answer that question because you haven't a clue. Are you just trying to show me that you can walk out that door and I cannot? But Miss Rosenbaum, you are so wrong. I too will walk out that door, to a new home where I will live quite comfortably for possibly a long time. So again, what have you gained? What were you expecting from your grand audience with the so-called butcher of Lyon? Who knows Miss Rosenbaum, I may actually out live you"

In that moment, Sarah realized Barbie was not like the others she had spoken to after their trials. He was still arrogant, he knew he was still able to belittle and intimidate a person by his biting words and evil stare. There was no doubt nothing the court could do would ever change or break him.

Attempting to choose her words carefully, Sarah began to speak. "Actually, I had some things I wanted to ask you, and some things I wanted to tell you. But I now realize none of that matters. But yes, now I can say I met the devil face to face, and I know there is a special place for you in hell."

Finishing her comment, Sarah stood up and walked toward the door Ishmael was holding open for her. Her skin crawled as she heard Barbie's hideous laugh echoing off the concrete walls of the interrogation room. It was an evil laugh, identical to that of Sgt. Wilhelm.

The day Barbie was transferred to prison, Sarah watched the American Military Police load him into an armored car. The entire time he attempted to belittle the men by making fun of everything they did. She wondered if he thought there would be some sort of monument to his greatness when he finally died, or if they would make his cell into a place to be revered by ardent Nazis forever. But she had been assured that when he passed he would be cremated like all the Jews he sent to the concentration camps, and that his ashes would be unceremoniously dispersed, so the world could never worship at the foot of his grave. The only place his evil soul would ever be welcomed was in the darkest depths of hell.

Chapter Nineteen
Why Me?

With 1989 drawing to a close, Sarah was extremely happy with her life, but realized there was a battle facing her she didn't want any part of. After a long night of sleeplessness, Sarah rolled over to look at the clock on her night stand. She shook her head with disgust when she realized it was only three o'clock. Slowly, she swung her legs over the edge of the bed preparing to quietly get up when Simon reached over and touched her.

"Another long night without sleep, my dear. You cannot keep this up. We need to see a doctor to find out what's causing you not to sleep. I will make an appointment in the morning."

Sarah laid her head on the strong shoulder of her husband as he now sat beside her.

Looking into his dark brown eyes, Sarah took his hand and placed it on her right breast. "Do you feel the lump?"

Taking Sarah into his arms, Simon kissed her on the forehead. "When did you first notice it?"

"On Sunday, when I was getting dressed. I tried to tell myself I had just imagined it and there was nothing wrong. But that evening as I got ready for bed, I realized it was larger than I thought, and it was certainly for real. I wanted to tell you but I couldn't find the words and I didn't want you to worry. I have an appointment Friday morning with an oncologist. I was going to tell you this morning over coffee, but now you know."

Simon held Sarah tight, as tears rolled down his face. "Honey, you have overcome other obstacles when others would have given up. You survived death every day in Dachau and you can survive this. We will fight it together."

Friday morning, a very frightened Simon drove Sarah to the Sheba Medical Center in Tel Aviv. Once they were registered, they were greeted by Dr. Adam Abend, the chief oncologist in the hospital. After a long discussion, Sarah went through a battery of lab tests before receiving a CT scan. Later in the day, Dr. Abend and his associate walked into the room.

"Well Sarah, we have done all the tests we needed to do. I'm sorry to say that my worst fears have come true. We have concluded with no doubt that you have advanced breast cancer on your right breast, and there are several small growths on your left breast that may be cancerous as well. The only way to get a handle on this and save your life is to do a double mastectomy. I wish I could tell you to go home and think about this and get back to me in a week or so, but that's just not feasible. Time is of the essence in your case if we are going to save your life. My team recommends immediate surgery followed by several rounds of chemotherapy. We can get you into surgery tomorrow afternoon."

Sarah closed her eyes for a moment as she fought back the tears that were threatening to gush forward like a bursting dam. Grabbing onto Simon, she shook her head. "No, no more pain, no more suffering. You and Simchah can have a good life, it is time for me to go to Galenka and the others, this I must do, it's my time."

Taken back by Sarah's statement, Simon placed his hands on her shoulders and looked deep into her eyes. "No Sarah, Simchah and I would have no life without you. You are our lives! Your time to join Galenka and the others will come soon enough, as it does for everyone. But today is not the day to make that decision. You are young, we are young, we have so much life yet to live and you cannot simply walk away from life like this. After all, did not Isaac and Galenka both tell you to survive, to live, to never give up? How can you turn your back on them now, Sarah? How?"

Dropping her head down to Simon's shoulder, tears began to flow as they hadn't in a very long time. Once again, she was angry at herself for crying, as she had promised she would never cry again. But how does one face a crisis as devastating as this, without feeling the pain and agony. The fear itself was so overwhelming. Simon held her tightly as he allowed his tortured wife to feel all the pain she had held inside for so long.

After several minutes she looked up at Simon and nodded her head. "I will fight, I will not let you or the others down, but you must make me a promise. When I'm strong again, and I will be, you must take me back to Dachau. I must visit the ghosts one last time."

Simon kissed Sarah and smiled. "First off, you could never let me down, and yes, Simchah and I will take you back to Dachau as you wish, whenever you feel you are ready. It's time you go back and make peace with your past."

The following afternoon as Sarah laid on a gurney waiting to be rolled into surgery, a Rabbi making rounds of the hospital stopped by to visit. Placing one arm around Simchah, and taking hold of Sarah's right hand, he said several prayers for a good outcome. When he was finished, Sarah looked up at the man.

"Tell me Rabbi, after all I have been through and survived, why me, why now?"

The Rabbi shook his head. "Only our God can answer that question my dear. As you have eluded to, he brought you back from the gates of hell and delivered you to the homeland of your ancestors. Little do you know what he still has in store for you, or what great things you might yet accomplish. Trust him, Sarah."

Before Sarah could reply, the surgical team arrived and rolled her into the operating room.

When everything was ready, the anesthesiologist placed a mask over Sarah's face. Smiling down at Sarah, the woman asked her to count backward from one hundred. As a cool mixture of oxygen and anesthetic drugs rushed over her face, Sarah began to count. When she reached ninety-eight she closed her eyes.

As the surgical team went to work, Sarah's mind spun in circles, stopping at scenes from her life like a slide show. She could smell and taste the birthday cake she was never able to enjoy. She could feel Isaac pulling on her arm as he yelled at her to run, as they raced through the forest away from the train, the Nazis, and her family. She could see the bodies of the farm couple the Germans had hung from the trees behind their house as a warning to others. But now they were looking at her with wide eyes, as if warning her not to enter their home. Suddenly, she was in Paris enjoying coffee and cakes with Rochelle, only to see the bloody body of her friend mangled on a roadway in Orleans. Out of the darkness came Sgt. Wilhelm, laughing like a madman. He carried the black box and the instrument he had shoved up inside of her. He was close, then very close, then he was beginning to undress her. She could smell the urine, body odor and his whiskey breath as he attempted to kiss her.

Sarah began to thrash on the operating table as she screamed at the top of her lungs. Desperately, she attempted to push the anesthesiologist away with her one free arm. "No, no. Stop it, stop! No, not again!" Sarah yelled, as she began to struggle against the ghost of Sgt. Wilhelm.

Immediately, Dr. Abend and his team stopped what they were doing, as the anesthesiologist fought to gain control of their patient. Sweat poured down Sarah's face as she gasped for air, still refusing to allow the face mask be placed back over her face. She screamed, as the pain from the surgery felt like hot irons piercing her body.

Dr. Abend placed his hands down on her shoulders, as he called out, "Sarah? Sarah, can you hear me? Can you hear me?"

Looking totally terrified, Sarah looked about the room. "No, no, I am not one of your test patients. Please, please don't kill me like the rest. I'll be good, I promise, please don't do this to me!"

Finally, one of the surgical nurses came forward, removing her mask. Looking down at Sarah, she smiled. In a soothing voice she inquired, "Tell me who wants to hurt you? Who wants to hurt you, Sarah? I won't let him touch you ever again. Just tell me who wants to hurt you."

Shaking with fear, Sarah fought to get the words out. "Sgt. Wilhelm, he's evil, he let Hintermayer, Dr. Hintermayer do surgery. He killed my little ones, he butchered them like animals. I fought for them, but they took them all away and they went up in smoke, they were just babies. Don't let him touch me. Don't let him hurt me! I want them all back, they did not deserve to die like that, I want them all back!" Sarah cried out, as tears poured down her face. "I want to live, I want to live! I promised Isaac, please keep Sgt. Wilhelm and the doctor away from me."

The nurse placed her hand on Sarah's cheek, wiping away the tears. "You are safe here, honey, no one is going to hurt you. I won't let them. We're going to give you something to settle you down so we can continue, you must relax now."

Dr. Abend nodded to the anesthesiologist to inject the drug she was holding in her hand into the IV. Slowly, Sarah's breathing and blood pressure began to fall as she once again closed her eyes. Shaking his head, Dr. Abend said. "This woman has been through a hell none of us will ever understand." Squaring his shoulders, and trying to regain his focus, his said, "Alright, put the mask back on and give her a higher dose, we need to get this finished."

After changing his gloves, the team went back to work, keeping a close eye on Sarah's blood pressure and pulse, since they had given her a much higher level of anesthesia.

Around midnight, Sarah began to moan slightly as she came out from under the heavy sedation she had been given. Once the nurses were satisfied with her condition, they allowed Simon and Simchah into the room. For Sarah, it was a glorious reunion after all she had experienced. However, an hour later she looked at Simon.

"You must call Ishmael. I need to speak with him."

When Ishmael came to the phone, Sarah said, "It was Dr. Hintermayer that performed the surgeries in Dachau when I was there. I don't know how I could have blocked that from my memory, but he came back into my mind last night. Find him! Then, when I am ready to travel, we will go get him. I want to be there when he's captured."

Ishmael listened to everything Sarah was saying. When she was finished, Ishmael continued. "Sarah, the executioner has beaten you to the punch. The good doctor was found guilty of war crimes and hung in Landsberg Prison in 1946. He's buried in the cemetery at Spottinger-Friedhoff. There were many horrific charges filed against him, and they included the bizarre surgeries and murders of all your children. He has already been dealt with, Sarah, you have no need to fret over him."

Sarah nodded her head. "Thank you, I only wish I could have been there to see him hang."

Ishmael smiled, knowing the death of Dr. Hintermayer would give her some peace. "So, now you have nothing to concern yourself with and plenty of time to get well. I know the chemotherapy will be tough, but you are one tough woman and you can do this. In time, you still have a desk in my office, but it can wait for now. When you are feeling somewhat better, and Simon agrees, I will send you files to read through."

The chemo treatments were extremely hard on Sarah. Throughout most of the time she could barely get out of bed, and when she did, she was too sick to do anything. After the second week of chemo, Sarah asked Simon to shave her head, as she hated seeing the large clumps of hair come out whenever she attempted to use a brush or a comb. When Simon was finished, she picked up a mirror and gasped. There in that reflection, was the Sarah from Dachau looking back at her. She trembled as Simon placed his strong arms around her.

But the worst was still yet to come. During the second round of chemo, she became so sick she wasn't able to keep down any solid food. She would lay in bed and sweat so much, Simon would need to change the bedding several times a day. Her complexion turned ashen gray as large dark circles appeared around her eyes.

Becoming seriously dehydrated and undernourished, Sarah was readmitted to the hospital. Doctor Abend stopped the chemo as he was afraid it was going to kill her if he continued. Three days after returning to the hospital, Sarah slipped into a coma.

Not sure of how to handle the situation anymore, Dr. Abend contacted Sloan Kettering Cancer Center in New York. After a long consultation, Dr Mark Moore flew to Tel Aviv to deal with Sarah's case, as he had dealt with several just like it over the last few years. After conducting a large battery of tests, he began a regimen of drugs he had found useful in his other patients. Seven days after slipping into the coma, Sarah regained consciousness. It continued being an uphill battle each day, until finally Dr. Moore decided Sarah was strong enough to finish her second round of chemo.

Early one morning when there were no nurses in her room, Sarah slid out of bed, making her way into the bathroom. Standing in front of the mirror, she took a deep breath before untying the straps from her gown. After closing her eyes, she let the gown drop to the floor. Sarah stood motionless for a few moments before opening her eyes to gaze at her body in the large mirror. As she gazed at the reflection in the mirror, Sarah began to sway back and forth before fainting, and collapsing to the floor.

In a split second, Simon was kneeling beside his wife. "What are you doing, Sarah? You should not be getting up by yourself like this. What are you trying to prove?"

As she trembled, she replied. "Help me up and take a long look at me. This is prisoner Sarah Rosenbaum." After a moment of silence, she began to yell, "This is what I looked like when Dachau was liberated. This is what we all looked like. This is what we looked like when we were stacked in piles outside the crematorium. This is what we looked like before we went up in smoke! This is what the Nazis did to us! I don't want to die this way! I don't want to die the way the Nazi's wanted me to die. Galenka, Raizel, Penina and Hadar all looked like me when they were taken to the crematorium. No, I do not want to die this way, I will not give the Germans satisfaction that they finally won. No! No! I will not die like this!" Sarah screamed, as she beat her fists against the mirror until it broke.

By now, several nurses, along with Dr. Abend had assembled near the bathroom, none of them sure how best to handle Sarah.

Shaking her head and gasping for air, Sarah leaned against Simon. Looking up at him she continued mumbling, "No, not like this, not like this. Dear God, not like this."

As she closed her eyes, Simon picked up his distraught wife, carrying her back to the bed, where nurses bandaged the cuts on Sarah's hands from the broken glass. After covering her with the bedding, Simon sat down beside her, asking everyone to leave the room.

Throughout the day, Sarah slept most of the time. She ate just a few bites of the food they brought her, but she said very little to anyone. Around midnight, she swung her feet over the side of her bed, then slipped on her robe and slippers before standing up. Taking hold of her rolling IV stand, Sarah slowly walked to the door of her room, looking down the corridor. Placing her hand against the wall for balance, Sarah began gingerly walking. As she moved forward, she kept repeating, "The kapos will not take me to be stacked by the crematorium, I will not go up in smoke. I will not go up in smoke!"

As one of the nurses attempted to grab hold of her, the charge nurse said. "Follow her from a distance, but do not touch her. Trust me, she knows what's best for her, better than we do. I believe the anger she is expressing is the best treatment she could have."

Day after day, Sarah went for walks holding onto Simon or Simchah, and at night continued her lonely walks by herself, always repeating the same message which unnerved some of the younger nurses.

When the chemo treatments were completed, Sarah insisted she be allowed to return home. Each day she continued walking and doing strengthening exercises, as well as eating a special diet that a Mossad doctor suggested for her. Slowly, Sarah's color began to return as well as her stamina and strength. Three months after surgery, Simon surprised her by taking her to the Mossad firing range, where she could visit with friends and keep her hand gun qualifications in good standing. It was the best therapy Sarah had experienced in a long time, as Mari and Josiah came by to visit. Once again, she felt like her life was beginning to take on a purpose.

One evening as Sarah and Simon sat together on their veranda, Sarah reached over, taking Simon's hand. Smiling she said. "You have been right all along, sweetheart. I must go back to Dachau, I must finish the journey. The circle must be completed."

Simon looked lovingly at his wife. "If you are sure, then we will go. We must wait a bit longer before we go, however, as you need to get more of your strength back first. We have waited this long, what will be a few more weeks or even several months. You must be strong to take this trip."

Nodding her head in approval, Sarah replied. "You are right about that. The ghosts of my past will be there waiting for me. If I'm not strong, I will not be able to confront them."

Sarah had honestly thought about going back for several years, though she hadn't told Simon, as the time never seemed appropriate. Some times she would just make excuses why they shouldn't go. But now she had faced death head on under her own terms and won, and she knew she might not be so lucky the next time around if her cancer returned. Somehow, facing the ghosts of Dachau did not appear to be as big of a challenge as she once thought it would be, and she needed to confront them before she left this world.

Over the next several months, Sarah's strength began to grow and she once again began to enjoy her life. Simon was overjoyed to see the resurgence of the woman he had loved for so long, taking on everything life threw at her. Ishmael enjoyed having Sarah back in her cubical studying files and working with teams as they scoured the globe, searching for elusive Nazi war criminals.

Chapter Twenty
Return to Dachau

It was four in the morning as Sarah stared out the window at the dark rain-soaked streets of Munich from her fifth-floor hotel room. Traffic was light this hour of the morning, as most Germans were still sound asleep. But for Sarah it had been a long restless night, tormented by dreams, faces and visions of past horrors at this place she would return to in just a few hours.

Dachau! For all intents and purposes, it was just another word for hell in her vocabulary. A filthy, rodent infested, diseased land of the dead, where only hatred and pure evil could exist. A place where you looked up to see the thick black smoke emanating from the tall smoke stacks if you wanted to see the faces of the people that had disappeared. A place where the few children there played hide and seek among stacks of corpses, never giving it a second thought.

Dachau! It was an appropriately ugly name for a place that destroyed all forms of human dignity. It was a place that destroyed all hopes, dreams, and beliefs that the God of Israel was watching over his people. It meant destruction of the human spirit and soul that existed inside each walking skeleton that eventually found death more appealing than life.

Walking up quietly behind his wife, Simon placed his strong hands on Sarah's shoulders as he gently turned her toward him. She trembled as she laid her head onto the sturdy shoulder of this man she had finally found peace with. Simon held her tight, not saying a word, as he understood the battle that was going on within his wife.

Shaking her head, she whispered, "I don't think I can go back there. I'm afraid I'm not strong enough. The thought of it scared me all night long."

Slowly Simon led her back to the bed where they sat down. "No one is forcing you to return, Sarah. All we have to do is opt out of the tour and interview in the morning. There is no doubt in my mind that everyone will understand. In fact, there may be others that will not go at the last minute as well. What you have accomplished since you were released from Dachau speaks volumes about your courage. You can go home knowing men like Klaus Barbie have been brought to justice because of your strength and courage. You have proven again and again that you are brave and courageous. More so than any other women I have ever known."

After composing her thoughts, Sarah looked at her husband. "But how can I look at myself in the mirror when we get home, knowing I was this close to Galenka, Raizel and Hadar but backed away.

Surely their ghosts will look back at me, wondering where my courage has gone. Wondering why I couldn't visit them when I was so close their spirits could reach out to touch me. But most of all, I think Simchah would feel tremendously let down. She has waited so long to come here with us."

Kissing Sarah on the cheek, Simon smiled. "You survived, sweetheart, you survived. They know your courage, they know what you have accomplished in your lifetime. Their spirits are with you always, even here in this hotel room, don't ever forget that. Now, there are still hours to sleep before we are to leave. Lay down next to me, close your eyes and try to sleep as Simchah is doing across the hall."

When Sarah awoke several hours later, she was filled with a sense of determination that surprised her, and Simon, especially after the long heart wrenching night. When Simchah joined them, Sarah explained what had gone on during the long night, and how she felt now. After giving her mother a hug, Simchah smiled.

"Mother, I too tossed and turned a good part of the night. I could not find peace with what I expect to see this day. But we will get through this together, as a family."

Sarah smiled as she kissed her daughter on the cheek, "Yes we will, my love, yes we will."

However, as they began their walk toward the elevator, Sarah felt a knot growing in her stomach. She was actually on her way now to relive the darkest days of her life. There was no way to know how she would react when she actually saw the main gate for the first time, and the thought of it filled her heart with anxiety.

Entering the lobby of the hotel, several reporters walked up to her, thrusting microphones toward her face as cameras whirled.

"Mrs. Waldmann, how are you feeling today, are you ready for the trip back to Dachau?" A young German female reporter inquired.

"Return? What do you mean? I have never left Dachau, it is in me as I am in it, every day of my life. The ghosts of the victims speak to me always. I'm just going back to see some old empty buildings," Sarah replied, as she brushed past the young woman.

Neither Simon or Simchah were sure what they should say as the bus left the hotel. It was clear that Sarah was deep in thought and they did not wish to disturb her.

Although there had been some quiet conversation between other passengers during the drive to Dachau, the bus became eerily silent as they approached the parking area. Stepping down from the bus, Sarah quickly reached out for Simon and Simchah as her knees buckled. She gasped as she shook with fear, unable to move. Standing in front of her like a dream out of hell was the main entrance to Dachau which represented everything sinister and evil the world could ever offer.

A slight breeze circled around the camp, filling Sarah's nostrils with a scent of death she had tried hard to forget.

"Do you smell it? Tell me you smell it, don't let it just be my imagination."

Simon was almost frozen in place as he stared at the rusty worn railroad tracks leading directly through the front gate of the camp. Simchah stared at the decrepit cattle cars sitting on the siding, trying not to cry as she imagined her mother inside as just a young girl, scared and unaware of what was happening to her.

Both Simon and Simchah stood motionless, their senses

overloaded as their minds attempted to process where they were, and what they were actually seeing. Simon shook his head as he looked over at his wife. "We are actually here. I'm not sure what I smell, I am not sure if I can comprehend any of this."

Simchah felt nauseated and dizzy for a few moments, before removing a bottle of water from her purse and taking a huge swallow. After placing the bottle back into her purse, she scanned the area very slowly. "My God, I feel evil all around me. I feel as if I enter those walls, I shall never come out the same." As another gust of wind blew past them, Simchah nodded her head. "I can smell it, Mother."

A moment later, Sarah took Simon and Simchah by the hand, leading them forward toward the entrance. Stopping by the large iron gate, Simchah read the words that were welded into it, "Arbeit Macht Frei." She remembered seeing photos of the gates in her history books, as well as listening to her mother and other survivors talk about them many times. Now there they were, directly in front of her.

Sarah remembered looking at the gates the day she arrived, wondering why soldiers would be shooting people if there was work and a new life waiting for them here, none of it made any sense then, and it still made no sense to her today.

"What a lie it was, that work will set you free. Nothing set you free here, it only destroyed everything and everybody. Why did our people go with them so willingly? Why did we allow ourselves to be fooled by them?" Sarah said angrily as she glared at the monstrous steel gate.

As the last person in the tour group passed by, Simon was surprised to watch Sarah spit on the gate as she said, "Galenka, forgive me!"

Walking slowly into the strange surroundings, Sarah was taking in every sight and sound, attempting to place her mind back into the camp when she was there. She shuddered as she remembered the stack of bodies where she sat holding Galenka's hand the day the camp was liberated.

To her left is where the survivors rose up, attacking the kapos when the Americans brought them back into camp. Today it was impossible to believe those ravaged week skeletons could have found enough strength to beat several of the men to death before the soldiers could stop them. She remembered looking down into Philip's bloody face, as he struggled to take in his last breath of air, before his eyes rolled back into his head and he died. She had not struck any of them, but neither did she try and stop anyone from taking out their vengeance on the hated kapos. It was Jew upon Jew that day, and only those that survived the camps could understand the reasons for their anger. Many survivors came to Dachau searching for absolution, but few if any ever found it inside these walls.

Turning to her right, Sarah looked at the spot where Klaus Barbie lined up the six women in front of her by the commandant's office. She could see herself kneeling on the ground, screaming in horror as the murderous bastard shot the six women. The faces of those terrified women frozen in fear still haunted her dreams. Although, like most prisoners, they all must have prayed over and over to die at some point. But when death was imminent, all of them found reasons in their hearts to survive, but they understood nothing could change the inevitable.

Simchah placed her arm around her mother's shoulder. "Tell me mother, what are you seeing, please share it with me."

Sarah shook her head, "My darling, everywhere I look I see evil. Everywhere I look, I see death." Pointing toward the crematorium, Sarah said. "See the soldier, he is going to throw the body of a child on top of the corpses. It's so small, they can shove it in the oven with an adult and get rid of it quicker. After all, it's just one more dead Jew for the accounting office."

After walking a short distance, Sarah stopped. "From right here over to the door of the crematorium, bodies were stacked, like so much firewood. We were dying faster than they could cremate us. I think as the end of the war neared, the soldiers quit pushing the kapos to work harder, as they began to realize they could never finish the job. I walked about the bodies as if it was a normal fact of life, and in all honesty, it actually had become that if you lived in a camp" Taking a few steps more, she said, "Here is where I sat holding Galenka's hand. There were already two more bodies on top of her. Even if the crematorium had been still operating, it would have taken maybe a week for them to get to her body."

Taking Simchah by the hand, Sarah slowly walked into Building X which had been the camp crematorium. The ovens were quiet now, but stopping just inside the door, she could see the dirty, sweating kapos, wearing face scarves and sliding bodies into the coal fired ovens. They dared not utter a word of protest, as a shot to the back of the head would make them the next candidate to enter the ovens, whether they were dead or alive. The smell inside the small building must have been ghastly for the workers. That is the reason why suicide rates for men assigned to the crematoriums were three times as high as the rest of the camp. Once you were assigned to the crematorium, there was no way of getting a job change, so suicide became the only way out for many of those men.

Sarah slowly stepped up to one of the ovens as she peered down at the rails where bodies were placed before being shoved into the all-consuming flames. Bowing her head, she placed her hands on the iron door while reciting a prayer from the Kaddish, as Simon held tightly to Simchah as she wept.

Leaving the crematorium, they turned to walk toward one of the barracks. Taking hold of Sarah's hand, Simon asked, "Where did Galenka go if she wasn't cremated. What happened to her remains and all the others? Where did they take her?"

Turning slowly, Sarah shook her head. "Gone, gone with the rest of them. In the days after the camp was liberated, people from the town and nearby areas were brought here by American soldiers to clean up the mess their army had made. They all wore face masks and gloves as they loaded bodies onto trucks. They all cried out in desperation, saying they were not responsible for the mess, that they were innocent, and why should they be punished by being forced to load the countless emaciated rotting bodies of our people onto the never-ending line of trucks. I only felt contempt for them because they knew what was going on here, and they just chose to ignore it. Where the bodies went, I don't know."

Walking toward one of the barracks, Sarah said, "Look, the prisoners are preparing for count. They will all line up in neat orderly rows. Watch the guards beating them with hoses and night sticks. The terrified people try every day to avoid the beatings and the vicious dogs. We were always scared when we came out for count. We never knew what the commandant might have planned for us, or if we would survive so we could eat the watery meal that had no taste."

Sarah looked all around her and shivered, as ghosts of women she knew reached out, trying to touch her. She could feel their bony fingers poking her and touching her face. She could smell their dirty unwashed bodies, covered with infected sores, their dead eyes staring blankly into eternity, asking her over and over, "Why did you survive and not me." Everywhere were guards, pushing and shoving the human corpses to cooperate and fall into ranks, as dogs nipped at their bony ankles. But not a sound could be heard today, only the sorrowful wind that whined through the deadly wire.

Just as Sarah felt like running back to the camp entrance. Galenka slowly walked through the crowd of ghosts. She smiled at Sarah as she held out both hands, as if wanting to give her a hug. Nodding her head, Galenka said, "My child, you have not forgotten us, you came back. We have all been hoping you would return."

Shaking her head, Sarah quietly replied. "I missed you so much. I have never forgotten you or all that you worked so hard to teach me."

Galenka nodded her head. "Your family is as proud of you as I am. You survived, Sarah, you survived."

Slowly, the apparition of her friend faded away, leaving Sarah shaken and short of breath.

Simon and Simchah reached out to catch her as she wavered on her feet. Gasping for air, she called out, "Galenka, Galenka, don't go. Come back, please!" Desperately, she reached out to catch Galenka before she was gone.

Looking at her family, Sarah whispered, "Galenka and the rest are all here, they have never left. Can you feel them around you? Can you feel their hollow eyes staring at you?"

Simon stood silent as he looked around and over his shoulder. "Yes. Yes, I can feel them all around. It's as if they were still alive."

Nodding her head in agreement, Simchah replied. "They have been all around us since we entered the camp. I could feel them. Some of them call out your name, Mother, I can hear them."

"Listen to them, Simchah. All they want is to be heard, they each have a story to tell. A story of loss, a story of pain, and they all ask the same thing. Why, why, why?" Sarah responded, as she once more took Simon and Simchah by the hand, leading them into the barracks

Standing inside the dreary building, everything seemed eerily strange to Sarah. Tourists stood near by clicking cameras and reading the tourist brochure they were handed, while shaking their heads.

Some were discussing dinner plans as restless children asked when they were going to leave. They were all so wrapped up in getting in and out of the camp, going on to their next tour, and wondering why they signed up for this stop during their busy vacations, that they were incapable of seeing what was right in front of them. All they had to do was stop and listen, stop and open their minds, stop and realize that human beings were here, and that human beings had perished here, human beings no different than any of them.

Pushing through the crowd of people, Sarah walked slowly down the aisle watching kapos fill their carts with the bodies of the dead, soon to be rolled over to the crematorium. Women barely alive laid on their mats, watching her walk by. As Sarah neared the back wall of the barracks, Galenka appeared in front of her again.

"Child, what are you doing in here, you know what this is all about. You know where you need to be, you must face your demons while you still have time, or you shall never get past it. You must go, go now," Galenka said boldly as she pointed her withered hand toward the yard.

Sarah shook her head. "I have thought about it many times, but now that I'm here, I don't know if I'm strong enough to do it."

Galenka smiled. "You were strong as a child, and you are stronger now. You have what it takes to face your greatest fears and you must."

"Come with me, Galenka, I need to have you there with me," Sarah asked softly.

"No child, this you must do on your own. You faced it as a child and survived, now you must face it as a woman, knowing you survived the evil this place thrust upon you," Galenka replied, as she continued pointing out toward the yard.

Suddenly, Simchah stood in front of Sarah, looking at her with a puzzled expression on her face. "Mother, did you hear what I just asked? Who was it you were just talking to?"

Sarah reached out for Simon with one hand as she placed the other on Simchah's cheek. "I have a place we must visit, let's go out into the yard."

Before they could turn to go, Simchah looked searchingly at the back of the barracks before taking hold of her mother's arm. "Mother you must answer me, were you actually speaking with Galenka?"

"Do not think I'm crazy my daughter. But yes, it was Galenka

I was speaking to. She has been walking near me the entire time we have been here. She wants me to remember everything, to see everything again, to face my fears. Now come, we must go," Sarah responded with a reassuring smile.

As they walked out back into the yard, several rude media photographers pushed and shoved some of the tourists, desperately trying to capture the expressions of the returning prisoners. Simon pushed one of the most arrogant photographers away from Sarah with the directive that if he returned, his camera would be destroyed. Simchah walked off to her left to read the sign explaining about the barracks. As she read, she felt a cold hand on her arm. Turning, she saw the apparition of a bedraggled dirty woman smiling at her.

"I am Galenka, Simchah. Learn from your mother, be there for her, she will need you."

Simchah was totally taken back by what had just happened. "What? What are you trying to tell me? Wait, don't go, talk with me please, why will she need me?"

But no matter how hard she pleaded, the vision of Galenka faded away until she was gone. Feeling light headed, Simchah sat down on a bench, trying to sort out what just happened.

Moments later Sarah and Simon approached the bench. Sarah slowly knelt down in front of her daughter as she took hold of her hand. "Are you alright darling?"

Simchah nodded her head, "Yes mother, I just needed to sit for a moment and have a drink of water. We can move on now." However, the acknowledging look her mother gave her was different from anything she had seen before, she knew they both now had shared the same thing, Galenka had spoken to her.

Sarah led Simon and Simchah over to an area in the yard where a small placard explained that this is where the punishment box had been located. Sarah could feel a coldness coming over her body as she looked at the ground where she had laid when she had been pulled from the box, and been horribly assaulted. In the distance she could hear the cruel laugh of Sgt. Wilhelm coming closer as his spirit appeared to circle around her. She once again could smell his foul whiskey breath and the stale urine as it splattered the box. But Sarah stood still and straight, refusing to show any emotion. Without a tremble in her voice, she called out, "You will have no power over me again, Sgt. Wilhelm. I have defeated you and you can no longer hurt me!"

As Simchah took her by the arm, she whispered, "It is alright, Mother, if you cry. What happened to you here was horrible, it's alright for you to feel the pain."

Closing her eyes, Sarah shook her head. "Darling, as I have said so often, I have cried an ocean of tears, and have felt the pain in my heart too many times. I shall not allow Sgt. Wilhelm to destroy me, I will not allow him to break me down ever again, I will not allow the bastard to have power over me the rest of my life. Today, my darling Simchah, I will stand strong. His evil no longer exists and I shall not cry. I have won."

When she finished speaking, Sgt. Wilhelm had disappeared, along with all the images and odors associated with him. A gentle breeze blew through the camp, bringing with it a scent of fresh air as if a new day were dawning. All she could see now was the woman they had pushed into the box that night, that pleaded her for prayers. She was smiling, giving Sarah the peace of mind she had searched for since that night so long ago.

Feeling better than she had in a long time, Sarah took Simon and Simchah by the hand, leading them a short distance to the massive fence that surrounded the camp. The terrifying electrical monster was quiet and harmless now, as it was the day the American Army arrived at the front gate.

Walking up to the fence, Sarah place her hand on a cold strand of barbed wire. Motioning her family to join her, Simchah and Simon stepped forward, placing their hands on the cruel wire. As Sarah reached over to touch one of the large white insulators on a nearby post, she began.

"It buzzed and snapped constantly, especially in the rain. You could feel the power running through it when you were several feet away from it. The power it had was as deadly as a rifle bullet could have been. If you ran into it, the power would kill you and toss your lifeless, burned body back a good six to eight feet, and death was instant. I stood right here on two occasions, contemplating a quick death. I had seen three people kill themselves this way. Afterwards, their bodies lay on the ground smoking as their muscles twitched. One man actually had his arm torn off by the explosive charge. Both times I stood here, I could see the guard in the tower preparing to shoot me if I moved any closer to the fence. Funny, I thought, why would they waist a bullet on a person when the fence would kill you just as quick. But that was the way of the Nazis. It was not for any normal person to understand."

Simchah hugged her mother as tears rolled down her cheeks. "Mother, I do not know if I would have been strong enough to survive what you did."

Holding her daughter, Sarah smiled. "Yes, darling, you have what it takes, you would have been a survivor for you are a strong woman."

Slowly, Sarah and her family began walking back toward the main gate where they had entered. When Simon strolled off to look at a display, Simchah turned toward her mother.

"I cannot lie to you. When I was near the barracks, Galenka did talk to me. I have never experienced anything like that in my life. I could tell by the expression on your face that you knew what had happened."

Sarah smiled slightly. "I did, but since we walked away from where the box was, they've all gone, they have all disappeared including Galenka. Was it all in my head? I'm not sure what to think right now."

Placing her hand on Sarah's shoulder, Simchah smiled. "No, they were here. Dad and I felt them, and I did talk to Galenka as you did, it was no dream. They were here for you, to help you come to grips with all you went through as a child. No Mom, they were real as can be. I will swear to it, and they will always be here, they can not escape their past, nor can they pass through the wire to find peace."

Arriving at the gate, Sarah stopped once again to look at the iron monster. The longer she looked, the more the rage inside her grew. Although visiting Dachau had brought her some peace, she could still not come to grips with how one person could have turned an entire country against its own people, strictly because of their religious beliefs. After all, what could a seven-year-old girl have done to threaten the welfare or security of Germany.

Since a large group of survivors had returned to Dachau today, several media reporters from around the world had set up a small interview area. One by one as survivors left the camp, reporters would ask them to stop and answer questions.

As Sarah stood staring at the gate, the woman reporter that had attempted to talk with her in the lobby of the hotel walked up to her.

"Mrs. Waldmann, now that you have finished your tour of Dachau, can you tell me what you are feeling?"

Sarah was about to turn and walk off as she had at the hotel, but Simon and Simchah motioned for her to answer the reporter.

After looking back at the camp for a moment, Sarah replied. "I feel as if all of that took place in another lifetime, to another person, yet I know it was me, and I know all the people that died here were real, they all did exist."

The reporter nodded her head, "Mrs. Waldmann, you moved to Israel after the war, and have only returned to Germany a few times to testify in war crime trials. Would you ever contemplate moving back to your homeland in the future?"

Sarah laughed. "Israel is my homeland. I was already living there for some time before independence was proclaimed. So, Israel and I are one. I have put much of Germany out of my mind, and I rarely think of it. I was only seven when we were taken from my home, so I accumulated more bad feelings about Germany than I ever had the chance to accumulate good ones. My family has no graves to visit, and today, I would still feel like an outcast. No, I would never return to live or visit here ever again."

"Just one more question before I let you go. Over the years you have testified in several trials against former Nazi war criminals. Do you plan to continue hunting down war criminals, or do you feel all the major ones have now been captured?" The reporter inquired.

Sarah glared at the reporter. "There is no such thing as major or minor Nazi war criminals. We will hunt all of them down to the last person and bring them to justice. Did you ever hear the Nazi's claim they had concentration camps filled with major or minor Jews?"

Clearly upset by Sarah's answer, the young German reporter told her camera man to stop filming as they walked away.

Before another reporter could manage to get Sarah off to the side, she grabbed hold of Simon and Simchah's hands and began walking toward their bus.

Sarah was tired and not feeling very well when they returned to the hotel. After taking her medication, she and Simon laid down for a nap before dinner.

Simchah used the time to stroll in and out of the shops lining the street near the hotel. Exiting a shop, she observed a one-armed older man standing on a street corner, pan handling for money. As Simchah approached, he turned to look at her. He had a large gash on his face that ran from his scalp down to his neck, running straight through what had been his eye, and he was missing several fingers on his left hand. Holding his cup toward Simchah, he said, "Help a war veteran, Fraulein, anything will help. As you see by my cup no one wants to help a Nazi soldier anymore."

Simchah went into her purse pulling out five marks. "Here is five, and there is five more if you will answer some questions for me."

Smiling, the man replied, "Ask what you will."

"Did you ever work in a concentration camp during the war?" she asked almost nervously.

The man laughed as he shook his head. "Ya, I get asked that a lot by visitors, especially those from Israel as you are. I recognize your accent, you see." After laughing a bit the man continued. "Nein, I joined the Wehrmacht in 1944 when I was seventeen. After I was trained, I was sent to the Atlantic wall in Normandy. We fought hard, but Hitler would not release the Panzers so the Allies threw us back farther and farther. My unit was withdrawn into Germany behind the Siegfried line. After a short leave I was reassigned to a new Panzer unit. We began training for the battle people refer to as, The Battle of the Bulge. It was Hitlers last gasp for victory, but it was doomed to fail. The winter was tough, we were short on fuel, and the Americans fought like wild animals, they just wouldn't give up.

Well, then Patton broke through and my unit was right in his path. We had big Panzer tanks, but he had so many Sherman tanks and artillery, that they crushed our armor." Holding up his left hand he continued. "An artillery round took off my fingers, destroyed my face, and tore up my intestines and stomach pretty good. I was left for dead in the back of one of our trucks for several days before I was rescued by American medics. They sent me to a field hospital to be fixed up as much as possible. I spent the rest of the war in a POW camp. But no matter how you cut it, the German people have little time for war veterans that were captured and can no longer hold down a job, just as they want nothing to do with S.S. soldiers or concentration camp guards. So, tell me this Fraulein, was it one or both of your parents that were survivors of Dachau?"

Simchah nodded her head. "My mother."

Looking down at the ground for a moment, the man responded. "I am so sorry to hear that. Germany cannot and will not do anything to ever repay those poor people. It's a tragedy that will mark out history forever, and sadly most German schools no longer teach kids about the war."

After handing the man the other five marks she had promised, Simchah smiled. "It really has been nice speaking with you. Take care of yourself."

The man bowed slightly before walking off down the street toward the next intersection.

Arriving back at the hotel, Simchah found her parents well-rested and ready to get something to eat. They walked several blocks before coming to a restaurant that other tourists had suggested to them. After a pleasant meal, everyone was enjoying a cup of coffee when two women approached their table.

The taller of the two women smiled. "Hello, I am Diedra, and this is my sister, Miriam. We were on the tour at Dachau today and saw you there. We listened to your interview with great interest when you were leaving. We have been searching for our brother for years without luck, so we ask every survivor we run across to see if they knew him."

Sarah pointed to the table across the aisle where no one had been seated. "Please pull some chairs over and join us for coffee, it would be my pleasure."

After the women were seated, Diedra began. "We were born in Germany near Aachen. Our father worked in a factory that made German war equipment. It was run by a man named Torberg that liked the lucrative military contracts, but hated the Nazis. It was on a Saturday that the S.S. troops arrived to clean out Jews around Aachen. My sister and I were down at Tritonenbrunner Lake with Torberg's daughter Suzanne, cooling off in the wonderful water. On the way back, Mr. Torberg grabbed us and took us to his factory, where he told us what had happened. He said our parents had been taken away, but he never saw our brother. We told him Ishmael had spent the weekend on a farm helping with field work. So, we had no way of knowing if they had captured him or not."

Sarah leaned closer to the table when she heard the name Ishmael. "Was your brother captured?"

Miriam shook her head as she continued the story. "Several days after the S.S. moved out, we drove to the farm with Mr. Torberg but no one was there and all the livestock was gone.

We stayed hidden in the factory for about a week, before Torberg took us to a monastery where a large group of Catholic sisters lived. Torberg promised them a truck load of food if they would hide us for several weeks, while he made plans to get us out of Germany. You see, England was still taking refugee Jews at the time. He was hoping to get us to England through the port of Antwerp in Belgium, where he also owned a factory. It was only about an hour and forty-five-minute drive, but we would have to cross the German-Belgium border that was controlled by the S.S. Since our papers identified us as Jews, the guards would take us away and all would be lost."

Diedra laughed heartily as she put her hand on Sarah's arm. "Mr. Torberg was a conniver to say the least. Part of the deal with the sisters for a truck load of food, included giving us full habits just like they wore, and teaching us English while we were there. When he had everything lined up, he placed us into the back seat of his car wearing the habits and holding rosaries.

Well, the S.S. guards were very used to seeing Torberg cross the border, and they knew of his factories, so they never checked his papers. When they saw us in the back seat, Torberg told the soldiers we had asked for a ride to Antwerp so we could move to England. Well, the German government hated Catholic sisters and priests and wanted them gone. So, the sergeant never asked for our papers, and instead, he opened the back door and told us to get on that ship and never come back to the Fatherland if we knew what was good for us. After we promised him we would never return, he slammed the door shut and told Torberg to get us out of there."

Everyone at the table broke out laughing as Sarah ordered more coffee. After placing her cup down, Diedra continued. "At the Antwerp factory, Torberg introduced us to his chief engineer, a man named Finkelman. Being Jewish, he and his family had fled the Aachen factory a year earlier in fear of the Nazis. Now, he feared

Germany might invade Belgium and they could still be captured if the ports were closed. So, about two months earlier, they had applied for permission to enter England with no more than five people in their travel group, and it had just been approved. The ship they were to travel on was scheduled to leave in two days. We said good bye to Mr. Torberg and asked if he would keep an eye out for Ishmael. We then stayed with the Finkelman's, who also had a daughter our age, until the ship sailed.

Arriving in Southampton, Finkelman went to work for a company that sent necessary products to Torberg for his factories. My sister and I knew enough English to get by, so we went to work in an English factory that was transitioning to make Enfield rifles for the Army. As all things go, we both were married, had families and moved on with our lives, never to hear of our brother or Mr. Torberg again.

Miriam and I often wonder and believe that Ishmael could have escaped and survived. He was very smart and resourceful in many ways. But as you are aware, when the war ended, Europe became a crossroads for misplaced persons going in every direction, and many people changed their names along the way."

Hearing what Diedra had to say about their brother, Sarah was shaking inside. She looked over at Simon for a moment before inquiring. "Diedra, what was your last name when you lived in Germany?"

Both Diedra and Miriam laughed. "I am so sorry," Miriam replied. "We never did tell you our last name, it was Stein."

Sarah gasped as Simon took her by the arm. "What, what is it?" Miriam asked, as she stared at the shocked look on Sarah's face.

"When I escaped from the train and made it into the Bohemian Forest with Isaac, we connected with a group of Jews that had been living there for some time. The leader was a man named Ishmael. No one used last names for their own protection. Throughout my period of hiding and trying to survive, Ishmael became a large part of our lives. He knew how to overcome nearly every obstacle that hindered us. But he was not able to save us when we were captured.

When I escaped from the Allied government after my release from Dachau, it was Ishmael that found me, got me out of Europe on a ship to Beirut, and helped set up an adoptive family for me in

Israel. When we parted in Beirut, he told me we would never see one another ever again. However, when I joined the Israeli Defense Force, I was picked to work for Mossad as I still do. I was shocked to find out that Ishmael was head of the department hunting down Nazi war criminals. So, he is my boss, my friend, and my savior. His full name as I know it is Ishmael Stein."

Miriam and Diedra sat motionless for a moment as they stared at Sarah. "Are you saying our brother is still alive after all these years?"

Sarah shook her head, "It's possible, there could have been other Ishmael Steins, but from what you have told me of your brother, it only seems to make sense that the two could be one in the same. I'll tell you what I will do. I only know how to get a hold of Ishmael when he's at the office. So, first thing in the morning, I will call him and ask if you are his sisters. We can meet back here around nine for breakfast and I'll tell you what I found out."

The sisters were nearly in shock as they walked out of the restaurant, hoping Sarah would give them good news in the morning.

It was about seven o'clock when Sarah dialed the number for Mossad. Instantly, the captain that answered the phone connected her to Ishmael.

"Good morning, Sarah. How are you doing? How did your trip to Dachau go?" Ishmael asked, as he smiled.

"I am feeling good, although I still get a little tired from time to time. Our visit to the camp was very interesting, and I could never be sorry that we came here. But now I have an important question for you my friend," Sarah stated, as her hand shook.

"If you need more time off, we can get along just fine until you are ready to return. I told you to take all the time you needed, "Ishmael replied, as he looked over a report on his desk.

"Thank you, Ishmael. But that's not what I wanted to ask you. What I need to know is this. Did you have any sisters when you were growing up? And if you did, what were their names?" Sarah asked, as she sat nervously waiting for his response.

Ishmael placed the report down on his desk as he sat quietly for a moment. "Why are you asking, my child. What difference could it possibly make to you on this trip?"

Sarah gritted her teeth, as this was exactly the kind of answer she had expected from her very private boss and friend. After taking a deep breath, Sarah replied. "Please Ishmael, would you just tell me?"

"That was a long time ago, longer than I care to think about," Ishmael began, as small beads of perspiration formed on his forehead. After staring up at the ceiling for a moment, he continued. "I had two sisters. When the S.S. came down the road to the farm I worked at, I ran. I ran faster than I had ever run before. I climbed a tree in the woods, and watched them take the farmer and his wife away, as they were also Jews. I went back to the house that night, grabbing some food, a pistol, ammunition, a blanket and clothing. I left quickly, hoping no one would see me and report the sighting to the S.S. or Gestapo. I hid out in an old barn near the woods for about a week. When I returned to our home, several of the neighbors that were still willing to speak with a Jew told me my entire family had been taken away, and that I had better leave before I was turned in to the Gestapo, as they now had an office in Aachen, and spies were everywhere. I didn't dare go into the house or be spotted near it, so I just left, crossing over into Belgium through the Ardennes. I never looked back."

As a tear ran down each cheek, Sarah asked again. "What were their names, Ishmael?"

Smiling at the memory, Ishmael replied. "They were my older sisters and they always took good care of me. They were Diedra and Miriam. Why do you need to know this now?"

Sarah's mouth became dry, leaving her unable to speak. Quickly, she handed the phone to Simon as she drank some water.

Taking the phone, Simon stated. "Ishmael, Sarah is a bit choked up right now. You see last evening during dinner, we began talking to a couple of women. They told us their story, including that they grew up near Aachen, had a brother named Ishmael, and identified themselves as Diedra and Miriam, and their maiden name was Stein."

Before Simon could continue, Ishmael dropped the phone receiver onto his desk as a flood of tears gushed forward. Ishmael had forgotten what it was like to have family, or what it was like to feel such emotion. After regaining a bit of composure, Ishmael picked up the phone and continued. "I need to know, did they say where my father worked and who he worked for?"

"Yes, they said he worked for a man named Torberg who

vehemently hated the Nazis, but ran some type of military equipment factories because the military contracts paid good money. One factory was in Aachen and the other in Antwerp near the port," Simon explained.

Shaking his head, Ishmael replied. "That is all totally correct. My God, my sisters are alive. When will you be seeing them again? Tell them I want to see them as soon as possible. If they can come to Israel with you when you return that would be all the better. I will work out all they need to get into Israel. Thank you, Simon. Thank you both for finding my sisters. Tell Sarah she will get a big hug when you return."

Miriam and Diedra were already seated in the restaurant when Sarah, Simon and Simchah walked in. The tension was so thick, Sarah almost felt physically ill. When everyone was seated, Sarah smiled at the women. "Ishmael has confirmed that you are his sisters."

Immediately, the two women began to cry as they hugged each other, saying Ishmael over and over.

After the women regained their composure, Sarah explained what Ishmael had told them regarding immediate travel to Israel. There was never any question, they immediately agreed to the travel arrangements.

As they ate breakfast, Sarah came to realize the trip to Dachau had most certainly been set in motion by a power much higher than anyone on earth. Once again, she felt sorrow for all the times she had rejected the God of Israel when she had been in Dachau. But it was at times such as this, that Sarah became to more fully understand that there is meaning to everything, and as Galenka had said so often, the God of Israel will reveal the reason for everything when the time is right.

As EL AL Airlines Flight 1253 touched down in Tel Aviv on a sunny Sunday afternoon, Ishmael and his wife Yvonne stood in a conference room near the gate where the plane would unload. Watching the aircraft taxi to Gate 15, Ishmael paced back and forth, getting more anxious by the minute, no matter how hard Yvonne tried to comfort him. It took about ten minutes before his aide Capt. Lucy Rachbon walked into the room.

"Sir, they are arriving in a cart as we speak, are you ready to see them?"

Smiling nervously, he nodded his head. "Yes, and make sure Sarah and her family come in also. They are responsible for all of this, they should be here."

The captain nodded her head as she slipped out of the room to await the arrival of the two airport carts. When they arrived, she greeted all of them. "Sarah, it's so good to have you and your family back home. We have missed you in the office." Turning toward Miriam and Diedra, she held out her hands. "Shalom, and welcome to Israel. Come, your brother awaits you."

Moments later, the two women walked slowly into the room, looking at their long missing brother. In turn, Ishmael also stood motionless, looking at his sisters in awe, as if they were ghosts. Seconds later they walked toward each other and hugged as tears of joy overcame them. Later, Ishmael stated he could not remember the last time he had been kissed so much.

After talking with his sisters for several minutes, Ishmael walked over to Sarah, giving her a tremendous hug. "Child, I always knew you were special. I had no idea why our lives kept colliding, but I always felt that someday you would do something great. And today, you have done the impossible, you brought my family back to me from the grave."

After shaking hands with Simon and kissing Simchah on the cheek, he escorted everyone out of the terminal to waiting limousines that took them to Mossad headquarters where a large banquet had been prepared by Mossad chefs.

The party went on for hours as Ishmael happily introduced his sisters to everyone. Sarah could not have been happier with the results of her trip to Dachau.

Chapter Twenty-One
You Can Not Hide

About a week later, Sarah once more returned to work. She had barely sat down in her cubicle when Ishmael came over and sat down beside her. "I have a mission for you, Josiah and Olga. I fear it will be a sad case, but the director has approved it, and the United States State Department will allow us to proceed." Opening a file, he handed Sarah a photo of a middle-aged man in an S.S. uniform. "That is S.S. Lieutenant Gunter Melnik. He was a Romanian turned Nazi and a true brutal anti-Semite. He worked at the Sobibor Camp in charge of slave laborers. He was known for his brutality and torture, especially in the use of the hard rubber truncheon he carried. It is estimated he was personally responsible for the deaths of over 1500 Jews. The prisoners called him Sandu the Savage."

Reaching into the file, Ishmael pulled out another photograph that he handed to Sarah. "This is a photo of him today, that was taken just a few weeks ago. He is a retired construction worker living in Pittsburgh, Pennsylvania, going by the name of George Masters."

Looking up at Ishmael, Sarah frowned, "He's an old man!"

Nodding in agreement Ishmael replied, "Yes, he's 85 years old, and in rather good shape. Two women that survived Sobibor and moved to the States after the war recognized him working in a church booth at a county fair. They found a deputy sheriff and demanded he be arrested. Of course, Masters and his wife vehemently denied the allegations. After Masters was taken into custody, it became apparent that his immigration papers from 1948 were not proper. It was then that we were contacted by the State Department and the two women. So, you will go to Pittsburgh and attempt to make heads or tails of the situation. It's important that everything be handled with kid gloves due to the man's age, and the fact that we don't yet know for sure he is this Sandu."

Arriving in Pittsburgh, Sarah and her team were taken to the State Attorney General's office, where they were given a run down on everything that had happened so far. Sarah and Olga chose to start the investigation by speaking with George Masters, to get a feel for the man, while Josiah went off to speak with state investigators.

Sitting down in an interrogation room, Masters glared at Sarah and Olga. "You are Jews are you not?"

Sarah nodded, "Yes, we are here to get to the bottom of this issue. We work for Mossad."

Masters grunted, as he rubbed his rather large nose. "I didn't do what these women accused me of. I was never in Sobibor, I was never in the German Army, and I was born in Russia, not Romania. You are wasting our time."

"Your accent is Romanian, not Russian," Olga replied, as she glared at Masters. "Plus, it would have been impossible for a Russian to have travel documents approved in 1946. A Romanian, possibly, a Russian, no. Your documents state they were approved in Munich, again, not possible if you were a Russian."

Masters leaned forward in his chair, slamming his fist on the table as he yelled. "I tell you again, I am Russian not Romanian, and my papers are accurate. You are all trying to hang an old man for something I never did."

Sarah stood up, pacing the room for a moment. Stopping, she leaned forward on the table, staring down at Masters. "So, why does your name not show up in the immigration files for 1946 through 1948 in Munich? Did you think we would not check?"

Masters ran his hands over his bald head and screamed in frustration. "You do not understand, you cannot understand. There were thousands of people like me that had nothing to go back to. Everyone was hurrying to get people through the paper work, maybe they did not log things properly, maybe they just didn't list some people, as there were so many thousands waiting for help. Why will you not believe me?"

"So, tell me then, where were you from February, 1943 through March of 1945?" Sarah asked, as she walked behind Olga and leaned up against the wall.

"As I told everyone already, I was fleeing the German Army as they over ran Mother Russia. What else could I be doing, I was just trying to stay alive," Masters replied angrily.

Olga jumped on his answer. "The Germans were turned back at Kursk in July of 1943, and from that point on they were in retreat. Just who were you running from, Sandu?"

Exploding in anger, Masters pointed his finger at Olga as he screamed. "I am not this Sandu, whoever he was. Why don't you find this Sandu and ask him all that you are asking me!"

Sarah walked slowly behind Masters and leaned over his shoulder. "I see you have the temper you were known so well for, Sandu. Are you still just as violent? Would you like to hit me with your truncheon? Would you like to grab me by the throat and throw me to the ground because I'm a filthy Jew whore?"

Masters turned toward Sarah and spit on her blouse. "I could still—"

As Masters stopped, Sarah leaned even closer, "You could still do what, Sandu? Crush me like a bug? Send my emaciated body to the ovens? Tell me, what could you do Sandu?"

As sweat rolled down his face, he shook his head, "I am not this Sandu you are looking for. Look, maybe I don't have all the dates just right, it's been a long time since the war. You must understand, we were all scared and just hoping to survive," Masters yelled, as he once more beat his fists against the table.

Sarah walked around to the other side of Masters leaning down against the table once more. "I too was scared. I ran from the Germans and hid where ever I could, and I was also in Dachau, but always I knew what year and month it was. That's how you survive. You sir, are a liar!"

Masters shook in rage as he glared at Sarah. "You are a bitch, a filthy Jew bitch. What right do you have to confront me like this? I am an American now!"

Before Sarah or Olga could respond, Masters jumped up, kicking the chair up against the wall. Do you want to take me on right now? Do you want to see who is tougher? Do you want to see what I can do to the likes of you? I am finished, take me to my cell!"

He had just finished speaking when Josiah and a U.S. Marshal charged into the room. Masters stood erect as sweat ran down his face. Clenching both fists, he glared at Josiah. "Jew boy, do you want to see what I am made of?"

Josiah stared back with anger in his eyes, as he held back the wrath that was beginning to boil over within him. "Have it as you wish, but you should know better by now than to ever underestimate your opponent."

Masters grunted, as he realized Josiah was much more than he could handle at his age. Holding out his wrists, he turned to the marshal. "Take me to my cell, I am through here."

As he left the room, he looked over at Olga who was standing a few feet away. After spitting on the floor, he yelled at her in a language Sarah did not understand. Once the door was closed, Olga smiled. "That was an old Romanian dialect. He told me to burn in hell."

Over the next several days, Sarah and Olga interviewed the two women at length. At the end of the second day, the older of the two women looked deep into Sarah's eyes. "You have not said as much, but it is evident that both of you survived concentration camps. You say you have been involved in arresting many war criminals. Tell me, what goes through you when you see these criminals again? Tell me you do not get physically sick, tell me you do not break out in a sweat, tell me your mouth does not go dry as you once again fear for your life. When I saw Masters standing in that booth at the fair, I wanted to vomit instantly. When he turned to look at me, I was so scared, I could feel those eyes penetrating right to my spine. Then he grinned that evil grin and my blood ran cold once more. He recognized me the second I recognized him. As we backed away, he laughed, he laughed loud and sneered as he watched us go. He knew he had intimidated us once more, and figured he would never see us again, due to our fear. But this time he had no rubber truncheon, no snarling dogs, and no soldiers with rifles. We were not going to let him get away. Never again would he hurt anyone. We had to act and we did. I always wondered what had become of Sandu the Savage, as he haunted my dreams over and over. Since his arrest now, I have been able to sleep. I cannot wait to testify against him."

After conferring with Ishmael and the State Department, the decision was made to file charges against Masters. After deliberations, The International Court of Justice in the Hague charged Masters with 1500 counts of murder, 1000 crimes against humanity and 100 lessor charges. His trial was set for the following year.

The city of Hague, in the Netherlands, was abuzz with reporters from all over the world as the trial of George Masters was set to begin. Sarah and Olga worked day and night getting documents in proper order for the prosecuting attorneys, and filling document requests from the defense.

Over the first two weeks of the trial, a parade of witnesses filed in and out of the docket, but Masters never flinched. It was emotionally draining on Sarah when Angela, the American born wife of this man now known as George Masters, gave her tearful testimony. Although Sarah was sure she knew by now that her husband was guilty, she still loved him and was willing to fight for her family.

On the second day of the third week, a male survivor testified that he had watched Masters beat two men to death with his truncheon by crushing their skulls while he laughed. The man had barely finished speaking, before Masters stood up and yelled.

"My name is Gunter Melnik, I came from Bucharest, Romania. I joined the German Army in 1940, after the German Army invaded our home. They released me from prison where I was doing time for murdering a Jewish shopkeeper. I helped them round up Jews from Romania and France before they sent me to work in Dachau and later Sobibor. Yes, I am guilty of the charges that have been brought against me. I wish to stop this trial for the sake of my family. Do with me as you wish."

Although Masters had changed his plea to guilty, the judges spent a week going over all the testimony before making a final decision. When they were ready, Masters was called back in for sentencing.

Sarah sat nervously in her chair, her eyes glued to the judges as they took their places. After everyone was seated, the lead judge told Masters and his attorneys to stand. After a moment of silence, the judge began. "Gunter Melnik, you have pleaded guilty to all the charges that were stipulated in the complaint. After much deliberation this court has found you guilty of 700 charges of murder, and 400 counts of crimes against humanity. We are sentencing you to 50 years in prison, to be served at the Dutch prison in Scheveningen. May God have mercy on your soul."

His wife and children cried as they watched him being taken out of the courtroom in shackles. Sarah had a very empty feeling in her chest as she listened to the sobs of his family. This man the family had looked up to and loved for all those years had turned out to be a fraud, and a brutal murderer. How could they ever reconcile all of that in their hearts? Her thoughts went immediately back to the wife and daughter of Sgt. Wilhelm, who both took their own lives when his past was revealed. How could anyone find peace with a situation like this.

Before leaving the Netherlands, Sarah and Olga took time to visit the home of Ann Frank in Amsterdam. Sarah felt a major kinship to Ann's story, as they were both just children when the Nazi's destroyed all that was good in their lives. They also visited the Hollandsche Schouwburg (Holland's Theater), a theater that was built in 1892 for the performance of plays and concerts. In 1941, the Germans renamed it the Joodse Schouwburg (Jewish Theater), as it became the collection point for Jews before they were sent off to the internment camps. Over 159,000 Dutch Jews perished during the war. Sarah and Olga knew that Holland had suffered the greatest number of Jews killed, by percentage of population, of any other country in Europe. Olga had known many Dutch women while she was in Sobibor. Knowing they had all passed through this theater and perished in the camp, made the visit very difficult for her.

Arriving at the airport, Sarah and Olga were more than ready to be leaving the Netherlands. They had worked through a tumultuous trial, visited places that brought back the horrors of the camps, and been treated badly by many members of the media for prosecuting an 85-year-old man. Worst of all, because of the media coverage, their photographs had been plastered in the newspapers and appeared nightly on television news broadcasts. There was no place they could go where people did not point and gawk at them, or wish to talk to them about their war time experiences. They both longed to be back in Tel Aviv with their families, where they could find peace and quiet.

Chapter Twenty-Two
A Battle Like No Other

About a month after returning from the trial, Sarah began feeling sick and lethargic much of the time. Once more, she immediately checked herself into the Sheba Medical Center in Tel Aviv. After interviewing Sarah, Doctor Abend ordered a battery of tests. After all the test results were compiled, Dr. Abend walked into Sarah's room. After greeting Simon and Simchah, he looked seriously at Sarah.

"I'm sorry to tell you, your cancer has returned. We have found it in your axillary lymph nodes under your right arm, and in your liver. It's extremely possible the cancer in the lymph nodes was there when we did your mastectomy, but was too small to show up. The cancer on your liver is what we would consider stage two, but it's operable. We sent your results to Sloan Kettering Hospital in New York last evening to get their opinion. I spoke with several of their doctors this morning, and they concur with our findings. So, we would like to operate on your liver, the day after tomorrow, to remove the lesions. Then we will go after your lymph nodes on Friday, which will be a much less dangerous surgery. We will be doing chemotherapy for both areas, and add radiation on the lymph nodes. How does that sound, Sarah?"

Sarah sat silent for several moments as she looked at her family.

"Tell me, Dr. Abend, what are the chances of beating this a second time. Please be honest with us."

Dr. Abend took a deep breath. "This will be a battle like no other you have ever faced. Your immune system never fully came back from your time in Dachau, and you have never gained all your strength back from your first surgery and chemo. Adding radiation to the mix will make you sick, and you will find it very difficult to keep food down. Of course, we will give you IV's and supplements to help you keep your strength up. There will be days when you are going to feel like you cannot go on, but they will pass. This will be a struggle, Sarah, but our team of doctors believes you can survive and go on to have a good life. There are never guarantees, of course, as everyone responds to therapy differently, and no two people have the same body chemistry."

The morning of her surgery, Ishmael walked into the alcove where Sarah waited to be wheeled into the operating room.

Shaking his head, he took hold of her hand. "Only Mossad gets permission to be in here, Sarah. Well, that and some serious persuasion, maybe."

Sarah laughed as she reached up for his hand. "Thank you for coming, Ishmael. This battle has me concerned."

Smiling, Ishmael replied, "Little one, must you always do things the hard way? You have always been a fighter, though, and I believe you will work your way out of this predicament just the same. You are in our prayers today and forever."

Sarah smiled as she looked up at this man that had always been there for her, and had saved her so many times. "This time I'm afraid, Ishmael. I think the odds are against me, and the fight will be too tough. I'm so tired, and so worn out, what strength do I have left? Most of all, I fear leaving Simchah and Simon."

Ishmael glared at Sarah as he pointed at her. "I will not have talk like that from you, my child. I simply will not accept it, not now, not ever. You will fight, you will fight like you did in Dachau, you will fight to survive like you did against Professor Felix. You must live, Sarah, for your family, for Isaac, for Galenka, and for me. You must survive, you have much to teach the younger generations, they need your voice, Sarah."

Before Sarah could respond, a surgical nurse walked into the alcove. "I'm sorry sir, it's time for her to go now. Everything is ready and the doctor is waiting."

Ishmael nodded his head as he smiled at the nurse. "Good, I have told her all I needed to say, she knows now what she must do."

As the nurse rolled Sarah toward the large swinging doors, Ishmael called out, "Survive Sarah, you must live."

Several hours later, Sarah opened her eyes in the recovery room. A young nurse standing aside the gurney smiled, "Hey, there you are. Welcome back, Sarah. How are you feeling?"

With her throat parched from lack of moisture, Sarah fought to reply. "Dizzy and mixed up!"

"That would be normal for the heavy sedatives they used on you. Dr. Abend remembered what happened during your last surgery, so he wanted you out as far as possible," the nurse replied while adjusting the flow rate on Sarah's IV. "Another hour and that feeling will go away. Then we will take you to recovery where your family is waiting."

Later that evening, Dr. Abend walked into Sarah's room. After checking on the IV's, he looked at Sarah. "The surgery went very well. We took a little more of your liver than we had planned, but we wanted to rule on the side of caution. I'm positive we have it all. We will continue as planned for your lymph node surgery Friday morning.

With both surgeries completed, Sarah felt extremely weak, and was not looking forward to the radiation and chemotherapy she was facing. She understood the treatments were not mandatory, and could be turned down if she chose that route, but she also understood that Simon and Simchah would be anything but pleased if she opted out.

The day Sarah started her radiation, Simon had coffee with Dr. Abend. "Tell me Doctor, what did Sloan Kettering have to say about Sarah's tests after surgery?"

Placing his cup on the table, Dr. Abend looked seriously at Simon. "They are not as optimistic as we are regarding Sarah's chances. They have pointed out several very small spots on Sarah's liver they feel could also be cancer, but they are not one hundred percent sure. Of course, the best way to find out for sure would be to do a minor surgery and take a biopsy after we are finished with chemo and radiation. Although, if those small spots are cancer, the chemo should attack them, just as it will the lymph nodes. Let's not put the cart before the horse, Simon. We will see where things stand after we finish the treatments, and Sloan Kettering agrees."

Simon nodded his head as he contemplated what he had just been told. "So, be honest with me. What are Sarah's chances of beating this a second time?"

Doctor Abend sat quietly for a moment as he took a swallow of coffee. "Not as good as I would like them to be. But she is exceptionally strong willed, we both know that. I'm thinking we should just wait on that question until we are deeper into her treatments."

Because of Sarah's weakened and critical condition, Dr. Abend ordered her to remain in the hospital. Over the next several weeks, Sarah lost an incredible amount of weight and her color once more became ashen gray. More often than not when her meals were delivered, just the smell of the food made her nauseous. Nights were the worst as she would have violent nightmares about Dachau. She would thrash about in bed, soaking the bedding with her sweat and blood, as her IV needles would come lose from her arm. Waking up, she would gasp for air and shake for hours, refusing to go back to sleep.

Simchah had basically moved into her mother's room to help take care of her. Night after night she held her mother after her dreams, attempting to comfort her. Sarah would look wide-eyed at Simchah repeating over and over, "Make them stop, make them go away. Please, I cannot do this!"

All Simchah could do was to whisper, "Shhh, you are safe, they were only dreams, they are only dreams, Mother, I'm here with you."

Most early mornings, as daylight crept through the curtains, Sarah would finally feel safe enough to fall back to sleep, but she always begged Simchah not to leave her alone. Simon would take over on weekends, allowing Simchah time to mentally regroup and see her friends.

Seven weeks into the treatments, Sarah spoke very little as she laid in bed staring at the ceiling. No matter what Simon or Simchah said to her, she rarely responded. One evening after refusing her dinner tray, she reached out to take Simchah's hand.

"I'm finished my love. What Dachau could not achieve, the cancer has. Tell your father that I love him. I will be with you always."

With that, Sarah went into cardiac arrest. Simchah screamed for help as the cardiac team came rushing into the room. They began CPR as the doctor prepared to give Sarah a shot of adrenalin directly into the heart. When she did not respond, they gave her a shock with the paddles that jerked her sickly body up from the bed. Instantly, an irregular heart rhythm appeared on the monitor.

Doctor Rachela, who was in charge of the cardiac team, watched the monitor. "Come on Sarah, you can do this. Come on, honey keep fighting. You have life left to live, you cannot leave Israel just yet."

Slowly, Sarah's heart returned to a normal rhythm, but she did not respond to verbal commands or touch.

Simchah stood paralyzed against the wall, her hands over her face as tears rolled down her cheeks. Taking a deep breath, she addressed Dr. Rachela. "Tell me what's happening. Is she going to survive? Will she be alright?"

Taking Simchah by the hand, the doctor responded. "Sometimes after such an ordeal, the brain in a matter of speaking shuts off to regroup. Her pulse and blood pressure are good, and we will watch her for a while before we get excited. Stay with her, and talk to her, even if she doesn't respond. We've called your father."

Simchah sat on the edge of the bed holding her mother's hand for several hours, talking to her and telling her stories. Just before Simon arrived, Simchah laughed as she squeezed her mother's hand. "Mom, remember when I fell off the monkey bars at school in second grade? You told me I was banned from playing on them forever. But as soon as my arm was out of the cast, I was right back on them. I bribed my teacher with cookies not to tell you. Daddy knew of course, and he was fine with it. And when I told you my black eye was from a softball game at school, actually it was from getting punched in the face by a girl I didn't like. Afterwards, we became good friends."

Simchah jumped off the bed and screamed, when Sarah instantly responded, "I know, Sasha told me that story."

Simchah grabbed her mother and held her tight, as Dr. Rachela and Simon walked into the room, smiling. "Ah, so you have graced us with your return," the doctor said. "How are you feeling, Sarah?"

Looking up at Simchah and Simon, Sarah smiled. "All I know is that my special angels are here with me, so everything is fine."

The next day, Dr. Abend ordered x-rays and other tests to see what the radiation had accomplished over the past seven weeks. He was sure Sarah could not tolerate much more and still get the chemo treatments she required.

He and his team were happy to see the spots on Sarah's liver had disappeared, and the area around the lymph nodes was looking much better. After conferring with Sloan Kettering Hospital, the decision to stop the radiation was made.

A few days later, Sarah was allowed to go home, returning to the hospital for her scheduled chemo treatments. Although they were incredibly rough on her, Sarah fought to live as hard as she had in Dachau. But now she had the love of her family and friends all around her to give her strength.

It took several months for Sarah to regain her weight and endurance after her last chemo treatment, but she was also happier than she had been in a long time, as Simchah and her husband Jon Gellner presented her and Simon with their first grandchild. A little girl they named Judith.

A month later, Sarah was called to Mossad headquarters for a special occasion, but was not told what is was. Upon arriving, she learned that Ishmael was retiring from his post after forty-six years. Since there were few Nazi war criminals left to capture now, his job was being integrated into a new security post that would be led by Josiah Shapiro. Sarah was pleased to hear the good news for these two men she had come to admire so much.

After the festivities were over, Ishmael took Sarah by the arm and led her out into a flower garden. After they had walked for a bit, Ishmael guided Sarah to a bench. "Well, my child, it has been a remarkable trip. Whoever would have thought we would come this far after our first meeting in the forest? In fact, who would have thought we both could survive the horrors of the Nazi's."

Sarah smiled as she squeezed Ishmael's hand. "If not for you my friend, I would not have survived. You always appeared to be in the right spot at the right time."

Ishmael grimaced as he looked up at the sky. "But I could not save you from Dachau and the horrors you endured. I have always regretted that. But things fell apart so fast, we were being overrun, and I was fighting just to stay alive, minute by minute. I had no idea what happened to you, until I heard through the network that you were in Dachau. I feared I would never see you again."

Sarah smiled at Ishmael as he wiped tears from his weathered face. "I survived because of all you taught me from the forest right up until Isaac and I were captured. It was you that gave me strength, even when I was ready to give up and die. Although I prayed to die, our God of Israel had other plans, just as you and Galenka tried to teach me. If I had not gone to Dachau, I would never have met Galenka or Raizel or Hadar. They all taught me so much, although I did not understand it all at the time. Without experiencing Dachau, I could not be the person I am today. Do not feel bad Ishmael, you did all you could for me, and it was supposed to be the way it was. We are family and no one can ever change that."

Ishmael nodded his head as he laughed. "Yes Sarah, we have changed very much since Paris. You have become a wise intelligent woman that I will always trust and respect. Thank you for all the wonderful memories."

As they stood up, Sarah looked at Ishmael. "In many ways you know me better than anyone on this earth. You know what I was like in the forest, in Paris and Normandy. I made bad mistakes, I thought only of myself, and people I cared for died because of my thoughtlessness. I have tried to do what is right since Dachau. I have tried to bring the butchers of that evil to justice and be a good influence on my daughter. Do you think my soul has found redemption?"

Ishmael hugged Sarah tightly, without saying a word. As he released her, he looked deeply into her eyes. "My child, your soul has been redeemed a thousand times over, and the God of Israel and all its descendants will bless you a thousand-fold. Find peace my daughter, may peace go with you."

Watching Ishmael slide into the back seat of the black Mossad limousine for the last time was very painful for Sarah. She knew he and Yvonne were very private people, and Ishmael's one wish now was to enjoy the rest of his life, and live it in peace.

Josiah walked up to Sarah as the limousine pulled out of the parking lot. "We shall all miss him and I hope I can honor him always in this new job. But I shall miss you most, Sarah. You taught me so much when we started the team, and I am proud to pass all that knowledge on to the new agents coming on board. You are welcome to visit us any time you wish."

Sarah hugged Josiah. "You will do well, you have always been a good agent. But now it's my time to leave Mossad, and put this part of my life behind me. Take care my friend."

As Simon drove from the parking lot, Sarah looked back over her shoulder. Her time in the agency had taught her a lot, and she was proud of what she had helped Mossad to accomplish. But now, like Ishmael, it was time to close the door on that part of her life. The things Ishmael had said to her had given her heart peace, a peace she so desperately sought.

Chapter Twenty-Three
Welcome Home

With their house sold, Sarah and Simon drove to their new home north of Tel Aviv, near the coastal town of Netanya, midway between Tel Aviv and Haifa. Sarah began a strict regimen of working out, that included daily swims in the warm waters of the Mediterranean. Slowly, her former strength began to return, and she thoroughly enjoyed the bicycle rides she and Simon took along the coast.

Whenever possible, Mari and Olga would drive over to Netanya to have lunch with Sarah, and share all the relevant gossip that was spreading through Mossad headquarters. The visits always included a short note from Josiah that Sarah especially enjoyed reading.

In March of 1992, Simchah announced she and John were going to have their second child. Sarah was excited with the news, but was well aware something was not right with her medically. She noticed from time to time that her left arm and hand were not responding properly. Several weeks later, she noticed there were times that her left foot did not operate properly when she walked or swam. Although it scared her immensely, she decided not to tell Simon about it, because he would drag her back to Sheba Medical Center in Tel Aviv immediately. Nevertheless, it all came to the forefront one morning in April, when Sarah collapsed in their kitchen and began to have a seizure.

Dr. Abend was sure he knew what was going on with Sarah, but he wanted to do every test known to man to make sure his diagnosis was correct before speaking with her family. After conferring once again with Sloan Kettering Hospital, Dr. Abend was ready to deliver the news.

Walking into Sarah's room, Dr. Abend shook hands with Simon before walking over to the edge of the bed.

"Well Sarah, I hate to bring you this news. Your cancer has returned, but this time it's much more serious. You have what is called a Glioblastoma, or brain cancer. It is already at stage three and this type of cancer grows very fast. Scientists have found that chemotherapy does little if nothing to stop the growth of the tumor. The only treatment that really works today is heavy doses of radiation."

Simon's knees buckled, as he grabbed for a chair to sit down. After taking a deep breath he looked up at Dr. Abend. "What will the radiation do? Will it kill the tumor?"

Shaking his head, Dr. Abend continued. "To be blunt, if the tumor is caught in the very early stages, we have had some success with the radiation. But once it has become stage three, there has not been much success in stopping its growth. There have been some cases where it has been slowed, but never eliminated."

Sarah sat quiet for several moments before speaking. "What will happen to me as the tumor grows? How much time will I have if I do nothing, compared to having radiation?"

"You will begin to lose more strength and your muscles will begin to deteriorate. In time, you will not be able to walk or take care of yourself. You will need to be placed in a cancer care unit. I would expect you to have four to six months of relatively good life, then after that you would go down hill rather rapidly. With the radiation, you will be sick most of the time and your quality of life will be diminished considerably. To be fully honest, I do not think the time difference will vary much. We can give you medication that will help control the seizures and the pain," he explained, "but I'm afraid there is little more we can do." Dr. Abend explained slowly and painfully. "I'm so sorry."

Sarah sat erect in bed with her eyes closed as she digested

everything she was just told. Taking hold of Simon's hand, Sarah replied. "I want my last months on this earth to count for something. There are things I still want to do, and I would like to see Simchah's new baby. I will take the medications, but I will not take the radiation. That is my decision."

Simon leaned over, kissing Sarah on the forehead. "It shall be so. I also want as much quality time with you as possible."

Returning to their home, Sarah invited Simchah and John to come for the weekend. Telling her daughter what was happening, and explaining what the future would be like was excruciating.

After Simchah composed herself, she looked at her mother. "Tell me what things you would like to do, we will arrange everything for you."

"I need to return to France and walk the beaches of the Normandy invasion. I want to see the bunkers and the cemeteries. I need to see where the Allies came ashore. I also must return to Orleans and find Rochelle's grave if it's possible. Someone must know where she was buried. Most of all, I must return to Straubing once more to see where I was born. I must take you all there, you must see it."

Simchah and John went to work making all the arrangements, with Josiah being their first contact. He was devastated to hear what was happening to Sarah. He immediately provided a private Mossad jet, a van and driver, a Mossad doctor, and all the necessary rail passes the family would require for the entire trip.

On the morning of June 6, 1992, Sarah strolled Omaha, Utah and Gold Beaches of the Normandy Invasion. She walked up to the gigantic pill boxes above Omaha Beach where she had once sold pastries to the soldiers. Sitting down on a short wall, Sarah looked up at Simon.

"This is where I sat when Field Marshal Rommel purchased muffins from me. The Germans ate pastries while the forced laborers struggled with the heavy wet cement and reinforcing bars. I felt like a traitor, yet we gathered a lot of important information."

Sarah sat quietly in a wheel chair as Simon pushed her slowly through the American Cemetery above Omaha Beach. Seeing grave markers with the Star of David on them, Sarah rose from her chair to walk over to them. Looking at Simchah, she said, "See, the names are no different. Here is a Goldfine, here is a Kravitz. They all died for us, and their blood ran red just as every other man buried here. We were all one.

Arriving at Orleans the following day, the city historian came to visit them in their hotel. They discussed everything that had happened on that fateful day in the square. Smiling, he explained to Sarah how the citizens of Orleans had rescued Rochelle's body before the Germans could take it. After breakfast the following morning, the historian led them to number one Boulevard Lamartine where the Grand Orleans Cemetery was located.

The caretaker led them to a grave with Rochelle's name on it. "The underground hid her body for two days until they were able to dig a grave late at night to bury her. There was no marker on the grave until after the Nazi forces were driven out. According to what I was told, they identified her from an ID card she had hidden in the false bottom of her shoe. We decorate her grave each year on the anniversary of the attack in the square. We consider her a hero."

Sarah knelt down on the cool grass and pulled some weeds out from the base of the stone. "I have come back for you, Rochelle. It was not supposed to end the way it did, you should never have been killed. You gave much of yourself to help me, and it cost you your life. For that, I am eternally sorry. We shall have time to talk soon."

Getting back in the wheelchair, Sarah looked at the caretaker. "And where are the graves of the others that died that day?"

"The Nazis loaded them on a truck and no one knows where they were taken. I'm so sorry to have to tell you that," the caretaker replied sorrowfully.

After resting for a few days, they began their long train trip to Munich. All the while, Sarah recounted to everyone how she had escaped from the Allied guards and met up with Ishmael. For the first time, Sarah was actually enjoying recounting her past after leaving Dachau.

Arriving at Munich, Sarah was feeling very sick and her color was beginning to change. The doctor ordered her to take a day off and gave her all the meds that had been prescribed, but it was evident Sarah was losing her final battle.

Sarah became uncomfortable as their new van passed familiar landmarks she remembered from her childhood, and the trip she made back to Straubing with the military police. At one point she felt like telling the driver to turn around and forget about Straubing, but she did not want to disappoint Simon and Simchah. This was something they were looking forward to.

The town had grown quite a bit since Sarah was there in 1945, but the main shopping district had not changed much at all. Sarah could almost see people she remembered walking from store to store with their children in tow. She wondered how many Jews might have returned to Straubing and stayed after the war, considering the welcome she was given.

Moments later, the van turned onto the street leading to her old house. Many of the small homes on the street she remembered had been torn down and replaced with larger more modern structures. As the van pulled up to the house, Sarah was stunned. The tidy, well-kept home she remembered, now sat empty in a very sad state of disrepair. The sign in the front yard stated that the land was for sale and the home scheduled for demolition.

Exiting the van, Sarah stood with her hands over her face as she stared at her childhood home. Simon and Simchah took Sarah by the arms as they walked forward. Entering the house, Sarah attempted to overlook the holes in the walls, and the spray painting that had been done by vandals. The handsome cupboards where her birthday cake was placed, now laid on the floor with the doors ripped off. The wind whistled through the broken windows as bugs flew freely about.

Going upstairs, Sarah peered into the bedrooms. No longer did her brother sit on his bed, and Rose's frozen body no longer stared from the bedroom doorway. Looking out the window, the beautiful back yard was now overgrown with weeds, and a junked car was parked on top of her father's garden. It was clear even the ghosts of her family had abandoned this home they loved so much. Or was it possible the ghosts of her family had driven out everyone that attempted to make a home here. Either way, there was nothing worth saving, and the house no longer served a purpose.

Coming down to the main floor, Sarah sat down on the steps. She remembered the first time she had mastered the climb and scared her mother half to death. Sarah laughed as she thought about the time she attempted to run away from Jonathon after taking his prized toy truck, and fell head first down these same stairs. It was a miracle she had survived to be seven.

Simchah came and sat down beside her mother as Simon leaned against the wall. "I'm sorry the house is not what you wanted it to be, Mother. But at least it's still here for you."

Smiling, Sarah kissed her daughter on the cheek. "It's not so bad, honey. Memories don't mind so much if there is a hole in the wall, or if a window is broken. They are all here to be remembered one more time. Sarah became quiet as she turned her attention toward the front door. There stood her family looking healthy and happy, dressed in their best clothing as if they were on their way to the Synagogue.

Slowly, her mother stepped forward and smiled. "Sarah, as usual we are always waiting for you. What is taking you so long?"

Taking hold of Simon's hand, Sarah said, "I have never been so blessed." Placing her head on Simchah's shoulder, she peacefully left this world behind. To this day, Simchah swears she saw a seven-year-old girl walking out the front door, holding tightly to her mother's hand as she looked back over her shoulder and smiled.

EPILOGUE

*S.S. Captain Herald captured in Italy was sentenced to twenty-five years in prison in 1955. She was released in 1980. She lived the balance of her life in Dortmund, Germany with her brother's family. She died in 2012 from a heart attack.

*S.S. Sergeant Alfred Wilhelm was convicted on charges of crimes against humanity and murder. He was hanged in Nuremberg, Germany in October of 1956. Sarah attended the trial and the execution as she promised. Wilhelm's remains were cremated and dumped into the North Sea, as were most executed Nazi's in the fifties and sixties.

*S.S. Corporal Kolmar was tried in France for crimes against humanity for his work with Prof. Felix. He was sentenced to five years in prison. Leaving prison, he moved to Casablanca, Morocco where he was murdered in 1967.

*S.S. Corporal Barnard from Dachau was killed in 1957 by a former Dachau prisoner in France. Barnard had moved there in 1946 using false identity papers.

*S.S. Doctor Hintermayer actually did exist. He was found guilty of crimes against humanity. He is most known for the experiments he conducted on Jews with extreme cold and extreme heat. He was hung in Landsberg Prison in 1946 for his crimes and is buried in Spottinger-Friedhoff cemetery in Germany.

*Klaus Barbie was an actual figure in the dreaded S.S. and was known as the butcher of Lyon. He was sentenced to life in prison, in Prison Saint-Paul in Lyon France. He died of leukemia on September 25, 1991. His statement to Sarah that he would out live her did not come true. Sarah passed away six months later.

*Dr. Joseph Mengele was an actual Nazi war criminal. Because of the hideous medical experiments he conducted on Jews in Auschwitz he was labeled, "The Angel of Death." The story of his death here is factual.

*U.S. Marshal Sam Swenson was indicted on charges of taking pay offs from Odessa to keep Doctor Mengele safe while in Miami. He was sentenced to fifteen years in prison. He was found hanging in his cell two days after being sentenced.

*Federal Attorney Ed Barimore ran the investigation that led to Sam Swenson's arrest. He retired in 1985 and became an advisor on several television police shows.

*S.S. Lt. Oscar Miller was found guilty of crimes against humanity for the deportation of 1000 Jews from France to extermination camps. He was sentenced to seventy-five years in prison in the Hague. He died of complications from pneumonia in 2001.

*Isaac Levin from Penzburg. His body was never found after his failed attempt to find Capt. Herald.

*Josiah Shapiro still works with Mossad and lives in Tel Aviv with his wife and two children.

*Caleb Schiff is buried in Tel Aviv.

*Ira Gutnick's body was brought back to Israel from Italy and is buried on his parents' farm.

*Mari Segal ended her service with Mossad in 1995. She went on to teach part time in a local high school. She passed away in 2009.

*Olga Armand quit Mossad in 1969 when she married. She is still alive today living in Tel Aviv. She has written several books about the Holocaust.

*Sariya and Yoram Pearlman, Sarah's adopted parents in Israel, broke off relations with her after the shootout in Nahariya. They were afraid she would bring violence to their home, and they believed hunting down war criminals was an evil occupation. They did not know Sarah had passed away until several years after her death.

*Ishmael Stein retired from Mossad in 1991 at the age of 65. He died in his sleep at the age of 84 in 2010. Both his sisters made one more trip to Israel for his funeral.

*Simchah (Waldmann) Gellner is still alive today living in Haifa with her husband John. They have three children.

*Simon Waldmann passed away in 2019 at the age of 89. He never remarried after Sarah's death. He traveled extensively after Sarah's passed, lecturing about the Holocaust at schools and conferences around the world.

*Sarah (Rosenbaum) Waldmann. Born May 10, 1932 in Straubing, Germany. Died June 11, 1992, in Straubing, Germany. Sarah's remains were transported back to Tel Aviv, Israel by Mossad. Per her request there was just a small gathering of family and close friends for a final service. She was cremated and buried in a small cemetery near their home outside Netanya. Simon was buried beside her when he passed. Ishmael honored Sarah by returning to her grave with a solitary red rose every year on the anniversary of her death, until he passed in 2010.

*The story on page 12 of the prisoners attacking and killing the kapos in Dachau at the end of the war is accurate.

*David Ben-Gurion was the preeminent leader of the Jewish community in Palestine from 1935. He became Prime Minister when Israel declared independence in 1948. He served until 1963.

NOTES

As World War Two came to an end, Allied Soldiers began liberating detention camps all across Europe.

It is estimated that Hitler's Third Reich operated 42,000 camps or ghettos throughout Europe from January of 1943, until its demise in May of 1945. They operated many different types of camps. Some were strictly detention or re-education camps, others were for slave labor, some were for political prisoners, and some were designated extermination camps. Many of the large camps such as Auschwitz and Buchenwald had several satellite camps for varied reasons. Today, most people believe only Jews were held and exterminated, however, that is far from accurate. Here is the most current list of who occupied, passed through, or were exterminated in those camps during the Third Reich's reign of terror.

This list was made available in March of 2020 by the American Legion:

> 6 million Jews.
> 5.7 million Soviet civilians.
> 3 million non-Jewish Soviet prisoners of war.
> 300,000 Serb citizens.

250,000 Roma (gypsies)

250,000 people with disabilities, living in institutions.

100,000 Jehovah's Witnesses, homosexuals and German political opponents.

There is a good possibility that many more may have perished that are known only to God. May they also rest in peace.

If you want to learn more about the Holocaust please read:

"The Holocaust," by Martin Gilbert

"Into that Darkness," by Gitta Sereny

"The Gates of the Forest," or "Night," or any other books written about the Holocaust by Elie Wiesel

"The House on Garibaldi Street," by Isser Harel, regarding the capture of Adolph Eichmann.

There has been much written about the ratlines, especially the monastery line. There are articles at smithsonian.com, the guardian.com, along with several books available through amazon.com